Suspicion of Vengeance

Also by Barbara Parker
in Large Print:

Suspicion of Malice
Suspicion of Betrayal
Suspicion of Deceit
Suspicion of Innocence

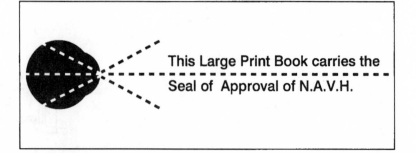

This Large Print Book carries the
Seal of Approval of N.A.V.H.

Barbara Parker

Suspicion of Vengeance

Thorndike Press • Waterville, Maine

Published in 2002 by arrangement with Dutton, a member of Penguin Putnam Inc.

Thorndike Press Large Print Mystery Series.

The tree indicium is a trademark of Thorndike Press.

The text of this Large Print edition is unabridged.
Other aspects of the book may vary from the original edition.

Set in 16 pt. Plantin by Al Chase.

Printed in the United States on permanent paper.

Library of Congress Cataloging-in-Publication Data

Parker, Barbara (Barbara J.)
    Suspicion of vengeance / Barbara Parker.
       p. cm.
     ISBN 0-7862-3751-1 (lg. print : hc : alk. paper)
   1. Connor, Gail (Fictitious character) — Fiction.
   2. Quintana, Anthony (Fictitious character) — Fiction.
   3. Women lawyers — Fiction. 4. Miami (Fla.) — Fiction.
   5. Large type books. I. Title.
   PS3566.A67475 S878 2001b
   813'.54—dc21   2001053454

For Milton Hirsch
lawyer and man of conscience,
intellect, and wit

And Abraham drew near and said, Wilt thou also destroy the righteous with the wicked?

GENESIS 18:23

PROLOGUE

September 1989

It was the first good luck in weeks. A soft rain after a dry spell, a portent of better days. The home owners had signed the listing agreement. The papers lay like sheets of hammered gold in her portfolio on the seat beside her.

Louise hadn't expected this. She'd driven way the hell out in the boondocks, almost as far as Lake Okeechobee, because the head of the agency didn't want to spoil his Saturday night. He found Louise at O'Haney's Pub around the corner from the office, finishing her second gin and tonic. She told him she would be happy to go, of course, no problem. Her job was hanging by a thread.

She put some gas in her Buick sedan, bought coffee and breath mints, and headed west. Suburbs fell away, and flat fields of sugarcane blurred past her windows, the sun red as blood on the horizon, dropping out of sight as Louise finally, after several wrong turns, reached a scrubby, two-acre plot of land with a concrete-block ranch house that might bring eighty thousand dollars, if they were lucky. The Jamisons were a husband and wife and their two little girls. They kept a Bible on the coffee table in the living room, and they brought Louise some iced tea and apple pie. She had expected them to ask for an estimate of how much the property was worth, then show her the door. But they wanted her to sell it for them. Louise had a listing.

She thought of stopping back by Haney's to see who might be there she could tell, somebody from the office, but just as quickly she put the idea aside. At this hour the bar would be too full of smoke and loud laughter and men who'd want to buy her a drink. Louise decided to go back to her apartment, tidy the place up, do her nails, and get to bed early. Tomorrow she would be at her desk by nine o'clock to catch the early customers.

Things were about to change for her, she could feel it. The Jamisons had brought good luck. They'd given her the listing. It was a sign.

At the end of the long gravel road Louise turned on the dome light and checked her hand-drawn map. Go left. The tires spun, then caught. Her headlights illuminated a narrow county road, strands of barbed wire, and an occasional pine tree or sabal palm. West Palm Beach was a glow on the horizon.

She thought of the pint of Bombay gin in the glove compartment. One eye on the road, she unfastened her seat belt and reached across the car. The little door fell down, and Louise felt for the bottle, then pulled it out. The amber lights on the dashboard showed the level: half gone. She couldn't remember when she had last opened it. Two weeks at least. The remembered taste of it suddenly sickened her. She punched the button to lower her window, intending to fling the damned bottle into the weeds. Good-bye, good riddance. The wind whipped her hair around her head. She veered left, tires rumbling on the rough pavement.

Her eyes went to the rearview mirror. Someone was behind her, headlights on high beam, closing in. A Palm Beach County deputy? Her heart leaped, and she swerved back to her lane and glanced at the speedometer. Sixty-five miles per hour. She slowed to the speed limit, fifty-five. One more DUI, they would send her to jail and take away her license. But she wasn't drunk, she reminded herself. Her last drink had been hours ago.

Louise shoved the bottle under her seat.

Her hands were shaking. She raised the window and looked into the mirror for the telltale silhouette of a light bar, seeing only the glare of headlights. There was nothing to illuminate the vehicle behind her. No moon, no other traffic on this desolate road.

Slowing to fifty, Louise expected the other driver to go around, but he kept a steady distance of four or five car lengths behind. The light in her eyes was an annoyance. She angled the mirror. Who was it back there? Migrant workers in an old car too wheezy to accelerate around her. Or kids out joyriding. They could be drunk, using the red beacons of her taillights to guide them back toward the coast. Louise had done that, focusing on someone else's taillights, hanging on to the wheel with both hands, praying to make it home.

She had gotten away with it a couple of times, but that had been in Martin County, where her husband was a captain in the sheriff's office. The deputies had known who she was. Here, she was on her own. She couldn't call Garlan for help. He was already using her last DUI as an excuse not to let the children get into her car. She had to visit them at the house. She had to knock on the door and wait for Garlan to open it, then go in and look at everything that used to be hers. He would let her take Alex and Jackie for walks or go upstairs to their rooms. The door to the master bedroom would always be closed. Garlan had set the terms, and she had been too weak to fight him. Her failures. Her guilt.

I can't forgive you for this, Louise.

But it wasn't his forgiveness she was after. It was her own. She knew that now.

"To hell with you, Garlan."

She would call the children tonight. That's what she would do. Garlan didn't want her calling too late, but she'd be home by nine o'clock; that wasn't late. She hadn't called them in almost a week. Hadn't seen them in . . . longer than that. Why?

She'd been afraid. Ashamed.

A longing for her children — to hold them, to kiss their faces, to say she loved them — suddenly overtook her, settling in to her heart, which ached with both regret and hope. She would call them. Alex was only nine. He would speak to her. Jackie might not. She was twelve years old and angry. Her father's daughter. *Oh, baby. I left you too, didn't I? What have I done?*

The lights in the rearview mirror grew brighter, and Louise heard the throb of a powerful engine. She eased her car to the right, but the other vehicle remained behind

11

her. For the first time, she felt a prickling of fear. They had to know she was a woman. They must have seen her shoulder-length blond hair.

It wasn't a small car, she could tell that much. Perhaps a pickup truck. They were popular out here, so many farmers. Louise wondered where she could turn off that wouldn't lead to a dead end.

"Jackass." She tilted her pump on its heel, pressing down on the accelerator. The lights fell back, then closed in again. The speedometer said seventy, eighty. The broken white line came faster. *Tick tick tick tick . . .*

She kept her eyes on the rearview mirror, watching to see what the other car would do. Gravel clattered under her right front tire, and she quickly pulled the wheel left. She'd almost gone off the road.

"Be careful!"

She dried her damp palms on her skirt and took her foot off the gas. Her heart hammered in her throat. Let the other car follow. So what? A few more miles, they would get to a main road. She stared into the darkness. There were no houses nearby, nothing, only the tantalizing glow to the east.

He was coming closer. Lights filled the in-

12

terior of her car. He struck her from behind, and Louise's head jerked. Then another tap, and his bumper settled against hers. She felt the sudden increase in speed. He was pushing her, shoving her car faster and faster. Her speedometer rose past seventy.

She tried braking, but it did no good. A burning smell reached her nostrils.

"Stop it! Stop!"

She stamped on the accelerator once more. The lights dropped back suddenly, very fast. And then Louise noticed the yellow sign, the sharp, left-turning arrow. It flew past her. The white line on the side of the road veered sharply. Louise slammed on her brakes, and the car swerved, fishtailed, and jolted over gravel and weeds.

She screamed and hung on, but the world swung wildly around her. Trees flew toward the windshield. Her jagged scream ended in an explosion of noise and tearing of metal.

Then nothing.

She became gradually aware of pain so intense it shocked her with its ferocity. Each breath sent fire through her flesh. Her bones flamed. Her eyes were filled with sticky warmth. She blinked. Saw a shattered windshield. A tree lying across it. A starburst of cracks. One headlight still on.

Blood in her mouth, flowing down her

chin. Her jaw wouldn't work. "Ehh. Ehhh." The words screamed in her mind. *Help! Somebody. Please help. Help me.*

Then her door came open, and her arm flopped out. The interior lights came on. She couldn't turn her head to see. Someone turned off the headlight.

His fist closed on the front of her jacket, and he pulled. She slid into the white-hot steel cogs of an immense machine of pain.

He stood over her, black sky behind him. Stars exploded into blue and fiery orange sparks. Her throat gurgled with a laugh.

It's you. I should have known.

He was wrapping a cloth around a metal bar. Raising it high. It came toward her, and the cogs of the machine bit into her skull. *Don't. Not yet. It isn't fair.*

There was a slow, ringing noise. A telephone. On her nightstand. She couldn't wake up. So sleepy. Fumbled for the handset, knocked her glass over. Heard it shatter. Warm liquid flowing over her.

Her daughter's voice. *Mama?*

Jackie. Is that you? The ringing stopped. *Wait. Please don't hang up.*

Water rushed in slow waves through a deep chasm, echoing, growing fainter. *Shush. Shush. Shush.*

The card. She'd bought it two days ago at

14

the mall. A funny card with a cat holding a flower. Still on her dresser. She'd meant to send it today. Honestly had meant to. *I'm so sorry. Oh, my babies. So sorry.*

The pain was gone now. She floated.

Forgive me.

CHAPTER 1

Sunday night, March 4

The porch lights were too bright, Gail thought. They turned the front of her mother's house into a stage set: wrought-iron furniture, the bricks and white wooden columns, the screen door with its metal silhouette of egrets. Between porch and driveway a live oak tree, fuzzy with air plants, interrupted the glare, and Anthony stopped his Cadillac in its shadow.

He turned off the engine and tilted his head toward the girl sleeping in the backseat. "Do you want me to carry her in?"

"No, it's okay. She can walk."

Neither of them made any move to open a door.

Gail touched his cheek. The late hour had put the stubble of beard on his face. She said softly, "What a fast weekend."

He turned his head to put a kiss in her palm. His lips were full and warm. "We should have stayed in Miami."

Anthony's law partner had invited them to a family weekend at his house in the

16

Keys. The house had unexpectedly filled with relatives and friends of relatives bringing enough Cuban food for a month. Gail and Karen had shared a bed in a guest room; Anthony had been exiled to Raul's boat with some of the other men.

"I miss you already,"she said.

He whispered in her ear. "Why don't you put Karen to bed and come to my house?"

She laughed. "I wish."

"Come on. I'll even let you sleep for a couple of hours."

"Karen likes me around in the morning."

"So do I." His smile was visible in the brief glint of light on his teeth.

"Well, you're not eleven years old. Anyway, I have to be in court at eight o'clock."

"*Ay,* Gail." He held her. "This is crazy, living apart."

"You were the one who threw my engagement ring into the pond."

"A mistake. I told you a thousand times."

"Really. Your aim looked pretty good to me."

Their rush toward marriage last summer had ended in a spectacular fight. Gail had shoved her engagement ring at him, and he had flung it into a water hazard on the golf course behind the Biltmore Hotel. It had taken them months to forgive each other.

Anthony wanted to start from where they'd left off. Gail wasn't so sure it could be done.

"When are you going to stop torturing me for that?" He rested his forehead on hers. "What if I found it? Would you marry me if I found it?"

"In all those weeds and muck? Not a chance."

"But if I did?" His black eyes seemed enormous, so close to her face. "Would you?"

"Maybe."

He whispered, "*Caprichosa*. I think you don't love me anymore." His breath warmed her cheek. He spoke to her in Spanish. What he wanted to do to her.

Her skin burned.

Then his eyes were shifting toward the house, focusing on something past the passenger window. "*Coño*. It's your mother." He popped the trunk release, opened the door, and got out.

Gail felt like a teenager caught necking past her curfew. Irene Connor stood at the edge of the porch in a bright yellow sweater, arms crossed against the chill. She was a petite, pretty woman with curly red hair.

"Hi, Mom."

"Hi, honey. I was about to wonder if you'd been in an accident or something."

18

Gail opened the rear door. "Karen, we're home. Wake up." She tugged the beach towel away. "Come on, sweetie, get up."

Karen yawned widely as she stumbled toward the house, eyes half closed, a long-legged girl in shorts and big sneakers. She was making a show of it, and it occurred to Gail that Karen hadn't been asleep at all. She eavesdropped without remorse, spurred by a squeamish but ravenous curiosity about her mother's sex life.

Anthony walked behind them with a suitcase and beach bag.

Irene held the screen door. She was frowning. "Anthony, dear, do you have a couple of minutes? I need to talk to you."

"Is something wrong?" He looked down at her, concerned.

"I want to ask a favor for a friend of mine. Her name is Ruby Smith. Gail, you remember Ruby, don't you? When we used to go up to Sewall's Point? The older woman who baby-sat for you and Renee?"

"Of course I remember Ruby. Is she all right?"

"She needs to find a criminal lawyer. I'll tell you about it inside. Isn't it *cold* tonight?"

Anthony sent an inquisitive look Gail's way, and she shrugged. Irene's gray cat scooted through the door as they came into the foyer. The tabby watched from the sofa. Irene straightened Karen's sleep-tangled hair. "It's bedtime for somebody."

"Not yet, it's too early. Can I have something to eat?"

A look passed between Gail and her mother, and Gail turned Karen toward the hall. "Go on, sweetie. Bath and pajamas first, okay? Gramma needs to talk with Anthony for a little while."

With a dramatic sigh, Karen vanished toward her bedroom.

In the kitchen, Irene offered to make coffee. Anthony preferred plain soda, if she didn't mind, or he would be up half the night. When her mother turned away, Gail caught him looking at his watch. He made a quick, guilty smile and smoothed his hair back. It fell into deep waves at his collar. Gail's fair complexion required sunscreen and a hat; Anthony's skin glowed with a dark tan.

Irene filled the glasses. "Have you ever been to Sewall's Point?" When Anthony replied that he wasn't sure if he had heard of it, she said, "It's on the intracoastal waterway near Stuart, about a hundred miles north of here, the next county up from Palm Beach. My parents bought a vacation house after Daddy came back from the war. Ruby worked for us. Later on, Ed and I bought the house from my parents' estate, and we kept Ruby on. The girls adored her."

Gail's memory produced a snapshot of a short, round woman, a frizzy gray perm, and a muumuu with big patch pockets. Ruby Smith had carried a box of Red Hots in one of them, which she would tap out into their palms if they'd been good. Her accent was twangy Florida Cracker, and her lap could hold three children at once. Ruby had cleaned house and cared for Gail, her sister, and the assortment of cousins and friends who would drop by.

Her mother said, "After Ed passed away, I sold the house, but I'd go visit my sister Louise and her family. Her husband was Garlan Bryce. He's the sheriff of Martin County now. You might have heard the name? My niece, Jackie, is with the city of Stuart police department, following in her father's footsteps, you might say."

Anthony sipped his club soda, gamely trying to follow this torrent of information.

"Louise died in a car accident," Irene said. "She was thirty-six. Did Gail tell you?"

He let out a murmur of condolence and said that yes, Gail had mentioned it.

"Anyway, Ruby and I have kept in touch. She's eighty-one years old, and I haven't seen her since my sister's funeral, but we've written. She lives in a retirement home now, and her eyes are so bad she can't drive. Except for church she hardly goes anywhere. She is the dearest, sweetest thing."

"Mrs. Smith doesn't sound like a person who would need the advice of a criminal defense attorney," Anthony said. "What's the problem?"

"Her grandson. His name is Kenny Ray Clark. Eleven years ago, he was tried for murder and sentenced to death. Ruby believes he's innocent. She asked me to talk to you about it."

Anthony raised his brows. "I think he's past any help I could give him."

The memory slowly reassembled itself in Gail's mind. "Kenny Ray. . . . Right, I remember. Ruby brought him with her a couple of times. He was kind of tall and skinny? He didn't talk much. That was ages ago. Did you ever tell me about his arrest?"

"Yes, but you were away in law school," Irene said. "Want to hear what else Ruby said? She said Jesus spoke to her and told her Kenny Ray was innocent, and if he was going to be saved, it was up to her to find a way to do it." Irene looked from Gail to Anthony and back again.

Gail nodded, unable to think of an appropriate reply.

Anthony appeared to contemplate the ice cubes in his glass. "What did her grandson do? Allegedly. Who was the victim?"

"A young married woman. Someone broke into her house and stabbed her to death. The real tragedy is, her baby died, too. He was in his crib and choked on his milk. Just awful. They wanted to charge Kenny Ray with *two* murders, but the medical examiner said the baby's death was an accident. The husband came home from work and found his wife and child both dead. Of course the community was up in arms, and the police had to find someone to pin it on."

"They don't put a man away without evidence," Anthony said. "What did they have?"

"A neighbor picked Kenny Ray out of a lineup, but he had an alibi. He was across town when it happened. A man in jail with Kenny Ray said he confessed, but would you believe someone like that?"

"The jury did," Anthony said. "They believed the snitch, and they believed the eyewitness. Prosecutors love eyewitnesses. They're better than a fingerprint. Is the case still on appeal?"

"I don't know," Irene said. "Ruby told me the Supreme Court turned him down a few weeks ago."

"Which Supreme Court? Florida? United States?"

"The U.S. Supreme Court, I think. Why are you shaking your head? Is that bad?"

"He's running out of time. I don't know what issues could be left to litigate."

"Oh, this is *terrible*." Irene reached across the table. "Anthony, could you take the case? Don't worry about your fees. Ruby has some money saved up."

"Irene —"

"She said she would spend it all if she had to, every last dime, but she needs to find the right lawyer, someone experienced and tough and smart. I told her I'd trust you with my own life, if I had to."

"Irene, thank you for your confidence in me, but I can't. I'm sorry."

"Why not?" Gail leaned crossed arms on the table. "It would be exciting."

"Exciting?"

"To save an innocent man from execution. Don't you get bored with all those white-collar, federal bank fraud trials you've been doing lately?"

A smile flickered at the corner of his mouth. "I can't take Kenny Ray Clark's

24

case because he already *has* a lawyer — a team of them. The state of Florida appoints capital appellate lawyers for everyone on death row, one of the few states that does. I'm surprised that Mrs. Smith didn't mention it."

"She did," Irene said. "She's just not satisfied with the job they've done so far. There he sits on death row, and she can't get anything out of them except 'We're working on it.' She wants to hire an expert."

"They *are* experts. They're dedicated professionals who do nothing but defend prisoners under sentence of death." Anthony spoke slowly, clearly, and Gail distinctly heard the creeping edge of impatience. "Ruby didn't hire them, and she can't fire them. They're her grandson's lawyers, and that is probably why they don't talk to her. Even if Kenny Ray hired a new lawyer, and it would be very expensive, how much could be done after eleven years of appeals that hasn't been done already?" Anthony waited for Irene to deduce the obvious. Kenny Ray Clark was out of luck.

Irene lowered her eyes. "I don't know what to tell Ruby."

When Anthony glanced at Gail, she shot him a look hard enough to make him sigh. He took Irene's hand in both of his and patted it gently. "Tell her you talked to me. Tell her I said that the best thing she can do is trust his lawyers, and not to look for someone to make miracles. They will do a good job for Kenny Ray — a better job than I could do. If there is any way to prove his innocence, they will find it."

"Do you think so?"

"Of course."

Leaning back in her chair, feeling distinctly let down, Gail noticed a movement at the crack under the kitchen door, a shifting of light, probably made by someone's feet. A cat. Or a creature equally as curious.

"Karen? Come in here."

The swinging door opened, and Karen walked through as if it were natural to have come the long way around instead of through the back hall from the bedrooms. She wore a long yellow sleep shirt and her hair was still damp. She kissed each of them in turn, such a perfect child, smelling of soap and shampoo. "I finished my bath."

Irene roused herself. "Sit down, precious. I'll bet you're starving. Let's see what I've got in the fridge."

Karen went to the cookie jar. "How do they execute people? In the electric chair?"

"You've been eavesdropping," Gail said.

26

"I thought we agreed you wouldn't do that anymore."

"I wasn't. I heard you talking. I can't go around with my hands over my ears."

From across the kitchen, Irene said, "They inject something in his veins to make his heart stop beating."

"Like, stick a poison needle in his arm?"

"That's right."

"Mother, please."

"Do you prefer that I lie to her?" Irene shoved a casserole dish into the microwave and punched numbers on the keypad.

Anthony glanced at his watch and pretended surprise. "Ah. It's almost eleven o'clock. I should be going."

Karen asked, "They won't kill him if he's innocent, will they?"

"Damn good question," Irene said.

"They don't believe he is innocent." Anthony put a hand on Karen's shoulder. "He had a trial, and the jury found him guilty."

"For stabbing that woman." Too late, Karen realized her mistake, and glanced at Gail. "I heard you all the way in my room. You were pretty loud."

"I'll bet. We'll discuss this later."

Karen turned a bright smile on Anthony. "Thanks for taking me to the Keys. I had a really nice time."

"You are very welcome, *señorita.*" He made a small bow. "Good night."

Gail and her mother walked with him to the front door, then onto the porch. Gail was still in her shorts, adequate for bright sunshine, too cold at this hour.

With an excited intake of breath, Irene grabbed his arm. "Anthony, do you suppose, before I call Ruby, you could speak to his lawyers? You know. Find out what's going on? What they plan to do next?"

"Yes, why not?" Gail said.

His quick glance meant only one thing: Stay out of this, *por favor.* He gave her mother a regretful smile. "No, I'm afraid I can't, Irene. Client confidentiality. Lawyers aren't allowed to discuss their cases, even as a favor for a client's grandmother." He bent to kiss her cheek. "Let me know what happens, will you? I wish I could have been of more help. It was good to see you, Irene. Next time, a happier occasion."

"I hope so."

When the front door had closed and they were alone, Gail said, "I can't believe the way you just brushed my mother off."

"I did not brush her off, Gail. I gave an honest, pragmatic opinion."

"All she wants is to help an old friend."

28

"I know that. I would like to be able to help, believe me."

"Really? You can't make one phone call?"

"No, I can't."

"Why not?"

"Because — as I just explained to Irene, if you were listening — they won't talk to me."

"They would if you got Kenny Ray's authorization."

"Oh. *Perdóname.* I didn't think of that." He fixed his dark eyes on her. "If Ruby Smith wants to know the status of his appeal, and she isn't getting information from his lawyers, she should ask her grandson."

"What a sucky attitude."

"I am sorry you think so."

"How much time would it take, for God's sake? Ruby would pay you."

Anthony extended thumb and last finger, miming a telephone at his ear. " 'Oh, it's you, Mr. Quintana, big shot lawyer. You want to know if we are doing our jobs. Yes, we are, and screw you.' But maybe you're right. Maybe they would talk to me. 'Mr. Quintana, we are so sorry to tell you that our client just lost his last appeal, but we hope the next one will work. Maybe we can get him a few more years on death row.' Gail, all I would do is raise this woman's

29

hopes, then have to explain why the jury found her grandson guilty on evidence too persuasive to ignore, and that the best she can do is pray. Maybe Jesus will speak to the appeals court."

Gail narrowed her eyes.

"Sweetheart. Please. She's an old woman who used to clean houses for a living. I won't take advantage of her." He gently squeezed her shoulders. "Don't be angry with me, *querida*. There are lawyers who would take her money and in the end, accomplish nothing. I'm not one of them."

Gail leaned against his chest. "This is so sad."

"I know." His arms went around her.

"It's got to be terrible for Ruby. Waiting for him to die. Believing in his innocence."

"Yes. It's very sad."

Gail knew that he didn't give a damn what happened to Kenny Ray Clark. He didn't care and didn't want to care. Anthony Quintana had not become successful by taking on lost causes, unless — as he had jokingly told her — the client had a big enough bank account or a big enough cause to make losing palatable. Anthony could demand monstrous fees for his services, but would not take a dime from people like Ruby Smith. Gail had to admire him for that.

His hands were warm on her back. He nibbled her ear. *"Ven a casa conmigo."*

"Good night, Anthony." She kissed him and gave him a little shove.

From the end of the driveway she watched until his taillights had turned the corner. Then she stood there and watched the empty street. Her mother would be in the kitchen waiting for her. Wanting to know what to tell Ruby. Gail wished she knew.

CHAPTER 2

Monday, March 5

The sky had been gray all morning. Heavy clouds, cold rain sliding down the glass. Kenny could see the sky, the way his cell was situated. He reached up and pulled a string. Fluorescent tubes came on. The lights running down the corridor were too dim to read by, and not much came in through the window, ten feet away past a second set of bars.

Next door the Mexican kid was crying again. He'd arrived two weeks ago, still didn't believe it. Give him a few years, it would sink in.

Kenny put his blanket around his shoulders and sat on the edge of his bunk. He picked up the envelope again. The mail room had slit it open and read the letter before they'd sent it on to G wing. Kenny had read it himself four or five times this week, trying to decide what to do.

He lay back with his pillow folded under his neck and shook the letter out of the envelope. Three pages. Lined paper from a pad, a bunch of pink roses at the top of each page. The handwriting was a little shaky, but not hard to make out.

Dear Kenny Ray, I hope you are feeling better and that you got that bad tooth out. I am doing as well as can be expected, so don't worry. Thank you for the sweet poem you wrote me — he skipped to the bottom of the page — *You always said you was innocent, and I wanted to believe it but in my heart I never did. Now I know that you were telling the truth.*

Before going on to page two, which he could almost recite, Kenny rolled a paper around some Top tobacco. Licked it closed. Lit it. He'd learned not to rush. Whatever there was, expand it to fit the time in front of you. Develop a routine. He tossed the packet to the footlocker, pulled in some smoke, and started to cough. He had to get up and hawk in the sink. Press the button to turn on the water. Rinse the sink. Metal toilet underneath, use the paper to dry the sink. Put the roll back.

Ruby wanted him to quit smoking, and he'd told her he had. It made her happy. Whenever she visited, and it wasn't too often because she couldn't drive anymore, Kenny would put on a clean shirt and brush his teeth so she wouldn't smell the smoke. His teeth and fingers were stained, but she couldn't tell. She couldn't read without a magnifying glass in front of her nose. He hoped he outlived her.

He went back to his bunk and adjusted the blanket and pillow. Picked up the letter. Page two. *This is how I came to know that you're innocent. You might not believe me, but it's the truth.*

He shook his head. "Ol' lady, what am I going to do with you?"

The heavy, metal door opened at the end of the tier. There were footsteps on concrete, the clink of chains. Three guards coming, maybe more. Usually it was only one.

The crying next door stopped. Kenny couldn't see because of the block wall that divided the cells, but he could hear him. Manuel getting off his bunk. Walking to the front of his cell, putting his hands around the bars.

The empty milk carton from breakfast was sitting on his footlocker, and Kenny reached over to tap the ashes off his cigarette.

I know you are innocent because the Lord told me so. I felt His holy presence and heard His voice. He spoke your name.

Kenny wondered what the Lord sounded like. If he had a deep voice.

He told me that you never killed that girl and

*they should not have put you on trial nor sen-
tenced you to death.*

"Why don't you tell the Lord to come on down and get my ass out of here?"

A couple of seconds later the guards walked by, four of them, and Kenny watched over his raised knees. They stopped at the next cell. He knew all of them but the young one with the blond crew cut.

The oldest, the sergeant, said, "Lucius? Come on over here." Lucius was supposed to turn backward and hold his hands next to the bean flap so they could put on the cuffs.

"Go away." His voice was muffled. "It's too damn cold to get up."

Kenny wondered where they were taking him. If they were going somewhere like the shower they only used the handcuffs. But they were carrying leg irons and a waist chain. Lucius couldn't be going to the visiting room because this wasn't the weekend, and weekend or not, he never had visitors. He'd been in here sixteen years, a lot longer than Kenny, and his folks never showed. His last appeal had been turned down by the Supreme Court. Kenny had a bad feeling.

"Come on now, Lucius, don't make us come in there."

Kenny's eyes went back to the letter. *I'm going to hire you a new lawyer. I don't think the ones you have are doing you any good.*

Lucius asked a question, but it didn't carry around the corner.

The sergeant said, "Goin' down the hall."

"Y'all takin' me to see the warden?"

"Don't know, podna, just following orders. Let's go."

"Is they a warrant?" His voice was thin as a wire.

"Stand up, Lucius. C'mon over here. Don't make us come get you."

I have enough money to pay for a good lawyer. Please don't tell me not to. I am eighty-one years old and I have my mind made up.

The guards were talking to each other. "He ain't coming out." "Yeah, he will. Come on, Lucius." "He ain't coming, I said." One of them spoke into his radio. "Go ahead. Unlock it."

"Oh, Jesus," said Lucius. "They's a warrant, ain't they? The warden gon' to read me the warrant."

"Come on, now. We gotta take you with us. Don't make it hard."

"Jesus, Jesus."

The young guard laughed. "Jesus ain't gonna help you where you're going."

The sergeant looked around at him. "Shut up."

The lock clicked, metal striking metal.

Manuel was crying again. His face would be pressed against the bars, tears making his fat cheeks all shiny.

Page three.

In my life I have tried to do the Lord's will, and He has shown me the way. I prayed for you to be saved, and I can already see you walking in the blessed light of His love.

The young guy stood back while the door came open, and the other three went inside. Lucius was fifty-two years old and weighed about a hundred pounds. They wouldn't have any trouble.

"Let go of the bunk, Lucius."

"Don't pull me, I can stand up."

"Then do it. We ain't got all day."

Metal clicked. They told him to turn around. Put his foot out. Now the other foot. Click. Click. Chain links whipped through metal and danced on the concrete floor.

Black guy at the end of the row called out, "Kick their ass, old man."

Trust in the Lord God, for He is your rock and your salvation.

Kenny threw the blanket aside and stood up. His legs were weak all of a sudden, and he leaned his forearms on the flat metal brace the bars ran through. He turned his head left to see what he could see. The guards were bringing Lucius out. The blond one pointed at Kenny and said, "Stand back." Kenny blew some smoke into the corridor and didn't move.

The leg irons made Lucius shuffle along, and his unlaced sneakers slapped on the floor. His hands were cuffed at his waist, curled around each other like he was holding on. The bright orange shirt was too big for him. He stopped outside Kenny's cell. He grinned, and his eyes rolled white in his face. "Bet you a smoke they's takin' me to see the warden. We gon' have us a tea party."

Kenny nodded. "Bring me a cookie."

"I will." Lucius seemed like he was hung up on what to say next. He ran his tongue over his lips. "Take care of yourself."

"You'll be back."

"Well. I hope so, but you know what they say. Third time's a charm."

Lucius had slipped past two death warrants already. For a while he just looked through the bars at Kenny. The sergeant put a hand on his shoulder. "Let's go, podna."

Someone shouted down the row, "Lucius! Stay strong."

When they were out of sight Kenny put his forehead against the metal and closed his eyes.

The kid said, "Where they going? What happen?"

His little brown nose was sticking out past the bars. Kenny wished he could reach around and break it. "Just shut the fuck up."

"*Y tu madre.*" Manuel went to turn on his radio, a spic station out of Jacksonville. Usually the other guys would be screaming at him to turn it down, but nobody was talking.

Kenny sat on his bunk and rolled another rip. Lit it. He looked down at the letter. *I felt His holy presence and heard His voice. He spoke your name.*

"Crazy old woman."

Kenny gathered the pages of Ruby's letter and tucked them into the envelope. He opened his footlocker and dropped the letter inside. He'd write her back tonight or tomorrow. Tell her to forget it. Don't waste your money on me, Ruby.

Eleven years on death row, only one way he was getting out.

CHAPTER 3

Thursday, March 8

Kenny Ray Clark's state-appointed lawyers worked out of an office in Fort Lauderdale, next door to the federal courthouse. A woman named Denise Robinson was handling his appeal. Over the telephone she had sounded African-American, northeastern, smart. And in a big hurry to get back to whatever it was she'd been doing. No, she said. She couldn't discuss the Clark case or any other case. Gail persisted: "Under the circumstances, I believe he'd allow it. Would you ask him?"

There was a long pause. Ms. Robinson said, "Our liaison's going out to the prison this week. He might have time to see Mr. Clark. I'll get back to you." She hung up.

Gail muttered, "Thanks for your call, Ms. Connor."

She had made Ruby a promise — not to take over the case, but to find out what was going on. Ruby had wanted to pay, but Gail had refused. This was a favor.

Ms. Robinson called back on Thursday morning. Kenny Ray Clark had signed a permission form. "He said he knows you. I'm going to quote him because it's kind of funny. He told our liaison, 'Yeah, Gail Connor, the skinny blond girl with a mouth on her.' " Ms. Robinson laughed as if they were sharing a joke.

How strange, knowing a man on death row. Gail could not imagine how a boy of twelve had metamorphosed into a killer. She corrected herself: an alleged killer.

In the same conversation Ms. Robinson quickly recounted the history of the case. After taking over from the trial attorney, CCR had appealed first through the state system, then up the federal ladder — district court, Eleventh Circuit Court of Appeals, finally the U.S. Supreme Court. The lawyers had claimed incompetent trial counsel, improper sentence, prosecutorial misconduct, judicial bias, et cetera, and they had been denied at every turn.

"You said 'CCR.' What is that?"

"Capital Collateral Representatives. It's the old name, what we were called before the legislature split us into three regional offices. They wanted to make us more efficient. Keep that conveyor belt moving."

Moving toward the lethal-injection gurney, Gail supposed. "What do you plan to do next?"

Ms. Robinson replied that a piece of good luck had just dropped into their laps — a new alibi witness named Tina Hopwood. She was saying that the police had pressured her not to testify at the trial. An investigator needed to go up to Stuart to interview the woman. Depending on what he found out, they might file a new 3.850.

"Thirty-eight fifty?"

"Three-point-eight-five-oh. Motion for postconviction relief. Look in the Rules of Criminal Procedure."

After venturing an opinion that Kenny Ray Clark was probably safe for at least another two years, Ms. Robinson relented: Gail could come by the office and look at the files that afternoon. Gail told her secretary to clear her schedule.

At noon she and Anthony met at their favorite Italian place in Coral Gables. As soon as the waiter had taken their orders Gail leaned across the small table and told Anthony about the new alibi witness.

"Tina wasn't Kenny's girlfriend, by the way. She and her husband, Glen, had rented him a spare room in their trailer. Anyway, Kenny was behind in his rent, and at ten o'clock on the morning of the murder, Tina threw him out. At that same time, an eyewitness put Kenny at the murder scene."

"Why didn't Tina Hopwood testify at trial?" Anthony broke off some bread, then looked around for the butter.

"The police forced her not to." Aware how unlikely this sounded, Gail added, "That's what she alleges. The point is, if Tina Hopwood is telling the truth, and if the eyewitness is mistaken, there's an innocent man on death row."

Anthony took a bite of bread. The gold at his wrist glittered. "What about the confession?"

"A jailhouse snitch. You know what their word is worth."

He looked at her, then said, "May I give you a little advice, sweetheart? Do what you have to for Ruby, then let it go. You should spend your time on your own cases."

"This is my case, Anthony. And stop being so damned condescending, will you?"

Gail hated to admit it, but he had a point. She had taken a risk opening her own office last year, and she was barely afloat. And why not, after the death of her sister, divorce, engagement to Anthony, breakup from Anthony, a pubescent daughter driving her nuts, a miscarriage, six months on antidepressants, and a frequent desire to throw herself in front of a cement truck. She was better now. She was beginning to think

43

she was going to be all right.

Following Ms. Robinson's instructions, Gail took the elevator up to the fourth floor. A sign on the wall announced OFFICE OF CAPITAL COLLATERAL COUNSEL, SOUTHERN REGION. Beside that was the seal of the state of Florida. An unmarked door opened directly into a room with stacks of cardboard banker's boxes and a huge copy machine. A young man in jeans and a T-shirt looked around as he continued to press buttons and flip pages.

"Hi. Need some help?"

It took Gail a second to realize that she had not inadvertently come in the wrong way. There was no reception area because the clients never showed up. She said who she was, and that Ms. Robinson was expecting her.

"Denise said to put you in the conference room. She's finishing up a brief. It won't take long." He led Gail around the corner past open doors and offices cluttered with papers. She heard someone on a phone call, saw a man typing into his computer.

"Can I get you anything? Coffee?"

"No, I'm fine. Thanks."

Left alone, she set her briefcase on the

floor. Law books occupied the shelves, but so many storage boxes were in the way it would have been hard to reach them. More boxes had been piled on a hand truck and stacked on a low blue sofa.

On the long table in the center of the room was one box with a piece of paper taped to the lid. Gail went over to read it. *D. Robinson.* She lifted the lid. Legal papers. The one on top was an inch thick. *State of Florida vs. Kenneth Ray Clark. Amended Motion to Vacate Judgment of Conviction.* Under that were more pleadings. Manila folders had been crammed in sideways. Gail walked her fingers over the index tabs. *Police reports. Witness list. Crime lab. Autopsy.* Until now, this case had not been real to her. She took out the folder with the police reports and flipped it open. The reports had been filed in chronological order, starting with the first officer to arrive on the scene, Deputy R. Adams.

On Monday, Feb. 6, 1989, at approximately 1817 hours, this deputy was dispatched to the residence at 2200 White Heron Way in Palm City w/regard to a complaint re deceased persons. On arrival at 1821 hours I observed complainant, Gary Dodson, standing in front yard holding his son (Darryl Dodson, w/m 03/11/88). Mr. Dodson was visibly upset and crying. I asked if he or the child needed medical attention and he kept saying "they're dead, they're dead," referring to his wife and child. I entered the home and found the wife, later identified as Amber Lynn Dodson (w/f 01/30/65) lying faceup on the bed, partially clothed. There appeared to be an electrical cord around her neck and several stab wounds to her torso.

A large amount of blood had pooled around the body. I exited the house and contacted Sgt. Hardy via radio and requested him to meet me at the scene. EMS along w/Martin County fire/rescue arrived at approx. 1823 hours. Paramedic Marsh pronounced the child at 1824. Paramedic Lee entered the residence and pronounced the

wife at approx. 1825. I began
my crime roster and proceeded
to secure the scene. . . .

Many more pages followed, written by
various other officers. Supplemental inci-
dent reports. Copies of pages from a pocket-
sized spiral notebook in which conversations with neighbors had been recorded.
Names, dates, times. Crime scene reports.
A scale drawing of the house. Typewritten
pages prepared by a Sergeant R. Kemp. A
report of a photo lineup, copy attached. Six
small faces, badly reproduced, impossible
to make out. One was initialed "DC" and
dated 2/20/89. *Dorothy Chastain positively
identified photograph #2, Kenneth Ray Clark,
as the man she observed on the victim's property.* A copy of the report had been sent to
Captain Bryce.

Gail slowly let the folder down on the
table, her eyes on the page. She had expected his name to pop up somewhere. This
was a Martin County case, after all, and the
sheriff's office had investigated.

The last time Gail had seen Garlan Bryce
had been at her cousin Jackie's graduation
from high school eight years ago. He'd been
Sheriff Bryce by then, a big man in a business suit and a Stetson, his military haircut

turning gray. After the ceremony they'd all gone back to the house, which his grandparents had built on the St. Lucie River. Friends, relatives, and local big shots had spilled out onto the oak-shaded lawn. Gail and Jackie had sat in a porch swing and talked. They'd caught up on news and promised to stay in touch. But they hadn't. Ever since Aunt Lou's death, the Bryces had kept their distance. Gail wasn't entirely sure what the story was, it had been so long ago, but she thought it started when Louise and Garlan's marriage went bad. Aunt Lou left him, and a few months later her car veered off the road and overturned. At the funeral Gail saw how Garlan avoided her mother. He'd blamed Irene for taking her sister's side.

"Ms. Connor. You must've found something *real* interesting. I called your name twice."

The woman standing in the doorway came in. She was in her mid-forties, Gail thought, and very tall, over six feet. Her long legs made her quick steps seem graceful. A white linen shirt hung loose over faded blue jeans. Her hair was pulled tightly back, shining, then escaping into a huge black puff. Each ear was adorned with several earrings. Behind gold-framed glasses, her large, slightly protruding eyes rested on Gail as if taking a reading. She extended her hand.

"I'm Denise Robinson. Sorry to keep you waiting. Things are crazy around here."

Gail nodded. "I hope it was all right if I looked through the box."

"That's why I left it there. You'll find only the basic stuff, but it gives you a good overview. That's what you said you needed."

"What about the trial transcript?"

"I didn't put it in."

"Well, could I see it?"

Ms. Robinson raised a brow. "It's two thousand pages. Do you have time for that? We can't make free copies."

"I'll do what I can today and come back tomorrow. What time do you close the office?"

"We *live* here. You think I'm kidding." Ms. Robinson finally smiled, showing a space between her front teeth. "Okay, I'll ask someone to dig out the transcript for you. Read and observe a bad defense attorney greasing the tracks toward a conviction."

"Who was it? The public defender?"

"If only. No, the PD would've done a decent job. One of their clients was a witness against Kenny Ray, so they had to conflict out. The judge appointed Walter Meadows. Aside from being a practicing alcoholic, he hadn't handled a capital case in twenty years."

"Why didn't the Florida Supreme Court order a new trial if Meadows was so bad?"

"You don't do much criminal law, do you? The Florida Supreme Court doesn't like to overturn convictions. They want to keep that train rollin' down the tracks."

Gail gave a quick shake of her head. "No, what was their basis for denying your claim of ineffective assistance of counsel?"

Apparently surprised that Gail had the brains to remember this, Ms. Robinson said, "Here's how it works. We don't file our motion in the Supreme Court. The rule says we have to file it in the *trial* court, right back before Judge Willis. Now, is Willis going to admit he was *wrong* to appoint Walter Meadows? Uh-uh. Judge Willis says, well, so what if Walt didn't do his own investigation? And if he didn't cross-examine that deputy, why, he musta had good reasons. It was all defense strategy. The jury might have voted guilty anyhow, so I'm gonna deny y'all's motion."

"He didn't say *that,* surely."

Denise Robinson gave a slow nod, and the black pouf of her hair went up and down.

"When we take it up to the Florida Supreme Court, all they ask is, 'Did the trial judge have *any* facts to support his decision, or was he *totally* off the wall?' "

"I see. He didn't sound irrational, so they affirmed his ruling."

"You got it." Denise Robinson tilted her head toward the box on the table. "What did you find in there that was so fascinating?"

"A name. Garlan Bryce. He was married to my aunt."

"Sheriff Bryce? We've met in court a few times." She gave Gail a sideways glance. "And he's your *uncle?*"

"By marriage. We haven't really been in contact since my aunt died. What did Garlan do on the Clark case?"

"Supervised. He was in charge of the Criminal Investigations Division. The lead detective was Ronald Kemp, but Garlan Bryce ran the show."

"Did Tina Hopwood say who convinced her not to testify?"

"It would probably have been Kemp, somebody working the case directly. I doubt it was Bryce — if that's your question."

"But he would have known about it, don't you think?"

"Of course." Denise Robinson sat on a

corner of the table. "You and Sheriff Bryce don't speak?"

"Not lately."

"Too bad. Guess I can't ask you to call him up. 'Uncle Garlan, what did y'all do to Tina Hopwood?' "

Gail smiled. "What did Ms. Hopwood say?"

"She was on probation for worthless checks at the time, and they threatened to have her thrown in jail. I haven't talked to her directly. She called Walt Meadows, and he got in touch with us. He's retired, but she didn't know who else to call, and I think Walt feels bad, somewhere in his pickled little brain, for how he messed up."

"Why do you think Ms. Hopwood waited eleven years to say anything about it?"

"Damned if I know. I just hope she doesn't change her mind." Denise pushed away from the table. "If that's it, I need to get back to work. Coffee machine's down the hall to your left."

"Wait. Could you give me an opinion about something?"

She turned around in the doorway. "All right. What?"

"Do you think Kenny Ray Clark is innocent?"

"Excuse me?"

"I think Ruby would be all right if she had some hope."

"Hope of what? That he actually, factually didn't do it?"

"Yes. What can I tell Ruby?"

"For God's sake, you *never* tell a relative the client is innocent. Don't even go there. They'll expect him to walk out the door, and it might not happen, then they'll hate you. I think the best she can hope for is a new trial. If Kenny gets a lawyer who knows his ass from his elbow, he might have a chance. Tell Ruby that this new information will give us more time. Other than that . . . I don't know. I can't say what's going to happen. Now if you'll excuse me. That brief won't write itself."

"Ms. Robinson —"

She turned around again.

"Could he be innocent?"

"He says he is. As his lawyer, I don't ask."

"But most of them claim to be, don't they? What do you really think?"

Her dark eyes flared with impatience. "I can't answer that. No, I'll be real clear. I *won't*. I'm not going to sell out my clients by dividing them into two neat little stacks, those that deserve my help, and those that don't."

"I would like to tell Mrs. Smith," Gail

said firmly, "whether Kenny has any chance of getting out of prison. I presume that innocence would make a difference."

"You presume. Let me tell you something, Ms. Connor. Guilt or innocence is not the point. The state is trying to kill my clients. I'm not asking that they be set free. I just don't want them dead. Who do you think they are? A bunch of Ted Bundys? My clients are more ordinary than you'd ever dream. Most of them are from poor and violent homes. They can hardly read and write. They're addicts and alcoholics. A few were juveniles at the time of the crime, and the Supreme Court says it's okay if we execute them. Half of the people sentenced to death are black, and the Supreme Court sees no problem with that. It sees no problem rejecting a claim of innocence, as long as the prisoner got a fair trial, but would someone tell me what that is? I've seen cops lie, witnesses make mistakes, and defense lawyers fall asleep. Killing people to prevent killing doesn't work, hasn't worked, and never will, but damn, it feels good. You sort through all that, and then we'll talk about innocence and guilt."

Gail could think of no response. Her cheeks burned from confusion and embarrassment. "I'm grateful for your time. If you would have someone find the trial transcript, I'll get to work."

Denise Robinson put a hand on top of her head and looked toward the ceiling. "Lord have mercy." With a low laugh, she said, "How I go on. Live, eat, breathe this kind of work, you forget how to talk to normal folks. I am sorry."

"I understand," Gail said. "You believe in what you're doing."

"Yes, I do."

For a long moment, Denise looked across the table at her, then smiled. "Why don't you sit down and let's talk for a little bit." She pushed a chair toward Gail, then found another for herself. She crossed her legs. "What law firm are you with?"

"I'm a sole practitioner." Gail sat down but could not relax. "I was with Hartwell Black and Robineau in Miami for eight years, handling major commercial litigation. Last year they offered me a partnership, but I said no and opened my own office. I needed a more flexible schedule. I'm divorced with a daughter, Karen. She's eleven now. Her dad's living in the U.S. Virgin Islands, so I'm it."

"I hear you." Denise's smile showed the gap in her teeth. "Hartwell Black, huh? That's starting at the top. What kinds of cases do you do now?"

"Basically anything that crosses my desk."

"But not criminal law?"

"I know nothing about criminal law. Well, that's not entirely true. I've picked up a few things from my . . . well, I guess you could say fiancé, but we're not in a hurry. His name is Anthony Quintana. You might have heard of him."

"I *might* have heard of him? Oh-ho, yes. If my clients could've hired Anthony Quintana, most of them wouldn't *be* my clients." She grinned. "You know the definition of capital punishment?"

"No, what?"

"Them without the capital gets the punishment." Pushing herself out of the chair, Denise said, "You know what? Before I leave you with all those files and things, you ought to say hi to Kenny." She laughed. "His picture's on the Department of Corrections Web site. You can leave your briefcase in here, it'll be all right. Come on."

Gail followed her out the door.

Denise glanced over her shoulder as she walked. "Ruby Smith had three children, and Kenny's mother was the oldest, Norma. She married a house painter and they moved around for a few years. Kenny was born in Arkansas, he and his older sister. Their father split when he was five. Norma's second husband beat her and the kids with anything in reach. A broom handle, a belt, an extension cord. He was sent to prison on drug charges. After that Norma lived with a man who started sexually abusing Kenny when he was nine years old."

"My God," Gail murmured. She had some knowledge of Ruby's family history but not this.

"It wasn't in the record. Kenny wouldn't let Walter Meadows bring it up in the sentencing phase. He was too ashamed. Walter should have pushed him, because the jury needed to hear it."

Denise led Gail into a cluttered office at the end of the hall. Windows looked out on the rough gray exterior of the federal courthouse.

"Norma found out, but she was afraid. She threw the kids in the car and came back to Florida. She was a heavy drinker, and it got worse. When Kenny was fourteen, she ran a hose from her exhaust through the car window and killed herself. It won't surprise you to learn that Kenny had some emotional problems as a teenager. A psychologist testified about that, but the jury didn't buy it. They recommended death ten-to-

57

two, and the judge concurred. He said that the victim had been strangled and stabbed to death in the course of a burglary, which made the crime particularly heinous, atrocious, and cruel. He also made reference to Kenny's prior record."

Denise moved some papers off a chair and dragged it closer so Gail could look over her shoulder. She kept talking as she tapped on her keyboard, going on-line. Her hair was a soft black cloud resting on the white linen curve of her back. Framed photographs filled a shelf over her desk: a young couple with a baby, a child riding a tricycle, a young woman in a cap and gown. A letter on lined paper was tacked to a corkboard. *Dear miss Robison! I thoagt you want to know they have tranfer me off the row, I am now at Sumter Corectinal . . .*

"He didn't have a long list of violent offenses, like armed robbery or sexual battery, as a lot of them do. It was mostly minor drug offenses or drunk and disorderly. Unfortunately, he was out on bond for an attempted burglary in the same area as the murder three months prior, but it hadn't gone to trial yet. Then there was the aggravated assault, which the prosecutor really drummed on."

The Web connection was made, and the

home page for the Florida Department of Corrections assembled itself.

"Kenny pulled a knife on another man outside a bar. He was twenty, they'd both been drinking, and who knows who started it, but his lawyer advised him to plead guilty to avoid jail time. At his murder trial, the prosecutor told the jury that Kenny had a violent criminal history, and that unless they recommended death, he was likely to be a danger to other inmates."

Denise clicked on the link *Death Row*. A long list of names appeared on the screen. She scrolled through it, lines flashing past. She slowed. "Here he is." She clicked on his name. "I think the photo is fairly recent. He's thirty-four now. He was twenty-two when he was arrested."

The screen went blank for a moment, then the face of a man appeared, text underneath. Gail didn't read the words. Her attention was on Kenneth Ray Clark, who stared sullenly back at her. He was all bones and angles, with hollow cheeks and temples, and prominent ridges around his eyes. The colors were vivid: brown hair, hazel eyes, purplish blotches underneath them on pale skin, a V-necked orange shirt.

Gail drew back from the screen. She didn't know him. This face wasn't familiar.

There was nothing here but low intellect and caged violence. But what was a man supposed to look like, who had been beaten and raped as a child? A man who had spent most of his adult life waiting to be executed. She felt ignorant and out of place.

Denise looked at her, then with a series of clicks, exited the site. For a while she sat with her hands in her lap, her gaze going out the window. "The first time I saw a death row inmate, it wasn't on the Internet, it was in a maximum security prison. I was so scared my voice croaked, and I couldn't hold my pen to take notes. You think I've always done this? Uh-uh. I'm a middle-class girl from Baltimore. My parents taught high school. I worked in oil and gas law in DC for ten years. Two kids, a nice house in Arlington. My husband died of a heart attack, forty years old. One day my son told me about a boy he'd met whose father had been sentenced to death in Virginia, and he was going to be electrocuted. He asked me if I'd help him. What was I going to say? No? One thing led to another, and I worked my rear end off, and got a stay of execution. He was resentenced to life. Maybe he'll be paroled, maybe not, but at least he's alive. I never went back to my old job. I applied for a job here. That was seven years ago. It's hard. When we lose a client, I cry. I do. I cry and then I get busy trying to save the next one. Sometimes we succeed."

Her eyes softened. "I'm sorry. I didn't mean to beat up on you before."

Gail smiled. "I'm tougher than I look."

"Yes, you are." Denise swiveled her chair around. "Listen. Kenny needs some help. I'm working eighteen hours a day right now, and so is everyone else. We have to file that motion as soon as possible. It could buy him some time."

"Wait. You don't want *me* to do it?"

"I have to tell you, we don't pay. All right? But it's just this one thing. If you don't want to continue on, we can try to find someone else to take over."

"Denise, I can't."

"Eight years with a major law firm? Don't tell me you can't."

"I do commercial litigation. My God. I'm not qualified to take on a death row appeal."

"It's not that hard. All you have to do is go talk to Tina Hopwood, look into the case a little bit, write the pleadings, and file the motion. If the judge grants a hearing, you argue it." Denise Robinson's eyes did not move from Gail's face. "I *know* you can argue."

Gail was shaking her head. "I'm sorry. I

don't have time. My own cases are so back-logged —"

"We've got forms, checklists, and tons of research materials. We can answer any question you have. That motion *must* be filed soon."

"I came here to discuss the case and report to Ruby Smith. That's all." Gail heard the plaintive tones in her own voice.

"I know. I know you did." Denise put her hand over Gail's and patted it. "You really want to do something for her? Or just talk about it?"

"This is crazy."

"No. I'll tell you what it is, Gail. We get civil practice lawyers from big law firms come in here, very big firms, that have a policy of so many hours of pro bono work. They come in, and they don't know who the client is. He's a name on a file. He's one inmate out of nearly four hundred. But they start working the case, and they start thinking about how this man got where he was, and the next man with similar facts and a better trial lawyer got life or an acquittal. They meet the client and find out he's been locked up ten years, and in that time he's learned how to read and write, and he has come to some understanding of the world. The lawyer wonders, what are we going to gain, killing this man? A lawyer who takes a capital appeal gets inside the system, really inside. And sometimes, not very often, he finds a man who shouldn't be there at all. Talk about joy. You don't know joy till you see that man walk into the light. But no matter how it ends, win or lose, whether the client gets a new trial or he's put to death, I've never had one of these lawyers — not one — come back and tell me, Denise, this was a waste of my time. Maybe they do only that one case, but they all say thank you. Now I see how it is. I understand. I didn't before, but I do now."

Denise Robinson leaned nearer, and Gail felt the pull of her bright eyes. "You want me to tell you that Kenny is innocent, and that you're going to win. I can't promise that, but you *will* have something worth fighting for. Justice. A man's life. A man's *life*. As a lawyer, ask yourself, what can I ever do in my career that will matter as much as this?"

CHAPTER 4

Friday afternoon, March 9

From his position at the edge of the fairway, Anthony could see the half-acre pond at the bottom of the slope. Banyans formed a dark, leafy backdrop, and the reddening sun glittered through their branches. Shadows extended across the grass. Beyond the trees soared the coral pink tower of the Biltmore Hotel.

A diver in full-body wet suit and mask slid under the water. Lily pads shifted. Another diver emerged carrying a mesh bag lumpy with golf balls. He spit out his regulator and upturned the bag over a wire basket. The balls rattled into it. The divers were using underwater lights, but they would stop working at sunset.

Anthony assumed they were former Cuban operatives for the CIA. The man who had hired them sat on a folding wooden chair and watched their progress. This was Hector Mesa, a small, gray-haired *mulato* in a suit and tie. His duties for Anthony's grandfather were undefined but of long standing. Ernesto had lent him to Anthony

64

for this job. Hector didn't know how long it would take, but Anthony had said it didn't matter. Hector's radio was tuned to one of the Miami AM stations that played old boleros and mambos on scratchy 78s recorded in the fifties. His foot, in its polished leather shoe, kept the beat.

A voice came from the other direction. *"¡Oye! Anthony! ¿Cómo va eso?"*

Anthony turned to see a wheelchair speeding across the grass. In it sat his grandfather, wearing his Panama hat and pointing a cane in his direction. Ernesto's male nurse pushed the chair, and Gail and her daughter ran to keep up. They had come through the wooden gate in the rock wall that surrounded the Pedrosa house. Its red tile roof and stucco chimneys rose above the trees in the yard.

Gail waved, and Anthony waved back. She looked like a teenager, such a bright smile, and her dark blond hair swinging around her face. Capri pants and white sneakers made her legs long and slender, and a loose blue sweater hid her breasts.

A golf cart went by and a man leaned out the side shouting at them to get off the fairway. Ernesto shook his cane at him. Out of breath, the nurse stopped the wheelchair a few feet into the rough. He helped Ernesto

65

stand up. Ernesto hated the chair.

"Mira las bellezas que te traje."

He could speak perfect English, but often his mind refused to remember this. Anthony nodded. "Yes, two beautiful ladies." He kissed Gail's cheek, then Karen's.

"What are they *doing?*" Karen asked, her eyes on the divers.

"Looking for golf balls. Go see how many they've found. You can have some if you want." The girl ran toward the pond.

Anthony saw Gail steady the old man with a hand on his arm, pretending that she needed his support on this uneven ground. "How in the world did you get permission?"

"The general manager was very understanding."

"I'll bet."

Ernesto laughed. "What does it cost to fish for golf balls? *Estás loco.*"

Gail whispered, "I agree with you, *Señor* Pedrosa. He's nuts."

"Anthony, *adentro.* Everyone is here. *Vamos a comer.*"

"Oh, Ernesto, could you tell them to go ahead and start without us? I have to see this."

She had something on her mind. Anthony said, "*Ahorita, abuelo.* We'll be there in a few minutes." Gail called for Karen to go with Ernesto. The nurse helped the old man back into his chair, turned it around, and checked for golfers before hurrying across to the gate in the wall. Ernesto held his hat on. Karen ran beside him, her pockets full of golf balls.

Gail turned around. "Did you tell everyone what you're doing out here?"

"No, only Hector. Those other guys won't talk."

"But Hector tells Ernesto everything, and Ernesto tells your grandmother, and she always confides in *Tia* Fermina, who would probably tell Uncle Humberto and Betty and Xiomara — Stop laughing. We have to go in there and have dinner with everybody. This is so embarrassing."

"What is? That I love you this much?"

She looked back at the house, hiding her smile.

Anthony whispered, "I'm going to find your ring."

"Good luck."

"Oh, yes, and then we'll see how much your promises are worth."

"I didn't *promise*."

"You did."

"Not in those words." She reached for his hand. "I need to talk to you before we go inside."

"We'll walk to the other fairway and back."

They went around the pond and into the trees. The banyans blocked the fading light with their heavy foliage and multiple trunks. Gail lifted a pile of leaves with one foot and sent them spinning. "Ernesto is in good spirits," she said. "He's almost giddy. What is it, his new heart medication?"

"No, I came over early, and we talked about the trip."

The trip to Cuba. Only a few people knew about it. Ernesto Pedrosa Masvidal had spent the past forty years condemning the regime, supporting secret raids, and bending American foreign policy. All that was over. The old tiger was worn out. Now he wanted to sit along the Malecón once more and watch the waves. To flirt with the women, to smoke a *robusto*, to drive into the countryside and for the last time fill his eyes and his heart with Cuba.

"Have you decided when you'll go?"

"Probably the middle of April," he said.

"That's so soon."

"The weather will be good."

She put her arm around his waist. When they passed behind one of the immense trees, out of sight of the men at the pond, Anthony turned her around and kissed her. Her mouth was warm and tender, opening for him. He thought of the small room up-stairs. He could make some excuse to the others. No one would look for them.

Pulling away, she said, "Anthony, I have to drive up to Stuart early in the morning and come back on Sunday. Mother's going to watch Karen. I was thinking . . . maybe you'd like to go with me. If you have time."

"I would like that very much — unless you plan to get separate hotel rooms."

She smiled. "No. Just one."

"Good. Let me pay for it, because I want something nice. On the beach. All right? You're going to Stuart to talk to Ruby Smith?"

"Yes, and to Tina Hopwood as well, and to as many other witnesses as I can find. I'm going to reinvestigate the case, and I'd really like your advice on how to do it."

"What?"

"Kenny Clark is probably innocent. The trial was a joke. I've read the transcript. I've read everything. I didn't get to bed until three o'clock this morning. Denise Robinson asked me to file a second motion for postconviction relief. I told her I would." Gail stopped, her eyes on him, waiting for a reaction.

Anthony said, "What do you mean? You're helping them out?"

"Yes."

69

"You're going to work on a *death case?*"
He had to laugh. "*Ay, Dios mío.* A capital
appeal. You don't know anything about it."
Gail's mouth compressed to a line. He put
his arm around her. "Sweetheart, I'm sorry,
but come on. It's not worth it."

"I'm not doing it pro bono," she said. "I
called Ruby, and she's willing to pay fees
and expenses."

"Oh, my God. No. You would take this
old woman's money? For what? Let his attorneys handle it. They're taking advantage
of you, using you like a law clerk."

The light was not so dim he couldn't see
the flush of anger on Gail's cheeks. "I already told Ruby I would file an appeal. For
God's sake, Anthony, give me some credit.
Denise has already given me checklists and
forms and copies of relevant case law, and I
thought — excuse me for presuming — that I
could get some input from you."

"No. I told you, I'm not getting involved,
and I don't want you to either. You complain you have no time for Karen or for me,
but you have time for *this?*"

"That's so selfish."

"I mean it, Gail. Tell Ruby you changed
your mind."

"I can't."

"What do you mean, you *can't?*"

Her chin lifted. "I've signed a notice of appearance."

"*Alaba'o.* You what? *¿Qué has hecho?* Do you know what this means? You would need a court order to get rid of this case!"

"Denise said that she could find someone else to take over, but for now, the motion has to be filed —"

"*Ay, mi madre,* she would say anything, they are so desperate over there." He was on the verge of incredulous laughter. It appalled him that Gail could be so gullible, so naive. Why would that woman with CCR have given a death case to a lawyer who was in no way qualified — The answer came to him.

"Did you tell Ms. Robinson that you know me? Did you mention my name?"

"Yes, so what?"

"Aha. This is why she wants you. Call her. Call her right now. Tell her she has to take the case back."

"I will not. I know damned well how to research the law, analyze a case, and write a brief. I've been doing it for *nine years!* You have no respect for my intelligence, my abilities —"

"Gail —"

"— or my commitment to something a little larger than my own immediate interests. What do *you* do? You hardly practice law anymore. When was the last time you took a case that really excited you? You're so busy chasing business deals —"

"*¡Espérate!* It's a crime to make money now? I have a law firm and two teenagers to support. You didn't complain about money when I took you and Karen skiing in Aspen last month."

Her eyes sparked with anger, and she squared her shoulders. "Oh, that is so low."

"I didn't mean that." He pressed his fingers to his forehead, then dropped his arms by his sides. "Gail, listen to me. A death row appeal can take all your energy, every hour in the day, everything you have. You can't possibly bill Ruby Smith enough to pay for the time you will lose. If you do this, you will regret it."

"I'm a lawyer. I want to practice the kind of law that *matters*."

He listed in his mind all the things that should matter to her, but this was not the time. He came closer, speaking softly. "Do you think this is because of losing the baby? You became so depressed —"

"Dammit, Anthony, would you stop treating me as if I were on the verge of a mental collapse?" She swept his hands aside.

He took a breath and let it out. "I give up. What can I say that won't set you off?"

She looked toward the pond, which caught the last shimmers of sunlight. One of the divers waded out of the water with a dripping bag full of golf balls. Faintly came the notes of an old bolero from Hector Mesa's radio.

With a small laugh Gail said, "Incredible."

"What is?"

"All the trouble you go to for me." Her eyes shifted back to him, wide and blue, full of repentance. "I adore you, Anthony."

His head throbbed. *"¿Me quieres? Tú me vuelves loco."*

"Do you still want to come with me to Stuart? You don't have to help on the case. I won't even talk about it."

"Yes, you will." He held out his hand. "And yes, I want to come with you."

They left after dinner. Martin County wasn't so far away, and not waiting till morning would give them two nights together, not one.

Anthony had driven the traffic-choked interstate many times to the Palm Beach County courthouse, or had arrowed directly to Disney World with his children.

Traveling north, he had noticed the subtle changes in the flat green landscape. More pine trees, fewer palms, fewer of the ubiquitous tile-roof, peach-colored subdivisions. But he had no clear picture of those small towns strung out along the Florida coast. He was more familiar with New York, Havana, or even Madrid.

The cruise control was set on seventy-five, and the Seville glided along in the flow of traffic. Anthony tapped the end of his small cigar at the crack in the window, and the ashes swirled into the darkness.

Gail's head was bowed over the files in her lap. A banker's box took up the middle of the front seat, and the five volumes of the trial transcript were stacked on the floor. That woman with CCR had let her borrow them. Anthony was still waiting to hear how Kenny Ray Clark had been wrongfully arrested and convicted for the murder of Amber Dodson. Gail had told him she wanted to put it all in order first. A rainbow of Post-it notes tabbed the transcript. She had done a chronology of the investigation, and a cross-indexed list of evidence and witnesses. It was exhausting to think about. She had barely spoken for the past hour.

He said, "What do they have to eat in Stuart? Is the food any good?"

"They have seafood. Steaks. The usual."
The map light shone on a newspaper clipping. POLICE CLOSE TO ARREST IN DODSON MURDER.

"Do they have Cuban coffee?"

"There must be a Starbuck's."

"They don't serve Cuban coffee at Starbuck's," he said.

"They have espresso," she said.

"It's not the same."

"Oh, please." She looked up. "I wonder if I should call Jackie."

"Does she know anything useful about the investigation?"

"If she does, it's secondhand from Garlan. I really should call, as long as we're in town." Gail got on her knees to find her purse in the backseat. She sat back down with her cell phone and address book. She pressed the numbers, then shook her hair back to put the phone at her ear. Voice mail must have picked up. She said, "Hi, Jackie, it's Gail. Sorry to miss you. Guess where I am? On my way to Stuart. Anthony and I decided to come up for the weekend. We're staying at the Hilton. Give me a call, maybe we can get together for lunch or something. I'd love to introduce you to Anthony. Say hi to Diddy and Garlan." She left her number and hung up.

"I feel so guilty," Gail said, putting her phone away. "Lunch or something. As if she's an afterthought. But really, we don't have much time to spare, do we?"

"What's your cousin like?"

"When you meet her, you might think she's distant, but it's just that she takes everything so seriously, her job most of all. I think even if Garlan weren't a cop, Jackie would be. She's fearless. Garlan gave her a hunting rifle when she was fourteen and taught her how to shoot. And she's Jackie, not Jacqueline."

"What a woman." Anthony sent some smoke toward the window. "What was the other name you said? Not her father, the other one."

"Diddy. He's Garlan's dad."

"Diddy? *Coño.*"

"I can't remember his real name. He's this little dried up man in blue jeans and a plaid shirt, playing the harmonica. There used to be cowboys in Martin County, did you know that?"

"Are there any Cubans?"

"I don't think so."

"Ah. So this is where all the Anglos went when we took over Miami."

"No, *querido,* it's where all the Yankees go to retire and play golf." Gail noticed an exit

76

sign and pointed. "That's where we get off. Martin Highway."

Anthony guided the car around the ramp, paid the turnpike toll, and turned east. Gail told him to keep going. The road would zigzag through Stuart before reaching Hutchinson Island, the long strip of land running along the intracoastal.

Gail had the weekend mapped out as carefully as the route. At eight in the morning she would meet the alibi witness, Tina Hopwood, for breakfast. Then she would go to the retirement home where Ruby Smith lived and get a deposit on fees and costs. At four o'clock she would drop by to speak with the eyewitness who had put Kenny Ray Clark at the crime scene. In the time left over, she would try to find the jailhouse snitch who said that Kenny Clark had confessed to him. The snitch's name was Vernon Byrd. Twelve years ago, he had been brought from prison to testify for the state. Where was he now?

Gail would locate Byrd and as many other witnesses as possible and get affidavits from those willing to give them. She had brought her laptop computer and portable printer. Her notary seal was in her purse. She was a mobile law office.

Anthony didn't know if she wanted him to

accompany her on these interviews. She hadn't said. He thought he might catch up on his sleep or take a long walk. He hoped the beach wasn't overrun with tourists. He liked to gaze at an empty ocean. He had thought seriously of buying a small island in the Keys. He had wondered what it would be like to retire at his age, forty-three. He didn't think that Gail would agree to such a life. She was rarely still for a moment. She burned with energy.

"What was your house like, the one on Sewall's Point?" he asked. Most of his own childhood — until Ernesto Pedrosa had kidnapped him out of Cuba — had been spent in his father's shabby, poured-concrete house in Camagüey province. "Was it like the houses in Palm Beach?"

"God, no, it was just an ordinary house." She bent over to pick up some papers from the floor. "Three bedrooms. A screened porch with rattan furniture. A wooden dock with a boathouse. We were on the intracoastal, not on the beach, so we didn't get waves."

"You had a boat?"

"My *parents* had a boat. Daddy loved to fish."

Anthony smiled at the word. *Daddy.*

"He named it the *Irene Marie*, after my

mother. Her big thing was decorating. She went wild on Sewall's Point. One summer she and Aunt Lou made these enormous wooden flowers and stuck them all over the yard. They'd been drinking. It's funny now, but at the time, I nearly died of embarrassment when my friends saw it."

The soft curves of her face formed a pale silhouette against the window. "Aunt Louise. She was so beautiful and funny. My favorite aunt. My God, she was just two years older than I am now when she died. Mom still misses her. I'm terrible for not keeping in touch with Jackie."

Anthony reached across the file box and pulled Gail toward him. *"Que mala eres."* He took his eyes off the road long enough to give her a kiss that ignited into desire. He wanted a bed, a room by the ocean. He wanted her. He wanted to throw these papers into the trunk and lock it. *"Tanto te quiero, mujer."*

She murmured against his lips, *"Te quiero más."* And then she was shoving him away, still smiling. "Later. I have plans for you." She picked up her pen and went back to her notes.

Anthony had met Gail Connor two years ago, and in that time he had constructed an outline of her life. Names, places, dates. He had heard about the class trip to London, ballet lessons, a debutante ball, private schools. She was the great-granddaughter of original settlers, as much of an aristocracy as could exist in Miami. Gail's mother had inherited their wealth, and her father had squandered most of it. Even so, the imprint of privilege remained.

Not knowing why, Anthony found all this intensely engaging. Perhaps because it was *her* life, and he wanted to possess even her memories. Or perhaps because it was so different from his own confused, even violent, heritage. His mother, a Pedrosa, carried the blood of Spanish royalty. His father, the descendant of slaves, had fought with Fidel in the revolution. Anthony's family had been shattered and torn apart. At times he could put his hand on his chest and feel his soul in pieces. But never when Gail was with him.

"Sweetheart, where am I supposed to turn?"

She consulted her map. "Just follow the road till I tell you. Look at this. We're going right through Palm City."

Hardly a city. Anthony glanced about to see only the usual ragtag assortment of suburban gas stations and strip malls, similar to those in any other small town.

"It's where Amber Dodson was murdered," Gail said, studying the map. "Here's White Heron Way. The eyewitness still lives there. I've never talked to an eyewitness in a criminal case. You can give me some ideas, okay? Tomorrow, after we talk to her, let's take pictures of the Dodson house. All right?"

"We?"

She looked at him. "Silly me. I forgot you don't want to get involved. I'll borrow your car and go by myself."

"No, I'll come with you."

"You don't have to," she said. "It's my case."

"*Bueno,* I'll go for a swim." What a difficult woman she was.

She told him to take the bridge across the river and bear right. Going through town, their progress was slowed by the car ahead of them. A New Jersey license plate, a gray-haired driver. Anthony accelerated around it, then shot past two other sluggish sedans. The road took them past a small airport, then curved north. Most of the traffic had cleared out.

"When are you going to see your client?" Anthony asked.

"I don't know. I haven't had time to think about it."

"You have to talk to him. Get his side of

the story. Get to know him. Have you ever been to Florida State Prison?"

"You know I haven't."

"Don't worry about being overheard. They will put you in a little room with him, very private. You'll probably be safe. They leave them in leg irons. Be sure to wear something plain. He hasn't seen a woman in a long time."

She looked around. "Will you come with me?"

"Why?" He laughed. "It's your case."

"Anthony, I'm not going alone. And you can help me talk to the witnesses tomorrow. Okay?"

"Say please."

Gail gave him a playful shove. "Oh, stop it."

At the next intersection he went past a car going thirty in the left lane. Old people. He saw the tops of four white heads and the driver's knuckles on the steering wheel.

Gail looked up from her map. "Take a right on Ocean Drive. That leads to the bridge over the intracoastal."

He glanced into the mirror. *"Ay, cara'o."*

Bright lights flashed into the car. There was a police car behind them.

Gail turned around. "What did you do?"

"Nothing. I was going the speed limit."

Anthony pulled into the parking lot of a bank and hit the button to lower his window. He turned off the engine and waited.

Blue and red lights pulsed in the darkness, headlights were on high beam, and a spotlight went on. He squinted into the side mirror. A figure in a dark uniform approached, then moved to a position behind the open window. All he could see was a navy blue shoulder. A slender arm.

"Sir, your driver's license and registration, please." A woman's voice, low and steady.

Anthony shifted to get to his wallet. "I wasn't speeding, officer. I am sure of that."

"No, sir. You ran through that red light back there."

"Red light?"

"Your driver's license, sir."

Gail leaned over his lap from the passenger seat. "Oh, my God. It's Jackie!"

The officer's face appeared as she came nearer to look around him. "Gail?"

Unbuckling her belt, Gail shoved the door open. She went around the front of the car, and they met at his window, where Gail held out her arms. "I don't believe it! This is so funny!"

Her cousin allowed a quick hug, then

glanced at the passing traffic. "Hang on a second." She went back and turned off the flashers and spotlight. Anthony got out and Gail made the introductions.

In Miami, and if this woman had not been in uniform, Anthony might have politely kissed her cheek. They shook hands. Her face was young and smooth. A little makeup would have made it pretty. She wore her hair in a single braid. Brown eyes moved over him in a neutral way. "Glad to meet you. So. You guys just got in?"

"We were on our way to the hotel," Anthony said with an innocent lift of his brows. "I was a little lost, and if I didn't see the light —"

Gail hugged her arm. "Jackie, you look amazing. How are you?"

"Good, good."

"Your dad?"

"He's fine. Busy over at the sheriff's office. You know. Hey, I got your message, but I was in the middle of a DUI."

Gail laughed, delighted. "I remember when you were six years old you said you wanted to be a cop. I never doubted for a moment you would. I bet you're wonderful."

"Well. I like it." To Anthony's astonishment, she blushed.

Fingers linked together, the two women smiled at each other. Gail tall and slender, with delicate hands and a small waist. Her cousin in a bulletproof vest. There was no way to tell what was underneath. Pepper spray and a Glock 19 rode on one hip, a radio and collapsible baton on the other. Light gleamed on the badge over her left pocket, an American flag was sewn on the right, and patches decorated her sleeves. The silver name tag said J. BRYCE. Anthony wondered how long it would take her to put him on the ground with a knee in his back.

She said, "Are you busy tomorrow afternoon? Diddy's having his birthday party out at the ranch. He just turned eighty years old, can you believe that? The historical society is putting it on. They're having barbecue, a band, games for the kids, a roping demonstration. See, Diddy hangs out a lot at the museum, telling stories about the way it used to be." She laughed and made quotation marks with her fingers. " 'Diddy Bryce, Martin County Treasure.' It'll be fun. I mean, if you're not busy."

"We'd love to come," Gail said. "What time?"

"It's on from noon till five. Drop by anytime." She pulled a pen and notebook from her left shirt pocket and wrote directions, then ripped the sheet out and gave it to Gail. "Call me if you get lost. I always keep my cell phone on."

The two women embraced again. "It's good to see you, Jackie."

"You too." She gripped Anthony's hand firmly, then let go. "See you tomorrow."

Jackie Bryce took a few steps toward her cruiser, then stopped, pivoted in her thick-soled black shoes, and came back, standing squarely in front of him. "You need to be careful on the road. Yellow means slow down, not speed up and get through it like down in Miami, okay? I'm going to let it go this time."

He made a slight inclination of his head. "Thank you."

"Sure. Y'all have a nice evening. Don't forget your seat belts."

She got back into her patrol car and pulled around the Cadillac. At the street a rear tire caught the curb, squealing.

Gail said, "Jackie really isn't as humorless as she seems."

"It's the rookie cop syndrome," Anthony said. "Did you notice the police department patch on her sleeve?"

"No, what about it?"

"City of Stuart. Sailfish Capital of the World. *Coño.* What a place."

CHAPTER 5

"Bonboncita, *let's not ruin dinner talking about this case. Where are your notes? Read them to me on the way to the hotel. Tell me how the police came to arrest an innocent man for murder.*"

"*It's complicated.*"

"*I'll stop you if I have any questions.*"

Monday, February 6, 1989

The city of Stuart is surrounded on three sides by the St. Lucie River, which curves up and over, then flows south to the intracoastal waterway. In the late 1800s roads were so few and the scrub palmetto so thick that pioneers built their houses facing the river and visited their neighbors by boat. When the railroad pushed through, commerce followed, and the main highway has become a multilaned corridor of shopping malls, branch banks, fast-food franchises, and car dealerships. But those who control things keep development reined in, and Martin County remains green on a coast increasingly buried in concrete.

Trains still run through the old section of

Stuart. The narrow streets and small shops have been preserved. The county courthouse is still downtown. There is only one felony judge, P.R. "Pat" Willis. He is the same judge who in 1990 sentenced Kenneth Ray Clark to death for the murder of Amber Lynn Dodson.

Amber's senior portrait from Atlantic Christian Academy, which appeared in news stories, shows a pretty girl with long blond hair. The thin chain of a crucifix gleams on her skin. She was married at twenty-two in her family's church. Her husband, Gary, seven years older, practiced law in Stuart. After the wedding they bought a house in an area called Palm City, across the south fork of the river. It was a typical 1960s ranch style, and pine trees shaded the yard. There weren't many young people on their street, but the neighborhood was safe and quiet, a good place for a family.

A murder was unthinkable.

Then the call came in to 911. Within half an hour, the street was cordoned off. Blue and red lights flashed in the darkness, and people poured out of their houses to see what was going on.

Several backup units followed, then a lieutenant and six detectives. The crime scene technicians arrived with their equipment.

Brass from the city of Stuart police department came by to see if assistance was needed. The Martin County sheriff would have been there, but he was in the hospital with a bleeding ulcer. By 7:30 P.M., the crime scene roster noted over thirty law enforcement personnel at the scene. The captain in charge of the criminal investigations division, Garlan Bryce, rushed back from a meeting in Vero Beach. He parked his unmarked Jeep Cherokee across the street, requested permission to enter the scene, then ordered anyone not essential to the investigation to clear out. Bryce went by the book and demanded that his officers do likewise. On the radio Bryce had already assigned the investigation to Sergeant Ronald Kemp, thirty-six, who had an unmatched success rate in closing cases.

The victim's husband had been put in the command van to keep him away from the scene, the neighbors, and the press. Bryce would speak to him, but he wanted to see Mrs. Dodson's body first.

It appeared that the attack had begun in the kitchen. Blood had fallen and dried on the white tile floor. There was part of a print made by a bare foot. Blood droplets. Swipes and smears. Then another footprint toward the hall, and drops leading away.

A crime scene technician stood back as

89

Kemp led Bryce down the hall. The men stepped carefully on the beige shag carpet to avoid the blood. Kemp stopped at the baby's room. He explained that Dodson had been in the front yard holding the dead child in his arms when the first deputy had arrived. The child had no visible bruises. There were two bottles in the crib, one of them empty. In a corner of the mattress was a pool of soured milk. The paramedics had found vomit in the child's nose and mouth.

"He died of positional asphyxia," Gail explained. "The ME said the baby got stuck between the mattress and the bars of his crib. He couldn't get enough air when he threw up his milk."

"Pobrecito. *And his mother, stabbed to death. Were all the knives in the kitchen accounted for?"*

"According to her husband, they were."

Bryce came out of the baby's room and the men continued down the hall. Kemp pointed out a quantity of blond hair on the floor. Bryce knelt to see skin attached to the roots, as if the victim had violently wrenched herself away from her attacker.

The master bedroom was at the end. The door was the same ivory color as the carpet and wall, and there were swipes of blood on the jamb. On the back of the door, Bryce could make out the slide of fingers and a larger smear about four and a half feet off the floor where an upper arm might have been braced.

The wheels of the king-size bed had been knocked out of their casters, and the nightstand had overturned. Blood at the foot of the bed appeared to have been deliberately smeared. No clear shoe tread or footprint patterns could be seen.

The victim lay diagonally across the bed on rumpled sheets and a pale blue comforter. An electrical cord was tied around her neck. Her bare feet pointed toward the door. Her legs were parted, and red silk pajama panties hung from one ankle. It took Bryce a second to realize that her matching top was not pulled down, but pushed up over her breasts. Her torso was red from her own blood. The blood seemed to glow in the white flash of the crime scene camera.

The medical examiner would later testify that he counted twenty-seven separate stab wounds, but that the victim's chest and abdomen were so lacerated that not all of them could be counted. He would find under her collarbone a small gold crucifix driven there by the force of the blows. Despite the position of the panties, there was no evidence of recent sexual intercourse.

The pool of blood on the sheets had clotted, and the clear serum, which had separated out, made a ghostly brown outline. Lines of cast-off blood went over the pillow, up the maple headboard and the wall, and across the ceiling to the approximate limit of where a raised knife would have thrown them. Her face was bloody but without cuts except for a deep slash on her chin. There were defensive wounds on her hands and forearms but so few of them, four or five, that Kemp's first thought was that the killer had kept stabbing the victim after she had lost consciousness or was already dead.

Kemp drew Bryce's attention to the electrical cord, which was attached to a small white alarm clock. The cord went around the victim's neck twice and had been pulled tightly, indenting the flesh. That the cord extended across the wounds indicated postmortem positioning. The alarm clock itself was not a digital model, but an older kind with hands, which had stopped at 10:23.

Bryce studied this awhile, then said it was time to get a statement from the victim's husband. Outside in the van he put his hand on Dodson's shoulder and assured him that they would not rest until they found the person responsible. Then the captain left the scene to Detective Kemp.

Kemp looked carefully at Dodson's hands and face. First apologizing that this was necessary, he asked Dodson to roll up the sleeves of his shirt. Dodson was cooperative. There were no scratches or bruises. His grief and shock appeared genuine but could have been caused by the death of his son. When told about the empty jewelry box on the dresser, Dodson confirmed that his wife had kept her jewelry in it. Kemp told him that no rings had been found on his wife's fingers, and Dodson said that she had worn two: an engagement ring and a wedding band that matched his. He began to cry.

A photograph taken outside the courthouse eleven months later shows Gary Dodson after his testimony. His parents walk on either side, and he appears to sag between them. He is a man of average height, perhaps a little too soft, his sedentary occupation taking its toll. At thirty-two, his hair is thinning. His cheeks are hollow, and his mouth is drawn inward. The reporter wrote that he broke down on the stand, blaming himself for leaving his wife and child at home that day.

The baby had kept them up most of the night with a stomachache, and Amber was so tired that Gary sent her back to bed and told her to sleep for a couple of hours. He called Amber's boss and the nursery to let them know. He left the house at 8:40 A.M. and arrived at his law office around 9:00 A.M., as usual, and just before 10:00 he called to check on the baby. The baby was finally resting, but Amber wanted to sleep till he woke up. Gary called her again at 12:30. There was no answer, and he assumed she had already taken the baby to the nursery and gone to work. It never occurred to him that anything was wrong.

Amber worked for a land development company, got off at 5:00, and would always pick up the baby on her way home. Gary arrived home at 5:50 P.M. and parked his car under the carport next to hers. The sun had gone down, and the yard was in shadow. He wondered why no lights were on. He walked to the kitchen door and opened it with his key. He called out, but there was no answer. Then he saw the blood on the floor.

Gail looked up from her notes. "What do you think so far?"

"Kemp verified this story, I suppose."

"He pulled the phone records and talked to

the nursery and Amber's employer."

"A thorough man. Kemp suspected the husband. When a woman is murdered, they always look at the man she was close to."

"Remind me to stay on your good side."

"No, no, sweetheart, you couldn't be anywhere else. What did the medical examiner say about time of death?"

The medical examiner in that district, Dr. George Snyder, did not always appear at death scenes, even homicides, but Kemp insisted. Snyder drove down from Fort Pierce and arrived shortly after 9:00 P.M. He pushed a long thermometer between the victim's ribs. He consulted his charts. The victim appeared to be about 64 inches, 110 to 125 pounds. Based on core body temperature, rigor mortis, lividity, and such other factors as body weight and the weather that day, he gave an initial estimate of time of death as two hours either side of noon, or between 10:00 A.M. and 2:00 P.M.

From long experience, Kemp knew that time of death is elusive. Snyder's estimate had supported Dodson's story, but Kemp didn't want to rule him out.

Just then Sergeant Miller in crime scene told Kemp to come take a look at the guest bathroom. They had sprayed the sink and shower with Luminol. Miller cut the lights, and another man turned on the battery-powered black light. The areas around the drains exploded into fluorescent purple.

Kemp asked Dodson for his consent to search the entire house and both cars. Dodson signed the form. Police found no bloody towels or clothing. Gary said he had not showered since that morning in the master bath.

Kemp's doubts about the husband lingered, but he knew that answers would not come as easily as he had hoped. By then it was nearly midnight. Dodson had already called his wife's family to tell them what had happened. His own parents were waiting to take him home with them, and Kemp told him he could go, but to stay close.

Meanwhile Kemp's partner, Tom Federsen, had been looking for the point of entry. The aluminum-framed awning windows operated with a crank, and they were open in the master bedroom. This was not unusual, as the temperature that day had not gone past the low seventies. Dodson said that he and his wife usually slept with the windows open, and they had been open when he left that morning and when he had returned. The screens were intact. Neither the front nor kitchen doors had been forced.

The sliding-glass patio door, however, did not appear to be sitting precisely in the track. Federsen asked if anyone had touched it. No one had. He took a strong light and went around to the back patio. He knelt down and saw shiny scratch marks on the bottom of the heavy aluminum frame. After photographs were taken, the door was dusted for fingerprints, and putty was used to make an impression of the marks, Federsen used a screwdriver to manipulate the door. He found that levering it up would lift it free of the lock.

Others on the team found fragments of white rock on the carpet near the door. More fragments were found on the patio. All pieces were photographed, plotted on the crime scene diagram, and sealed into plastic bags. The thick grass revealed no footprints. Toward the left, or west side of the house, was the master bedroom, where an old room air conditioner hung out the wall. Beyond that, a hedge, then the street. To the right was a utility shed, the carport area, and another house some twenty yards away. Directly behind the Dodsons' house was a four-foot chain-link fence, then pine woods.

About fifty yards away Fletcher Road ran parallel and ended a quarter mile east at a small county park. The killer could have left his vehicle on the road or at the park and come through the woods. Kemp ordered the road sealed off. He wanted photographs of tire tracks, if any, before more vehicles passed through. A more thorough inspection would have to wait for sunrise.

Earlier, teams had been organized to canvas the neighborhood. Had any of the neighbors heard or seen anything unusual during the day? Any strangers going through? They suspended their efforts at 11:30 P.M.

Amber Lynn Dodson's body was taken away at 3:15 A.M. Kemp and his team remained on the property for another five hours.

"Gail, does CCR have copies of the crime scene photos?"

"They have the autopsy photos. I didn't ask what else they have."

"When you speak to Denise Robinson on Monday, find out. You want every photograph taken by the police."

"All of them?"

"Every photograph. Videotapes as well, if they made them."

"That's going to cost a lot."

"I told you. Capital appeals are expensive."

That morning both *The Stuart News* and *The Palm Beach Post* ran the story on page one. MOTHER MURDERED, BABY FOUND DEAD IN PALM CITY. The story was repeated on all three local TV stations. Calls from alarmed citizens flooded the sheriff's department switchboard. In a press conference, Captain Garlan Bryce said they were working on several leads. He reassured the public that the person responsible would be arrested and brought to justice.

Kemp spoke with the victim's parents. The Mayfields had moved to Stuart in the late 1950s. Fred worked at the Evinrude plant, and Rose owned a small shop downtown, Mayfield Antiques. They said their daughter and son-in-law's marriage was happy. They knew of no one who would have wanted to harm Amber. Everyone loved her.

Gary Dodson's secretary confirmed that Dodson had arrived at the office just before nine on Monday morning, and that he had not left during the day. He had taken his lunch downstairs. Kemp sent a detective to speak to the waitress in the coffee shop. She remembered selling Dodson a cup of coffee around nine o'clock. He came back for lunch. Police searched nearby trash bins and found nothing relevant. If the time of death was accurate, Dodson's alibi would hold.

Interviews with neighbors continued. The retired couple living next door, the Grigsbys, had left at 7:30 A.M. on Monday for the Sandpiper Restaurant, which offered a senior citizen breakfast on weekdays. They had not noticed anything unusual at the Dodsons'. Mrs. Grigsby said that the widow across the street, Mrs. Chastain, had gone out of town on Monday afternoon. Her daughter in Atlanta had just had a baby. Kemp left his card in Mrs. Chastain's mailbox.

Wednesday, February 8

There were several reports of strange vehicles in the area the morning of the murder. At the county park, a dark-colored pickup truck with fender damage. Driving through the neighborhood, a car with tinted windows, two black men inside. A silver Honda Prelude in the Dodsons' driveway that morning.

The Honda belonged to Amber's younger sister, Lacey Mayfield. Detective Kemp remembered seeing it at the Mayfields' house when he and his partner had gone over on Tuesday to speak to Amber's parents.

On the second visit, the house was full of friends and relatives. Kemp and his partner asked to speak privately with Lacey Mayfield. She was twenty-one years old and lived in an apartment near the fitness studio where she worked. Lacey had called Amber's work that morning to talk about a party for their parents' anniversary. Told that Amber was at home with the baby, Lacey decided to drop by and say hello. When she arrived at 9:30, Amber's car was there but she didn't answer the door. Assuming that Amber was sleeping, Lacey drove straight to the studio in time for her ten o'clock class. Except for lunch, she had been there until 4:00 P.M. When Kemp asked why she had not mentioned this before, Lacey said she had forgotten.

Kemp learned what he could about the victim. After graduating with honors from high school, Amber Mayfield had enrolled at Indian River Community College, lived at home and helped with expenses. She had dated, but there had been no serious relationships. Mr. Mayfield's layoff at Evinrude had depleted family savings, so Amber put her plans for university on hold and found a job. Her employer, JWM Corporation, was building houses west of the turnpike in an area called River Pines. Amber worked as a receptionist.

While waiting at the sales office, Kemp picked up a glossy brochure. Amber Dodson's photo appeared inside in a swimsuit. She had excellent legs. So did the man in the picture, handing Amber a towel. Blond hair, age around thirty. The caption read: RIVER PINES FOUNDER J. WHITNEY MCGRATH ENJOYS SWIMMING AT THE CLUB.

Amber's supervisor was Vivian Baker, director of sales, an attractive brunette in diamond earrings and a business suit. Ms. Baker told Kemp that Amber had been well-liked at JWM, her work had been satisfactory, and there had been no rumors of affairs or financial difficulties. She knew of Gary Dodson but had never met him. Until the previous summer he had worked for Mr. McGrath's attorneys in Palm Beach. She said that Mr. McGrath rarely came to the site and did not know the victim personally.

Kemp wanted to speak to McGrath. Ms. Baker refused to give out his address and phone number. Kemp explained the penalties for obstructing a criminal investigation.

McGrath lived on Jupiter Island.

"Have you heard of Jupiter Island?"

"No, where is it?"

"On the ocean between Stuart and Palm Beach. Mega-rich, but very anonymous. The highest per capita income in the U.S."

"Kemp suspected McGrath was involved with the victim?"

"Apparently, but McGrath said he hardly knew her. By the way, there is — or was at that time — a Mrs. McGrath."

"That always complicates matters. I have a question about Amber's husband. Why does a lawyer working for a firm in Palm Beach own such a middle-class house?"

Gary Dodson's firm, Hadley and Morgan, had maintained a branch office in Stuart to handle the affairs of its clients in Martin County. They needed someone to fill out the real estate department, starting at forty thousand per year. The pay was low, but legal positions were scarce for new lawyers. Gary Dodson had been working for the firm three years when he met Amber, who had come to deliver some papers from River Pines.

In one of several interviews, Dodson told Kemp that he had left Hadley and Morgan on July 15 because they wouldn't offer a partnership. He opened his own office in

Stuart the first week of August. At the time, Amber was staying home with the baby, who had been born in March. By September, with Dodson's new practice still struggling, Amber wanted to go back to work. Kemp wrote in his report that Dodson seemed embarrassed about his lack of success. He wondered if the happy couple had argued.

Kemp made another visit to Amber's workplace. Bypassing Vivian Baker, he spoke to two young women in the accounting department who had known Amber. One of them recalled that Amber had made a comment about her husband's impotence. Kemp wrote in his notebook, "Noodle-dick." The women didn't know if she had a lover.

Friday, February 10

The media covered the funerals of Amber Lynn Dodson and her baby son, held at the First Baptist Church. Her husband sat with his head bowed and his eyes closed. Her father silently wept. Her mother fainted and was helped back to her seat by Amber's sister, Lacey. The crowd was estimated at more than three hundred.

Afterward, surrounded by cameras, Captain Garlan Bryce said that the investigation was proceeding, that the police would be thorough, and he could not share any information. Again he promised an arrest. An editorial in that morning's *Stuart News* had questioned whether any progress was being made.

The team doubled their efforts. They were all going on four to six hours of sleep a night, Ron Kemp on even less. Every pawnshop within a hundred-mile radius was contacted. Officers leaned on informants. Every lead was pursued. They combed through records of similar crimes in the area. Burglaries, loitering and prowling, knife assaults. Sheriff Carr could be heard yelling in his office.

All fingerprints found in the house were being run through data banks. None had been found on the clock, sliding-glass door frame, or the shower door. The ME had found no skin under Amber Dodson's fingernails. The small white particles found on the carpet and back porch had been identified as crushed coquina rock, commonly found at construction sites.

Gary Dodson allowed the police to examine his financial records. There was no life insurance on his wife and only ten thousand dollars' worth of equity in the house.

Dodson had moved out and planned to sell it.

Whitney McGrath referred all requests for interviews to his attorneys, who insisted he had no further information.

Tuesday, February 14

Eight days after the murder, Detective Kemp was told that a woman waiting in the lobby had information on the Dodson case.

Dorothy Chastain had just returned from the birth of a grandchild in Atlanta and had found Kemp's card among the mail her neighbors had collected. She lived at 2205 White Heron Way, across the street from the Dodsons.

The morning of the murder, Mrs. Chastain was sitting at the living room window waiting for the friend who would drive her to the airport in West Palm Beach. Around ten o'clock, Mrs. Chastain saw a young man walk furtively — Kemp wrote the word in his notebook — around the hedge on the west side of the Dodsons' house, then go into the backyard. Kemp's notes describe the man as "white, 20–30 y.o.a., med. ht/wt, very long br. hair, clean shaven. Boots, blue denim jacket."

Over the past week the investigation team

had listed 173 men who had been arrested for burglary, loitering and prowling, or knife assaults in the county within the past three years, who were not currently incarcerated. Kemp had put twenty men at the top of the list and sent detectives to talk to them. Mrs. Chastain's information narrowed the possibilities.

One of the men on the list was Kenneth Ray Clark, a twenty-two-year-old day laborer whose last known address was a trailer park off Cove Road, south of town. Two things grabbed Kemp's attention. First, Clark had been arrested three months previously for an attempted burglary of a residence a quarter mile from White Heron Way. Seeing police, he'd tossed a Baggie containing five grams of marijuana. Clark had bonded out on all charges, and the case was set for trial.

The more compelling fact was that on the booking form Clark had listed his employer as "JWM Co." Kemp showed his photograph at the River Pines construction trailer, where the supervisor told him that Clark and a friend of his, Glen Hopwood, had been let go about three months before for selling marijuana on the job.

In addition to the more recent charges, Clark's priors included a juvenile burglary, a couple of DUIs, a resisting without violence, and an arrest two years ago that Kemp noted with interest: an aggravated assault with a knife. Clark had been put on probation.

Mrs. Chastain was asked to wait while Kemp and his partner assembled a photo display. She picked out one of the six but wanted to see him in person to be absolutely sure.

"Stop. The Department of Justice has put out advisories, don't do this, but the police continue to do it. The photograph she ID'd was Kenny Ray Clark, no?"

"Of course."

"And the other five were a refrigerator, a fire hydrant, a nun, a cowboy, and a German shepherd. Then they brought him to the station on a pretext and put him in a lineup. None of the other five in the lineup was in the photo display. Of course she would pick him out."

"She said she was absolutely certain."

"Certainty does not mean accuracy. All right, go on."

Wednesday, February 15

Detective Kemp drove Mrs. Chastain to the sheriff's department headquarters the next morning and took her into a room where she could view six men through a two-way mirror. She pointed to number four. She had previously stated that the man she had seen was of medium height and weight with very long brown hair. This man's hair was only to his shoulders, and he was six feet tall. Nevertheless, Mrs. Chastain was certain that he was the one she had seen going behind the Dodsons' house. She was also sure of the time — five minutes past ten. She had been looking at the clock and worrying she might miss her flight.

"If she was looking at the clock, how in hell did she see a man fifty yards away across the street? Did the defense attorney bring this out at the trial?"

"No."

"Que idiota."

Kemp took Clark into an interview room, where Clark told him that on Monday a week ago he had been hanging drywall from eight in the morning till four in the afternoon at a new building going up in Fort Pierce, in the next county. When asked who could confirm this, Clark gave the name of the crew boss. Kemp asked Clark to wait while he checked it out by telephone.

Kemp had a feeling in his gut that Clark had been lying, and his spirits rose when the crew boss said that Clark had been laid off on February third. When Kemp came back into the interview room, Clark said he had mixed up his dates. He'd meant to say that on the morning of the murder he'd been at home till around ten o'clock, then had gone to see a friend of his, Lougie Jackson. Kemp tried to question him further, but Clark insisted on leaving.

Captain Bryce told Kemp not to make an arrest until they had more to go on.

Thursday, February 16

Another detective had good news. He had shown a photograph of Clark's blue Chevy truck to the fisherman who had been at the county park the morning of the murder. The man's original statement had mentioned a dark-colored truck with fender damage, make unknown. Clark's truck had a missing rear bumper, but the man was "pretty sure" it was the same vehicle.

The evening of February 16, Detectives Kemp and Federsen went to Clark's previous address, a trailer owned by his friend Glen Hopwood and wife Tina. Glen was in jail in Palm Beach County, unable to make bond on a felony drug charge. Tina was a nurse's assistant at a retirement home in Stuart. Kemp's report stated that Kenny Ray Clark had been living in the Hopwoods' spare bedroom, but on the morning of February 6, Tina Hopwood evicted him. Kemp wrote, "Hopwood stated she has no recollection of what time Clark left."

Friday, February 17

Kenny Ray Clark moved in with his girlfriend, Carol Malloy, who lived in Jensen Beach, in the northeast part of the county. They were in bed asleep at 6:30 A.M. when someone knocked loudly on the door. They ignored it. A second later a muffled voice shouted "Police!" A moment after that the door crashed open, and a SWAT team poured in. The woman kept screaming while Clark was put on the floor and handcuffed.

A search produced carpentry tools and a wood-handled hunting knife with a six-inch blade. Clark's pickup truck was towed to a police facility to be examined for trace evidence.

News cameras and reporters were waiting at the entrance to the county jail when the convoy arrived. They panned on the police car going by, catching a glimpse of a wiry, bare-chested young man in the backseat. He leaned forward as if to hide his face, and his hair swung over his eyes. The lens of the TV camera reflected back, distorted by the curve of the glass. These few seconds were played over and over again in slow motion on every broadcast.

At the press conference, Sheriff Carr, with Captain Garlan Bryce at his side, thanked Ron Kemp and the rest of the investigative team for their outstanding work. The sheriff announced, "We are confident that we have apprehended the killer of Amber Dodson."

CHAPTER 6

Saturday morning, March 10

"I don't know who that lady across the street thought she saw, but I know one damn thing. It wasn't Kenny. No way."

Gail's digital recorder sat in the middle of the table among the plates and napkins and coffee cups. The waitress had brought breakfast, but no one was eating. They were at a booth in the back, away from the noise of the grill and the half dozen customers in the place. The diner was too run-down to attract much of a crowd.

Anthony sat to Gail's left, and she couldn't see his reaction to what Tina Hopwood had just said. So far Tina Hopwood hadn't said much. She seemed to be waiting for them to accuse her of some crime. She was thirty-four, but pale, smoke-damaged skin made her look older. Her hair was long and unnaturally black, an odd choice for eyes clear as seawater. Her T-shirt repeated the cartoon on the van in the parking lot: a smiling poodle in a footed bathtub, bubbles rising and popping over its head. CLIP 'N'

DIP PET GROOMING.

Gail said, "At the trial, Dorothy Chastain said she saw Kenny at just past ten o'clock. You say he was with you. You would have testified for him, but the police pressured you not to. Is this correct?"

The strangely pale eyes flared with anger. "They threatened to have my probation revoked if I got on the stand. They said I was trying to protect a killer."

"What were you on probation for?"

"Writing bad checks." Tina Hopwood swung out an arm to pick up her coffee. "I paid back every last cent, over three thousand dollars in restitution. I worked a lot of overtime."

"Have you had any arrests or convictions since then?"

"One speeding ticket. I don't get into trouble. I have two boys, I own a house and a business. I groom pets for some of the finest people in the area." Pride sent a flush of color into her cheeks. Tina Hopwood locked eyes with Gail, then Anthony, daring them to criticize.

Anthony sent a warm smile across the table. "You have two boys? How old are they?"

He had promised to let Gail ask the questions, but she was glad he jumped in. A change of approach was needed. His voice conveyed intimacy, and laugh lines curved around his mouth. His chocolate-brown eyes could make a nun swoon. Gail waited for Tina to say something.

She was still hiding behind her coffee cup, but she raised a shoulder in a shrug. "Michael is sixteen; Jerrod is fourteen. They're good kids, and I love them to death. I divorced their father eight years ago, and I've been on my own ever since."

"Oh, but you have done very well. I have a teenage son myself. He says he wants a dog, but I don't know."

"He has to be responsible for it," she said. "He can't expect you to bathe and feed it. Dogs are like children, they need attention and love. But they give more than they get, unlike most two-legged creatures."

"Ah, yes. Very true."

Tina Hopwood smiled back at him.

Gail felt the little nudge on her thigh and started over in a more conversational tone. "Tina? Back in February of 1989, where were you working?"

"At a retirement home in Stuart called Bella Vista, basically mopping floors and emptying bed pans. I'd wanted to be a nurse, but I got pregnant in high school, and there went that idea."

"You married Glen Hopwood?"

"Yes, in 1985. We bought a double-wide south of town, near Cove Road. It had a leaky roof and bad plumbing, but Glen knew how to fix things. Glen usually worked at a marina his uncle owned in Port Salerno. It was close enough that he could walk whenever his car broke down, and it did a lot. Those were hard days."

"How did Kenny Ray Clark come into the picture?"

"We all went to Martin County High. The guys didn't hang out then, but they wound up working the same construction site. One day I get home and they're drinking beer out in the yard, and Glen tells me Kenny's going to be renting the spare room. Well, okay, Glen, thanks for asking. I think Kenny paid forty dollars a week."

"The police reports say that Kenny worked at River Pines, but was let go a few months before the murder. Amber Dodson worked in the office there. Did he ever mention her name?"

"No. At the trial they made it sound like he broke into her house because he knew her. He didn't. River Pines was a huge project, and if you worked construction, you were at River Pines. My ex-husband, Glen, was out there, and he got Kenny a job. They both got fired, though. Glen was selling weed to some of the guys, and the crew boss figured Kenny was in on it, since him and Glen hung out together. I never seen a man with worse luck than Kenny Clark."

"Did either of them ever mention the name of the owner, Whitney McGrath?"

"I never heard of him."

"All right. How long did Kenny live with you and Glen?"

"About a year and a half."

"Were you all using drugs? I'm sorry, but I need to know."

"Do you have to record this?"

Gail turned the machine off.

Tina Hopwood broke the corner off a piece of toast. Her inky black hair framed her face. "It was recreational. That's what Glen and I had in common in high school, an appreciation for a good line of coke. After we got married, we were using when we could afford it, but mostly it was weed and beer. When I got pregnant with Jerrod, I cut way down, but Glen wouldn't. He started selling. He'd get stuff for the rich beach kids who didn't want their parents to catch them in East Stuart. Kenny didn't do drugs, but he would if Glen gave it to him. He looked up to Glen in a way. I think Kenny moved in with us so he could have a family. It wasn't great, but it was better than he grew up with. Do you know that he got beat so bad with the buckle end of a belt that he still has scars on his legs? His mother killed herself when he was fourteen. The newspapers called Kenny a career criminal, but most of the stuff he got into, it was from tagging along after somebody else — like my dear ex-husband."

"Where is Glen now?"

"In prison. He robbed a gas station. He won't get out for a long time. I wouldn't care except for my boys."

"May I turn this back on?"

"Sure."

"Tell me what happened the morning of the murder."

"Well, Kenny came home about four in the morning, waking the kids, banging into things. He'd been out partying, and he never could hold his liquor. He went in the bathroom and threw up. I got the kids back to sleep, but I was so mad I just laid there and boiled. Glen wasn't there at the time. He was in jail, I forget why. Kenny owed me rent money, but he'd give me these big puppy dog eyes. 'Oh, Tina, don't put me out, I don't have nowhere to go, I'll pay you Friday, I swear.' Then he lost his job. I was about to snap. That morning, I dropped the boys off at my mother's house and clocked in at work, but then I told my boss I had a family emergency, and drove back home."

"What time did you get home?"

"About nine-twenty. It only takes fifteen minutes when there's no traffic. Kenny was still asleep in his clothes and boots, dead to the world. I started putting all his stuff in plastic trash bags and carrying them out to his truck. He wouldn't wake up, so I threw some ice water on his neck, and he jumps up and starts yelling. I told him to get out. He begged me to let him stay, but I said forget it, buddy, I had enough of this shit. So he left and moved in with his girlfriend."

Exhaling a breath, Tina Hopwood looked at the ceiling. "I keep thinking, if I hadn't been in such a bad mood, if I'd stayed at work and not woke him up, none of this would've happened. Anyway, about ten days later these detectives from the sheriff's office knocked on the door. I'd just put the kids to bed and I was watching TV. They said they were investigating the murder of Amber Dodson, and they wanted to know about Kenny. I told them he moved out that same morning, the day she died. They asked me what time. I had to think about it for a while, then I go, ten o'clock. They say, are you *sure*? Yes, I'm sure, because I went straight back to work, and I got there right around ten-fifteen. Kemp did most of the talking. He said, that can't be right. We have proof he killed that girl. A neighbor saw him there at ten o'clock, so you're wrong. I said, I'm not wrong, she is."

"Do you remember the detectives' names?"

"Ronald Kemp and Tom Federsen."

"Okay. Go on."

"They left, but two hours later, they came back and asked me the same questions all over again. Kemp says, 'You're lying. You're trying to protect that piece of shit.' I said, 'No I'm not, you're the piece of shit.' He pushed me into a chair. He said, 'You're on probation for a felony. I could have your ass back in jail in two minutes, bitch.' I said, 'For what,' And he goes, 'For possession of the drugs that we could find if we looked. Are you going to help that murdering slimewad or are you going to tell me the truth?' "

Tina Hopwood turned her seawater eyes toward the window. Her lashes were spiky black. "It's funny how your mind can make you believe whatever you need it to. I thought about my kids. What would happen if I went to jail. When Kenny's lawyer called me and wanted me to testify, I said no. I told him I thought Kenny was guilty, and I *did*

120

think that. There was this thing that him and Glen got into one time that made me justify it to myself and say, well damn, he had it in him to kill that girl."

"What do you mean?"

It took her awhile to reply. "It was on Fourth of July weekend, so it sort of sticks in my mind, you know? That Friday, Glen got home from work and told Kenny that this guy he knew wanted him to chase some Mexican squatters out of a shack in an orange grove, and bring a friend. They'd split a hundred dollars. I said, 'Glen, don't do that,' but he went anyway. They were gone almost all night. I woke up when Glen opened the door to our room to get some clothes. He was all covered with mud, and I said, 'Glen, my God, what happened?' He told me, 'Nothing, go to sleep.' He took a shower, and then I went out in the living room, and they were drinking a bottle of Black Jack and smoking a joint. I said, 'What did you all do? Tell me right now.' He says, 'Tina, shut up or I'll shut your mouth for you.' And Kenny just sat there and wouldn't look at me.

"I knew they'd done something terrible, and I kept waiting for the other shoe to drop. Kenny Ray started drinking real heavy and missing a lot of work. Later on, when the cops told me Kenny murdered that woman, it was in my mind that he could have done it."

"Who were the Mexicans? Migrant workers, do you think?"

"I guess. We never talked about it again."

"Tell me what made you decide to help Kenny after so many years."

"It started because of my younger boy, Jerrod. Over Christmas break he was staying the weekend with a friend. They had this brilliant idea. Hey, let's go throw rocks at cows. Don't ask me why they thought that would be fun, but they did. So they went out to a pasture and climbed through the barbed wire. The owner must've seen them, because a sheriff's deputy showed up. He pulled out his gun and told them to lie on the ground. He called for backup, and they made the boys turn out their pockets and take off their shoes. They didn't find anything, but they arrested them for criminal trespass. It was real late that night before they called me, and when I saw Jerrod, he was so scared and mad, madder than I'd ever seen him. I said, honey, I understand, because I did understand. We had a long talk, and I told him about the past. Not everything, but a lot. I told him, 'I am so blessed to have you and Michael. So blessed.'

"I hadn't thought about Kenny in a long time. He was in prison, Glen was in prison, and I was getting on just fine, my new business and all. You get out of a bad place, you don't want to go back there. But when I was talking to Jerrod, this light went on. I remembered how they treated me, what Kemp said. How he made me feel like a criminal. Scared and dirty. He made me think I was wrong, but I wasn't. Kenny didn't leave my place any earlier than ten o'clock, and even if he did, he was so hung over, he wouldn't have gone out looking for a house to rob. It doesn't make sense. Kenny wouldn't hurt anybody, not like that. He made some mistakes when he was young, but he's not bad. He's not."

The sunlight had shifted its angle on the table. The digital numbers moved silently in the display. Gail looked at Tina Hopwood. "Is there anything else you want to add?"

She wiped her eyes on a napkin and shook her head.

Gail turned off the recorder. "I'll send you a draft of the affidavit. If you have any changes, let me know."

Tina said, "Clean up my language, okay? You know, make it sound halfway intelligent. And tell Kenny I'm sorry. I didn't mean for this to happen. I swear to God I didn't."

They sat in the front seat of Anthony's car and watched the Clip 'n' Dip van drive away.

"What do you think?" Gail asked.

"I don't know."

"Yes, you do. You believe her."

"What matters is whether the judge believes her." Anthony started the engine.

"Kenny is innocent," Gail said. "I'm sure of it now."

"You're going to need more than one affidavit to overturn a death sentence."

"But I do feel hopeful, don't you? I think we have some good news for Ruby."

"Listen to me." Anthony put the car back into park and turned to her. "Don't allow your emotions to take over. Remember these words: 'Ruby, I will do everything in my power.' Leave it at that."

"I can't believe you really maintain such detachment with clients."

"Detachment? No, it's professional distance. You're a good lawyer, *corazón*, but this isn't another of the commercial lawsuits that you are used to."

She smiled at him. "Would you like to come in as co-counsel?"

"No, thank you." He nodded toward the slim leather portfolio on the floor. "Did you bring the fee agreement for Mrs. Smith to sign?"

"Yes, I did."

"How much are you going to charge her?"

"Are you *sure* you don't want to co-counsel the case?"

"Try to get at least seventy-five thousand dollars."

Gail let out a whoop of laughter. "Oh, my *God*."

He stared at her, then said quietly, "It will cost you at least five thousand just to copy the existing files, not to mention the thousands of copies you still have to make. Crime scene photographs. Travel expenses, long distance charges, Federal Express. A private investigator. What about your time? Expect to put in hundreds of hours —"

"For a hearing on one motion?"

"How optimistic. What if the judge says no, and you have to appeal his order? Ask her for more money."

"Denise Robinson said they would take the case back if it got complicated, and I'm going to hold her to it. Ruby knows this. I refuse to gouge her on fees."

"No me digas más." Anthony looked over his shoulder and backed the car out of its parking place. "I offered a suggestion, you don't want to take it, okay."

Gail could feel her temper bubbling. "There's a difference between offering a suggestion and giving orders."

He braked at the road, waiting for traffic to clear. "You know something? When you don't agree with me, it's your case. If you do agree, it's ours. Have you noticed that?"

"Fine. Stay out of it, then."

He laughed. "How?"

Ruby Smith lived in a two-story brick building called Sunset Villas. The lobby was blandly institutional, but the place was clean, and the staff seemed competent. It could have been worse, Anthony thought. Many old people spent their declining days in miserable poverty. This woman was not rich, but she had the money and strength of will to look out for herself.

Gail had told him that diabetes and a bad heart had sent Mrs. Smith to the nursing home. Her three surviving children helped out, but they had scattered to other states. For companionship she had the other residents, a TV, and a turquoise parakeet, which chattered from its cage on a small table by the window. A fresh breeze drifted through.

Smile lines had been permanently etched on the old woman's face, and her brows seemed suspended above the frames of glasses so thick they enlarged her faded blue eyes. The lady's feet, in their socks and pink terry cloth slippers, were propped on a footstool. A walker was within reach. She sent Gail into the tiny kitchen to pour three glasses of iced tea.

Anthony was directed to bring the large tin from the table holding the bird cage. "You ever try peanut brittle? The doctor won't let me have sweets anymore. My pastor's wife brought it over." To be polite, Anthony took some. The candy was flat, with peanuts in it. It cracked when he bit it, and he caught the pieces against his chest.

Mrs. Smith laughed. "Careful. You like it?"

"Yes, very unusual." He added a small lie: "Delicious."

Gail had told him that Ruby Smith used to live in a small white frame house in the old section of Stuart, not far from the river. She and her late husband had built it with their own hands, Ruby doing most of the work because he'd had a leg shot off in Korea. Ruby had tended him in his last illness, cleaned other people's houses until her body gave out, and never complained. She told the children in her care that everything that happened was part of a divine plan. Gail said she had believed that, as a child.

When Mrs. Smith wasn't looking, Anthony put the remains of the peanut candy in his shirt pocket. As he had expected, the women spent a while talking about old times. From one end of the sofa he listened to stories of Gail's childhood that he'd never heard before. Gail herself sat on a chair pulled close to Ruby's, and from time to time she would turn and smile at him to show he was included.

"How do you like living in America?" Mrs. Smith asked him.

Anthony replied that he had been here for thirty years, was a citizen, in fact, and had two children. He took their pictures out of his wallet and showed her. Ruby picked up a magnifying glass and squinted through it. Angela, who just turned eighteen, studying ballet. Luis, a sophomore in high school. Ruby asked questions about his family in Cuba and was astonished to hear that he planned to take his grandfather there next month. He told her that it wasn't so dangerous anymore.

The talk gradually turned to the subject at hand. Her grandson. The man on death row.

"Poor Kenny Ray. He's had a hard time

of it. His stepfather was evil through and through. When my Norma walked out on him, Kenny Ray wasn't but ten years old. Norma wanted to live with us, but her dad wouldn't hear of it. He said she made her bed, and she could lie in it. Norma wasn't much of a mother, you know, but my husband was a fool. We lost her, and all them kids suffered, Kenny Ray most of all. We took them in, but I should've seen where he was heading."

"Oh, Ruby. You can't blame yourself."

"Not a one of us can't look back and see things we ought to have done different, but what's past is past. The Lord has given me another chance. He set my feet on the path and led me to you. Norma is gone, but we're going to save Kenny. You're his instrument of salvation."

The weight of this trust settled down on Gail. "I'll do my best, but Ruby, it won't be easy." She leaned closer, elbows on her knees, and spoke about appellate procedure, the difficulties of overturning a conviction, the time it would take. Ruby listened attentively, asking a question now and then, wanting to understand. Gail answered without hesitation. She said she had hope. She said she believed in his innocence.

Listening to this, Anthony felt a jolt of unease. Gail was committing herself to this case as though her own life were at stake. The odds against her were high, but she didn't see this. Or seeing, she had decided not to care. There would come a time when the hard truth would make itself known, but for now, in this small room, with an old friend whose last wish was to save her grandson, hope was not such a bad thing to have.

The palm fronds outside the second-floor window shifted in the breeze, and the curtains moved inward. The sun fell in lacy patterns on the floor.

Gail said softly, intently, "Ruby, I'll do everything I can for him. I promise."

"That's plenty good enough," said Ruby.

"I suppose we should be going," Gail said. As if it were an afterthought, she opened her portfolio and took out some papers. "I brought the fee agreement with me. I'm sorry to have to charge you, but the costs will be pretty high. I'll need ten thousand dollars to start with."

Anthony nearly leaped to his feet. Only ten thousand? *¿Estás loca?* Ask for fifty! He shifted on the sofa and cleared his throat. If Gail noticed, she pretended not to.

The amount seemed to stun Ruby Smith

as well, for a different reason. "My word." She waved a hand. "No, no, it's all right, if that's what it costs, I don't begrudge a penny. If you need more later on, you ask me." She pointed toward her desk and told Gail where to find her checkbook and pen.

"What else am I going to spend it on? Dance lessons? I'm eighty-one years old. I might kick the bucket tomorrow. My kids don't need it. This is for Kenny Ray." She wrote out the check and signed the papers. "There you go, honey. Now when y'all get home, give Irene and Karen a big kiss from Ruby. And tell them to come see me!"

"I will." Gail bent down to hug her. "Good-bye. We'll call you again before we leave."

"Come here, Anthony, you get a hug too. Now help me out of this chair, I want to walk you to the door."

Anthony took her arm, and Gail positioned the walker. The old woman leaned heavily on it. "Gail, you be my boy's champion. Like it says in Psalms, 'Plead my cause, O Lord, with them that fight against me. Let them be as chaff before the wind.'" A smile beamed from her wrinkled face. "It's a glorious day. I want to shout."

CHAPTER 7

Saturday afternoon, March 10

Under a boundlessly blue sky, pine hammocks and sabal palms dotted the monotonous landscape. A few head of cattle watched the car pass. Gail knew that the first Bryces in Martin County had once owned all this land. Looking at a map she could see how Bryce Road would go under I-95, then veer south, join a small county road, and eventually vanish in endless flat plains of sugarcane. Lake Okeechobee was a blue curve on the left side of the map.

Anthony was cursing in Spanish at the rocks that clattered on the undercarriage of his new black Seville. As they drove west, Gail told him that she didn't plan to ask the sheriff any questions. It would be useless. But she would tell Jackie why they'd come to Martin County, so she wouldn't find out later by accident.

"Why don't you ask her to help you?"

"Help with what?"

"She knows people here," Anthony said. "You don't. Ask her how to find the snitch who said Kenny Clark confessed to murder."

"Jackie's father arrested Kenny. That would be a little dicey, don't you think? Getting her involved like that?"

"She works for the city police, not the sheriff's office. All she has to say is no."

"True," Gail said reluctantly. "We'll see how it goes."

At the ranch, which used to belong to Diddy Bryce, they parked among the other cars inside the wire fence. Further on were pine trees, a long tin roof glinting in the sun, and some outbuildings. A dozen horses cropped the grass in a paddock. A gravel road led toward an open gate where dozens of balloons danced on their ribbon tethers.

The gate was tended by women in matching green T-shirts, and a sign announced that ten-dollar donations to the historical museum would be gratefully accepted. Gail had left her purse under the seat and had only a few dollars in the pocket of her shorts. Anthony reached for his wallet.

"Gail!" She looked around. Jackie was jogging toward them, wearing jeans and a white cowboy hat. Her hair swung at her shoulders.

"Hi. I was about to think you wouldn't make it." Pearl buttons accented her blue denim shirt, and a wild turkey feather decorated her hatband. She put an arm around Gail's waist and spoke to the women selling tickets. "This is my cousin Gail from Miami, and her friend Anthony."

"Well, then, you-all can go in for free."

"No, I'll pay." Jackie bumped Anthony aside with a hip and laid a twenty on the table. The woman waved them through. In a low voice Jackie said, "People are always offering to do me favors. I never say yes. They'd expect me to forget I saw them run a stop sign or something. Why don't you come over for dinner tonight? Or just come over, if you get too stuffed on barbecue this afternoon."

"Oh, I'd love to, but we've already got plans." Gail didn't elaborate. They planned to drop in to talk to the eyewitness, Dorothy Chastain, at five o'clock. "Is your dad here?"

"He was, but he got a phone call. I think he'll be back."

Jackie pointed things out. A picnic tent with tables and chairs, another for food, a third with crafts for sale: quilts, wood carvings, toys, fishing lures. The band played country music from a stage erected near the tin-roofed, concrete block building that Jackie called a barn.

Gail doubted that Anthony had any more

of an appetite than she did; room service had brought lunch. She put a hand on his shoulder. "Anthony, would you find us something to drink?" A hint to leave them alone for a minute. She smiled at him.

He smiled back, then asked Jackie what she wanted. "Nothing for me, thanks." He walked into the crowd. Gail saw a couple of women stare at him. He was worth looking at: the way he moved; the dark hair that waved back from his forehead; the full mouth. He wore three rings, a gold bracelet, and a lizard-strap watch. The white shirt, rolled casually to the elbow, had been purchased at the Prada store in New York.

"What a babe," Jackie said. "Are you guys reengaged yet?"

"He's trying to wear down my resistance," Gail said.

"I wouldn't have any."

"Who are you going out with?"

"Nobody, really. Well, this guy in fire-rescue, but" — she grinned — "the man can put out fires, he just can't light them."

Gail hugged Jackie's arm. "I wish you'd come to Miami. We'd have a good time."

"Maybe I will. I've got some vacation days coming."

"Listen," Gail said, "there's this case I'm working on —"

But Jackie's attention had been drawn to the stage. The band had stopped, and two of the members were carefully hoisting an old man up the steps by his elbows. Gail shaded her eyes. "Oh, my God. Is that Diddy?"

"Sure is. Still kicking. He sold the place about five years ago, but he loves to come out here and play cowboy."

Diddy Bryce put his harmonica to his lips and reedy notes came out in a lively tune. A guitar and banjo played backup. From time to time the old man stopped to shout instructions to what Gail finally realized was an imaginary dog chasing a fox.

"Git 'im! Cut 'im off!" More reedy notes on the harmonica, then another shout, "In the woods!" The banjo player stepped forward to do a solo, and Diddy Bryce's toe tapped as he played along. "Git 'im! Go'n, boy!" He stopped abruptly, grinning and pointing upward. "Treed 'im!"

The audience laughed and applauded.

Diddy held on to the microphone. "Used to be all kinds of wildlife in them woods yonder. Foxes and bear and coons and wildcats. Gators too. We still got gators in the ponds and canals, so watch out when you go skinny-dippin'." The crowd laughed. "Back when my pa was a young man, 'fore there was fences, he run about two hunnerd head of cattle free-range, and he'd round 'em up with cattle dogs. They had their dogs and their bullwhips. My arm ain't so good anymore, but here's my sidekick, Rusty Beck, to show you how it's done."

While Diddy talked, volunteers had been moving the crowd back from the stage, and two boys had dashed around setting empty soda cans on the ground. A chestnut horse trotted into the clearing. The rider kept his fist tight on the reins, and the horse pivoted, kicking up dust. The man threw a leg over the pommel and slid off.

Rusty Beck carried a leather bullwhip and a knife in a sheath on his belt. Sleeves rolled past his biceps showed off hard, ropy muscles and a tattoo of an eagle on his right arm. His hair was tied back in a graying ponytail, and the sun picked up the red in his goatee and mustache. A hat with a silver band shaded his eyes.

Gail stood on tiptoes to try to locate Anthony in the crowd, hoping he could see this. When the boys had led the horse away, the man made a quick movement like throwing a ball overhanded. The whip uncoiled with the crack of a rifle shot. Walking in a slow circle, his arm moving rhythmically, he snapped the long whip to left and right. The crowd moved back. He turned quickly and one of the soda cans leaped up in a puff of dust. Sharpened steel glinted at the tip of the bullwhip. The dented can fell back and spun. The man sent another one flying, and as it descended, he cut it wide open. He worked his way across the open ground, his steps accompanied by loud cracks. Cans jumped and clattered.

Gail spotted Anthony shouldering his way slowly through the crowd, smiling his apologies. Taking a shortcut, he appeared at the edge of the clearing with two large paper cups. The bullwhip cracked over his head, and he froze.

A line of small explosions cut off Anthony's path. People moved back, laughing in alarm. Anthony turned slowly to face the man with the whip and stared at him through his sunglasses. Dirt leaped up within a few inches of his polished shoes, and grit dusted his pleated trousers.

Gail grabbed Jackie's arm. "He's going to get hurt."

"No, he won't, but it's rude." Jackie yelled, "Rusty, stop showing off!"

Laughing, the man turned his back, and the long whip came down on another soda can. Anthony stood still for a moment, then stepped away. The crowd applauded, but his lips were pressed too tightly to return their smiles. Reaching Gail, he gave her one of the cups.

Jackie looked toward the stage. The man was getting back on his horse. "He always does that, and usually it's one of his friends in on the joke. I'm sorry it was you."

Anthony made a slight shrug. "Who is he?"

"Russell Beck — Rusty. This is his property. He's the one who bought Diddy out. I should tell him to watch his manners."

The band was playing again. Anthony nodded toward the pine trees at the other end of the barn. "Let's stand over there." As they walked, the noise diminished. "There's a sign by the food tent. The catering has been donated by the JWM Corporation. That stands for J. Whitney McGrath, no?"

"That's right, but everybody calls him Whit."

"You know him?" Gail asked.

"We say hello. He keeps a couple of horses in the barn. Rusty looks after them."

Jackie caught the glance that Gail and Anthony exchanged. "Why'd you ask about Whit McGrath?"

Gail explained. "His name showed up on a murder investigation in Palm City twelve years ago. I'm representing the man who was convicted of the crime, Kenneth Ray Clark. His grandmother is Ruby Smith. She used to babysit for us. Do you remember her?"

Jackie slowly shook her head. "Not really."

"Well, Ruby asked me to help Kenny Ray. He's been on death row for eleven years. The victim was Amber Dodson. Her name might be familiar. She was twenty-four, married, stabbed to death in her own house. Her baby died of accidental suffocation."

"Right, right. It's an old case. The guy who killed her was a local, a laborer or something. And you're his lawyer?"

"I'm going to file an appeal. I believe he's innocent. This morning we talked to a woman named Tina Hopwood. She could have given Kenny Clark an alibi, but the lead detective threatened to have her probation revoked if she testified. The case was handled by the sheriff's department. Jackie, I wanted to let you know up front because technically it puts me and Garlan on opposite sides."

"Who was the detective?" Jackie asked.

"Ronald Kemp."

"I've met him." Her brown eyes revealed nothing else. If she had an opinion of Kemp, she wasn't sharing it. "Why are you telling me all this?"

"Because I need help locating someone. I thought that since you're with the Stuart PD, you might know. But don't, if you'd rather not."

"Who is he?"

"Vernon Byrd. He's also a jailhouse snitch. He said my client confessed. I think he was lying."

"I know Vernon," said Jackie. "He's about six two, three hundred pounds. His street name is Peanut. We busted him last month for disorderly intox. It took four officers to get him cuffed. He hangs out at the Cherokee Lounge, sort of a bouncer. I could get a home address for you."

"Wonderful. Are you sure it's all right?"

"What do you mean?"

"All right with Garlan."

"I don't see a problem. If you've got questions about procedure or need an address, something like that, I could help you. But I can't go behind anyone's back or give out information you're not entitled to."

"No, of course not," Gail said.

"So you really think your guy didn't do it?"

"That's what we think, but we can't prove it yet. There was an eyewitness, a woman who lived across the street from the

141

Dodsons. She saw a man fitting my client's general description in their yard, but we think she was wrong. I'm going to talk to her about it later today."

Jackie hooked her thumbs in the back pockets of her jeans. She was a couple of inches taller than average, and her body gave the impression of quick, agile strength. "This is good stuff. I don't get to investigate homicides. Most of my work is fairly routine, you know, being on road patrol." She rocked on her boot heels. "Are you sure it was a break-in? I guess they looked at the husband."

"He was the first suspect," Anthony said. "He's a lawyer, Gary Dodson. He sold the house, but he still practices in Stuart. Do you know him?"

"Only the name. He runs ads in the newspaper. Cheap divorces and wills and things like that. Were he and his wife having problems?"

"His alibi checked out," Gail said. "He was at work by nine o'clock, and Amber died between ten and two."

"Only if you believe the medical examiner," Anthony said. "Time of death isn't that reliable. In fact, *querida,* you should let an independent forensic pathologist look at the ME's notes."

"You still think Amber's husband did it, don't you?"

"I think he's the most logical choice. Well? Do you want me to talk to a pathologist? I have one in mind. I would trust his opinion."

Gail wondered how much it would cost, then decided it didn't matter. "All right, fine."

"That's not a bad idea," Jackie said. "I went to a seminar on homicide investigation, and one of the speakers was this FBI expert who said it's useless to talk about time of death. There are so many factors that can throw you off. Body weight, air temperature, blood loss, even whether the person had been exercising."

"Exactly so," said Anthony.

The hat made a shadow across Jackie's face. Under the brim her eyes turned to Gail. "What was it you were saying about your client's alibi witness? The police threatened her?"

Gail said, "Kenny was renting a room in Tina Hopwood's trailer. She could have gone on the stand and contradicted the eyewitness, but she didn't. She told us that Detective Kemp accused her of lying and said he would 'discover' drugs in her house if she gave Kenny Clark an alibi, so Tina kept her mouth shut. She couldn't go to jail. She had two kids to support. She's coming forward now because . . . well, I suppose you could say it's a guilty conscience."

"Okay. So who was the guy in the yard? Did the victim have a boyfriend?"

"Who knows? According to one of her co-workers, she wasn't getting much from her husband."

"Were there any other suspects?"

"Amber's sister was on the list for a while. Lacey Mayfield. Do you know the name?"

"Sure. She works at Mayfield Antiques on Flagler Avenue in the old downtown. The Mayfields have owned it for years."

"Lacey came by Amber's house early that morning, but she was asleep, so Lacey left and went to work. She was there the rest of the day except for about forty minutes when she went to lunch. Supposedly."

Jackie looked past Gail and called out to someone. "Hey, Dad. You missed most of the party."

Garlan Bryce was heading in their direction. He wore boots and jeans, the attire of the day. The weight of fifty-five years had slackened the skin on his jaw and put pouches under his eyes. He was a little grayer, a little heavier, but no less solid.

He nodded at them. "Gail. It's been awhile."

"Hello, Garlan." His cool manner unsettled her, but she calmly introduced him to Anthony. There were polite handshakes.

"Got a minute? There's something I'd like to discuss." He looked at his daughter. "You come too." Without waiting for a reply, Bryce walked over and moved one of the sawhorses that barred the wide entrance to the barn. Anthony took Gail's cup and tossed it and his into a trash barrel. She sent him an inquiring look, and he shrugged.

They followed the sheriff into what could have once been a storage room. Scraps of lumber and metal were strewn about. Light came weakly through dirty, web-draped windows. Jackie appeared unsure what was going on.

Garlan Bryce closed the door. His gray eyes fixed on Gail. "I'll get to the point. An elderly lady by the name of Dorothy Chastain called the office a little while ago. She said a lawyer from Miami was going to come to her house and question her about the Clark trial. This lawyer wanted her to sign an affidavit. Mrs. Chastain wasn't sure if she should. I was just over there. I told her she didn't have to talk to anybody."

The sheriff turned his head toward his daughter. "Did you know about this?"

"No, sir. Well, some of it. We were

145

talking when you arrived."

Gail was about to explain but Anthony was quicker. "Ms. Connor and I are reinvestigating the Clark case. With all due respect, sheriff, the police have no right to interfere."

"Mrs. Chastain is a state witness. If you want to talk to her, you need to get an okay from the prosecutor."

"No, we do not. The trial is over."

"If you disturb this lady again," said the sheriff, pointing stiffly at Anthony, "I will not take it lightly. I got to her house, she started crying. She thought she'd done something wrong. It was hell getting her calmed down. You stay away from her."

Gail broke in. "Garlan, it's my case. Anthony is advising me. I've been retained by Kenny Ray Clark's grandmother."

With a short laugh, Bryce shook his head. "Ruby Smith. Well, that explains how you got into it." He tugged on the front of his vest. "Ruby hired you to file another appeal, did she?"

"Ruby believes that Kenny is innocent, and there's a good chance she's right." Gail hesitated, then said, "Garlan, we have information that your lead detective, Ronald Kemp, threatened a potential defense witness to keep her from testifying."

"What witness? Who are you talking about?"

"Tina Hopwood."

"Who?" He tilted his head.

"She rented a room in her trailer to my client."

"Oh, for the love of Christ."

"Did you know what Kemp planned to do?"

His lips thinned against his teeth. "My officers do not threaten witnesses."

"I believe that this one did, Garlan. Look. I'm not trying to attack you or your department. I'm just trying to get to the truth."

"Is that so? Let me save you some time. We don't throw people in jail who don't belong there. We want to get it right, because if we don't, some defense lawyer or judge down the line is going to give us problems. We do not put together a half-assed case and cross our fingers the jury will see it our way. We don't make an arrest until we have evidence. We had evidence when we arrested Kenny Ray Clark. We had a great deal of evidence. I don't doubt for one second that he's right where he belongs."

The air in the small room seemed to be running out. Gail said, "I'll need copies of the crime scene photos. Who do we ask?"

"Get a court order." Garlan Bryce headed

for the door, then paused as his glance fell on his daughter.

"I won't be long," she said.

He opened the door and was gone. Jackie let out a breath.

"I'm so sorry," Gail said.

Jackie looked fiercely at her. "You didn't tell me everything. You didn't say you suspect my father of framing your client."

"No one suggested that."

"My father has more integrity than anyone I know. He would never allow a witness to be threatened, and if it did happen, and he found out, he wouldn't stand for it."

Quietly, Anthony said, "Jackie, you're a police officer. You know how these things go. They were dealing with a violent, highly publicized murder that had to be solved. Any investigator with Kemp's experience would know how to bend the rules, and his supervisors would expect him to."

"Not in my father's office."

Anthony sighed.

Fear of being rebuffed kept Gail from moving. "Jackie, I didn't know Garlan would react this way. Never mind Vernon Byrd, I'll find him somehow. Just don't let this come between us. Will you call me sometime? Please. We won't talk about this case."

Jackie stared past her. After a long moment she said, "I'll call you."

The quick tap of her boot heels receded on the concrete floor of the barn.

Anthony said, "Welcome to Martin County."

"Dammit." Gail sat heavily on a stack of roofing shingles, not caring about the dust. "Could that have gone any worse?"

"Well. It appears that a gap of several hours has developed in our schedule. It's a beautiful afternoon. Perfect beach weather." He stroked her hair, then bent to kiss the crown of her head. "On second thought, why don't we go back to the room?"

"And do what?"

"I could think of something."

She looked up at him. "Be serious."

"I am serious. You kept me up all night."

"Excuse me? I kept *you* up?" She let him kiss her, then held him down by his shirt collar. "We could look at the trial transcript."

"Mmm. How exciting."

"You said you wanted to see it."

"Give me a summary. I'd like to hear how a case as weak as this one resulted in a sentence of death. You have as much time as it takes for me to drive back to the hotel." He pulled her up and brushed the dust off her bottom. "Let's get out of here."

"No speeding," Gail said. "I don't think Garlan's in the mood to cut you any breaks."

CHAPTER 8

"It doesn't seem reasonable, does it, that Kenny Clark sat in jail for a year before the case went to trial?"

"A year? It's not that unusual, querida. There is no bond in a capital case, and if the cabrón who represented him believed in his guilt, well, let him sit."

Judge P. R. "Pat" Willis, a small, tidy man whose Cracker accent was not out of place in Stuart despite the influx of Yankees, ran his courtroom with brisk efficiency. He ordered that no one mention the Dodson baby's accidental death, as it would have been highly prejudicial to the defendant. The chances were slim, however, that the jurors did not already know about it. Jury selection began the week of January 8.

The trial was not televised, but the news media gave it heavy coverage. As a witness, Gary Dodson attended the trial only on the day he testified. He avoided the press. His bowed head and slumped shoulders said enough.

The victim's sister was a swirling vortex of

rage. Reporters sprinkled her comments into their stories for heat. "Kenny Ray Clark is guilty, and he should be put to death by stabbing, like he did to my sister. He stabbed her in the heart. He strangled her. He let her baby die. I want him to pay." In her photos she has long hair, like her sister, but Amber was the pretty blond one. Lacey was in the courtroom every day with her parents, Fred and Rose Mayfield. They all sat in the front row, directly behind the prosecution table, holding hands.

Joseph J. Fowler, the state attorney for the Nineteenth Judicial Circuit, did not usually try cases himself, but he took this one. He was up for reelection in the fall. Two of his top assistants sat with him. One of them was a woman named Sonia Krause, who would eventually take over Fowler's job.

The other table was reserved for the defendant and his court-appointed attorney, Walter Meadows. Photographs show a man in his late fifties, overweight, wearing a rumpled gray suit. At breaks he goes outside to smoke a cigarette. In the afternoon he closes his eyes during part of the state's case. The judge inquires if he is asleep. Then inquires again. Meadows replies, "No, your honor. Wide awake."

"I have known such attorneys," Anthony said. *"They drink at lunch. They don't know how to prepare a case because they usually plead a client guilty. They don't investigate because there isn't enough money. How much did Meadows earn?"*

"Forty-five dollars an hour."

"Clark got what he paid for."

The newspaper sent a sketch artist into the courtroom. The picture of the defendant adds ten years to his age. Kenny Ray Clark's hair is short and spiky; the shading on his lean face looks like stubble; his eyes veer away. Tattoo-smudged hands rest on the table. The artist has drawn them large enough to break bones.

The trial began promptly at 9:00 A.M. on January 15. After opening statements, the first witness was called to the stand: Sergeant Ronald Kemp of the Martin County Sheriff's Office, trim, articulate, professional in manner, holder of commendations, graduate of FBI seminars. With the prosecutor asking a question here and there, Kemp took the jury step by step through the investigation and the evidence that had led them to their man. The eyewitness ID. A confession. The lack of an alibi. Mr. Clark had claimed to be hanging drywall the day of the murder. That lie had been quickly exposed.

On cross, the defense attorney laid the groundwork for a later attack on the eyewitness, Dorothy Chastain. He wanted the jury to think that Kemp had used the photo display to plant Clark's image in her mind. Kemp's patient explanations emphasized that the police had followed accepted procedure.

The only concession that Walter Meadows got from Kemp was that the police had not found any of Amber's missing jewelry in the defendant's possession.

The next day was taken up by detectives from crime scene. The prosecution didn't dwell on the physical evidence, perhaps because Fowler knew they had nothing conclusive. Even so, the state scored some points. Joe Fowler unsheathed the defendant's hunting knife and left it on the low wall of the jury box. Light glinted on its blade. An expert testified that the fragments of coquina rock found on the carpet at the Dodson house were consistent with those found in the tread of the defendant's tires. The long screwdriver taken from the toolbox had been tried on a piece of test aluminum, and the marks were consistent with those on the sliding door. The jurors were shown glossy color enlargements of the knife, blood spatter, a screwdriver, aluminum, and rocks.

To his credit, Walter Meadows managed to obtain an admission that "consistent with" did not mean "the same," and that some other screwdriver could have been used. None of the tools found in the Dodsons' utility shed had been examined.

Luminol had shown blood on the knife seized from the defendant, but in too small an amount to be tested. Meadows said, "Give me a simple answer. Was any of the victim's blood found on the knife or on anything whatsoever that belonged to Mr. Clark? Yes or no."

"No."

The next witness was the fisherman who had seen a pickup truck at the county park. His original statement to police had mentioned fender damage; at trial he was certain about a missing rear bumper. Meadows was able to bring out this discrepancy, a small victory.

The state called Vernon "Peanut" Byrd, resident of the "dirt section" of Bahama Street in East Stuart, more recently a resident of the Glades Correctional Facility. Shortly after the defendant's arrest, Byrd and Clark had shared a cell in county lockup. On the stand Byrd freely admitted

his convictions for possession of crack cocaine and dealing in stolen property. He
denied that anyone had promised him le-
niency if he testified. He had been asked to
show up and tell what he knew.

"Kenny said he didn't want to kill her, but
she kept screaming." Byrd provided details.
The red silk pajamas. The clock cord tied
around her neck.

*"How could he have known about the pa-
jamas and the clock?" Gail wondered. "They
weren't in any of the newspaper stories."*

"The cops told him."

"Oh, really."

*"Baby, you have an unrealistically high
opinion of the police."*

*"I sincerely doubt they would frame an inno-
cent man."*

*"They didn't. They believed Clark was
guilty. He murdered Amber Dodson. Why
should a technicality like due process stand in
the way of justice?"*

Meadows went after Byrd's unsavory
background, hoping the jury would believe
he lied to secure favorable treatment. As the
witness was still in prison, the impact of that
argument was lost. It would not be until
Kenny Ray Clark had been on death row for

a year that Byrd was paroled. The state attorney would deny any connection.

Day four of the trial began with the prosecution's most devastating witness. A reporter for *The Stuart News* wrote, "Dorothy Chastain, 58, a neighbor of Amber Dodson, supplied eyewitness testimony placing Kenneth Ray Clark on the victim's property." In the accompanying photograph she wears a dark suit and white blouse. She is serious but not severe. She could be a librarian, a high school principal, a lay church worker. Her glasses overpower her nose, and her chin recedes. She is all eyes.

Fourteen pages of the transcript were taken up by Joseph Fowler chatting with the witness about her background, her family, her education, her hobbies. His purpose was to show her as a reliable, intelligent woman with no axe to grind. She was here to do her civic duty. Fowler introduced photographs and a drawing, then asked her to show the jury where she had been sitting and to estimate distances. She didn't have to estimate. She had used a tape measure. She had also reenacted her observations with a stopwatch.

Her responses were direct and simple. Looking out the window for her ride to the airport, she had noticed a young man with long brown hair, wearing a denim jacket, standing near the hedge across the street. He came around the hedge, looked over his shoulder, then walked quickly behind the Dodsons' house. She never left the window. Her friend arrived and tooted the horn, and she had to go. It was 10:12. "I should have called Amber to alert her. I feel so bad."

"Mrs. Chastain, you have testified that you saw a man going behind Amber's house at approximately five minutes past ten."

"At exactly five minutes past ten."

"Exactly. Did you see that same man at a later time?"

"Yes, I did."

"Where and when was that?"

"I saw him on Wednesday, the fifteenth of February, at the sheriff's office."

"Under what circumstances?"

"Detective Kemp asked me to view a lineup. I picked him out."

"And were you certain, when you picked the man out of the lineup, that he was the same man you had seen going behind the victim's house?"

"Absolutely certain."

"Do you see the same man here in the courtroom today?"

"Yes, I do."

"Can you point him out to the jurors?"

"Right over there. The young man in the dark blue suit."

The prosecutor must have allowed the jury sufficient time to follow the imaginary line that ran from the witness's extended finger directly to the defendant, who had been told by his counsel not to look away when this occurred. But what did the jurors read into that cool, unwavering stare?

"Let the record reflect that the witness has indicated the defendant, Kenneth Ray Clark. Thank you, Mrs. Chastain. I have no further questions."

Meadows rose from his chair and took his notes to the lectern. The difficulty of his task must have weighed heavily: impugning the veracity of an honest, well-meaning citizen. "Mrs. Chastain, you described the man to the police one way in your initial statement, and then you pick out a man who looks different. I don't say you're lying. I suggest that you are mistaken. The truth is, you just can't be sure. Isn't that true?"

"No, I'm very sure. There is no doubt in my mind."

"Isn't it true, Mrs. Chastain, that you never saw my client actually enter the house?"

"Yes, that's true."

Meadows's reference to "my client" was a

misstep that he quickly tried to correct. "And isn't it also true that this person — whoever he was — could have gone over the fence and never entered the house at all? You wouldn't have seen this, would you?"

"No. All I saw was him going behind the house."

Meadows tried to shake her memory, but she held fast. His extended attack, and her calm rebuttals, served only to reinforce her credibility as an impartial observer of the facts.

Week two began with Dr. George Snyder, the medical examiner. The judge had allowed into evidence only a few of the autopsy photographs, taken after the body had been cleaned. Their only purpose, he said, was to prove that she had been stabbed. When the photographs made their way down the jury box, someone was heard to mutter, "Oh, Jesus." One of the women began to cry.

The ME testified that the defendant's knife, with a serration near the top of the six-inch blade, was "not inconsistent with" and "could have inflicted" the injuries.

"But Dr. Snyder, the deepest cuts on the body are only five inches deep. The murder weapon could have been some other knife entirely. Isn't that true?"

"It's possible, but a six-inch blade entering the body at an angle would penetrate less than six inches."

"Doctor, you stated in the autopsy report that the cuts are smooth. Are you saying that a serrated knife would make smooth cuts?"

"What I said, counselor, was that the extensive lacerations make it impossible to say precisely what kind of knife was used."

Switching directions, Meadows probed at the time of death, probably hoping to show that even if Kenny Ray Clark had walked through the Dodsons' yard, the victim could have died earlier or later. He waved Snyder's own report at him, in which the ME had estimated that death had occurred between ten and two. However, the jurors could not have forgotten Kemp's testimony about the clock that had stopped at 10:23.

The state did not consider it worthwhile splitting hairs over time of death. They had physical evidence tying the defendant to the scene. They had the defendant's statement to his cell mate. They had his lies to the police. They had an eyewitness. And they had the bereaved husband, who had found his wife's mutilated body.

Gary Dodson's answers were hesitant and short, as though he could not bear to relive the experience. Halfway through his testimony the judge asked if he needed a recess. Dodson said no, he could go on. To establish the identification of the victim, Joe Fowler showed him one of the autopsy photos.

"Yes. That's her. My wife. Oh, God. Amber. Amber."

The Palm Beach Post reported that weeping could be heard throughout the courtroom. Meadows rose only long enough to say he had no questions of the witness.

After Dodson had made his way out of the courtroom, Joseph Fowler announced, "The state rests."

"Que comemierda. *Meadows was afraid of alienating the jury! I would have asked for a recess so Dodson could blow his nose, then I would have taken him apart.*"

"*Too bad you weren't there.*"

"*Yes, there would have been an acquittal, and this very weekend, we would be in my bed, not on our way to a hotel room.*"

Meadows had a dilemma: whether to put his client on the stand. His client demanded to testify. Kenny wanted to swear he had never confessed to his cell mate; that he had left the Hopwoods' trailer at ten o'clock; that he didn't own a denim jacket; that his statements to the police had not been lies but faulty recollection. That he hadn't done it. However, Meadows knew that Joe Fowler was as dangerous as Kenny Clark was impetuous and unaware. It would be a disaster. Meadows persuaded his client to remain silent and allow his friend Lougie Jackson to establish his alibi.

Jackson was a friend from high school who had moved to Port St. Lucie, just across the county line. He testified that he was working nights, and Kenny woke him up at ten-thirty on the day of the murder. Jackson had seen no blood on him. They'd had a couple of beers together, and Kenny Ray Clark had gone on his way.

Joe Fowler did not dignify this testimony by attacking the witness himself. He sent his female assistant to do it.

"You're a good friend of the defendant, aren't you, Lougie?"

"Yes, but I wouldn't lie for him. And I'd appreciate it if you'd call me by my last name."

"Isn't it true — Mr. Jackson — that in 1984 in St. Lucie County, you were convicted of possession of cocaine with intent to distribute?"

This was the first Walter Meadows had heard of it. Gamely he tried to rehabilitate the witness on cross-examination, but skepticism was written all over the jurors' faces.

Closing arguments began the next morning.

It was a two-foot putt for the prosecution, but Joseph J. Fowler went over every detail of the crime and investigation. He methodically laid a foundation for the jury's only logical choice: a verdict of guilt. He proposed an explanation for the lack of blood on the defendant: Clark had showered at the Dodson home, then had changed clothes in his truck. In rebuttal, Walter Meadows argued that the state had failed to prove its case. That there was no physical evidence. That his client had been on Lougie Jackson's front porch drinking beer at 10:30. He couldn't have murdered Amber Dodson and have driven to Port St. Lucie all within twenty-five minutes. Reasonable doubt existed.

The jury was out for three hours. When the clerk announced the verdict, the defendant dropped into his chair. The Mayfields ran to embrace the prosecutors. Spectators applauded and cheered until Judge Willis gaveled everyone quiet. He announced that court would reconvene on Monday to consider the sentence.

Walter Meadows objected. This wasn't enough time. He hadn't prepared. The judge said that defense counsel should have known to prepare, and there would be no extensions. Guards fingerprinted and handcuffed the defendant before taking him back to his holding cell.

The sentencing phase took three days. The prosecution relied heavily on the opinion of a psychologist, who said, "This is a violent man. If given a life sentence, he would be a danger to other inmates. If he ever got out, he could kill again."

Gary Dodson took the stand to talk about his wife, their marriage, their hopes for the future. How much he missed her. There was still no mention of his son, but the jurors were in tears.

Meadows arranged for Kenny Ray's sister to fly in from Mobile, Alabama, to testify about their childhood. The beatings. How Kenny Ray had caught the brunt of their stepfather's rage. She did not mention the sexual abuse. Kenny Ray had forbidden anyone to bring it up. Ruby Smith came next to say that at heart, he was a good person, and he had suffered much as a child. Meadows excused her, but before leaving the stand she turned to the jury. "It's not right to kill. God makes that decision, not man. Please let him live. If he did wrong, he can repent and be saved."

Each side made a closing argument. Joe Fowler took off his glasses and approached the jury. Speaking without notes he went through the evidence, recounted the witnesses' testimony, and paid particular attention to the husband's grievous loss. An hour and a half later he summed up with these remarks:

"Mr. Meadows will ask you to recommend a life sentence. Is that justice? Is that what this crime demands? Ladies and gentlemen, this murder was not only premeditated, it was vicious. Amber Dodson's crucifix was driven into her body from the force of a knife entering her flesh over twenty-seven times. Do not doubt she suffered. She suffered alone and in great terror and pain. Her husband was robbed of his wife, her family of a beloved daughter and sister. I ask you, if the death penalty is not appropriate here, then where would it be appropriate? We as a society have a right to demand retribution. To say yes, this young woman's life mattered. To say yes, where the crime is this cruel and the loss so great, the penalty of death is the appropriate, moral response of a civilized society. I ask you — I beg you — to remember, to honor, this young woman. Justice demands that Kenneth Ray Clark pay the ultimate price for his crime."

Joseph J. Fowler must have stood silently looking at the defendant for several long moments, letting his words sink in, before returning to his chair.

Five years later, when Denise Robinson filed the first motion under Rule 3.850 in an attempt to overturn the conviction, she stated that Walter Meadows had been drunk. The defendant had smelled alcohol on his breath. If only the defendant had complained to the trial judge. If only.

"Ladies and gentlemen of the jury. Thank you for your time and attention. You have a momentous decision before you. Momentous. Whether to take or spare a man's life. You have found him guilty, this young man, Kenny Ray Clark. My client. You have heard the evidence. You have heard from Amber's husband. You know how he felt, losing his wife. It was indeed a terrible loss. Yes. I submit to you, however, that this does not justify the taking of another life, when that life — the life of my client — was twisted by the beatings of his stepfather and addiction and suicide of his mother. It was a sad and violent childhood. Not a normal life. But to deprive him of it won't restore

Amber Dodson to us. An eye for an eye, and we're all blind. With mercy in your heart, I beg you. Spare a man's life. A human life. For every life is precious. The quality of mercy is not strained, but droppeth as gentle rain. Thank you."

This was the totality of Walter Meadows's argument on his client's behalf.

The jury came back with a recommendation of death, ten to two. Judge Willis pronounced sentence then and there. Kenny Ray Clark screamed at the judge, "They set me up! They're liars!" He was dragged away. "I didn't do it! I'm innocent! You're going to kill an innocent man!"

The Mayfields stood hand in hand on the courthouse lawn, facing the cameras. Lacey Mayfield was beaming. Her father read a statement. "All we want to say is, thank you, God, for guiding Mr. Fowler. Thank you to the sheriff's department and the judge and the jury. Thank you all for your prayers. We are sorry for Mr. Clark, and we bear no ill will toward him or his family. We hope this verdict will enable our daughter to rest in peace."

Gary Dodson smiled as his parents hugged him. "It's over. It's finally over."

Not quite. It was 1993 before the Florida

Supreme Court affirmed the conviction. By law, the case was then assigned to a team of state-funded appellate lawyers, the Office of Capital Collateral Representatives. They would not raise the question of guilt or innocence: that issue had been resolved. They would raise issues of due process. They would allege ineffective assistance of trial counsel and look for new evidence.

The Rule 3.850 motion was filed in 1994 and summarily dismissed by Judge Willis in 1995. A year later, the Florida Supreme Court reversed, ordering that Willis hear testimony.

Lacey Mayfield appeared at the hearing in 1997. In this photograph she is heavier. She wears a T-shirt with the logo of NAVA, the National Association for Victims Advocacy. "What about our rights? Don't we count? My family's lives have been destroyed too, and we need the pain to end. We need closure. How long do we have to wait?"

Judge Willis ruled that Walter Meadows had done an adequate job and that in any event, nothing he had done, or failed to do, would have changed the verdict. Motion denied.

CCR appealed to the state supreme court, which affirmed in 1998. The governor signed a death warrant. An appeal to the federal district court resulted in a stay, and within a year the court had granted a petition for *habeas corpus*. Quirks in the schedule sent the case flying to the Eleventh Circuit, which reversed. Two years later, the case reached the end of the line. The U.S. Supreme Court refused to hear it.

The Stuart News ran the story on page four of the local section, along with another reprint of the victim's high school portrait. Her sister vowed to go to the governor. "It seems like everybody has forgotten what happened here. We haven't. As long as Kenneth Ray Clark is still breathing, and my sister is dead, it's a slap in the face of justice."

Eleven years had passed since sentence had been pronounced. This was about average. Some inmates had been on death row more than twenty years, and it was not unreasonable to imagine that Kenny Ray Clark could reach middle age before the execution took place. If it took place at all.

In 1997, as Walter Meadows was retiring from practice, he sent some of his old files down to Fort Lauderdale, care of Denise Robinson. She found, among the disorderly papers, a letter-size envelope with the name Carol Malloy typed on the front as though the address were to be filled in later. Inside the envelope was another, smaller envelope containing a letter from Florida State Prison, written by Kenny Ray Clark.

Denise had shown the letter to Gail. "Here. Read this. And ignore the bad spelling."

June 8, 1991

Dear Carol,

I have wrote you about ten letters since last year. I sent them to the apartment and to your folks house but no luck. Have you moved? Please send me your new adress.

You heard alot of lies about me, but this is the truth. I AM INNOCENT! The Florida supreme court will decide the apeal and I pray to God they will let me out, it was a mistake from start to finish.

It might take a year or maybe two and I wish you would wait for me but I understand if you can't. Please write back if only to say hello and how are you doing. It is depressing in here and knowing a letter is on

171

it's way from you would mean alot. Will you send me a picture? If you don't have one that's okay cause I see your beautiful face whenever I close my eyes. You are the one true love of my life.

This is the month of June, do you remember we talked about if we got married it would be in June? I said I will love you forever and I still mean it. I LOVE YOU.

Please write back if I haven't bored you too much. I will never forget you and I hope you feel the same. Stay sweet.

Sincerley,
Kenny

After finding the letter, Denise Robinson called Walter Meadows to ask why it was still in the file. Meadows said he had spoken to Carol Malloy. She had received the other letters but had thrown them away unopened, and she didn't want this one either.

CHAPTER 9

Saturday night, March 10

Officers on the Stuart Police Department rotated from shift to shift — days, nights, midnights. Jackie Bryce had been on nights for a couple of months, working three to eleven. Some of the road officers complained when they rotated around to nights because it cut into their social life, but Jackie couldn't say she had much of that. Unless she went out, which wasn't often, she would sit around the house in her jeans and a T-shirt and read. The current topic was bloodstain interpretation. Some of the detectives had been talking about it earlier in the week, and Jackie had borrowed a book from her father's study. The book was open on the circular oak table beside her bowl of cereal. As she sliced a banana she read the section on impact spatter.

Road patrol was where everyone started, but Jackie wanted the detective bureau before she was thirty. It wouldn't happen any faster for her than for anyone else. Garlan had made it clear to Chief Pitts: no favors. That was all right, but Jackie could see how her relationship with the sheriff of Martin County was having an opposite effect. The brass didn't want anybody to think she had an advantage, so they cut her no slack whatsoever.

Jackie wrote a few words in her notebook. *Medium velocity: diameter 1–4 mm, usually blunt force injury.* She looked up at a movement across the kitchen. Diddy had come downstairs in his old bathrobe. His hair was damp, sticking to his head.

He shuffled across the room in his slippers. "What a day."

Jackie smiled at him. "It was a great party."

"Is there some cake left?"

"You'd better not have anymore. Did you take your pills?"

"I will before I go to sleep." He found a bowl in the dish drainer and filled it with corn flakes. "I saw your cousin Gail today. Why didn't she come say hello?"

"They had an appointment to go to."

"She favors Louise, don't she?" Diddy poured the milk. "Your ma was slim like that, and the same color hair. Who's that man she was with?"

"Her boyfriend. His name is Anthony Quintana."

"He looks Spanish."

"He's Cuban."

"Same difference."

Jackie shook her head and went back to her book.

"Ain't she married?" Diddy pulled out a chair.

"She got divorced a couple of years ago."

"I can't keep up. After your ma died, her folks didn't visit no more. I used to like her sister. She was cute. What was her name? Gail's momma."

"Irene."

"Did they come to see you?" Diddy's hand shook. He ducked his head to get the spoon closer to his mouth.

"Who? Oh. No, they came to investigate a homicide that happened in 1989. Gail has a client on death row. She says he's innocent." Jackie took a napkin out of the holder and put it on Diddy's lap.

"Is that feller a private eye?"

"He's a lawyer. Why are you so curious?"

"Rusty wants me to find out."

"Tell Rusty to mind his own business." She ate a piece of banana.

"Why are you mad at Rusty?"

"You saw what he did with that bullwhip."

"Got some dust on the feller's pants is all."

"Rusty needs his butt kicked." She leaned

over to look into Diddy's bowl. "Is that nonfat milk?"

"Yes, boss. Who got killed?"

Jackie had learned to follow the wandering path of her grandfather's mind. "A woman who lived in Palm City, Amber Dodson. Somebody came into her house and stabbed her. They're trying to find out who really did it."

"I remember. It was in the news. She was all cut up. Terrible."

Jackie and her grandfather ate their cereal, and for a few minutes metal clicked on china in two rhythms, one quick, one slow. She closed her book. "Diddy? I might go to Tampa and visit Alex. Would you be okay here by yourself when Dad's at work?"

"I reckon so. A girl ought to see her brother." He chased a corn flake with his spoon. "You coming back?"

She put a hand on his arm. "Of course I am." The flannel robe was frayed at the cuff. He had a new one but he wouldn't wear it.

"Alex went to Tampa and stayed there. He don't hardly visit."

"He writes you letters. He calls."

"Your mother left home too. She oughtn't to have done that." The old man's mouth opened, and his eyes darted around the kitchen. "Jesus. I can't remember. Did she die?"

"Thirteen years ago."

"That's right. Don't seem that long. I guess I'm tired. What a day."

Jackie collected their bowls, then bent down to kiss his white-stubbled cheek. "It's past ten o'clock. Why don't you go to bed?" She turned on the water in the sink.

He shuffled toward the hall. "You're a good girl, Jackie."

"Remember to take your pills."

Until a year ago, Jackie had rented an apartment in a new development off Kanner Highway. The walls were white, the carpet was beige, and the refrigerator was chronically empty. There was very little furniture. The men she dated would leave before dawn. One day she gave the keys back to the rental agent and went home to the house on the river, which had been built by her grandmother Bryce's folks. The house was two stories with a wraparound porch and yard full of shade trees. She lived in the apartment over the garage. It would have been too humiliating to move back into her old room upstairs. Garlan wouldn't let her pay rent, so she put money toward groceries and the light bill. She kept an eye on Diddy.

Sometimes she would take him out to the ranch to pretend he still owned it, and Rusty would bring him home.

Rusty Beck was the son of one of Diddy's old friends. Charlie Beck threw Rusty out of the house at age sixteen, and Diddy let him live in a spare room in the barn, doing odd jobs and growing up wild as a weed. When the old man died, Rusty had inherited his grove land, then sold it and quit any kind of work. He built a cabin, raised a few horses and some cattle, and rarely came into town. Rusty seemed to like being alone out there where he could do anything he pleased, which included running his speedboat flat out over Lake O, hunting wild boar, gigging frogs, drinking cheap beer, chasing women from Indiantown, and otherwise raising hell. He liked Diddy, but everybody else kept their distance, like walking around an alligator sunning itself on a canal bank.

It bothered Jackie that Rusty had asked about Anthony Quintana. She wished she hadn't said anything, because Diddy might repeat it. Rusty was ticked off at Quintana for standing up to him, and if he got the chance, he would push him again. Jackie didn't think it would be easy. Most men, if they heard a bullwhip cracking over their heads, would run, and everybody would have a good laugh. Quintana wasn't that way. Meeting him the first time, Jackie had made a quick judgment: a hot-looking guy with too much jewelry and a shiny car. The truth was something else. There was more to Gail too. Jackie had always liked her, although she'd thought she was frivolous, even shallow. But she'd shown up on this old murder case, talking about saving her client from death row. Proving he was innocent, getting him out. She'd faced down Garlan Bryce. That took some guts.

On her way downstairs, after making sure that Diddy's pill box was empty in the section labeled SUNDAY, Jackie noticed the patch of light that fell across the old braided rug in the hall. Her father was in his study.

She knocked on the door. He looked up, and the lamp flashed on his glasses.

"Come on in."

She sat on the arm of the sofa. "You're working late."

"I've got a meeting tomorrow morning at eight o'clock." He nodded at the book. "What is that?"

She showed him. "It's one of yours. A couple of the detectives were talking about impact spatter, so I wanted to look it up."

"Good idea. Learn as much as you can.

You could wind up needing the most ob-scure bit of information." Police reports were stacked on the desk. The ice had melted in his glass of bourbon. He said, "Got something on your mind?"

Jackie said, "I wanted to ask you about the Dodson case."

"What do you want to know?"

"Yesterday Gail talked to Tina Hopwood. At about the same time the eyewitness says she saw Clark, Tina Hopwood says he was with her. She supposedly told this to Ron Kemp, but he threatened to pull her in on a probation violation if she testified in court." Jackie could read nothing in her father's face. "What about that?"

"Who are you asking for? Gail Connor and her pal?"

"No, Dad. It's for me."

He laid his glasses on the desk and leaned back in the chair. His weight made the leather creak. "Going into that investiga-tion, Ronald Kemp was the best we had on the force. If you want to learn something, read the file on that case. It's a model of police work."

She smiled. "Kemp did it, didn't he?"

Her father looked at her awhile. "You find this amusing?"

"No, sir."

"Never approach your job with anything less than the utmost seriousness and respect. Whether the victim is a young child or a crack addict, he or she deserves a methodical, thorough, and aggressive investigation. It's never easy. It's never to be taken lightly. If you believe otherwise, you're in the wrong career."

"Yes, sir."

He rocked slowly in his chair. "Let me fill you in on the Hopwoods. She had a criminal history. So did her husband. He was a drug dealer in the Port Salerno area, and he's now serving time for armed robbery. These are the people that Clark ran with. When Ron and his partner went to their trailer, the place was filthy. Tina was drunk and verbally abusive. Was Ron nice to her? I doubt it. Did he get the truth? I'm sure that he did."

Anthony Quintana's words drifted into Jackie's head. *You know how it works.* Kemp with enough experience to bend the rules. Garlan expecting him to.

"What did you say to the state attorney?"

"What would have happened, Jackie, if I'd gone to the prosecutor and said, you know, my officer was leaning on a possible defense witness because she was lying to us, and maybe you ought to disclose that fact to the defense lawyer. And say the defense lawyer went to the judge about it. 'Judge, judge, we've got some police misconduct in this case.' What might have happened?"

Jackie didn't like the condescension in his tone, but she gave the reply he was after: "Clark could have walked."

"That's right. And then I or Ron or Sheriff Carr would have had to explain to Ms. Dodson's family that after several thousand man-hours of work, a positive ID, strong physical evidence, and a self-incriminating statement to his cell mate, we're so sorry, but we had to let the guy go. That was unacceptable."

Several seconds ticked by. "I understand."

Jackie slid from the arm of the sofa onto the seat. A memory flickered in her mind. Standing in the hall. Her mother in here. Her father's voice: *That is unacceptable.*

"No investigation is perfect," he said. "We do the best we can, and we stand behind each other. Loyalty. You're on a team. Remember that."

"Yes, sir."

"What was Gail doing at the ranch? What did she want with you?"

Jackie brought her eyes up from the floor. "An address. She wants to talk to the man

Kenny Ray Clark supposedly confessed to."

"Supposedly. Whose side are you on?"

"I'm not on a side."

He tapped his pen up and down on his reports. "Are you going to help her out?"

"No. I'd rather not get involved."

He nodded, still looking at her. "Anything else you need to know?"

Unbidden, from years away, the words came into her head. *Why did my mother leave?* Jackie picked up the book from the sofa. "No. I guess that's it. Good night."

"Sweet dreams." He smiled at her but he didn't lift his arm as a signal to come around the desk and kiss him good night. They had stopped doing that years ago. He put his glasses back on and picked up his pen.

She sat for a long time in the dark on the wooden steps that led up to her apartment. The air grew chilly, and she pulled her hands into the cuffs of her sweatshirt. She thought about what she had said in the barn to Gail and Anthony. *My father would never.*

But he had. He had known what Ron Kemp had done, and he had condoned it. Kemp telling that woman she was going back to jail. Telling her whatever was necessary so she wouldn't get on the stand and screw up their case. That wasn't bending the rules, it was fracturing them. Kemp had believed he was right. That was all Jackie could give him.

Maybe he *was* right.

Clark had made a statement to Vernon Byrd, his cell mate. Kemp wouldn't have invented that. They'd nailed Clark already. Clark had simply run his mouth. Perps would do that. Stupid, but they did it.

Kemp had lived with the case, knew the facts, knew the evidence. Gail had just come into it. Anything against her client, she would ignore. Jackie had seen how defense lawyers would pick and choose the facts that suited them. At trial some of her own cases, good solid arrests, had gone down the tubes. A lawyer twisting the facts. Cop treated as the bad guy.

Jackie retied a sneaker. Brushed some leaves off the step.

She thought about Vernon Byrd. Three hundred pounds of red-eyed mean. Hung out at a pool parlor, earning table time in exchange for keeping the drunks and whores off the premises. He'd been paroled after only a year on a heavy narcotics conviction. Why?

For a few more minutes Jackie sat and listened to the slow, winter chirp of the crickets, then got up and went inside.

There was a photograph in the top drawer of her dresser. All the family had gotten together at the Connors' house on Sewall's Point on the Fourth of July. Jackie had just turned twelve, and Alex was nine, still a little kid. The snapshot showed her mother, her brother, herself, in the back of Uncle Eddie's boat. Their mother with her arm around each of them. Her cheek pressed to Jackie's head, her honey-blond hair spilling onto Jackie's brown bangs. Laughing. Always laughing. So beautiful. And the smell of alcohol on her breath. Dead at thirty-six that September, smashed in her car, drunk.

A long time ago, visiting Aunt Irene, Jackie had seen this snapshot and asked to have it. She'd never told her father. He had used the word disappointment. *Your mother was a disappointment.* An embarrassment. Louise had left him, betrayed him, walked out on her kids. *No sense of responsibility.*

Why had she left? No one had ever explained, and Jackie had always considered it disloyal to her father to ask.

Jackie wondered if her mother had talked to Aunt Irene. Sisters shared things like that. And maybe Gail knew. It was possible that everyone knew but her.

CHAPTER 10

Sunday afternoon, March 11

Before coming up to Stuart, Gail had done a title search on the Dodson house. It showed that a few weeks after the murder of his wife, Gary Dodson had put the house on the market, and in the years since then it had changed hands three times. This could only be explained by bad karma. The narrow street was not prosperous, but pretty enough, shaded by tall pines that left a layer of brown needles on the shingle roofs. Boats were stored in some of the side yards, and shiny SUVs announced the presence of families.

As they reached the house on the corner, Gail saw the FOR RENT sign. The place was vacant. "That's lucky," she told Anthony. "Park in front so I can get a clear shot of the driveway." No one was about except for some kids on bikes and an old man next door adjusting a sprinkler.

Gail got out and aimed her camera. One-story white house, green trim. Hedge to the left. Weedy flower beds. To the right, the driveway ended at a double carport, one side enclosed by decorative concrete blocks. On the other side, a door to the kitchen. Amber's husband had come through it that night and found blood on the floor.

Anthony walked toward the west side of the house. Gail followed. Sunlight gleamed on his hair and picked up the narrow gold stripes in his shirt. Sandspurs had attached themselves to the hems of his trousers. Lovely trousers. A lovely fit. She zoomed in, then pressed the shutter.

Stopping between the house and the hedge, he turned around, looking across the street. The eyewitness lived in the house directly opposite. "Take a picture."

"She might be watching us."

"She doesn't know who we are," Anthony said. "We could be real estate agents."

With a flutter in the pit of her stomach, Gail raised her camera. "If Garlan throws us in jail for trespassing, I'm making you pay my bond too."

"Garlan Bryce can't do a damned thing to us."

"This isn't Miami, *Señor* Quintana."

Gail swung around to shoot the west side of the Dodson house. A row of windows, all cranked tightly closed. A rusting air conditioner held up by angle iron. The algae on the concrete pad underneath it was dried and cracking. No one had lived here for a while. Gail shaded the glass to look through the windows, but the blinds were shut.

Around back, more photos. The patio had been enclosed, making it impossible to see the sliding-glass door where the killer had entered. The woods behind the fence had turned into more houses. She focused on the kitchen windows. Another air conditioner. The utility shed. They continued around the house.

The elderly man stood in the driveway, apparently waiting for them to come out from under the carport. He wore a bright yellow golf shirt and plaid pants. A cotton fishing hat shaded his eyes. The sprinkler next door waved slowly back and forth over the grass.

"You folks looking to rent the place?"

"Are you Arthur Grigsby?"

"I am. How'd you know that?"

"My name is Gail Connor." She gave him a card. "This is Anthony Quintana. We're investigating a homicide that took place here twelve years ago. Your name was in the police reports. Do you have a few minutes to talk to us?"

He studied her card, then nodded and took them over to his house.

"Bess? Got a couple of folks here that want to know about the Dodson murder."

His wife poured iced tea on the back porch while Arthur Grigsby settled himself into a folding chair. He tipped his hat back and interlaced knobby fingers across his belly. He answered the question that Gail had just put to him. "I didn't know Gary too good. I liked his wife all right. She'd be out strolling the baby and stop to chat. You remember Gary and Amber, don't you, honey?"

Bess Grigsby sat down with her cigarette. "Sure I remember." Her voice was a sack full of rocks. "Art thought Amber was the cutest little thing on two legs."

"She was, next to you."

Bess winked at her husband.

Gail glanced across the table. Anthony's dark eyes danced with amusement. She asked, "How did the Dodsons seem to get along with each other?"

"They got along all right," Art Grigsby said.

"Oh, Art. They fought all the *time*."

"I never heard him yell at her."

"Okay, he didn't yell. She yelled." Bess crossed her thin, darkly tanned legs. A leather thong sandal dangled from one foot.

"What did they fight about?"

"Please. Stupid stuff. She played the

stereo too loud. He never wanted to go out. There wasn't enough money. Of course there wasn't. Look at the cars. He had a BMW, and she had a Mustang convertible. And the way she dressed."

Art said, "They had big plans to remodel the house, then he left his job. Had a nice job in a big firm, but he wanted to start his own. Didn't work out so good."

"Uh-uh. He didn't quit, he got fired."

"He did? Gary told me he quit."

"Amber said he got fired."

"A man ought to know if he quit or got fired, honey."

"Gary? Admit he was a loser? Ha."

"Now, Bess, have some pity for the poor guy."

She blew her husband a little kiss. "You're sweet. Wrong, but sweet." Her laugh sent the rocks rattling in her throat.

Gail remembered that Gary had worked at the Stuart branch of a high-priced Palm Beach firm. "Did Amber use those exact words? They fired him?"

"They fired him, they let him go, whatever. Next time I saw her she was going on and on about his new law practice, lah-de-dah. That girl could put on such an act." Bess Grigsby reached to tap her cigarette over the ceramic coconut ashtray. Wrinkles crisscrossed her brown forearm. "She's dead. I shouldn't talk that way."

Anthony said, "Do you think she could have had a lover?"

"I don't know. Gary kept her on a short leash. I could hear him out there in the garage. 'Where've you been? You're ten minutes late. Go change that skirt, it's too short.' If she was fooling around, she didn't do it here."

"She wasn't that kind of girl," Art said.

Bess rolled her eyes and blew smoke toward the ceiling. It drifted past a mobile of painted tropical birds.

"Did you tell this to the police?" Anthony asked.

"What's to tell? That they acted like married people?" She nudged her husband's thigh with her toe and laughed.

Gail asked, "What was Gary like?"

Art Grigsby answered. "He kept pretty much to himself. Never did come over to chew the fat or get neighborly, you know, like ask how the game went or to borrow a tool or something. But I liked him okay."

"Oh, *please*. He was a sanctimonious *twerp*. Gary was the kind of guy who'd walk across the yard to pick up a leaf and accuse you of dropping it. He kept firing the yard men because they couldn't edge straight enough for him. The place looks like shit now, but when they lived there, you couldn't find a *speck* of dust. Amber showed me the pantry. Gary wanted all the canned goods lined up like soldiers exactly half an inch from the front of the shelf, and don't let me see the applesauce next to the peas. Applesauce goes with the *fruit*."

Art Grigsby chuckled. "Hell to pay around here if I tried to tell Bess where to put the applesauce. Hoo boy."

"Did it ever occur to you," Anthony asked, "that her husband might have killed her? When you heard she was dead, what did you think?"

The Grigsbys looked at each other across the table. Art said, "Bess and I had a few go-arounds about that. I won five dollars off her when they got the guy that did it."

His wife held her hand out and motioned for him to give.

"Nope. It's not over yet. Anyhow, Gary was at work."

His wife exhaled smoke to the side. "He could've hired a hit man."

"Bess watches too much TV."

Gail sent a quick glance toward Anthony, then said, "Mrs. Grigsby, do you think that your neighbor, Dorothy Chastain, could have been mistaken?"

"Ha! She's never wrong about *anything*, is she, Art? I hired a girl to come in to cook dinner for him when I had to be out of town visiting my sister, and Dotty spread it around that Art had a girlfriend. I let *her* have it. Bitch."

"Now, honey. Dotty didn't mean anything."

Anthony made a slight shrug. Nothing more could be learned here. Gail stood up. "We should be going. Thank you so much for your time."

At the front door, Art Grigsby shook their hands. "Come back and see us. We like company."

Anthony said, "It was a pleasure to meet you."

Bess Grigsby gave him a long, sideways look. "Love your accent. Where are you from, by the way? If you don't mind my inquiring."

He made a polite smile. "Cuba."

She snapped her fingers. "I knew it. *Cubano.*" Then another gravelly laugh. "Art and I went to Havana on our honeymoon. *Cha-cha-cha.*" Arms overhead, she swiveled her hips.

Her husband nodded. "I thought that fellow would've been executed by now. The wheels of justice grind slowly. It's a good thing for him, by golly, especially if you folks are right."

They walked slowly to the car, Gail leading because Anthony had his eyes on Dorothy Chastain's house. He said, "Look. She's watching us. As soon as we leave, she will call the Grigsbys to find out who we are."

Across the street, a woman stood at the living room curtains.

Anthony leaned against the rear fender of his car and raised his foot to pick the sandspurs off his cuffs. "Let's talk to her. We won't have this opportunity again."

"She won't call the Grigsbys, she'll call the sheriff."

"I think not. Now that we have spoken to her neighbors, she is curious about us."

Gail let out a breath. "Fine. You ask the questions, then."

"Me? It's your case."

She gave him a look. He smiled, the corners of his mouth going up, eyes hidden behind his dark glasses. She said, "You won't get through the door, but if you do, this was your idea."

He got through the door. Both of them did. It took an apology for disturbing her and regrets for any prior misunderstanding.

But this was a matter of utmost importance, a man's life in the balance, questions that only she could answer.

Dorothy Chastain took them into her living room, where crocheted throws protected the brocade sofa, and silk flowers grew from every marble windowsill and mahogany side table. She smoothed her skirt under herself as she sat. She was taller than Gail had expected. Even at seventy, she was assured in her movements and deliberate in her speech. She was cautious but not fearful. That she offered them nothing to drink said clearly that she didn't want them to stay longer than the five minutes Anthony had promised her this would take.

He sat forward on the sofa, hands loosely clasped. "For now, we are simply trying to gather the facts. We've read the police reports, of course, but they don't contain every detail. I hope you can help us."

"It has been a rather long time," said Mrs. Chastain. Her hair had been gray in the photograph; now it was white. Her glasses bore curved reflections of the living room window.

"If you would just tell us what you saw that day." Anthony beamed a look of concern toward the woman — brows lifted, lines across his forehead.

Mrs. Chastain said she'd seen the young

man coming around the hedge, waiting, looking over his shoulder, then going behind the house. She gave details of his clothing, his build, his hair. The time of day, the distances. Gail noticed how re-remarkably similar it all was to the words in the transcript. She had seen this happen in her civil trials. A story told over and over eventually becomes a memory of itself.

Returning from the birth of a grandchild in Atlanta, Mrs. Chastain had found Detective Sergeant Ronald Kemp's card among her mail. "So I drove over to the sheriff's department the next morning, a Tuesday, and asked to speak with him. He came out and introduced himself and took me into the criminal investigations office. His desk was in a cubicle, with other cubicles in the same room."

"Did you sit at his desk?" asked Anthony.

"He took me into another room. Or that was later. I'm not sure. It's been so long. But I did pick out Mr. Clark's photograph."

"Who else did you speak to?"

"Oh, there were quite a few people."

"Do you remember anyone specifically?"

"Let's see. I met Sheriff Bryce, although he wasn't sheriff then."

"He was Captain Bryce. Did you talk to him about the man you had seen?"

If she had, Gail noted, the conversation was not anywhere in the police reports.

"We didn't talk in depth. He was primarily speaking with Detective Kemp."

"Was this before or after you viewed the photographs?"

Mrs. Chastain gazed away, thinking. "I don't remember."

"All right. Let's go back to the time that you were standing at your window. Did you see anyone else in the Dodsons' yard that morning?"

"Anyone else? No."

"Any cars in the driveway?"

"I saw Gary leave at the usual time."

"Did you see Amber's sister?"

"Yes, that's right. What on earth was her name?"

"Lacey Mayfield. Can you remember when you saw her and what she did?"

"Let's see. It was after Gary left. And certainly before I saw Mr. Clark in the yard. I don't know exactly. She parked in the driveway. She got out, knocked on the door." Mrs. Chastain's eyes closed, and her glasses tilted upward. "She looked through the front window. She walked around to the side of the house. Then she came back, got into her car, and drove away."

Anthony was silent awhile, leaning his

forearms on his thighs, gazing past the silk flowers on the coffee table. "Did you tell Detective Kemp that you had seen Amber's sister?"

"Why, you know, I don't think we ever discussed it."

"Would you say that Lacey Mayfield walked into or across the same area where you saw the man in the denim jacket?"

"Yes, approximately."

Gail could see what Anthony was getting at. In the week that Mrs. Chastain had been out of town, she had confused the details of the two incidents.

He said, "All right. Let's go to the time when you went to Detective Kemp's office and viewed the photographs. When you got there, what happened?"

"Well, he took me to his desk, and we talked for a while. The younger detective was there too. What was his name?"

"Tom Federsen?"

"Yes. We talked, I can't recall what about, and then Captain Bryce came in, and we were introduced. After that, Detective Kemp took me into a conference room. I waited for quite a while. They brought me some coffee. Then I saw the photo display."

"Who showed it to you? Detective Kemp?"

She nodded.

"Who else was there?"

"He and Detective Federsen sat at the table with me, and Captain Bryce was standing to one side. Detective Kemp took a card out of a file. There were six photographs on the card. He said to take my time and tell him if I recognized any of them."

"Were the men all similar in age and appearance?"

"There were six young men, all of them white and clean shaven."

"All with long hair?"

"No, but Detective Kemp said that didn't matter because people's hairstyle can change. I studied the men very carefully. I didn't want to make any mistakes. My eyes kept going to photo number two."

"How sure were you at this point? Fifty percent? Sixty?"

"More like eighty. I said that I truly believed the second photo was the man I'd seen in the Dodsons' yard."

"What did Detective Kemp say to you?"

"He said I'd been very helpful to the investigation, and would I mind coming back to view a lineup? I said I'd do whatever I could to help. I felt so bad about Amber and her baby. What a terrible thing. My heart broke for Gary."

"Yes, of course. To lose both of them."

Anthony waited a few beats. "And you went to police headquarters again the next day, didn't you?"

"That's right. Detective Kemp came and picked me up. That was when I saw Mr. Clark in person."

"Where did you see him?"

"They had a two-way mirror like on TV, and I looked through it. The lights were very bright. They stood in front of a wall with height measurements on it. A chill went right down my spine. It was him. Seeing him in person, I knew it was the same man."

"You had no hesitation at all? You came into the room and immediately pointed him out?"

"I took my time. They said not to rush. I said, 'It's number four.' 'Are you certain?' I said, 'There is no doubt in my mind.' "

"You initially described the man as medium height and weight with very long hair. Mr. Clark is six feet tall, and his hair was to his shoulders. Did you notice the difference when you saw him in person?"

"The face was the same. I got a clear look at him the morning of the murder, but it's difficult to judge height."

"Did you ever think, even briefly, that the person you saw was a woman?"

"A woman? Goodness, no. It was a man." Mrs. Chastain pushed herself out of her chair and walked toward the window. "Come here, Mr. Quintana, I'll show you where he was, and how he walked behind Amber's house."

Gail followed them to the window, standing close enough to hear the conversation. Thin white curtains were drawn back, allowing a clear view of the street and the house on the other side.

"Mr. Clark was over there by the stop sign, near the hedge. He looked around furtively, like this, you see? Then he walked toward the back of the house."

"That was suspicious. Did you call Amber?"

"No, I . . . I thought of calling her, but my friend came to pick me up just then, and I didn't have time."

"You stood here for several minutes after the man walked out of your sight. That's what you said at the trial."

Slowly, Mrs. Chastain replied, "Yes. That's true. I had time."

"Was there a reason you didn't call her?"

"I should have. I know I should have. I just — didn't want to be a bother. Amber had made it clear to me in no uncertain terms that she didn't appreciate intrusions."

"Amber had accused you of . . . meddling? Of being nosy? Spying on her?"

"I never spied on her. I tried to be a good neighbor."

"So you didn't call her. You must regret that decision now."

Head bowed, Mrs. Chastain said, "Not a day goes by I don't think about it."

"Yes, it would be painful, knowing that as you stood here, just as we stand here now, a stranger was breaking into her house. Stabbing her to death."

"I can't tell you how awful I feel."

"But you made sure that her killer was brought to justice. At least you did that for her. That's what you wanted to do, wasn't it? For Amber?"

"Yes. I did." She put her fingers under her glasses to wipe away tears on her cheeks. "I just don't see why you think he could be innocent. I saw him."

As Dorothy Chastain stood by her window and wept, Gail could imagine what a jury would have done, hearing this. They might not have been so convinced she was right. Maybe it hadn't been a man she'd seen going around the house, but a woman — Lacey Mayfield, dropping by to check on her sister. If she had seen a man at the corner, he could have been anyone. Mrs.

Chastain went out of town for a week, and she forgot the details. The two events got mixed up in her mind. She felt so guilty about not calling Amber that she ID'd the first photo that looked plausible.

But Anthony Quintana hadn't been asking the questions that day. It had been Walter Meadows, a court-appointed hack who overlooked the obvious, fumbled the cross-examination, and delivered his final argument half drunk. The jury had believed Mrs. Chastain. They voted to send Kenny Ray Clark to death row.

Sunday evening

This far up the coast the land pitched more abruptly into the ocean. The waves didn't curl gently as they did on Miami Beach; they boomed. The sea foam rushed toward the land, digging at the shore and leaving a low shelf of sand as it fell back. A cold front had moved through, turning the sky to lead and chilling the air. A gust of wind flapped the edges of Gail's jacket and spun her hair around her face. Not much daylight remained. They wanted to be together one more night, then drive back before dawn, in time for Gail to have breakfast with Karen.

They walked north past an empty lifeguard stand, a sand-washed boulder, bits of driftwood. Gail took her hand out of Anthony's for a moment to pull her scarf closer. The wind cut through her sweater.

"Are you cold?"

"Yes, but it feels good. By July we'll be crying for this weather." She slid her arms under his jacket and around his waist. His muscles were tight and defined. "You feel good too."

He kissed her. His lips were cool until he opened his mouth, and the heat flooded into her. She clung to him. There were a few people out walking, but she didn't care what they thought.

He held her face. "We lasted the weekend together without a fight, did you notice? I think we could make it maybe thirty years, what do you think?"

"Hmm. That's a long time."

"True, but this is a pretty good start, no? Are you busy this week? We could get married."

She laughed and shook her head.

"When? Tell me."

"I don't know."

"Tell me a month. May. June. September. Anything."

The wind blew her hair into her eyes, and

she brushed it away. "Where's my ring?"

"I said I'll find it."

"When you do, we'll talk." She took a step backward and skidded when the sand gave way.

"*Ay, cuidado.*" Anthony grabbed her hand and pulled her up the slope before the next wave could soak her feet. He locked his arms around her waist and pressed his hips tightly to hers. "You can't get away. You know this, don't you?"

She made a show of shaking her head. "You don't *own* me."

"Oh, yes. You are mine. You don't go anywhere without my permission."

"In your dreams, buddy."

"I want to hear you say it. 'I am yours, Anthony. I can't live without you.' Come on, say it." His breath was hot in her ear. "*Soy tuyo, mi amor.*"

"Oh, stop. You are so rotten, Anthony!"

"*Sí, Anthony, papito, tú eres mi dueño, no puedo vivir sin tí.*" He nuzzled her neck, licking the skin under her ear.

Gail noticed an older couple walking by, smiling. She gave Anthony a quick kiss. "All right, we'll get married — as soon as you find my ring and Kenny is out of prison. Deal?"

He dropped his arms and looked skyward

as if checking the heavy clouds for rain. "Do you not realize, *señora,* how long it could take to get him out of there? *If* he gets out of there."

"Fine. Let me just get this motion filed and done with. That should be only a few more months. And what do you mean, *if?*" Anthony turned his head to look at her. Gail said, "Given what we've learned this weekend, I'm definitely optimistic. You aren't?"

He shrugged. "You have something to work with. I am optimistic to that extent."

She studied his face. He was serious. "We have a good case," she said.

"If you subpoena Dorothy Chastain as a witness, and even if she says to the judge what she said to us today, it would be useless. The judge won't disregard the jury's prior decision to believe her. So all you have is Tina Hopwood. And maybe the snitch, if you can find him yourself, because your cousin is too much under the thumb of her father to help you."

"Kenny is innocent."

"Perhaps he is, but it doesn't matter. The burden of proof is reversed. Your client is guilty until *proven* innocent, not *maybe* he's innocent."

"It doesn't matter?" Gail could feel the

slope of the sand shift under her feet, and she held on to Anthony's arm. "I can't lose this case. I won't."

In the fading light his eyes had gone black. She looked into them like looking into a chasm.

"Don't think about winning or losing. If you let yourself worry that you're the only thing standing between your client and disaster, you begin to panic and you won't be effective for anyone. Even the most brilliant lawyer can fail. Sometimes it's a matter of luck, of timing. It's out of your control. All you can do is fight like hell and then let it go."

"I refuse to *let it go,* Anthony."

"All right." His voice was soft. Placating.

"*You* can let it go. That's how you are. I can't detach myself that easily. I can't give up and see an innocent man put to death. I refuse to let it happen."

He reached out and brushed her cheek with his fingers. "It's getting cold. Why don't we go in?"

The truth snapped on like a light. Anthony assumed she would lose. He would stand by to offer his advice, maybe question a witness or two, but he wasn't about to scuff his shoes by walking the same rocky path that she, against his wishes, had chosen to take. *Let this be a lesson to you, bonboncita. Listen to me next time.*

With his hand still caressing her cheek, Gail wondered what would happen to them if they woke up one day, married, and the distance between them had not narrowed but widened? Would Anthony give her a reassuring pat as he walked out? Or fail to see it at all and wonder what she was complaining about?

She pushed these thoughts aside. If that day ever happened she would deal with it, but not now. She took his hand and kissed his palm. "I love you, Anthony."

He put his arm around her and they turned toward the hotel.

DEATH WARRANT
STATE OF FLORIDA

WHEREAS, KENNETH RAY CLARK did on the 6th day of February, 1989 murder Amber Lynn Dodson; and

WHEREAS, KENNETH RAY CLARK was found guilty of murder in the first degree and was sentenced to death on the 31st day of January, 1990; and

WHEREAS, on the 20th day of November, 1990 the Florida Supreme Court upheld the sentence of death upon KENNETH RAY CLARK and Certiorari to the United States Supreme Court was denied on the 29th day of December, 2000; and

WHEREAS, it has been determined that Executive Clemency, as authorized by Article IV, Section 8(a), Florida Constitution, is not appropriate; and

WHEREAS, attached hereto is a copy of the record pursuant to Section 922.09, Florida Statutes;

NOW THEREFORE, I, WILLIAM D. WARD, as Governor of the State of Florida and pursuant to the authority and responsibility vested by the Constitution and Laws of Florida do hereby issue this warrant directing the Warden of the Florida State Prison to cause the sentence of death to be executed upon KENNETH RAY CLARK, in accordance with the provisions of the laws of the State of Florida.

IN TESTIMONY WHEREOF, I have hereunto set my hand and caused the Great Seal of the State of Florida to be affixed at Tallahassee, the Capitol, this 12th day of March, 2001.

GOVERNOR

ATTEST:

SECRETARY OF STATE

CHAPTER 11

Monday, March 12

Biscayne Academy was closed for a teacher planning day, so Gail brought Karen along to the office with her. She turned her over to her secretary, Miriam, who put her at the extra desk and gave her a stack of folders and color-coded labels. After that, there were copies to make and papers to file. At eleven, Karen was remarkably thorough and quick. With no client appointments today, Gail planned to catch up on some work she had let slip, starting with complaints in two auto-accident cases.

The list of paragraphs from a standard complaint scrolled across her computer monitor. She hated personal injury law but couldn't afford to be picky. Recently she and two of her friends in the building had been discussing a partnership. The idea was beginning to appeal to her.

The door swung open and Karen came in with her hands behind her back.

"Miraculo change-o. I now present you with . . . your *lunch*. Ta-dahhh."

Gail laughed. "Amazing! Hang on, I'll

just be a minute." She clicked on a paragraph. *Plaintiff has incurred substantial medical costs . . .* "How are you doing out there, sweetie?"

"I'm almost finished." Karen sat in a client chair, tossed her hair over her shoulders, and unpacked the bag. Sandwiches, sodas, little cups of coleslaw. She shoved both of those in Gail's direction. "Mom. Do you remember we talked about a trip for spring break? You said you'd take me and Molly somewhere, and I get to pick."

"Umm-hmmm."

"You didn't *forget*, did you?"

Gail glanced around from the monitor. "No, I didn't forget."

Karen took a bite of sandwich. "We could go to Key West. That would be fun."

"Key West will be *mobbed* at spring break. What about a place right here on the beach? You like the beach, don't you?"

"We go all the *time*."

"You've never been to Busch Gardens." Eyes on the computer screen, Gail reached for her soda. "Aunt Patsy and Uncle Kyle live a few miles away from there. We could stay with them."

"Mom, you keep naming places *you* want to go."

"I keep naming places that I can afford."

"You *promised*. We won't eat much, I swear. We can cook in the room."

Gail smiled at her. "Okay. We'll go to Key West — assuming we can find a room at this late date. And don't start complaining if I bring my laptop and a box of files."

"Is Anthony coming?"

"What's wrong with Anthony?"

"Nothing, he's just *there* all the time."

"No, he's not coming. I told you, he's taking his grandfather to Cuba that week." Karen didn't dislike Anthony, but she missed her father, who managed a resort hotel in the Virgin Islands. At a distance, Dave's shortcomings weren't so obvious.

Her intercom buzzed. An outside line was flashing. Gail didn't want to pick it up. Miriam had been told to inform everyone — with the exception of Anthony or her mother — that Ms. Connor was in conference.

"Yes?"

"Kenny Clark is calling. From the *prison*."

"That's strange. How'd he get access to a telephone?"

"I don't know, but he says he has to talk to you."

"Okay, I'll take it." Karen was staring at the speaker. Gail picked up the handset to close off the sound. "Hello, Mr. Clark? This is Gail Connor."

"Hey. How're you doing?"

"Fine, thank you. What a coincidence. I just wrote you a letter this morning." Her mind caught up to the tension she'd heard in his voice. "What's going on?"

"The reason I called . . . I'm in the assistant warden's office. He just read me the death warrant."

This made no sense. "Excuse me?"

"The death warrant. They set it for April the eleventh."

"Set . . . what?" A crazy thought ran through her mind: someone was playing a joke.

"The execution," he said. "It's April eleventh."

Gail stood up and began to walk back and forth behind her desk. "How can they? We're going to file an appeal. They don't sign warrants until after the appeals are over."

"Well, they did it. I can't talk long. I need to call my sister. They give me two calls. One to my lawyer and one to a family member."

"Of course." Gail pressed her hand to her forehead. "I should come see you."

"How about tomorrow?"

"Tomorrow?" She grabbed her desk diary and turned it around. Lunch with the VP of a bank — a potential client. Wednesday was busier still, and there were depositions on Thursday. "I suppose so. What time is best for you?"

"It don't matter." He made a humorless laugh. "I'm not going anywhere. One more thing. Do you mind calling Ruby? Tell her not to come up here. She'll want to, but she's gonna start bawlin', and I don't need to see that right now. Tell her . . . I don't know. I'm okay, and I love her. You know. Make it sound good."

"I'll tell her. Wait. Kenny? I'm very encouraged by what I found out over the weekend. We'll discuss it when I see you. And don't worry."

"Yeah. I have to go. Thanks."

Gail listened to the disconnect, then hung up. Her wrist was so weak she nearly dropped the handset. There was a small calendar printed on a page of her desk diary. She counted the days, doing it twice to be sure. Twenty-nine. Four weeks from tomorrow. Less than a month to find new evidence, to prepare a motion, file it, argue it, and if it was denied, to appeal it . . .

"This can't be happening." She hit the speed-dial for Anthony's cell phone and was dimly aware of Karen asking her a question. She waved her quiet. Anthony's voice came on the line, telling her to leave a message. "Dammit." She remembered he was in trial today. At the tone she said, "Anthony, it's me. Kenny Clark just called. They've signed his warrant. I can't believe this. Call me back as soon as possible."

"Mom?"

Gail hung up and remembered Karen was there. What had she overheard?

"Mom, what happened? Are you okay?" Karen's blue eyes widened.

"It's all right. Really. A client of mine."

"The one on death row?"

"Yes, he called to ask a few questions."

"What's a warrant?"

"Just a legal term. Listen, Karen, I have to go out of town, probably in the morning, but I'll be home for dinner."

"Are they going to execute him tomorrow?"

"No, sweetie, they aren't going to execute him at all. You just sit and finish your lunch, okay? Stay there." She went out, closing the door on her way, then hurried to Miriam's desk.

Miriam whirled around in her chair. "What happened?"

"*Shhh*. The governor signed his death warrant and they've set the execution for April eleventh. Karen is not to know about this. I just don't think it's appropriate. Do you?"

"No, no, I don't." Miriam whispered, *"Ay, Dios mío."*

"I have to go see him tomorrow. Cancel everything on the schedule and move it somewhere else. I don't care what excuse you make up. Never mind the hearing, I'll find someone to cover it. Next, call my travel agent and ask how I get to the prison and back. It's way the hell up the state, almost to Georgia. Do I fly into Jacksonville or what? They have my charge cards on file."

While Miriam got busy, Gail took her cell phone all the way out into the corridor so Karen couldn't possibly hear, and called Denise Robinson. While it rang she stood at the window at the far end and gazed northward. The flat land vanished at the farthest point of a cloudless blue sky. Three hundred miles past that lay a place she had never really thought about, until little more than a week ago.

The receptionist said that Ms. Robinson had a meeting out of the office. Would Ms. Connor care to leave a message?

"Get me someone else, then. Anybody. The client you gave me just got a death warrant, and I have no idea what to do next."

Tuesday, March 13

Interstate 10 out of Jacksonville, then south on 301 to Lawtey. West to State Road 16, then northwest toward Raiford. The rental car agent drew the route with a yellow marker. He said she wasn't the first lawyer to ask directions to Florida State Prison.

When she thought she was close, Gail stopped the car at a Handy Way convenience store at the intersection of SR 16 and an even smaller county road. The store was part of a gas station with two islands out front under a metal roof. There were pay phones at the edge of the parking lot. Gail's cell phone wasn't set up to work this far north. She used her calling card and dialed a number at the prison, letting them know she'd be there shortly. It was 11:43 A.M.

Gail went inside and bought a cup of coffee and a prewrapped tuna sandwich. Standing beside her car she ate a quarter of it, but had no appetite and walked to a trash barrel to throw the rest away. She came back and watched a mud-spattered pickup truck pull in next to a pump, its owner getting out, a man in overalls and a camouflage-print jacket. Passing Gail, he nodded politely and smiled. How neighborly. How strange.

There was a church across the road. Woods. Empty fields. The sky was gray, promising rain. A few cars went by, the hum of their tires growing louder, then fading. The clerk inside the store had said that Florida State Prison was less than half a mile away. Gail shivered in the chill, damp air and sipped her coffee, arranging her thoughts. She didn't want to get back in the car until she was ready to go.

The route had taken her through several small towns. The people looked different. They were whiter. They dressed strangely. They lived in wood or brick houses, not stucco and tile. If Anthony were here, she might have told him, We aren't in Miami anymore, honey. This is the *South*.

A billboard outside Lawtey: Christ on a cross. *I Am the Way, the Truth, and the Light.* At the bottom, these words: *Brought to you by Harris Bros. Electric.*

Everything struck her as bizarre, even comic. Her head felt detached from her body, probably due to a lack of sleep. Going over her notes until four o'clock this morning, then lying in the dark making lists in her mind. At dawn, turning the alarm off before it sounded. She had managed to doze for an hour on the flight up.

Gail thought of calling Anthony, then

dumped that idea. She had spoken to him twice yesterday, and neither conversation had been friendly. First: "*Esto es increíble. I can't talk now, I'm in trial. I'll call you later.*" Second: a barrage of Spanish that she might have found colorful, had she been able to understand it. This part had come through perfectly: "For an intelligent woman, your naïveté is beyond belief. Didn't I tell you not to get involved?" She'd retorted, "Oh, isn't *that* helpful?" "What do you want me to do, Gail? You put yourself in this situation, you want me to get you out of it? Is that what you want?" She'd told him what to do with himself. He hadn't called back.

She asked her friends in the building to cover her court hearings, cancelled appointments with three potential clients, and left instructions with Miriam: Arrange with a copy service to copy the files in the Clark case *immediately*. Print out every case cited in any brief or court ruling. I need a list of private investigators who work in Martin County. Keep track of your time and add it to Mrs. Smith's bill.

In her phone call to Ruby, Gail had not mentioned money. What could she say? You have put me in charge of your grandson's defense, and I don't know what the hell I'm doing, but send me another ten thousand dollars, maybe twenty. She could hardly remember what she'd said to Ruby, beyond passing on Kenny Ray's message and telling her not to worry. Ruby had said, "The Lord sent you to save Kenny Ray, and I have faith."

Gail had little more than Denise Robinson's checklist. Denise had been so sorry, so very sorry, but she didn't have anyone else to give the case to, they'd gotten two more death cases this week. And just as Gail had been forming the words to say she didn't give a damn what cases had come in, that she couldn't do it, no, it would be a disservice to the client, she might as well stick the needle in his arm herself, just at that point Denise had said, "I know how frightening this must be for you, Gail, but you're all that Kenny Ray has right now. His life is in your hands. You're doing a fine and noble thing."

Denise had faxed her a copy of the death warrant and an official letter notifying Kenneth Ray Clark's attorneys of the execution date. Denise had received these from the governor's assistant general counsel in charge of capital cases, who hadn't yet heard that CCR was off the case.

Someone must have passed the word.

Shortly thereafter, Gail received a call from a clerk at the Florida Supreme Court. Was Ms. Connor aware that a death warrant had been signed? What were her plans? Did she foresee an appeal? Perhaps she would like to call back and set a tentative date for oral argument before the court.

The woman had been courteous, informative, unhurried. Gail had not heard such a sympathetic manner since the doctor had come out to tell them that Grandfather Strickland's cancer was inoperable.

The death warrant had a black border. Gail had pulled it off her fax machine and laughed. A black border, as if that improved the cheesy typeface and outdated legalisms. Whereas, whereas, and therefore. It was surreal. It was hideous.

Gail checked her watch. 11:51 A.M. She finished her coffee and threw away the cup. Her client was waiting.

The prison came into view, a low, sprawling building on acres and acres of open land. Every surface was painted a sickly green, even the guard towers with their dark windows. Razor wire glinted across the parallel rows of high, chain-link perimeter fence.

As instructed, she parked near the administration building, located outside the fence, then walked to the main gate and picked up a telephone. She told the voice on the other end who she was. A minute later the gate slid back. She walked through. It closed behind her. The next gate opened, and she walked up the steps to the glass doors. The entrance was a rectilinear, early sixties design with brushed aluminum letters across a concrete overhang.

Her mouth was dry as dust, and her heart pounded erratically.

She went through yet another gate, then signed in at a counter where guards in brown uniforms looked at her from behind tinted glass. She surrendered her driver's license. A female guard took her into a room and patted her down, even looking inside her shoes. Her portfolio and the folders inside it were searched quickly, efficiently, then handed back to her after she had walked through a metal detector. Gail had left her purse in the trunk of the rental car.

A guard escorted her through another gate, then up some steps. Everything was beige. The pipe handrail, the linoleum squares on the floor, the paint-thickened walls, the old-fashioned loudspeakers bolted to the ceiling. Huge fans stirred the air, making a constant, low roar that echoed on metal and concrete.

They came to a glassed-in room with banks of video monitors. The guard waved to a video camera, and a door clicked open. They went through it. The guard slammed it shut. Gail looked to her right. The main corridor, interrupted by more gates, extended several hundred yards. Aside from one man in a red jumpsuit pushing a dust broom, the vast corridor was completely empty.

Gail commented on that fact. The guard told her she wouldn't see any population inmates wandering around. This was a maximum security prison, and all one thousand prisoners were on permanent, twenty-four-hour lockdown.

A man proud of his work. He might have given her the tour if she'd asked.

He showed her to a small, narrow interview room and told her to sit on the other side of the desk. It was attached to the wall, and half of it folded down. The guard dropped it into place. Gail waited, staring at a door with a window in it.

A few minutes later she heard the rattle of chains and saw movement through the glass. The door opened and they brought in Kenny Ray Clark. His wrists and ankles were cuffed, and chain clattered on the floor as he walked. He wore blue cotton pants and sneakers. His shirt was the same bright orange she had seen on the death row Web site, a vee of white at the neck. One of the guards pulled out the chair, and Kenny Ray sat in it, leaning a shoulder against the wall. Tattoos of naked women and snakes climbed up his arms and vanished under the sleeves.

He was giving her the same close inspection. She had dressed carefully: a navy pantsuit, flat shoes, and a shirt that buttoned at the neck. No makeup, no jewelry except a watch. Her hair was brushed smoothly behind her ears.

"Hello, Mr. Clark. I'm Gail Connor."

He had to lift both hands to take hers. "Hi. You don't have to call me Mr. Clark. It's Kenny." He turned his head and sniffed through his nose as though he might have a cold.

"I talked to Ruby," Gail said. "She sends her love. She has faith everything will work out for you."

He nodded but said nothing. Hazel eyes stared dully out between ridges of cheekbone and brow. A memory flickered in her mind. "We met when we were kids. Do you remember?"

"Sure. It was at your folks' house. Ruby

brought me over there." Kenny slouched further into the chair. "So you turned out to be a lawyer. I'm not surprised. And you have a daughter. Right?"

"Her name is Karen. She's eleven."

"Eleven. Hey. Same number of years I've been a resident of the Hotel FSP." He coughed to one side.

Gail opened her portfolio and rummaged around for the crumpled pack of tissues she had seen among the various junk at the bottom. "Here."

"Thanks." He blew his nose. "I get a cold every winter. Clockwork."

"Will they give you something?"

"By the time they get around to it, I'm over it."

"How are you otherwise? All right?"

"A little tired. They moved me yesterday, so I didn't get my usual beauty nap."

"Moved you? Oh, yes. To Q wing." The other name for it circled in her mind: death watch.

"It's not bad. The cell's bigger. The TV works. But if I want the channel changed, I have to ask the guard to do it. That's a drag."

Gail's ignorance must have been written on her face. Kenny smiled. "The TV is outside the bars. Right now I've got all my other stuff with me, but pretty soon, they'll take it away. My magazines, my photo album, my extra shorts. It's a psychological thing. Cut the ties, get you ready to go. They've got a moke sitting out there twenty-four hours a day, keeping an eye on me, in case I try to off myself before they can do it. I'm not used to so much personal attention. They aren't the same guys as over on G wing. The guards on G wing know me pretty well, and the prison likes to put you with strangers."

She listened with agonized fascination. He leaned on his forearms, and chain rattled across the desktop. "I was about to ask for a new room anyway. Accommodations here aren't the best in the world. In the winter there's ice in the toilet, and in the summer we sweat like pigs. It can be up in the nineties, even at night, but they don't allow fans. The room service sucks, and all the maids look like men. The cell on Q wing is a little warmer. They gave me an extra blanket last night. Another good thing is, there's a friend of mine over there, Lucius Brown. But they're going to kill him next week."

Gail reached into her portfolio. "I — I wrote out some questions for you."

"What kind of questions?"

She opened the folder. "About your background, your family, and so on. I've read the psychological reports and the transcripts from your sentencing hearing, but they don't tell me enough."

"You know my family. Ask Ruby."

"I'd rather hear it from you." She took out six pages held together with a paper clip. "Please finish this as soon as possible. Don't mail it. Denise Robinson says the liaison with her office can pick it up and fax it to me."

Kenny Clark pushed the questions back across the desk. "Not interested."

"What do you mean?"

"I wrote you a letter over the weekend. I want to drop my appeals."

"Why?"

"I guess you got to be in here to understand why."

"You can't do that."

"It's my decision, not yours."

As if she had not heard him, Gail said, "Tina Hopwood wants to testify at your hearing. You can't give up now. You might get a new trial."

"Yeah. Chances are I'd be convicted and sentenced to death like the first time, and here we go again."

"Not if you had a competent attorney.

Meadows bungled your defense. You shouldn't be here."

"So what?" He put both hands on the desk, and the chain rattled across the edge. "Don't you know anything? Innocence don't mean nothing. The system don't give a crap. All they care about is, Did the innocent person get convicted according to the rules? If so, he stands a snowball's chance in hell. I know the law, okay? They never admit they made a mistake." Kenny Ray flipped the stack of questions with one finger and sent them into her lap. "Whyn't you go on back to Miami?"

Gail caught the pages before they fell to the floor. "Yesterday you told me to come see you."

"The warden handed me the phone and said call your lawyer."

"I didn't come all this way for you to tell me to turn around and go home."

"If Ruby had wanted to save my ass, she should've hired somebody who knew what they were doing."

Suddenly angry, Gail leaned across the desk. "It's true that I haven't done a capital appeal, but I'm a damned good lawyer. Denise Robinson is guiding me every step of the way."

"Oh, Jesus. Most of those people over

there are former prosecutors, don't you know that? They're on the state payroll. I should've fired her too. I'd be better off handling my own damn case."

"It's a little late to start now, isn't it? You're under a death warrant."

"The old reaper gets all of us sooner or later. Maybe it's my time."

"I refuse to accept that."

"Christ almighty." He leaned against the wall again and let his head fall back against it. "I'm tired. I'm tired of being in a cage twenty-four, seven. Tired of being in this place. The food is the worst they can get. They make money from what we don't eat, cause they sell it for slop to the farmers. They don't allow carbon paper, to keep us from filing motions. That's their game plan, to wear you down, and it gets to a point, you don't care. By the time they take you to death watch and put everything you own out there in the hall, and a stranger watching over you, making notes on when you take a piss and when you fall asleep, you're ready to check out. Some guys are bugged up, and maybe that's a good thing. The prison sends these quack doctors around to say they're sane enough to be executed, and they die laughing."

Gail's words stumbled over each other.

"All right. Look, I'm going to try the best I can. Everything that can be done. Denise said — Maybe we can get you resentenced. Not to risk another trial."

"Sure, that'll work. Get me life without parole. They'll make me sign a confession to something I never done. This way the state don't admit they screwed up, and I get to live. What a deal. I won't take it."

They stared across the desk at each other. He took a breath, snuffling again. "You know what my sister said when I called her yesterday from the warden's office? She said, I hope you ask forgiveness for what you done. I hope you find peace. Man. What a shock. I told her, hey. You're not coming to my party next month. How about if you come, Gail? You ever see a man get the needle? They say it don't hurt." He held out his arms, and the chain slid across the desk. Each wrist was enclosed in pitted black metal. He closed his hands tightly. The veins stood out clearly under his tattoos. "They stick one here, one over here."

"Stop it."

"I'm gonna have me some fried eggs and bacon. Hot biscuits. And some fresh-brewed coffee. All we get is stuff that tastes like they washed socks in it. You make sure I get real eggs, not that powdered shit."

231

"I won't let you give up."

"You got nothing to say about it. Would you be a witness? Would you be there?"

"Yes. If you want me to. But it isn't going to happen, so stop whining. We have a lot to do."

He looked at her and shook his head. "You're nuts."

"I promised Ruby."

"Ruby's nuttier than you are."

"If you gave up, it would kill her too."

Head against the wall, Kenny closed his eyes. For a long time he was silent, and Gail could think of nothing to say. When he spoke again the defiance was gone. "What I don't want is, I don't want to think that some miracle will happen and I'll walk out of here a free man. I don't want to start believing that."

"Don't, then."

His eyes came open. He jerked his chin toward the papers. "It would take me past my execution date to answer all them questions."

"Write fast."

"It's hard to write with the pens they make us use. Flex pens. They're a bitch to hold."

"Do you complain about everything?"

"Yeah." He grinned. Gail put her own

pen on top of the papers. "Forget it," he said. "They do a strip search before they put me back in my cell, and they'd take it away."

"That's ridiculous. You need a good pen."

"You be sure and tell the warden for me."

"I will."

Kenny's laugh turned into a cough. He took a breath. "Well. What's Tina up to these days?"

"She grooms dogs for a living. Clip 'n' Dip Grooming Service. She bought a house. Her boys are sixteen and fourteen now, doing well in school. She wanted me to tell you she's very sorry."

"A little late for sorrys. That's good about her boys, though. And her house. Yeah, she always wanted a house for the kids. What happened to Glen?"

"She divorced him. He's in prison for armed robbery."

"That's no surprise. Glen was always kind of wild. Well, me too. Young and wild and stupid. I must be stupid to be in here." He smiled, ducking his head to hide the stains on his teeth. "You don't have to agree with me."

Gail returned the smile, then said, "Can we talk about your case now?"

"Aren't you the workaholic? That's okay with me. I'd rather spend the time with a pretty lady than back in my cell. You think I don't remember you, but I do. Always ordering the other kids around. The girl who made up the rules." Kenny Clark's smile told her he meant no offense. "Is Karen as tough as you are?"

"I'm afraid so."

"Too bad you got divorced. I mean, I guess it's too bad. Have you got somebody new lined up?"

"Sort of. His name is Anthony Quintana. He's a criminal defense lawyer."

"Yeah? Is he any good?"

"He's brilliant."

"Is he helping you out? I hope?"

"He gives me advice." Gail forced herself to smile. "We should get started. I need to ask you some things. The first question isn't about your case, but I need to know. Tina Hopwood told me that on the Fourth of July weekend in 1988, you went along with her husband, Glen, to chase some Mexican migrants out of an orange grove. She said something terrible happened that night, but neither of you would talk about it. What was it?"

"I don't remember that."

"You have to be straight with me, Kenny. I don't want any surprises if we get a clemency hearing."

His bony shoulders lifted and fell. "Don't worry, nobody busted any heads. They'd moved into this old vacant house on some guy's property, so we told them to clear out. Except they weren't Mexicans, they were Guatemalans. They got in their car and that's the last I saw of them."

"Whose property was it?"

"I don't know." He added, "I swear."

"All right." Gail clicked her pen a few times, eyes on her notes. "We need to locate new witnesses, people never called before. There has to be someone."

He rolled his head back and stared up at the ceiling. "Check with Lougie Jackson. His house is where I was at after I left Tina's. He had some of his friends over, and they might remember me. My trial lawyer never asked them to testify. I told him to, but he didn't."

"Okay, I'll look for them. Do you know their names?"

"No. Lougie might know. If you can find Lougie."

Gail wrote it down, then said, "The snitch who testified against you was Vernon Byrd. You shared a cell with him. He said you told him about the victim's red underwear and the clock cord around her neck. How could he have known about that?"

"From me." Kenny grinned at the surprise on Gail's face. "I found out from the cops. When they were interrogating me, they gave me a lot of details about how Amber Dodson was killed. I talked to Byrd about it, but I never said I killed her. I never said I stabbed her to stop her from screaming. He made that up. The son of a bitch lied because he wanted to get out of jail. I could have explained that to the jury, but my lawyer told me not to testify. He said the jury wouldn't believe me, and I'd only make it worse."

Gail bounced her pen on her legal pad, thinking of the many ways in which Walter Meadows had screwed his client. "I'm going to find Byrd and talk to him."

"Hold a gun to his head. That's the only way he'll come clean."

"I'll have to buy one. What do you recommend?"

"Hey, I was kidding. Keep away from guys like Vernon. You hear me? Don't make me come after you, girl."

"I hear you." With a smile Gail turned a page in her notes. "You and Amber Dodson were both working at River Pines, but you never met her."

"Never. She was in the office. That was off limits to workers."

"Do you ever recall seeing the developer? His name is Whitney McGrath. Blond hair, good-looking? He'd have been around thirty."

"Yeah, he came out a lot. I remember him. Rich asshole. Excuse me."

"He told the police he rarely came to the site."

"That's a lie. When I worked there, before I got fired, I saw him around a lot. Did he know Amber Dodson?"

"He said no, but I'm going to check it out."

"Why the hell didn't my first lawyer ask me any of this?"

"Meadows was a drunk. If we can get you a new trial, you'll have the best."

"You?"

"Not me. Anthony Quintana. I'll twist his arm."

"Hey. Your brilliant boyfriend."

"What I really hope for," Gail said, "is to prove that you're innocent. If we can do that, you're out of here, but for now, let's just think about a stay of execution. That would give us more time."

"Prove that I'm innocent? How you going to pull that off?"

"Find the person who did it."

"You're too much." Laughing softly,

Kenny Ray Clark leaned against the wall again and rolled his head into a comfortable position.

His eyes shifted to her. "Why are you doing this? Helping me."

Gail played with her pen, turning it around and around before setting it on her notes. "I've asked myself that too. I care very much about Ruby. She was so good to us and I never really knew how good, until I had a child of my own. Maybe it's a way to say thank you, that's all."

After a few seconds, Kenny said, "Yeah, she's a sweet lady. I've caused her some heartache."

"You can make it up to her, Kenny. Just want to live. Okay? Come on, let's get back to work."

"Slave driver."

CHAPTER 12

Wednesday, March 14

Anthony Quintana had dinner with his grand-parents, and afterward helped the old man up to bed. They talked over a few more details about the trip to Cuba before Ernesto nodded off. Anthony went back downstairs to the study and called Hector Mesa's beeper, leaving the numeric code that would let Hector know he was wanted at the Pedrosa house.

Anthony sat at his grandfather's desk, and as a favor to his grandmother, went over some of the family's corporate accounts. He lit a cigar — not one of the Dominicans in his grandfather's humidor but one of his own Romeo y Julietas. Ernesto stubbornly refused to buy Cuban-made cigars.

Ten minutes later a knock came at the door.

"Entra."

Hector showed no surprise at the imperti-nence of Anthony occupying Ernesto's chair. He silently crossed the thick carpet and sat in one of the leather armchairs, hands folded in his lap. He was wearing the usual dark suit and tie, and his black-framed glasses hid his eyes. If he was annoyed at having been dragged out of his usual Wednesday night domino game, he kept it to himself.

In Spanish he said, "You wanted to speak with me, sir?"

He used the word *señor*. To say *Anthony* was too familiar and *Señor Quintana* too formal. Hector referred to the old man as *Señor Ernesto*, not appropriate for the grandson, for whom Hector had only conditional respect.

"I have a job for you — if you want it."

Anthony lifted his cigar from the ashtray. He didn't offer one to Hector, who would in any event have refused. Hector didn't want to be treated as an equal; he preferred the role of faithful, noble, and potentially deadly guard dog.

As the smoke drifted upward, Anthony said, "First tell me how the search is going. Are you close to finding Gail's ring?" He knew the answer because he had already asked his grandmother, who knew everything.

The little man squared his shoulders, ready for a tongue-lashing. "We have found nothing but golf balls and rusted cans. I don't understand it. The divers marked the bottom, and they searched every inch carefully. You saw them."

Rocking back in the chair, Anthony wondered if Hector was lying. He could have pocketed the ring, not to sell but to cause problems with Gail. Hector didn't like Gail. No. It was more accurate to say that Hector didn't believe she was the best choice Anthony could have made. On the other hand, Hector would lie to the Virgin Mary, but not to Señor Ernesto's grandson, when Señor Ernesto himself had ordered Hector to find the ring.

As a boy in Havana, Hector Mesa had shined rich men's shoes for pennies. One day he demanded that Ernesto Pedrosa give him a job washing his limo, and Ernesto had done so, admiring the boy's spirit. After the Revolution, Ernesto brought him along to Miami and lent him out to anticommunist paramilitary groups, where Hector learned other sorts of jobs. But those days were past, and Hector's talents were going to waste.

"If I may be permitted? I have a suggestion." Hector's thick gray brows rose, furrowing his forehead.

Anthony lifted a hand from the desk, waiting. "Well?"

"A duplicate. The jeweler has a copy of the design? It would be expensive, but —"

"I can't do that. It isn't the money, Hector. She would know."

"There are ways of making it seem that an object has been submerged for months, even years. I know people who could do it."

Of course he knew them: his former-CIA pals. Two of them had been diving in the pond on the golf course. "Tell them to try again. The ring is there, deeper in the mud. They missed it."

He shrugged. "As you wish. And the other job?"

"I think, Hector, that you will find this more to your liking."

Anthony told him about the murder case in which Gail Connor had become involved. He told him about the victim, her bloody and violent death, and the evidence that had led to the arrest and conviction of Kenny Ray Clark. Now, unless something extraordinary happened, Clark would be executed on Wednesday, April 11. Four weeks. A stay might be granted *if* enough new evidence could be found. Anthony believed he could persuade Gail to let someone else take over at that point. If Clark were executed on schedule, and Gail believed that her inexperience was in any way to blame, she could sink into another depression, and her health, her law practice, and their relationship would suffer. It was damned bad timing that the governor had signed a death warrant so soon.

"You see the problem, don't you, Hector?"

He nodded slowly. "Your trip with the old man. Yes. An execution would be inconvenient."

A heavy crystal ashtray sat on the desk, and Anthony rolled his cigar on its edge, dislodging the ashes. "Inconvenient. I wouldn't have chosen that word, but you're right. There's no choice about the trip, I have to go." It had taken months to arrange. If it was postponed, Ernesto might not live long enough to go. He was eighty-four years old, and his heart was failing.

"I don't know if Clark will ever get out of prison, and frankly, that isn't my concern. I want a stay of execution, if at all possible, and that requires a good investigator. Will you do it?"

Hector stared at the wall behind the desk. A tattered flag of Cuba hung there. "Maybe. If Señor Ernesto doesn't need me for anything. I should ask him."

"Yes. Ask him, by all means." Anthony knew as well as Hector that the old man had nothing planned, but protocol had to be observed. "If you can take the job" — Anthony picked up the brown mailing envelope on the desk but hesitated in passing it over — "these are my notes, an outline of what I've just told you. There's a list of things to do in order of priority. First, find Vernon Byrd." For the pleasure of seeing Hector's reaction, Anthony added, "Byrd is a bouncer at a pool hall in the black section of Stuart. His arrest record is in here. He's over six feet tall, three hundred pounds. They call him 'Peanut.' He could give you some trouble."

A smile flickered across Hector's lips. He held out a hand for the envelope.

Anthony took a smaller, heavier envelope from his breast pocket and handed it over without comment. Five thousand dollars in cash. To state the amount would have been an insult. Hector slid the envelope into his jacket. He would use it wisely, and if he ran out, he would ask for more.

"Work as quickly as you can. If you need extra help, hire it. With some of the witnesses, an American investigator would be a good idea. That place up there, those people — they aren't what you're used to. Stay in contact with me. If Gail asks you to do something, put her off. Check with me first, but don't tell her about it. She's a little sensitive in that way." Anthony leaned over to stub out the remains of his cigar. "I think that's all. Do you have any questions?"

"No, not at the moment." Hector was trying to hide his joy. He stood up and waited to be dismissed so he could get to work.

"Good night."

"Good night, *Señor* Anthony."

Señor Anthony? Surprised by this, he watched Hector leave the room, the carpet deadening his footsteps. The door clicked shut behind him.

Hector might have asked a certain question before leaving. Anthony had expected him to. *Is this man guilty of murder?* But the question had not been asked, and Anthony realized why. Of all the issues that might have piqued Hector Mesa's curiosity, this was the least important.

Gail opened the front door for Anthony but avoided his kiss. They went through the living room and into the wood-paneled den that used to be her father's, but which she had turned into a second office. Papers were laid out across the sofa, banker's boxes sat on the floor, and files were stacked on a corner of the desk. Her laptop computer was on. She had been working when he called, asking to come over, to talk.

"I see the files have arrived," Anthony said.

"This isn't all. Most of them are at my office. Seventeen boxes. Miriam spent the day organizing everything." Gail crossed her arms. She was wearing jeans and a thin pink sweater. No bra. Barefoot. Her hair was uncombed, and mascara had smudged her eyes. She was beautiful. "Sorry to rush you, but I have a lot to do tonight. What did you want to say to me?"

He smiled. "I came to apologize for our little disagreement yesterday. You caught me at a bad time, in the middle of a trial. Gail. Sweetheart." He put a hand on his heart. "I am sorry. Forgive me."

Letting out a breath, she looked toward the ceiling, then at him. "Do you want some coffee or something? I just made a fresh pot."

"Is that brandy still in the cabinet there?" He took off his suit coat and laid it over the arm of the sofa. His tie had been off since he'd left the federal courthouse. Gail leaned over to reach into the bottom of the bookcase. The seat of her jeans was soft and faded. She blew the dust out of a liqueur glass and poured.

"Thank you," he said.

She kissed him on the mouth. "I am glad

246

to see you, you jerk."

"How sweet you are," he said. "Tell me about your meeting with your new client."

"Kenny's all right. He's afraid to get his hopes up, but he's taking it pretty well. Better than I would, but he's had eleven years of practice. We talked for almost three hours. I typed up my notes, if you want to see them. He gave me some leads on witnesses."

"Excellent. I just spoke to Hector Mesa. He's going to help you out."

"With what?"

"Reinvestigating the case. He's very good. You're lucky he has time to do this." Anthony sipped his brandy.

"My God, Anthony, he was a paid assassin for Omega 7."

"Where did you hear such a thing?"

"You told me yourself."

"Did I? Well, Hector never took money. He was a patriot. Don't worry, he won't shoot the judge."

"This isn't funny. Maybe I don't want to work with Hector. I have a list of people that Denise recommended."

"No, no. How long will it take you to find someone else, explain the facts —"

"You're missing the *point*."

He made a small shrug of surrender. "I

should have called you. But I happened to see Hector on my way out, and I thought, well —"

"How much does he charge?"

"Nothing. He's doing it as a favor to me. Give him his expenses, if you insist." Anthony turned a chair around and sat in it, crossing his legs, holding the brandy glass on his knee.

"You are such a liar. Don't think for one minute that I'm letting you pay for this."

"All right, then. Hector can give you a bill when he's finished. You pass it on to Ruby Smith. All right?"

"Fine."

"Good. I told him to start by finding Vernon Byrd."

"I'm already ahead of him." Gail went over to the desk and looked through some papers, then wrote something on a legal pad. She tore off the page. "Here. Give this to Hector. And tell him to call me. I don't want him doing *anything* without my prior approval."

Anthony saw that she had written Vernon Byrd's name and an address in Stuart. *"Alaba'o.* Where did this come from?"

"Jackie. She called this afternoon."

"What a surprising woman. Most police officers would have turned their back. And if their father is the sheriff, forget about it. Why is she helping you?"

"She probably feels bad about the way Garlan jumped all over you. But I think the real reason is, she's a rookie on road patrol, and we dangle a homicide in front of her. It's too good to resist. She wants to get together for lunch next time I'm in town."

"When is that?"

"Friday." Gail took the sheet of paper out of Anthony's hand and went back to her desk. "I also need Lougie Jackson's address. Jackson was an alibi witness at the trial. The jury didn't believe him, but there were other people at his house who might remember that Kenny was there. It would help if Hector could find them."

"As long as you're going back to Stuart, get another check from Ruby Smith."

"I have it on my list." Gail gave him the paper again, which he folded and put in his shirt pocket.

"And don't forget to prepare a motion and order for the crime scene photos."

"It's done. I've typed up affidavits for Tina Hopwood and Bess Grigsby to sign, and I'm also going to ask to take new depositions of Ron Kemp, his partner Federsen, and Garlan Bryce. And maybe Dorothy Chastain, too. Why are you shaking your head?"

"I doubt the judge would allow it."

"That's probably true," Gail said, "but the more he denies us, the worse it looks, like the police are hiding something."

"Don't waste your time on strategies that won't pay off. You have enough to do already. The state is going to fight to preserve this conviction. They will say that the evidence you found is too late. They won't believe any of it. You show them black, they insist it's white."

"I *know*."

"You mustn't invest all your emotional energy in a case like this one. The odds aren't good."

"Anthony, *please* stop being so negative."

He looked at her awhile, then set his glass on a shelf. He tugged on her wrist. "Come here." She sat on his lap, and he locked his arms around her. Her hips pressed down warmly. "You're tired. Did you sleep last night?"

"No. I kept hearing gates clanging shut."

"*Pobrecita.*" He kissed the back of her hand. "I should have warned you."

"What a grim place. It's like some horrible sci-fi movie. You hear these huge fans going, and voices echoing in the cellblocks. A thousand men but you don't see anyone because they're all on lockdown. At the far end of the corridor is Q wing. The death chamber. It's right next to G wing, the old death row. Fifty inmates there, the other three hundred and twenty in a new prison up the road. G wing couldn't hold them anymore. Oh, the guards were very nice, answering all my questions. They said they still have Old Sparky, and they can roll it out and hook up the wires, if anyone prefers electrocution to lethal injection. Kenny was moved to Q wing on Monday. That's how they get a man used to dying. They separate him from everyone he knows, and they take what little he has away from him. There's a science to it, you see. It's like a machine, everything so organized and precise and soulless."

"Don't think about it anymore." Anthony stroked her arm, going up under the sleeve of her shirt. Her skin was satiny. "I worry about you, sweetheart."

She hugged him. "I know you do, but I'll be all right."

"You have to rely on me a little more. Anything you need, ask me. Will you? Anything." He kissed her, taking his time, feeling the tense muscles in her back begin to let go. "Why don't you put all this away for the night?"

"I wish I could."

"Yes. Put it away. Come over to my house. I'll get you up early. Make you some coffee."

Her laugh was warm against his neck. "You're so bad, tempting me like that."

"I never see you anymore."

Through her shirt he kissed one breast, then the other.

"Anthony, I can't go with you. Not tonight."

He made a small groan of disappointment. "Then why don't we make love right here?"

"Here? God, no. Karen might be listening."

"We'll be very quiet." He bit her earlobe, put kisses down her neck.

"It's so late."

"You don't have a few minutes for me?" He unsnapped her jeans.

"Anthony, stop it." She pushed herself off his lap and shook her hair back from her face. "Is this what you came over here for?"

"I came to offer my help."

"And I should show my gratitude."

Heat rushed into his face. "You're right, it's late." He got up and put on his coat. "When you have time, call me. Maybe after April eleventh."

"That's a terrible thing to say!"

"Buenas noches, señora."

He was in his car turning left onto Biscayne Boulevard when his cell phone rang. He knew who it was. He turned off the ringer and dropped the phone back into his pocket.

The Rickenbacker Causeway led from Miami to Key Biscayne, and the bridge arched over the bay. As Anthony's car swept down the far side of it, he kept one hand on the steering wheel and reached into his pocket. The message light was blinking.

"¿Qué quiere esa chica?" He flipped open his cell phone, dialed a code, and listened. Her voice was in his ear, hushed with remorse.

"Guess who? . . . I'm sorry, Anthony, but what did you *expect?* Karen's such an eavesdropper, and I have all this work to do. . . . I do *not* want to have a two-minute fuck with you. . . . No, I take that back. I would love it. . . . I'm sorry. You're trying to help me, I know you are. . . . Call me as soon as you get this message. Ten minutes, then I'm turning my phone off and going to bed. I'm so tired. . . . Love you. *Buenas noches.*"

There was a click, then silence.

He looked at his watch. *"Ay, Dios."* He hit her number on the speed-dial. It rang,

253

but there was no answer. He waited for the tone.

"Sweetheart, my phone was turned off, and I just saw the light blinking, and I called you right away, but it was too late. . . . I'm sorry, too. . . . Here, listen. I'm kissing you good night. . . . *Duérmete bien*. Sleep well. *Te quiero, mi cielito*."

CHAPTER 13

Friday morning, March 16

Leaving home at six o'clock in the morning put Gail at the courthouse in Stuart before eight. She was waiting at the door to Judge Willis's office when his judicial assistant arrived. The woman's name was Ms. Huff. Gail told her she wanted to set a date for the Rule 3.850 hearing in *State vs. Clark*.

The hearing had to be put somewhere in the twenty-six days remaining until April 11. Gail needed as many of those days as possible to prepare her case. But the hearing couldn't be too close to the execution date. If Judge Willis denied relief, there had to be enough time left to appeal.

Gail had already spoken to the "death clerk" in Tallahassee, a woman named Marcia Turner, who kept track of all capital cases in Florida. Ms. Turner had told Gail that the justices liked to hear oral arguments at least ten days before executions. This meant by Friday, March 30. Gail told Ms. Turner that this didn't give her enough time to prepare for the hearing before Judge

Willis. With some reluctance, Ms. Turner tentatively set it down for 10:30 A.M., Monday, April 2 and asked Gail to have her brief in by 5:00 P.M. on Thursday, March 29. The Attorney General's Office could file their answer on Friday, and the justices would review the case over the weekend.

Thus the hearing in Judge Willis's court would have to take place no later than the morning of March 29. There was no way to know how he would rule, so Gail would have to be ready not only with the motion under Rule 3.850 but the appeal as well. The motion could run two hundred pages exclusive of exhibits, attachments, and citations. The brief for the Florida Supreme Court could be another hundred, with more exhibits, attachments, and citations.

If Willis denied relief, Gail would immediately file the appeal, with a copy for the clerk, a copy for each of the seven justices, and a copy for the Attorney General. Thousands of pages, everything bound, indexed, and referenced.

Denise Robinson had given Gail some bad news: Kenny had already had one appeal to the local U.S. district court, and he wouldn't get another one, not since the Anti-Terrorism and Effective Death Penalty Act of 1996. Congress didn't want those little federal judges throwing monkey wrenches into the system, issuing stays of execution. Gail would have to make a choice. She could go to the Eleventh Circuit Court of Appeals in Atlanta, the same three-judge panel that heard Kenny's first appeal — and turned it down. Or go straight to the United States Supreme Court. It depended on how things worked out. In either event, the federal appeal would be in the form of a petition for writ of *habeas corpus* and/or petition for *certiorari*. Gail would prepare those in advance as well. The federal clerks would also expect to get courtesy copies of everything filed in the state court. More typing, more printing, more pages, and by then, costs in the multiple thousands of dollars, never mind the spinning numbers on the attorney's time clock.

Sometime before oral argument in the Florida Supreme Court, Gail would lodge the petition for *habeas* in the federal court system. The clerk would hold onto it. The moment the Florida justices ruled against her, if they did, the petition would be filed and the gears of the federal appeals process would engage. The case would proceed upward, Eleventh Circuit to U.S. Supreme Court. Or bypass the Eleventh Circuit. It depended.

Rules and protocol, deadlines and page

limits, finding the federal issues. There was a system to this. Figuring the angles, pulling back on the cue, letting go at the right speed and force, balls clicking, hitting the rails, bouncing gently, ball in the pocket. She prayed to make the shot. Miss, and her client would be dead.

Gail had gone past panic to a state of extreme concentration.

She told Judge Willis's JA that oral argument in the Florida Supreme Court was set tentatively for Monday, April 2, and that she would like the 3.850 hearing early on the preceding Thursday.

Ms. Huff said she needed to check with the judge. She went into chambers and after some murmured conversation returned to say that Thursday morning was impossible, as the judge was in trial. What about Friday, March 23, a week from now? Gail said there was no way she could be ready by then.

There was more conversation in chambers. Ms. Huff came out again. She was trying to remain patient with the idea of a hearing dropped into the middle of the week on short notice. Would Wednesday, March 28, be all right? Gail said she preferred the afternoon. They went back and forth for a while on whether Gail really needed four hours.

A short, white-haired man in tie and shirtsleeves appeared at the door of chambers to listen to the conversation. Gail assumed this was Judge Willis. He worked at his teeth with a toothpick, trying not to be obvious about it.

Finally he said, "You know, Ms. Connor, this is the second 3.850 motion in this case. I'm supposed to hold a hearing on whether you get a hearing at all."

"I'm aware of that, judge, but we're under warrant, and there isn't much time. Do you have two dates open?"

His judicial assistant muttered something and shook her head.

The judge said, "Well, Joan, let's just put it down for March 28, two o'clock in the afternoon. We'll go past five if we have to, but I hope this doesn't take too long. My wife and I have tickets at the Lyric Theater that night. Can't remember what's going on, but she'll have a fit if we're late. Let's try to get this wrapped up by six o'clock at the very latest." He told Gail to file her papers by 5:00 P.M. on Monday, March 26, to give the state attorney time to reply.

"I'm due to retire next month," he added. "Your client was my first capital case on the criminal bench, and he's going to be my last. How about that?"

"What a coincidence," Gail said. She reached into her briefcase and took out some papers. "As long as you're here, judge, would you mind?"

The first was a motion for an order allowing her to take depositions. "Mrs. Chastain has new information. Her ID of my client was tainted, and I need to establish that on the record. Officers Kemp and Federsen were involved in preventing an alibi witness from testifying. I believe Sheriff Bryce knew about it, and I want to establish that."

The judge tossed his toothpick into the trash under his JA's desk and took the motion from Gail. He read it and shook his head. "You'll have to request a hearing. If I signed this *ex parte,* the prosecutor would throw a fit. But let me tell you right now, I won't grant your motion. Mr. Clark's trial attorney had every opportunity in the world to delve into the ID issues when he deposed these witnesses eleven years ago."

Gail had not really expected him to allow depositions, but she had not known a hearing was required. She handed him the other motion. "This one is just routine, really. It's so I can get all the crime scene photographs from the sheriff's office."

"Ms. Connor, what did I just say? A

hearing is required on motions for discovery."

"When? There isn't *time*. We're under a death warrant."

"I don't make the rules," he said, "but I expect lawyers to comply with them."

Her mind spun. "Okay. What if I have someone from the state attorney's office call you and say it's all right? What about that?"

Ms. Huff bit her lips on a smile and pretended to be busy at her computer.

Peeved, the judge said, "Why can't you get the photos from CCR? They have them, don't they?"

"I need to see *all* of them."

"Crime scene photos aren't new evidence. You could have had them before. I won't grant this motion either."

Gail's pulse picked up. "I'm not saying the photographs are new evidence, I'm saying they might lead to evidence the police missed that *would* be new. It's no burden on the sheriff's office to give me the photos. Judge Willis, please. My client is facing imminent execution. I wouldn't ask for the photographs if I didn't honestly believe they contained crucial new evidence."

The judge held up his hands. "Tell you what. You run over to the state attorney's office and have somebody call me. If they have no objection, I'll sign it." He called to her as she hurried across his office. "Now you be sure and get that brief in on time, Ms. Connor. I hate to rush, and something like this throws everybody off schedule."

"Yes, judge. Thank you." She groveled her way out the door, biting her tongue. Screw the schedule. Screw the judge's theater tickets.

Gail took copies of the motion and order next door to the state attorney's branch office. Joseph Fowler, the original prosecutor on the case, had retired. One of his assistants, Sonia Krause, had become the state attorney of the Nineteenth Circuit, at the main office in Fort Pierce. Gail supposed she might see the woman in court on March 28. Krause had been second chair at the Clark trial. Gail expected no cooperation, but finally someone came down to see her, an attorney in the criminal trial division. He took the pleadings, went back upstairs, and came down again fifteen minutes later. "This isn't proper procedure," he said, "but we're going to extend you the courtesy." She thanked him profusely, went back to the courthouse, and paced for almost an hour outside Judge Willis's chambers waiting to see him.

The judge shook his head, uncapped his pen, and signed the order. "Must be your lucky day, Ms. Connor."

She returned once more to the state attorney's office and gave a copy of the order to the woman behind the desk. Raising a brow, the woman gave her a date-stamped receipt.

At the post office Gail sent copies of everything to the Attorney General in West Palm Beach, overnight delivery, certified mail. They would be arguing against her in the Florida Supreme Court, should she lose in the trial court.

Gail took two Excedrin, got back into her car, and headed for the Martin County sheriff's office.

In a small way, the Holt Justice Center reminded Gail of Florida State Prison. Many acres of empty land, many fences and coils of razor wire. But that was the county lockup. The sheriff's office was in the low building at the other end of the parking lot, flags out front.

The information desk was just off the lobby behind glass doors. Gail spoke to a woman in a green uniform, stated her purpose, and asked to speak to someone in crime scene. With a copy of the order in her hand the woman said to have a seat. Gail wandered to the window, then thumbed through a brochure on the Sheriff's Youth Ranch. Garlan Bryce's photograph was on the wall, one face among sixty-six other sheriffs of Florida counties.

"Ms. Connor?" A man in a long-sleeved striped shirt had come through a door to the back. He was around fifty, thin and wiry, with curly gray hair receding from his forehead. There was a holstered gun on his belt. At the counter he held up the order by its top edge.

"Is this yours?"

"Yes. I represent Mr. Clark." The man said nothing, so she went on, "There's a hearing March 28, and I want to make sure I get copies of the crime scene photos as soon as possible. All of them. How long will it take?"

"Usually ten days to two weeks."

"It can't be done sooner?"

His mouth smiled but the pale gray eyes were cool. "You asked how long it takes. That's how long it takes."

"You'll see that the order says 'immediately.'"

"Here's how it works, Ms. Connor. Somebody in crime scene has to find the time to drop whatever they're doing to go over to another building, where we keep our evidence vault. They have to locate the negatives. They fill out the paperwork and request a pickup from the commercial lab we use. The lab picks up the negatives. When they're done, they bring them back. Like I said, ten days to two weeks."

"May I ask your name?"

"Lieutenant Ronald Kemp." He wanted her to say something about it.

"I see. Do you drag your feet on all court orders or is this one special?"

"Do you think you should be treated special? There are other requests ahead of yours, just as important. We'll get to it when we get to it."

She stared back at him a moment, then took the order out of his hand and turned to the woman behind the desk. "Would you please let Sheriff Bryce know that I would like to speak with him? Again, my name is Gail Connor. He knows me."

"He's in a meeting," the woman said. "Do you want to leave a message?"

Kemp leaned against a file cabinet with his arms crossed, waiting to see what Gail would do.

"I'll wait."

She sat in one of the fake leather armchairs by the glass doors. Kemp went back to work. After ten minutes of doing nothing,

Gail went into the lobby and returned a few phone calls. She had just disconnected from a call to a client in a mortgage foreclosure case when she heard heels on the tile floor.

The sheriff had come out a door further down the hall. He was wearing his cowboy boots, a brown suit, and a cream-colored Stetson hat, apparently not planning to stick around.

Her heart pounded. She was sure that Dorothy Chastain had called him to complain. *Those attorneys from Miami forced their way into my house.* Garlan was going to pull out his handcuffs, arrest her, throw her in jail —

"I'm on my way out," he said, "so I don't have much time."

Relief made her dizzy. She cleared her throat. "Garlan, I'm trying to get copies of crime scene photographs in the Kenny Ray Clark case —"

"Gail, let me say this once, and please listen. This office does not put anyone's request at the bottom of the stack. Nor do we cut breaks for anyone. However, if a judge tells us that a certain case is a rush, we respond accordingly. The crime scene department will have the negatives ready for pickup early next week. If you go back in and get the phone number of the lab from the desk clerk, you can make your own arrangements as to how fast they pick them up and how fast you get them."

Garlan Bryce was a slab of polished stone. He said, "I hope this is acceptable."

"Yes. I appreciate it. Thank you, Garlan."

He touched the brim of his hat. "Good day."

Gail drove directly to Atlantic Photo, which did the processing for the sheriff's office. She asked to speak to the manager. When he came out she gave him a copy of the order and a check for five hundred dollars as a down payment. She gave him another hundred cash to treat it as a rush, and he promised her the prints the day after he picked up the negatives.

What was to be found in the photographs, Gail didn't know, but any straw floating by was worth grabbing at. It would be impossible, she thought, as she hurried to her car, to give these errands to anyone else. Not a paralegal or secretary or even an investigator. The attorney herself had to be there to shove, whine, and cajole.

With this small success, her spirits rose.

The Clip 'n' Dip van was waiting for her

in the parking lot of the Target store over the bridge from Stuart. Gail apologized for running late. Tina Hopwood said it was okay, she'd just gotten here herself; her client had changed her mind on the color of polish for her poodle's nails.

Her pink smock was flecked with dog hair. She sat in the front seat of Gail's Acura to read the four-page affidavit, which she signed at the end in loopy script, dotting the *i* with a circle. Her black bangs hung in her eyes. "You made me sound real good," she said. She gave back the pen and the affidavit. "What are you going to do with this?"

"File it with the motion as an exhibit." Gail slid it into a folder, which she dropped onto the backseat. "You won't have any trouble making it to court for the hearing, I hope."

"I'll be there. I'm gonna look that bastard Detective Kemp in the eye when I tell the judge what he did to me. Is Kenny coming?" Gail replied no, that Kenny would remain at the prison since his testimony wasn't needed. Tina squeezed her wrist. "You tell him I said to be strong. I'm praying for him." She turned to open the door. "Gotta run. Three dogs and a cat this afternoon."

Just as Tina Hopwood started the engine of her van, Gail knocked on the window, and Tina rolled it down.

"Do you remember you told me about some migrant workers that Kenny and your ex-husband chased out of an orange grove?" Tina said yes, she remembered. "According to Kenny, nothing happened, no one was hurt. But you said that Glen threatened to hit you when you asked about it. You're sure about that?"

"Positive. Why?"

"I'm worried that Kenny's lying to me."

"He is," Tina said. "What difference does it make? That was thirteen years ago."

Gail said, "I can't be blindsided. We're going to get some publicity. If one of these people sees it on TV and says Kenny beat him up, the state attorney would use it against us. I wonder if Glen would talk to me — in confidence of course."

"He might, if you put some money in his inmate trust fund."

"Where is he?"

"Union Correctional. Call me, I'll give you his ID number."

Another scrap of good luck. UCI was only a mile from Florida State Prison. Next time Gail went to see Kenny, she could talk to Glen Hopwood as well. But probably wouldn't. Time was too precious, her resources too few. She couldn't follow every last thread.

★ ★ ★

The Grigsbys took Gail out on the back patio again, and the three of them had some lemonade. She didn't object when Bess Grigsby stirred in some Absolut Citron for flavor.

Gail had brought only one affidavit. It was Bess who had observed problems in her neighbors' marriage; Art Grigsby's opinions were less certain. Gail said, "You don't mind, do you, Art?"

"Heck no, my feelings aren't hurt," he said. "Bess has the brains in the family."

"I don't know if the judge will consider this," Gail said, "since technically it could have been discovered before, but no harm in trying."

Bess Grigsby put her cigarette in the coconut-shell ashtray to read the affidavit. She slowly turned the pages.

"Hoo boy," Art said, reading over her shoulder. "There's some pretty strong words in there. You make it sound like Gary did it."

Gail felt their resolve slipping away, and she held on. "No, I'm not saying that. I want to show that the police failed to pursue other leads. They rushed to judgment with my client."

"What if Gary gets mad and comes

knocking on the door?"

"Oh, Art, don't be such a weenie." Bess held out her sun-browned hand. "Give me the pen."

Art took a swallow of lemonade. "My wife's one hell of a woman."

She did a shimmy, then picked up her cigarette. "You know it, sailor." Her laugh rasped from her throat, and blue jays outside the screen fluttered and settled back on the lawn.

Gail put the affidavit away. She would notarize it later and send Bess a copy. "There's something I meant to ask last time. Did you know any of Amber's friends?"

"Friends. Hmmm." Smoke drifted upward.

Art Grigsby nudged his wife. "Bess? Who was that girl with the red Corvette?"

"Art always notices girls in sports cars."

"She used to come by a lot before Amber had the baby. They worked together. She used to take Amber to work sometimes. I'd go out for the paper and see her drive up. Sure. A cute little blond girl, real friendly. Come on now, honey, what was her name?"

"You're such a sucker for blondes." Bess Grigsby swung her bare foot. "Before the baby. Hmmm."

"Janey . . . Joanie." Art interlocked his fingers on top of his bald head. "No, it was two names, wasn't it, honey? Judy Sue . . . Betty Ann . . . Hold on now, it's coming."

Rolling her eyes, Bess reached for her spiked lemonade.

He clapped his hands together. "Mary Jo. That's it. Am I right or am I right?"

"Arthur! You old smarty-pants." His wife pinched his cheek.

With a grin, Art Grigsby nodded at Gail.

CHAPTER 14

Friday afternoon, March 16

The historic section of downtown Stuart ran parallel to the tracks of the Florida East Coast railroad. The tracks, the main street, and several other roads met at a tangle of asphalt that the city had tried to make less confusing by means of a traffic circle. Gail went around and around the fountain, spotting the restaurant where she would meet her cousin but finding nowhere to park. This was still high tourist season, and the warm, sunny weather had filled the shops and outdoor tables.

Finally she veered off and drove for a couple of blocks along the tracks. The street would dead-end at the river. A black pickup truck was close behind her, so she swung into a tight U-turn and pulled off the road. Hers was the only car on that side, and she noted with approval the lack of parking meters. She didn't know how long she and Jackie could talk. Jackie would go on duty at three.

Gail had debated with herself what to say to her, how to get past that awful confrontation in the barn last weekend. Jackie would never go against her father, of course, but still it had to mean something that she had called with Vernon Byrd's address.

Locking her car, Gail heard the clanging of a crossing gate. Lights flashed at the intersection. She walked slowly in that direction. A moment later came the heavy thrum of a diesel engine. She saw bright vertical headlights. The train moved forward slowly, unstoppably. A forgotten thrill surged through her. As a child she had gone with her father to the railroad tracks in Miami. He had put a nickel on the smooth, shining steel and stepped down off the ties. She had waited, waited, watching the lights grow nearer, feeling the ground shake, the sudden wind and terrible noise, and there had come with it the hideous, wondrous thought of being swept under those clacking, massive, dreadful wheels.

Without realizing, Gail had wandered to the middle of the street. As she followed the progress of the engine, she turned. A pickup truck was directly behind her, not coming fast, but closing the distance. She hurried out of the way. It was the same shiny black truck she had seen before, a big Ford with knobby tires. The side window was down, and the driver rested his hard-muscled arm on the frame.

He was looking at her. A cowboy hat with a silver band shadowed his face, but she saw the reddish-gray goatee, a lank ponytail. The train thundered past, visible through the windows. The truck moved down the street. Chrome exhausts. Gun rack. A Confederate flag sticker in the back window. Brake lights went on. The crossing gates were lifting. The black truck vanished into traffic.

It took her a minute to remember his name. Rusty Beck.

At the end of the block she rounded the row of shops, crossed Flagler, and stepped onto the sidewalk outside The Jolly Sailor. An awning curved around the corner, and potted palms and hanging baskets of flowers formed a cheerful divider.

A young woman in a white shirt and jeans waved from one of the tables. Her hair was in a thick, glossy braid. When Gail reached her, Jackie gave her a quick hug. "It's nice out today," she said, "but we can sit inside if you'd rather."

"No, this is perfect."

While studying the menu Gail said that she would be here all weekend, since there was so much to do on the Clark case, and that Irene would arrive with Karen this evening. They were staying on the beach. Why not come over for breakfast tomorrow morning?

"I'd like that," Jackie said.

The waitress arrived with some water, speaking to Jackie by name. This was a small town, Gail reminded herself. They ordered fried grouper sandwiches. For a while they talked about Karen. Then Jackie's brother in Tampa. What it was like being a cop in Stuart. As the conversation bubbled along, Gail thought it was propelled mainly by the desire to avoid a topic that neither knew how to bring up.

Gail couldn't stand it anymore. "Thanks for Vernon Byrd."

"No problem," Jackie said.

"I've hired an investigator, someone Anthony knows. His name is Hector Mesa."

"That's good."

"In case your dad mentions it, we ran into each other this morning. I went by the sheriff's office with an order for crime scene photos. I talked to Ron Kemp first, and he was less than cooperative, to put it mildly. Garlan said I could have them. He even said to make my own arrangements with the lab, since it was a rush." Gail wanted to let Jackie know that she held no grudges. "He did me a favor."

Jackie nodded.

"I'll have them next week. Do you want to see them?"

"No, I don't think so."

Gail wished she hadn't asked. "I understand."

Jackie's hands rested on the edge of the table. Short nails, pale polish, a plain stainless-steel watch. Her forearms were smoothly muscled. Not bulky but strong. She said, "My father didn't tell me to stay out of it."

"That's okay."

"It's not like he orders me around."

Unsure where this was going, Gail remained silent, watching the thoughts move like cloud shadows across her cousin's face. Jackie's hair was parted in the middle, and the freckles she'd had as a child hadn't entirely vanished. A few of them still dotted her cheeks.

"What you said about him doing you a favor? That's not what it was. He was just doing the right thing, that's all."

"That's usually enough," Gail said. "But you'd be surprised how rare it is."

The waitress brought their lunch, and for a while they talked about fishing. Jackie liked to go when she could. "Your dad was a great fisherman. What was that boat they used to have? The *Irene Marie*. I have a picture of my mom and Alex and me on the boat. Do you remember my mother?"

"Of course I do. Aunt Lou was wonderful."

"I don't know. She drank too much. When I was twelve she walked out on us."

From Jackie's tone she might have been talking about someone they hardly knew, but Gail could sense something going on under the surface. "She couldn't have *walked out* on you. I mean, not in that sense."

"One day I came home from school and she was gone. She moved to West Palm Beach, and we hardly saw her. She died two months later in a car crash. She was speeding and went off the road at a sharp curve. They found a bottle of gin in her car. Alex says our dad threw her out, but he makes up memories because he needs them to be true. I think it's better not to fool yourself."

Searching for the right reply, Gail said, "It's probably more complicated than that. My husband and I split up. There wasn't much warning, everything just fell apart. Jackie, I know that Aunt Lou wouldn't have left you and Alex and not given a damn what happened to you."

Jackie wasn't convinced. "Then why did she leave?"

Gail realized that she didn't know why. Garlan and Louise had been having problems, but that wouldn't be news to Jackie. "When you come for breakfast tomorrow, why not talk to my mother? I have things to do, but you stay and visit. Mom adores you, and Aunt Lou was her favorite sister."

"I might." Jackie stared out toward the fountain, a girl with a vase on her shoulder, water splashing merrily at her feet. "How's your case going?"

"Not too badly, under the circumstances. My motion has to be filed in ten days."

"Is that enough time?"

"No, but it's all I've got."

"You still think he's innocent?"

"I believe so, yes."

"Maybe he's lying to you. Maybe that woman is too. Tina Hopwood. How can you tell?" Jackie's brown eyes were direct and unwavering. "You're his lawyer, and you have to believe him."

"If Kenny Ray Clark were on trial again, and he had a halfway competent lawyer, he'd be acquitted in five minutes." She let Jackie wait. "Want to hear why I think so?"

"All right."

She knew somehow that Jackie wouldn't

run to Garlan with what she told her, so she told her everything, facts and inferences tumbling out. It was good talking about it. Anthony would understand the legal points better, but he would be too ready to hand her his own opinion, and Jackie simply listened.

Pushing her plate aside, Jackie leaned on an elbow facing Gail. She spoke quietly, aware that other people were nearby. "You still think it was someone she knew."

"Probably. It usually is."

"But not her sister."

"Not if Mrs. Chastain saw Lacey arrive and leave within minutes," Gail said.

"And Gary is off your list too," Jackie said. "So where does that leave you?"

"With the same question I started with a week ago. Who was Amber Dodson? A girl from a respectable, middle-class family, who graduated from a Christian high school. A good girl, but not too good. She was wearing a red silk top and panties when she died, but she complained that her husband was impotent. After she had the baby, why did she go back to work at River Pines, way out on Martin Highway? For the money? She was a receptionist. She didn't have friends there. The girl she knew, Mary Jo, had moved on. So what was the attraction?"

Jackie said, "It had to be a guy. It's always a guy."

"How well do you know Whit McGrath?"

"Not very. If he were sitting at that next table, he might say hello, he might not. You think she was doing it with *him?*"

"His director of sales, a woman named Vivian Baker, told the police that McGrath hardly knew Amber, but the sales brochure had a picture of them at the pool in swimsuits. She also said he rarely came to the site, but he did, a lot. One lie, why not two? Something was going on. Tell me about McGrath."

"Well, like I said, he keeps a couple of horses out at Rusty's ranch, and I used to go out there a lot, because it used to be Diddy's, you know, and Rusty said we could use it as long as we wanted to. When I was a kid, and I'd go out there to take care of my horse, I used to run into Whit, but not lately. Yeah, he could've modeled in that sales brochure. He looks the part. He plays tennis, he skis. He flies his own plane, he crewed in the America's Cup. He has businesses all over the country, houses in New York and Colorado, and he's gone most of the time. He does things like hang gliding in the Andes. That was in the paper. Most of what I know I hear around town."

"Amber Dodson must have been dazzled."

"No doubt."

The waitress came along and cleared their plates off the table. Jackie barely noticed. The waitress had to ask twice if she wanted dessert. Jackie didn't. They both ordered coffee.

When the waitress was gone, Jackie said, "Your theory is, they were having an affair, and he killed her to keep his wife from finding out."

"Is that plausible?"

"Maybe. It was her money he started with."

"Really."

"Her name is Taylor Vandiver McGrath."

"Taylor?"

"They call her Tay. She's so Palm Beach. You hardly ever see her in Stuart. We're too provincial. The McGraths had money, but they weren't stinking rich, like the Vandivers. They have two kids, teenagers, in private school. River Pines was Whit's first project, and he was only like twenty-eight when he started buying up property. He wants to make it into a town, if he can get it past the county commission."

"How old is he now?"

"Forty-two?"

"Still good-looking?"

"He has dimples and shaggy blond hair."

"I'm going to be sick."

Jackie smiled. "Anthony's the babe." She looked at her watch. "I should get going. I'm on duty at three o'clock." She took the check out of Gail's hand. "Let me. You're in my town."

"Thank you," Gail said. "Thanks for everything."

"Glad I could help."

"Want me to keep in touch about all this?"

Jackie stood up and aligned her white plastic chair to the table. "Sure."

The brass bell over the door rang out melodiously when she entered. Display cases shone with silver and china, and the various pieces of antique oak or mahogany furniture smelled of lemon wax. There were reasonably priced small items as well, and Gail browsed among them. She picked out a charmingly silly 1950s plastic bracelet for Karen and a porcelain bluebird for her mother. She intended to leave with some information as well, if she could get it.

Behind a low divider in the back, a gray-haired woman worked on account books. There were two customers at the cash register near the door. Gail waited until they had gone out, then took her purchases to the front.

At twenty-two, Lacey Mayfield's photograph had appeared in newspaper stories during the Clark trial. Now her figure was full and soft, hidden under a blue jumper and white cotton turtleneck. A gold barrette held her mousy brown, chin-length hair back from her face.

The purchases added up to $63.50, and Gail used a credit card. She said yes, thank you, when asked if she would like them gift-wrapped.

"You're Lacey Mayfield, aren't you?" The woman said that she was. "My name is Gail Connor. I'm a lawyer and I wonder if I could ask you a couple of questions."

"About what?"

"Well, I know the whole situation is painful for you, but I represent Kenneth Ray Clark. His grandmother, who lives here in Stuart, used to work for my family. She hired me to handle his appeal."

Blue eyes stared at her. "So he's filing another appeal. Why am I not surprised?" Lacey Mayfield turned to find a box for Karen's bracelet.

Gail said, "I'm sorry for the pain your family has been through. I know it's hard to lose a sister this way. I lost mine. I know what it is."

"How long did it take for her killer to be executed?"

"He died before he went to trial."

"You're fortunate." She laid the small box on pink paper, which she folded quickly, expertly. Her hair swung against her jaw. "That's my mother at the desk back there. I bring her with me to give her something to do. She can't keep a job because of her nerves. Dad works but he's had two heart attacks. Amber's death hit them very hard."

"Yes, I know it must have."

Lacey Mayfield affixed to the wrapped box a gold sticker with the name of the store. A vee of blue ribbon made an instant bow. "You're the first of his lawyers to speak to us. None of the others cared to."

Gail hadn't thought, before walking in here, that this would be so difficult. "I wonder if you could tell me something. Amber had a friend named Mary Jo, a blond girl who drove a red Corvette. They worked together at River Pines before Amber had her baby. Do you know Mary Jo's last name or where she is?"

The porcelain bird vanished into a nest of tissue paper. "Mary Jo? It doesn't sound familiar. Amber and I didn't have the same friends. She was three years older. What's this about?" She put the bird in a box and taped it shut.

Gail said, "I've been looking into the case, and I'm certain that Mr. Clark didn't kill your sister. Someone else did, and I'm trying to find out who. Maybe she was in a dispute with someone at her job. Mary Jo might have some information."

A sheet of yellow paper flew off a stack of them. Lacey Mayfield slid scissors down the middle of it. "Another innocent man on death row. I get so sick of hearing about innocent men on death row." The paper quickly went around the box. Fold. Fold. Tape. "What was it this time, a mistake or a frame-up by the police?"

"A series of mistakes," Gail said. "One of them was made by the eyewitness, Mrs. Chastain. She lived across the street from your sister. She'd been out of town for more than a week when she picked my client's photograph out of a display, plenty of time to forget important details. It could have been you that she remembered. You walked around the house. You had long brown hair at the time. Mrs. Chastain could easily have been confused."

"I didn't walk around the house." Lacey

attached another gold sticker and ribbon.

"You went to the west side, didn't you? At Amber's bedroom window?"

"Yes, but she was sleeping, so I left."

"How did you know she was asleep? Could you see her through the window?"

"They were closed, and the curtains were drawn. I knocked."

"Loudly?"

"I wasn't trying to wake her up. I just thought she didn't hear the doorbell." With a sudden, knowing smile, Lacey Mayfield put a hand on her hip. "If you think she was already dead, you're wrong. Gary called her at ten o'clock and spoke to her on the phone."

"That's true." Gail had forgotten. She hesitated a moment, then said, "Did you ever own a denim jacket? My client didn't. Mrs. Chastain saw a denim jacket that day. Was it yours?"

"No. I never owned a denim jacket, and I would swear it on the Bible." Lacey May-field shook open a small shopping bag with a loud crack of paper. "This is unreal. Every time I think it's over, here we go again. This man is guilty of murder. My God. Why can't you *see* that? Everybody else does. You probably *do* see it, but you're being paid to overturn his conviction no matter who it hurts. You might as well spit on my sister's grave. I'm not going to tell my parents you came in here, it would probably give my father another heart attack." Lacey Mayfield's voice had begun to tremble with emotion.

Gail picked up her credit card receipt.

"Are you doing this because you feel *sorry* for him? Why does everybody feel so sorry for the criminals and not the victims? Kenny Ray Clark put himself where he is. He was a career criminal before he killed Amber, and he's been playing the system all his life. Why should he get to live when she's dead? He gets to watch TV and eat three meals a day. He can read books and write letters and go outside to exercise. He isn't suffering. He won't suffer when they execute him. He'll just go to sleep, like when a vet puts a dog to sleep. He killed more than my sister. He killed her husband and baby. He killed my mother and father. I've been through two divorces. He needs to die. He needs to get what he deserves, and shame on you. Shame on you."

Gail took the shopping bag. "I'm sorry for your loss, Ms. Mayfield."

"No, you aren't."

The bell tinkled again as Gail left the shop.

There was a trash can at the end of the block, and she dropped the bag into it and kept walking. The gifts were too weighted now with anger and woe. To see them again would be to think of a family condemned to grief. Grief had taken over their lives, had become their lives, and not even the death of Kenny Ray Clark would release them.

Gail was halfway to the hotel when she remembered why she had gone into Mayfield Antiques in the first place: not to argue with Lacey Mayfield but to obtain one small piece of information. She had come away with nothing.

That morning, hearing about Mary Jo Whoever from the Grigsbys, Gail had intended to find the woman quickly, see if she had anything to say, and if not, move on to someone else. But she was stymied. Gail knew her own personality: the sort of person who would not proceed to *B* until she had accomplished *A*. Now what? Let Hector Mesa find Mary Jo. But Hector was busy dealing with a jailhouse snitch, looking for more alibi witnesses, and getting current addresses for every last one of the jurors, in case any of them could be persuaded to sign an affidavit. *If I had only known that sleazeball Detective Ronald Kemp had beaten* the alibi witness with a rubber hose, I would never have voted to convict. If only I had known . . . fill in the blank with whatever other facts could be hurriedly assembled.

The clock on the dashboard said 3:15 P.M.

The bridge heading east was just ahead, and Gail braked to avoid it. Horns blared. She swerved quickly into a gas station, realizing she had been paying no attention and could have been rear-ended. Catching her breath, she parked and turned off her engine.

She had thought of someone who had to have known Amber's friends. She unfolded a map of Stuart and opened her address book. Gary Dodson had sold the house where his wife had been murdered, but he still practiced law in Stuart. Gail had found his office address through the Florida Bar.

His office was not, however, in the same high-rent bank building as before. Gary F. Dodson, P.A., was located in a fading, dusty, two-story frame house within blocks of where Gail had just had lunch. Traffic rushed past on U.S. 1 at the end of the street. A concrete walkway led to a porch, a door with flaking green paint, and a buzzer. A hand-lettered index card taped to the glass said RING FOR ADMITTANCE.

A living room had been made into a

waiting room. Stairs vanished upward on the left; a heavy, middle-aged woman in a brown cardigan sweater sat behind a desk on the right. She took her finger off the door-release button when Gail came in.

Gail asked if Mr. Dodson was available. She laid her business card on the desk and said it was a personal matter. The secretary glanced at the card and lifted the telephone. From along a narrow hallway came a distant, muffled ring. While the woman murmured into the mouthpiece, Gail took in details as her eyes adjusted to the dim light: dark wood furniture; out-of-date magazines on a marble-topped end table; an indifferent oil painting of sunset on a beach.

"Ms. Connor?"

She turned. A gaunt figure in a dark business suit stood in the entrance to the hall. One side of his mouth lifted in a tentative smile, creasing his cheek. "I'm Gary Dodson. You wanted to see me?"

Momentarily confused by his appearance, it took her a second to say, "Yes. How do you do?" The man in the photographs had been young and robust; this could have been his father. His hair was still black but so thin on top that the scalp showed through.

Dodson took her down the narrow hall to

his office. It was cramped and even more poorly lit than the front room. There was one tall, wood-framed window, but curtains had been drawn over it to keep out the afternoon sun. As her eyes adjusted Gail could see that every file folder, book, and piece of paper lay at exact right angles to the surface upon which it had been placed. Dodson went around his desk to sit in the black chair behind it. From below came a strange odor of dust, mildew, and rot, as though the subflooring had been flooded but never properly dried.

Gary Dodson propped her card on his brass pen holder, taking some time to get it exactly in the middle. "Civil trial practice. Commercial litigation. You're a sole practitioner? So am I." His smile left a long crease in his cheek.

"It's a constant fight for clients," she said.

"Yes indeed. Isn't that so?"

His skin seemed unnaturally pale, and Gail wondered if he lived upstairs, rarely going out, sending his secretary to do his shopping. The afternoon sun found a crack in the drawn curtains and sent a column of light angling to the floor. Cold air blew silently from a vent.

"Mr. Dodson, this has to do, in a way, with your wife. First let me say how sorry I am for your loss. Not only your wife but your child as well. Twelve years have passed, but it's something a person doesn't get over easily — if at all."

With elbows on the arms of the chair, the points of his shoulders rose as if suspending his desiccated body between them. He began absently to scratch at a scab on his hand. "That's very kind of you to say, Ms. Connor."

"I'm in Stuart because I've been retained by a relative of Kenneth Ray Clark. Based on a reinvestigation of the case, I am convinced that Mr. Clark was nowhere near your house when your wife was killed. This must come as a shock, of course, but I assure you it's true. I'm going to file an appeal, but the governor has signed his death warrant. We don't have much time."

"You say . . . Clark wasn't there? My neighbor saw him."

"Mrs. Chastain was mistaken." Gail added, "It happens more frequently than police or prosecutors will admit."

The music that had been playing in the background finally worked its way into her consciousness. The radio on his credenza was tuned to a "lite FM" station — slow, soothing instrumentals that could drive her insane.

Beside the radio was a gold-framed photograph of a young blond woman holding a laughing baby on her lap.

Swiveling his chair, Dodson saw what she was looking at. "There they are. Amber and Darry. That's short for Darryl. They're beautiful, aren't they? I never got married again. I didn't have the heart for it. I loved my wife and child very much." He rocked slowly in his chair, leaning his head on his fist. His starched white cuff was fraying at the edge, and the button was cracked.

"I read about the warrant in the newspaper last week. They said the execution date had been set. April eleventh, isn't it? I'd almost forgotten that Kenneth Clark is still alive. I get so busy with my work, you know how that goes, and I hardly think about it anymore."

"I'm trying to save his life," Gail said. "He truly is innocent."

"Is he? Then he might end up being executed. The innocent perish and the guilty prosper. File the appeal if you like, it's all the same to me." He said, "I've had enough of death."

The constant chill breeze from the vent had its effect, and Gail crossed her arms. Her lightweight tweed jacket did little good. She crossed her legs as well, but her slacks failed to keep her ankles warm. "I wonder if you remember one of Amber's friends, a girl named Mary Jo, who used to work at River Pines with Amber? She drove a Corvette."

"Yes, I remember her."

"Do you know her last name?"

He pursed his lips, then said, "Hammond. Mary Jo Hammond. I believe they met at Indian River Community College, and it was she who suggested that Amber apply for the job at River Pines. Mary Jo was in accounting."

This was promising, Gail thought. "Where is Mary Jo now?"

"She married some fellow named . . . Danziger. Can't remember his first name. He owned a night club in West Palm. Amber and I went to the wedding. I think they moved to South Beach, in your neck of the woods. Does this relate to your client in some way?"

"Possibly. I hope that Mary Jo might tell me who Amber knew at work. My theory is that she wasn't killed by a stranger — such as Kenny Ray Clark. When a woman is the victim, and she is attacked in the way that Amber was —"

"What way is that? She wasn't raped."

"I know, but . . . her pajamas were left in a suggestive position. She was stabbed repeatedly, many more times than necessary, in the chest and abdomen. Forensic psychologists would say that this indicates an emotional connection. I'm sorry to ask you this, but is there any chance that your wife was involved with someone?"

Shaking his head, Dodson continued to pick at the scab. "The police asked me that too. No, my wife and I loved each other. We were very happy."

Gail could see dark, dried flesh under the nail on his forefinger. All his nails were long and yellowed, and they had cracked off unevenly, leaving some with points at the corners. She quickly looked away.

"Mr. Dodson, you used to work in the Stuart office of Hadley and Morgan, based in Palm Beach, and one of their clients was Whitney McGrath, who developed River Pines. In July 1988 you left Hadley and Morgan to open your own practice. Amber had stopped working at River Pines when she was pregnant, but she went back in September of '88, when Darry was six months old. Is that right?"

"You've been doing your homework."

"Did Amber know Whit McGrath?"

"Naturally. She worked for him — rather, for his company, JWM."

"Were they on good terms?"

"As far as I know."

"Is it remotely possible she could have been involved with him? And that you might not have been aware?"

Dodson's forefinger slowed on the back of his hand. "You believe that Whit McGrath killed my wife?"

"I don't know if he did or not. I'm looking into possibilities."

"Point one: That isn't a possibility. Point two: I don't discuss my clients." Dodson opened a paper clip and cleaned under his nail.

"You're . . . Whit McGrath's lawyer?"

"Yes."

"Really."

"Not his *only* lawyer. Mr. McGrath has several."

"How long have you represented him?"

"Oh, it's been quite awhile, ever since I opened my own office."

"I see." But Gail did not see. Why would Whit McGrath hire this man whose office, whose very appearance, screamed failure? Was Gary Dodson telling the truth? Was he sane?

"What kind of cases do you handle for Mr. McGrath?"

"Various matters."

"Like what?"

Dodson raised a finger in admonition. "Do you talk about *your* clients, Ms. Connor?" The line in his left cheek deepened as he smiled in that lopsided way. "But as to your first question. The answer is no. My wife and Mr. McGrath were not involved. Amber was a loving and faithful wife and mother."

"Of course. I'm sorry."

His intercom buzzed. He picked it up, then checked his watch. "It's only four o'clock, Nelda. Have you finished everything? . . . Yes, all right, go ahead, but make a note on your time sheet."

He dropped the handset back on the phone, then swung his chair toward Gail. "It's Friday. They always want to leave early on Friday, don't they?"

At the other end of the hall a door opened. A momentary noise of traffic, then a closing door. The click of a lock. Then nothing.

The light through the curtains had shifted, falling now in a Z-shaped line across his desk. Across his hand. His fraying cuff, his terrible nails.

Gail stood and put her purse over her shoulder. "Thank you for your time, Mr. Dodson. I should be going." She backed toward the hall. "Don't get up. I'll show myself out."

★ ★ ★

She had parked across the street. The sun shone brightly, but a chill had entered her bones. It took her a minute of sitting in the hot car before she felt warm enough to turn on the engine and open the window.

She put the car into gear and glanced automatically in the rearview mirror. There was a pickup truck at the end of the block pointed in her direction. A black one, riding high off the ground. The sun glanced off its windshield, but she thought she could make out the shape of someone inside. Rusty Beck.

She hit the gas, and her tires squealed out of the parking place.

The truck didn't follow. She looked back several times, but it wasn't behind her. By the time she reached the bridge to Hutchinson Island, her nerves had settled, and she began to feel foolish. It had been an ordinary pickup truck, nothing more. Her fright had turned it into an apparition.

CHAPTER 15

Saturday morning, March 17

A good morning to sit on the beach. Bright and sunny, about seventy degrees. A few people were in swimming already. Jackie thought they were probably Canadians. The locals had more sense, waiting till May.

Irene leaned back on a wooden lounge chair and Jackie sat on the edge of the one next to it, facing her. Karen was walking barefoot in the surf, looking for shells, the wind blowing her sun-streaked hair around her head. She was mad at her mother for not sticking around. The three of them had taken the weathered gray boardwalk over the dunes of sea oats and sea grape, then gone down the stairs to the sand. The hotel was behind them, across the road.

Jackie would have invited Irene and Karen to her house, if it had been hers. It was her father's house. Jackie hadn't told him where she was going this morning and didn't plan to. She was aware of withholding a lot from her father lately.

At breakfast, Gail had taken three calls on

her cell phone, walking away to keep Karen from hearing. Jackie knew what it was about. Gail was looking for witnesses. She had a week to put her case together before her papers were due in court. She was running flat-out. Everything else in the world but breathing came second. It was hard to explain it to an eleven-year-old, when you didn't want also to explain that your client could be executed if you didn't run fast enough.

Settling back on the chair, Irene kicked off her sandals. Her toenails were painted bright blue with yellow flower stickers on the big toes. She wiggled them. Her feet were small, like the rest of her. "What do you think? Karen painted them for me."

"They're cute." Jackie smiled, then said, "What are you doing this afternoon, Aunt Irene? If you're not busy, bring Karen over to the station. I'll show you around."

"What a good idea. I'm sure Karen would go for it."

"She can see the inside of a patrol car."

"Hey, what about me?"

"You too." Jackie unlaced her sneakers and set them under her lounger with the socks rolled inside. "I remember the day they assigned me a car. At first they put you with a partner so you can learn, but then they let you go out on your own. I drove by a bank with a lot of windows, and I saw my reflection. I'm like, wow. I drove around the block so I could see myself again. A cop car, and this woman in a uniform carrying a gun, and she's got her sunglasses on. I go, hey, you're looking *good*. I ran up onto a curb and almost hit a light pole."

Aunt Irene laughed and reached over to squeeze Jackie's hand. "You're such a treasure. Now why haven't we visited more?" She patted Jackie's bare knee. The sun came through the straw brim of Irene's hat and made flecks of light on her face. Irene was almost sixty, but she had pretty blue eyes, and she wore mascara and lipstick and bright pink earrings.

"How are you, darling? All right?"

Jackie picked a shell out of the sand and brushed it off. "I guess Gail told you we talked yesterday."

"About your mother, you mean." Irene watched the water. "I still miss Louise so much. There were four of us kids, you know. She was the baby. Our parents had the place on Sewall's Point, and one Thanksgiving Lou was driving from FSU, and your father gave her a speeding ticket. That's how they met, but you've heard that story. They married when she got out of college. She was only twenty-two."

Jackie could see it was no use talking to Aunt Irene, who refused to say a bad word about anyone, much less her favorite sister.

But Irene went on, "They weren't suited. She married too young, and it didn't work out. It happens in a lot of marriages. She left your father but she never meant to leave you and Alex. That simply isn't true."

Jackie tossed the shell into the dune. "In the two months before she died, she came to see us maybe four times. One other time, Dad took us to her apartment. She'd been drinking, so he brought us home."

"That must have hurt you terribly." A breeze picked up the hem of Irene's yellow cotton dress, and she tucked it under her knees. "What you need to understand is that your mother was so depressed. She could hardly function. She'd sleep twelve hours a day. I tried to get her some help, but she wouldn't follow through on it. You know she was a real estate agent, don't you? After she and your father split up, she found a job at a Century 21 office in West Palm through some friends. I don't know if she made a single sale. She borrowed some money from Ed and me to get by. I wanted her to come stay with us, but she said no, she couldn't be that far away from you kids. Darling, you were always in her thoughts."

"What happened between her and my father?" Jackie said. "Please don't tell me it's the usual thing between a husband and wife. I'd like the truth."

For several seconds Irene stared out at the ocean. "She fell in love with someone, and it ended very badly."

"Oh, I see." Jackie made a soft laugh. "She cheated on him. I was wondering if that was it."

"That's awfully judgmental." Irene swung her legs off the lounge chair. "Listen to me, Jackie. Your mother wasn't in the habit of looking for other men. She stayed married for fourteen years to a man she admired but couldn't please. Louise wasn't perfect, but Garlan expected perfection, and she suffered with every failure."

"Are you blaming *him?*"

"I'm not trying to place blame, only to explain to you how things were between them. You said you wanted to know, so let me finish. They had come to a rough spot in their marriage. They might have worked it out if . . . this other thing hadn't happened. The man was a builder. I think that's how they met, but I'm not sure. He was younger, and he was also married. Your mother would never have gone after him, but he pursued *her*. He flattered her, made reasons to see her, and sent her anonymous little gifts. She was in her mid-thirties, and all of a sudden a handsome young man wanted her. Louise was so innocent, really. She let herself believe he loved her. She thought he would leave his wife. For a few months she was head over heels, but it dawned on her that he'd just been using her. He'd never loved her. Louise called it off, but inside, she was devastated. She told your father everything and asked him to forgive her. He wouldn't. He said he could never feel the same about her again, that she had betrayed him. After that, Louise decided she had to leave. She wanted you and Alex to come with her, but Garlan was angry and hurt, and he wouldn't allow it. He hired a lawyer. Another woman might have fought back, but not Louise. She just crumbled. She blamed herself for everything."

Irene took Jackie's hand. "Oh, you mustn't think she didn't care. She did. She loved you and Alex more than anything. She would have found her way back to you, I'm sure of it. If only there had been more time."

Jackie finally took a breath. "What was his name?"

"She wouldn't say."

"Did she tell my father who it was?"

"No, she was afraid of what he might do.

Garlan thought she was protecting this man, so of course that made things even worse between them."

"Do you think she killed herself? Did she drive off the road on purpose?"

"Of course not. It was an accident, that's all. A tragic, senseless, horrible accident that took her away much too soon. Oh, Jackie, darling, should I have told you all this? I think I've made you unhappy."

"You haven't. I'm glad you told me."

"Please don't blame your mother. Don't blame anyone, you'll destroy yourself that way. We're all so flawed, and we have to forgive each other."

Jackie hugged her. "I love you, Aunt Irene."

Irene held her tightly, then kissed her cheek. "Your mother would be so proud of you. She loved you very much. Don't ever doubt that."

Jackie had to pull away and stand up. She looked out at the sea for a while, then reached down and picked up her shoes. "I think I'll go. If you want to bring Karen to the station, come about two-thirty. Call me."

"We'll see you then."

Jackie started to leave, then said, "Aunt Irene? Gail should tell Karen what's going on. It's not right to try to protect her, because she's going to find out anyway. Eleven is old enough."

Jackie went up the steps over the dune, then down to the road. The sound of the surf receded. The sun was warm on her back.

She remembered that last summer. The afternoon heat, the unmoving air. Walking into the barn, hearing voices. Her mother's soft laughter. Whit McGrath in his boots, tall and blond, looking around to see who was there, tugging on Jackie's braid. *Hey, little girl. You're growing up as pretty as your mama.* Her mother turning away to pet his chestnut horse in the stall.

By September she was dead. Aunt Irene had said not to blame anyone. But someone had to bear responsibility. Her mother, for needing someone? Her father, for not loving her more? Or Whit, who wanted her? Maybe they were all to blame.

Gail had been right: It was more complicated than Jackie had thought. She had wanted an answer and still didn't have one.

Her phone rang as she was upstairs in her garage apartment working her way through some leftover potato chips and reading about the effect of cold weather on the rate of decomposition. *The most commonly applied rule of thumb is that the body cools 1½ degrees Fahrenheit per hour —*

Eyes still on the page, Jackie picked up the telephone. It was Gail.

She said, "I've found Mary Jo."

"That was fast. How'd you do it?"

"Well, actually, Hector did. It seems that Gary told me the truth. Mary Jo and her husband left Stuart in 1988 and moved to Miami to open a bar on South Beach. It didn't last long, though. The bar went bankrupt, the husband ran off with another woman, and Mary Jo went to Fort Pierce. That's not far, is it? How long would it take to get there?"

"This time of day about half an hour."

"She said I could come by. Want to go with me?"

Gail let Jackie drive. They would go right up the coast, and Jackie knew the way. Besides that, she could probably get away with speeding. Neither of them had much time. Gail would talk to one of the jurors at two o'clock, and Jackie had to meet Irene and Karen at two-thirty.

They got into Jackie's Isuzu Trooper and headed north. Fort Pierce was in the next county, another little coastal town full of tourists and boats.

It occurred to Gail, as Mary Jo Hammond opened the door, that if Amber Dodson hadn't died, she might have ended up just like this. Divorced, thirty-six, living with an adolescent son in a modest house in a new development, working as a computer systems administrator. Still a good figure, keeping herself up. She had acrylic nails and highlights in her blond hair.

"Amber was crazy about Whit. She had these fantasies that he would leave his wife for her. I don't *think* so. She started going out with Gary Dodson to make Whit jealous. He was a lawyer and not bad looking. Her parents pushed her to marry him, so she did. Slid right into it, which let me tell you is how most of us do it, right?"

"What about after she got married? Was it over with Whit?"

"No." Mary Jo snorted a laugh. "If he needed a quickie, and she was there, he'd call her into his office and she'd get on her knees. I said, 'Amber, wake *up*.' But I don't think she cared."

Jackie sat at the other end of the kitchen table with her chin in her hands, a perfectly blank expression on her face. Gail had told her to jump in if she had any questions, but so far she had said nothing.

Gail asked, "Could the baby have been Whit's?"

"Uh-uh. He had a vasectomy after his two kids. But after Amber got pregnant, which was totally unexpected, by the way, Gary made her quit work. Then Gary got fired. He started his own law practice, but he wasn't making much money, and Amber was going crazy at home. I was living in Miami Beach then, but she'd call me and talk for hours, how her life was so boring, and how Gary was such a dud. She wanted to leave him but she didn't have any money, and Gary couldn't afford alimony and child support, and there was no way she'd live with her parents again. I got sick of listening to it, so finally I told her not to call me anymore."

"She went back to River Pines," Gail said. "Do you know if she and Whit had become involved again before she was killed?"

"I have no idea. I hadn't spoken to her in a long time when I heard she was dead. It was on the news, they arrested the guy that did it. But you say he didn't. Holy shit. I bet it was Gary."

"The police checked him out," Gail said. "He was at work."

Jackie finally spoke. "Why do you think it

was Gary? Was he violent?"

"She said he wasn't, but . . . I didn't like him. He was weird."

"Weird?"

"Yeah. Like this Seiko watch he gave her for Christmas. She thought it was cheap so she wouldn't wear it. He took it out in the carport and laid it on the concrete and smashed it with a hammer. He never screamed at her, but they argued a lot. Afterwards he'd go into the spare room and sit there in the dark and . . . you know." Mary Jo looked around to make sure her boy was still in the kitchen making his sandwich.

Gail and Jackie exchanged a glance. Gail said, "Let's go back to what you said before, that Gary was fired from the law firm. What did Amber tell you about that?"

"She said they made him resign, which is the same thing. They found out he did something shady for Whit McGrath, and they told him to leave."

"Something shady? What does that mean?"

"Jesus, if I can remember." She tapped on a front tooth with one of her long red nails. "Amber made it sound shady. Some trick they pulled on a real estate deal. Gary did . . . whatever he did, and the law firm found out and fired him."

★ ★ ★

On the way back to Stuart, Gail said, "Well, that was certainly interesting."

Jackie skillfully gunned her SUV around a slower car on the narrow road. The intracoastal was on their left, old frame houses on the sloping ground to their right. She said, "And you got what you were after. Amber Dodson was involved with Whit McGrath."

"Yes, but Mary Jo can't say they were involved around the time of the murder, which is what I need. Hector is looking for Vivian Baker. She was working at River Pines as the director of sales when Amber died. She isn't there anymore. Maybe she'll talk to me. I should also check into why Gary was fired, don't you think?"

Eyes on the road, Jackie said, "I would."

"It could explain why Gary Dodson started working for Whit McGrath, if he wasn't lying to me about it. Gary was fired because of something he did for Whit, and Whit was making it up to him. Maybe. I wonder what he did? You know, Jackie, if it was *illegal,* as opposed to just *shady,* that might be something else to look into." They passed a long line of palm trees, and shade and sunlight rapidly alternated. "I wonder who I know with connections at Hadley and

312

Morgan in Palm Beach."

Jackie was holding the wheel with both hands, concentrating on the road. Gail had noticed that she was even quieter than usual. She didn't seem to be in a bad mood, just preoccupied. Gail wondered if it had to do with the chat with Irene after breakfast. Gail had no idea what Irene might have said, but as soon as she got back, she would ask her. It would be rude to start questioning her cousin.

They crossed the county line doing about sixty. A Martin County sheriff's deputy going the other way lifted a hand in salutation. He must have recognized the white Trooper belonging to the sheriff's daughter. Jackie glanced at her speedometer and slowed down. "Oops."

"I don't think he would have stopped you for speeding," Gail said.

"Yeah, but it sets a bad example."

Gail couldn't hold back a smile. "You're such a Girl Scout."

Jackie slowed to thirty going through a neat little trailer park with tiny plots of grass. The trailers were turquoise and pink single-wides that might have been there for forty years. A hurricane storm surge would have tossed them away like so many toys. The view went straight down the intracoastal, Hutchinson Island on the left, vanishing in the distance.

"Why don't you ask Whit McGrath why Gary got fired."

"How? Go knock on his door?"

"There's a big event going on tonight at the River Pines Club. He's unveiling Phase Two, a complete build-out of River Pines. It's supposedly invitation only, but I think you could walk in if you look like you belong."

"Great. 'Mr. McGrath, is it true that Gary Dodson is one of your lawyers? Why would you hire such a loser? What illegal or unethical act did Gary Dodson do for you when he was employed by Hadley and Morgan? Did Amber want money to keep quiet? Is that why you killed her? Or was it because she was tired of being on her knees, and she was going to tell your wife?' "

Jackie's smile broke into a laugh.

Gail said, "Maybe I'll just go there and watch."

"Tell Anthony to come too. It doesn't take that long to get here from Miami."

"He's trying very hard to stay out of this."

"All he has to do is show up. It's good to have a guy with you. That way you don't look as obvious. You'll have someone to talk to."

Gail thought about it. "That's true."

Jackie dropped her at the same shopping center parking lot where they had met two hours ago. "Call me later," she said. "And tell Whit that Jackie Bryce says hello."

Gail made some other stops before going back to the hotel. She sat in the kitchen of one of the jurors on *State vs. Clark*, explaining, persuading, finally begging him to sign an affidavit. To her surprise, he did. He would not have voted to convict Kenneth Ray Clark of murder, and recommend death, if Tina Hopwood had testified that Clark had left the trailer at 10:00 A.M. on February 6.

Driving away from the man's house, in a much better frame of mind, Gail knew she had added a few grains of sand to the scales. But it wasn't enough. Proof of innocence was required. She needed to name the killer.

The second juror spoke through the screen door and said she didn't want to get involved. A third said he couldn't afford to take the time off to testify. Gail left a copy of the proposed affidavit and her business card.

Hector Mesa had located four others in the area, but Gail had not been able to reach them by telephone, and there was no time to send letters. Hector was still working on finding Lougie Jackson's friends, and if one of them could be located, Kenny's alibi could be buttressed by additional testimony.

Her last stop was Sunset Villas Retirement Home.

She knocked at the open door to Ruby Smith's room, then went inside. Ruby put away some letters she was writing and lifted her arms. She hugged Gail tightly around the neck, and Gail remembered being hugged like this twenty-five years ago. She pulled a chair close and sat down.

"When's Irene coming over to see me with that sweet little girl of yours?"

"Tomorrow," Gail told her. "Mom wants to take you to lunch after you come back from church. Would that be all right?"

"I'll cancel all my other dates," Ruby joked, then her expression grew serious. "How are you doing, honey? How's the appeal coming along?"

Gail took her time, telling Ruby everything, not wanting to give her false hopes. She thought that Ruby should be prepared for the worst, if it happened.

"Oh, don't be so downhearted." Ruby took Gail's hand. "I'll tell you something. Jesus spoke to me again. It was last

Wednesday. I was just sitting here, about to go to bed, and the room got so bright, and I heard his voice. 'Fear not.' Just those two words. Fear not."

Gail nodded, unsure what to say. "Did anyone else hear this?"

Through the thick glasses, Ruby's faded eyes seemed to smile. "No, precious. I'm not going crazy. I have hope that Kenny Ray will be all right, I guess that's what I'm trying to tell you, and you shouldn't be afraid to hope for the best, either. We're not driving this bus, we're just along for the ride." She squeezed Gail's hand. "When are you going to the prison again?"

"Next week," Gail said. "After I write the motion to overturn his conviction, Kenny needs to sign it." Another flight to Jacksonville, another rental car. "Ruby, I need to get a check from you."

"Yes, you do." She took her old leather-covered Bible from the TV table next to her chair. A check protruded from between the gilded pages, and Ruby tugged it free. "Here. I already made it out."

Fifteen thousand dollars.

"I put in the extra five because I know it can't be cheap for you, all this work you're doing." She closed her Bible and folded her hands on top of it. Her nails were ridged with age, and heavy veins showed through the nearly transparent skin. With some hesitation, Ruby asked, "Will that be enough?"

Gail stared down at the check. The first ten thousand had vanished like dust blown from the palm of her hand, and fifteen more wouldn't last much longer. But it was impossible to ask for more. Anthony Quintana would have something to say about it — if Gail decided to tell him.

"Yes. It's fine." She bent down to kiss Ruby's cheek. "Thank you."

CHAPTER 16

Saturday night, March 17

Sunset at River Pines put a warm glow on the beige stucco houses and sent long shadows across immaculate lawns. The main road curved past the landscaped shopping center, past the Pines Riding Academy, and eventually around the golf course to the River Pines Club. With its columns and tile roof, it resembled a Mediterranean villa. Anthony and Gail sat on a tree-shaded bench by the tennis courts and watched the side entrance. There was a portico and under it, a woman taking names.

Gail had told Anthony the dress code: casual chic. He wore a cappuccino brown jacket and pleated pants with an open-collared black silk shirt. His narrow snakeskin belt with the gold buckle was a work of art. Gail had asked him to look in his closet for her short black sleeveless dress and matching high-heeled sandals. This would have been perfect for an evening affair in Miami. But they were not in Miami. The men and women walking through that door might have been going to a business meeting. Gail remembered now what Jackie had told her: McGrath was seducing the local politicians and chamber-of-commerce types before the commission voted whether to approve Phase Two.

Anthony spread his arms out lazily on the back of the bench, an ankle on his knee. "Are we going in or not?"

"In a minute. I'm waiting for that woman at the door to take a potty break."

"Gail, she's only there to write name tags. 'Hello, I'm . . . Billy Bob."

"Be nice." Gail crossed her legs and tugged her skirt down, hoping the bench didn't snag her hose. "What do you think of River Pines?"

"I've seen it all over South Florida."

"You think I'm on the wrong track with Whit McGrath, don't you?"

"Dodson killed his wife. When the pathologist finishes with the autopsy reports, and tells us that the time of death was off, I want to hear you say, 'Oh, Anthony, I was so wrong. We should have spent two hours in bed instead of enduring that party.' "

The woman at the door got up from her table and went inside. Gail grabbed her purse. "Come on, let's go."

Hand in hand they hurried across the grass and under the portico. On the table was a list of names with check marks beside them. Gail quickly wrote her and Anthony's names on stick-on tags and patted one onto his jacket and the other onto her dress. They vanished among a crowd of a hundred other people.

A piano played light jazz, and servers passed through with trays of hors d'oeuvres. A line had formed at the bar. All activities were pushed to the perimeter because the middle was taken up with a table at least ten feet on each side, illuminated by spotlights. Holding on to Anthony's shoulder, Gail followed in his wake as he eased through the crowd to get closer.

It was a scale model of River Pines in its final incarnation, if McGrath got the permits he wanted. There were clusters of homes and condominiums in gated communities, three golf courses, a movie theater, riding trails, shopping areas, and schools. Everything radiated from a town center that featured a hotel and conference center curving around a man-made lake. More colonnades and stucco and barrel tile roofs — Boca Raton washing northward.

Barely moving her lips, Gail read aloud, " 'River Pines. Florida's New Home Town.' Oh, my God. It's a *city*."

Anthony leaned close to her. "You don't

like it? You wouldn't want to live here?"

Gail stood on tiptoe. "I wonder where he is." All she had was Jackie's description: early forties, shaggy blond hair, and dimples. Her eyes swept over the crowd. A smaller group gathered in the back of the room near the piano. She saw the top of a man's head, the light picking up golden streaks in his hair. Someone moved out of the way. The man was sun-bronzed and lean, dressed in a navy blue jacket and tan slacks. White shirt, no tie. The clothes looked as though he'd had them for years, but they draped wonderfully well. He gripped a friend's shoulder and laughed in that booming, confident way of men who couldn't care less.

"That's got to be him," she said.

"Go find out," Anthony told her.

"Want to come with me?"

"It's your case." Standing behind her, Anthony put a kiss on her neck. His lips moved at her ear. "Come back and tell me that such a man could feel threatened by a girl like Amber."

"You're going to apologize when you find out I'm right," she said.

Anthony gave her a little shove. "Go on."

Gail maneuvered around the scale model and walked toward the piano. Even over the music she could hear Whit McGrath laughing. A server passed by, and Gail took a tiny pastry shell filled with caviar and sour cream. She nibbled it while McGrath talked about himself. How his parents, living on Jupiter Island, had sent him to prep school in Palm Beach. How he'd been suspended for hoisting an inflatable doll up the flagpole.

"My dad said one more stunt like that, you're going to Martin County High. That's just what I wanted! All my buddies were here. I passed out cartoons of the headmaster with his pants down, and bam! They expelled me. The next year at Martin County I played running back and we won the state championship. I said, 'Thanks, Dad.'"

Everyone laughed. Dimples appeared in his cheeks and lines fanned out from the corners of his sea-blue eyes. His lower lip was full and rosy. Gail had no doubt that Amber Dodson had wanted J. Whitney McGrath. Wanted him bad.

Standing with her weight on one hip, holding on to her narrow purse strap, Gail wondered how to break in. Then McGrath noticed her. He waited until one of the other men had finished a joke, then gave him a clap on the back and said there were people he had to talk to.

He headed for Gail, coming closer, reading her name tag. "Gail Connor." He raised his eyes. Even his eyelashes were blond. "Hi. Whit McGrath. Now where have I heard your name?"

"I don't know, but I'm Jackie Bryce's cousin."

"Hello, Jackie's cousin." His hand was big and warm.

"She said to tell you hello."

"Did she? Tell her I said hello right back." McGrath had a slow, lazy smile. "Aren't you the lawyer who's working on the Clark case?"

"Where'd you hear that?" Gail wondered if Gary Dodson had told him.

"Gee, I don't remember."

"Could we talk for a minute? Maybe over there?" Gail nodded toward a vacant area near some planters with bird-of-paradise.

He glanced at his guests. "Do you think they can find the bar without me?"

As they walked, Gail said, "I can't discuss the details, but I've uncovered evidence that Kenny Ray Clark is probably innocent. You knew the victim, and I was hoping you could help me out."

"Me? I barely knew Ms. Dodson. She worked for the sales office. All I remember is a cute little face at the reception desk. 'Morning, Mr. McGrath.' 'Hi, Amber.' " He lifted a hand as though she might still be there. "My God. What a tragedy. I was there at the trial for a couple of days, and I have to say, the case against your client was pretty compelling. What makes you think he's innocent?"

Gail said, "There were several mistakes in the original investigation, but I don't want to take up your time with that. What I wanted to ask —"

"No, it's okay. I'm curious." Whit McGrath was standing so close that Gail had to tilt her head up to look at him. There was a little flat place on the bridge of his nose, probably a collision with a sailboat jib or a ski pole. "You said you had evidence?"

"I'm sorry, I can't discuss the details of the case. You understand. I just wanted to ask you a couple of things about Gary Dodson." There was only a blank look in reply, and Gail added, "Amber's husband?"

"I know who he is."

"Mr. Dodson told me that he's been your lawyer ever since he opened his own practice. Is that true?"

"Not *my* lawyer. The company uses him now and then, but the general counsel is with a firm in Fort Lauderdale."

"Oh. I thought you used Hadley and Morgan in Palm Beach."

"Your information is a little dated," McGrath said.

"Apparently so." Gail made a mental note.

"So what's your question about Dodson? Or have I answered it?" McGrath moved in a little closer.

"Why do you — rather, why does your company use Gary Dodson?"

"Why not? I'd met him at Hadley and Morgan, and when he opened his own office, I told the personnel office to toss him some business. Sometimes one of the employees might need a real estate closing or a will, nothing too complicated." McGrath touched Gail's shoulder, his voice at such a low level she had to watch his lips to catch the words. "Then after his wife and baby died, the poor guy went to pieces, so we kept him on our referral list. I felt sorry for him."

Gail moved back a little, her shoulder blades brushing the wall. "Hadley and Morgan asked him to resign. Do you have any idea why?"

"Gee, I sure don't. That's the first I've heard of it."

"Mr. Dodson was working on something

for you at the time. Do you know what it was?"

"For me?" McGrath crossed his arms and stroked his chin. He wore a stainless-steel Rolex Submariner scuffed from long use. A plain wedding band. His hands were tanned and muscular. "Dodson didn't work for me directly. My company retained the firm, and he worked for one of the partners. It couldn't have been important or I'd have been told."

"Did Amber ever talk to you about her husband's leaving Hadley and Morgan?"

"As I said before, Ms. Dodson was an employee, not a personal friend."

Gail did no more than look at him, but her knowledge must have communicated itself in the lift of her brows.

Whit McGrath swiveled slightly, facing the crowd. "Okay. Okay, I get it." He smiled so that anyone watching might have thought they were having a pleasant conversation. "You want to point fingers at somebody else. Create some doubt, get the public all excited. I don't know who you've been talking to, honey, but it stops. Now. You've got balls, interrogating me at my own party. Before you go, Ms. Connor, hear this. If you throw mud in my direction, if my name is used in any way in your attempt to free a convicted murderer, I will sue you for slander. I will have your license to practice law. My attorneys will sue you until you bleed. I'll do it for sport." He was still smiling.

Stunned, Gail could only stare up into his face.

"Got that?" He patted her shoulder as he stepped away.

She watched him greet an older couple walking toward him, open his arms wide. A handshake. A kiss on the woman's cheek. Arms around their shoulders, turning them toward the scale model of River Pines, his hair shining under the lights.

Anthony was looking across the room at her, dark eyes holding a question. Gail moved toward the exit, and he followed.

They got out of the car where the road turned to gravel and ended at a barbed-wire fence. Ahead of them lay a vast flat field of dirt, weeds, and rocks. Brush had been scraped into piles, but a few pine trees remained, dark silhouettes. A rusting NO TRESPASSING sign with bullet holes in it hung on the barbed-wire fence, but the gate was open. They walked through it and down a gentle incline.

"Is this what you expected to see?" Anthony asked.

"I don't know what I expected," Gail said.

They followed the uneven gravel tracks that appeared to end a couple of hundred yards further on. Gail picked her way carefully in her high heels. A three-quarter moon hung over the tree line to the east, and the sun lingered as a diffused orange glow. The temperature had dropped, and she crossed her arms.

"It's so weedy," she said. "Nothing's been done out here in years, you can tell."

"They can't continue without the permits." Anthony pivoted as he walked. "While you were enjoying your chat with Whit McGrath, I talked to a reporter from *The Stuart News*. McGrath's company — he and a few other big investors — began to purchase property in the mid-1980s. They acquired over two thousand acres. They wanted to build a planned city. Phase One was approved before the county Master Plan went into effect, but Phase Two was held up by newly elected county commissioners who wanted to hold the line against development. Most of the retirees and the wealthy along the coast support them, but younger families are moving in, and there's very little housing. For years, McGrath has been funding the campaigns of the opposition. Now they have a majority. It comes up for a vote next month. McGrath has the state agencies on his side. He's a friend of Governor Ward and one of his biggest donors in the last election. A coincidence, of course."

They had reached the middle of the field. Bird calls came from the woods.

"The reporter told me that JWM is deeply in debt. McGrath needs this vote to go in his favor."

"And he'll probably get it," Gail said.

"Probably." Anthony took off his jacket and draped it over her shoulders.

His body heat was trapped inside, and Gail held it close. "Aren't you going to ask me if I think he killed Amber Dodson?"

"I know what you think."

"He was lying to me," she said. "I could smell it on him."

"Lying about what? His affair? That shouldn't surprise you. If you pursue this, you use up time that would be better spent preparing your case. The hearing is in less than two weeks. Sweetheart, what are we doing out here? Let's go back to the hotel."

With no more than a nod for reply, Gail looked around her at the torn landscape. "What did Amber know? Whatever Gary was doing for Whit McGrath, she must have known about it."

Anthony reminded her that Dodson had been fired seven months before his wife's murder. "That length of time," he said, "would seem to rule out a connection between the two events."

"You're just stuck on Gary as the bad guy," she said.

From her memory of the scale model and the position of the access road, Gail could see where the buildings would go. She pointed them out to Anthony. Over there, the cinema. Further on, the entrance to the town center. Gail wanted to soak in as much as she could. Soon it would be too dark to see, and they would have no choice but to leave.

They went around some pine trees and stopped at the rocky edge of a small lake about fifty feet in diameter, with a precipitous drop at the sides, as if the ground underneath had caved in.

"This is going to be the lake in front of the hotel," she said. "Ugly, isn't it? They'll Disney-fy it and top it off with that horribly ostentatious fountain."

Anthony tossed a rock. Silver ripples moved outward to the mildewed and weed-choked shoreline. "Ah. I meant to tell you. Hector's divers didn't find your ring."

"I figured that," she said.

"They will look again, but what will you

do if it can't be found?"

"Me? Nothing. What can I do?"

"Do you want another one?" Anthony dusted his hands and turned to look at her. As Gail tried to think of what she felt about that, he walked over and took her by the lapels of the jacket, pulling her closer. He shook her gently. "Answer me."

"Another one?"

"A new one. If I can't find yours, may I buy you a new one?"

It wasn't a simple question. She slid her arms around his waist. "Anthony, please don't ask me that now."

"You keep putting me off."

"Just let me get past this appeal. I already have too much on my mind."

"How hard is it to say one word? Yes? No?" He held her chin, forcing her to look at him. The weak light from the dying sun was behind him, and his eyes were black pools. "If you don't tell me, you can walk back to the beach. Yes or no."

"All right, then. No, I don't want a new one. I want the ring you threw away."

"Why? Why must you have that particular ring? They're all the same."

"Not to me." She kissed him. "You wore that diamond on your own hand, and I want it."

He laughed, but not happily. *"Tú eres imposible.* Let's get out of here." Gail felt his body suddenly tense. He was looking past her, frowning.

She turned. A hundred yards away, on the access road where they had left his car, another vehicle had come alongside it. Headlights, higher than those on the Cadillac, shone directly into the field. It was a truck, but at this distance it was hard to discern anything more than the shape.

Then the lights moved down the incline, and she saw it clearly: a black pickup truck with a high suspension and knobby tires.

Anthony muttered, "He's probably going to tell us we're trespassing."

"I think it's Rusty Beck." When Anthony looked at her, Gail said, "The cowboy at the ranch, remember? Showing off with the bullwhip?"

"How do you know his truck?"

"I saw him in it yesterday. He might have been following me."

Anthony was about to reply, but the headlights, steady until now, began to bob up and down. The truck had picked up speed, bouncing over the ruts in the ground. The pitch of the engine rose. The lights grew brighter, picking up the disbelief on Anthony's face.

"*¿Qué está haciendo ese tipo?*"

He grabbed Gail's arm and pulled her off the gravel tracks. The truck flew by them, swerved, and slid sideways, raising a cloud of dust. The rear wheels spun, then caught, and the truck circled back. The dust caught the beams of light. Rocks clattered in the wheel wells.

The engine roared, and the truck hurtled toward them again. It fishtailed across the ground, sending rocks flying. Gail cried out from a sudden pain in her thigh and protected her face with her arms.

"Get behind there!" Anthony pointed at a rotting pile of tree trunks and branches. In the gathering darkness Gail didn't see the hole. She stumbled into it and lost one of her shoes. His jacket slid off her shoulders.

The black truck cut off their escape and went into a tight turn. Anthony yelled, "I'm going to make him come after me. When I do, get into the trees!"

"No!" Coughing on dust, she held on to his arm.

"*Suéltame.* Let go!" He jerked free of her.

The headlights lit his face, then swung away. The truck was circling again. Anthony picked up a jagged white rock a foot in diameter. The wheels locked. The truck slid to a stop, driver's side toward them, and dust boiled from the undercarriage. A spotlight came on. Gail shielded her eyes.

The engine had quieted to a steady growl. A man's voice called out, "This is private property. You got no business here."

Anthony shouted, "I know your name. Russell Beck."

A laugh came from behind the spotlight. "I know yours too, slick."

"Why don't you get out of that piece of shit truck and talk to me like a man?" Anthony threw the heavy rock aside and strode forward, one hand raised in front of his eyes. The beam of light swung, then went dark, but for a quick moment Rusty Beck had been visible, reaching for the gun rack.

"Anthony!"

The barrel of a shotgun slid through the open window, and Anthony froze. The low rumble of the truck didn't hide the metallic sound of a shell being racked into the chamber. "Come on. You want a piece of this?"

Gail yelled at him, "Garlan Bryce is my uncle! I'll have you arrested."

"I'm scared now." The shotgun jerked toward the road. "Get on out. I see you again, no telling what might happen."

Anthony's chest was moving quickly with his breathing. He spun around and came back to Gail. "Are you all right?" She could only nod. "Where is your shoe?"

"I don't know. Never mind." One foot of her panty hose was shredded.

He found her shoe, and Gail held on to his arm to put it on. Her hand was shaking so badly she kept dropping it. Her fingers wouldn't work.

Rusty Beck said, "Hot damn. You got some legs. Bend over again, let me see your panties."

Gail murmured, "Anthony, don't say anything. Don't. Please don't."

"Put your shoe on."

"I'm trying to!"

He did it himself, roughly, but she knew that his anger wasn't for her.

"I dropped your jacket." Gail pointed, and he went to pick it up. The imprint of a tire ran across the back and sleeve. He balled it up and threw it.

They walked in the beams of the head-lights. Their shadows stretched out ahead of them. Rusty Beck turned on his radio to a country station. He gunned the engine, then put on the brakes, again and again, urging them on. Gail held tightly on to Anthony's arm and kept her eyes on the Cadillac. They walked up the slope and through the gate.

Rusty Beck's shotgun was out the window again, and the spotlight created a bright pool of light.

Anthony took out his car keys and aimed the automatic door release. He walked Gail to her side of the car and opened her door. He went around and got in. Closed his door. Stuck the keys in the ignition. Not rushing, not one tremor in his movements.

Rusty Beck gunned his engine. Tires screaming, the truck swerved around them, kicking up gravel. Its taillights receded on the long, straight road. The last remaining light of day allowed Gail to see Anthony's expression. He was still looking after the truck, and his eyes could have vaporized stone.

She let her head fall against the headrest. "Should we call the police?"

Anthony's lips thinned against his teeth. *"La próxima vez, tendré más que una roca."* He swept the keys from the ignition, found one he wanted, and reached across Gail to open the glove compartment. He threw aside a map and took out a black leather pouch.

She knew what was in it: a nine-millimeter pistol with seventeen rounds in the magazine. Lurching forward, she fell on his arm. "Don't! Anthony, my God!" She hung on, wrestling him for the gun.

"Gail! Stop it." He ripped it away from her. She crawled across the seat, going for his hand. Her shoulder hit the horn.

Laughter burst from her throat. "Don't go after him. Oh, my God. Anthony." She hiccuped a laugh and tried to catch her breath. "I'm defending a man on death row, and you're going to shoot someone for chasing us in his truck! I can't stand it. Please don't kill him. Don't!"

Anthony tossed his gun pouch into the backseat, then took Gail by the shoulders and shook her. "In case he came back! He has a shotgun. I wasn't going to follow him."

She started to cry. "You're not going to kill him?"

"*Niñita. ¿Qué piensas?*" He drew her into his arms, holding her closely, murmuring to her that he was thinking no such thing.

"You wouldn't. Would you?"

"No, sweetheart. Never." He kissed her lips and smoothed her hair back from her face, then kissed her again. "Baby, are you all right? Are you sure?"

"He ruined my ten-dollar panty hose." She laughed, then blew her nose on the handkerchief he gave her. "I'm sorry for dropping your jacket."

"It wasn't your fault." He held her face. "I love you."

"You scare me more than Rusty Beck does. Promise me you won't do anything stupid."

"Of course I won't."

"Promise me!"

He traced an *X* over his heart. "*Te prometo*. All right?"

The moon had set when the wood-hulled fishing boat came out of the channel into the Atlantic. The engine throbbed steadily, and small red and green running lights were the only indicator of its position. A mile off-shore the boat began slowly to rise and fall in the swells of deeper water.

Three of the men on board wore ski masks. Hector did not. He wanted Vernon Byrd to see his face. Before they had knocked him unconscious, Vernon had said *brother*, but Hector was not a brother. Afro-Cuban, yes, but not black. A Cuban would not let himself be called by a ridiculous street name. Peanut. Where was his dignity?

Vernon Byrd was conscious now. Aware of his situation. The ropes around his body were attached to a wire, which ran through a pulley, then to the drum of an electric motor. The pulley hung from the end of a davit that could swing out over the water and back. The equipment was for picking up heavy fish. Not as heavy as Vernon, and the electric motor had made a funny smell lifting so much weight. Another rope ran from Vernon's ankles to a concrete block, which Hector had set on the flat wooden gunwale. Hector had told Vernon that if he moved his feet, the block might fall in, and the combined weight could be too much for the welds that held the davit together.

Leaning against the gunwale, Hector talked to Vernon Byrd, whose bare feet dipped in and out of the sea as the boat rocked. Vernon Byrd only listened; duct tape had been wrapped around his mouth and head. Hector told the man what they knew about him. His family. His failed career as a boxer. His time in prison. The woman he kept that his wife didn't know about. What they would do to her. It was better not to say too much. Let his mind work.

The starlight let him see Vernon's face.

"Don't cry, Peanut. We aren't bad guys. We give you a choice." Hector took some money out of his coat pocket and focused the beam of a small flashlight on it. "Look, Peanut. You see this? A thousand dollars. It's for you. What do you choose? This? Or you want to go swimming? Which one? This?"

A nod.

"Very good. This lady I told you about, you go to her office, you sign the affidavit. If she says go to the court and testify to the judge, you go. It's easy. You say, your honor, there was no confession. I wanted to make a deal with the police, maybe they recommend parole, let me out early. That's the truth, isn't it, Peanut?"

He nodded.

"Tell the truth, you get the prize. But if you fuck up, you get something else. Will you remember what I have told you?"

Another nod.

"I want to be sure." Hector pushed the concrete block overboard. There was a splash, and Vernon's feet jerked downward. Muffled screams came from under the duct tape. Hector made a small motion with his hand. The electric motor hummed. The wire paid out, and Vernon disappeared. Water churned.

Hector took off his glasses and wiped salt water off the lenses. Put them back on. Waited. Watched the bubbles.

"Arriba."

The motor reversed, straining. The boat tilted. Vernon's chest was heaving. Hector motioned again, and he sank to his neck. "Will you remember, Vernon?"

The duct tape across his mouth went in and out. He nodded wildly. A wave splashed over his head.

Hector told the men to bring him in. The motor smoked. Vernon Byrd came up, and they swung the davit. Hector cut the rope to the concrete block. The rope snaked over the side and vanished into black water. Vernon Byrd slid to the bottom of the boat like an immense fish.

Icy pinpoints of stars glittered above the eastern horizon. No sound but the distant *shush* of waves on the beach. Anthony didn't know what time it was. A couple of hours before dawn, probably. Wrapped in the thick hotel robe, hands in its pockets, he sat on the balcony outside his room.

The alarm was set for six o'clock so that Gail could be back in her own room before her mother and daughter awoke. They knew she was here, but it was a matter of courtesy, Gail had said.

She had fallen asleep in his arms. Anthony had not slept. He had stared at the ceiling thinking of what to do about Rusty Beck.

When Gail had undressed, he had noticed

the bruise on her thigh, a purple blotch as wide across as a man's fist. Gail had said never mind, it's nobody's fault. An accident. *I can't deal with this now.*

To calm her, Anthony had let it go. He had taken her to bed and put a soft kiss on the bruise, then a kiss for the other thigh, one for each hipbone and breast, hiding his rage in passion.

What to do.

It would be useless to rely on the police. Useless and unimaginative. Anthony had come up with a dozen ideas of what to do with Rusty Beck, knowing he would follow through on none of them. Gail had enough on her mind, not to worry what he might do.

Do nothing. Except to ask Hector to keep an eye on her.

Restless, Anthony got up and walked to the balcony railing. The tiled patio was cool under his feet. How black the sky. Sooner or later lights would wash out the stars, and concrete would fill in the green spaces, as it did on the rest of the coast.

He rested his arms on the railing and thought about McGrath. For the first time, he thought that Gail could be right. McGrath could have brushed Amber aside if sex had been the only thing between them. But if Amber's husband had helped McGrath commit some crime, and if Amber had known about it, and this knowledge had jeopardized his plans for River Pines, then yes, that could have been fatal.

Why wasn't Gary dead too? He had kept his mouth shut.

Anthony couldn't see Whitney McGrath attacking a woman with a knife. He would have sent someone else. Twelve years ago, had Rusty Beck kept his hair long? That would be something to check out.

But something didn't fit. The sexual connotation of twenty-seven stab wounds to the central body mass. So much blood. And the red satin panties dangling from one ankle. Only a man obsessed would have done that. A rage so intense it had driven her crucifix under her collarbone.

Pacing back along the railing, tapping his hand along its surface, Anthony found himself once more thinking of Gary Dodson. He hadn't been able to satisfy his wife. He had compounded that weakness by being fired from his job at the Palm Beach law firm and failing at his own practice. Amber had been infatuated with McGrath. Gary was jealous. In the kitchen that morning they had argued. Gary exploded. He reached for a knife. Simple. Except that he had an alibi. So far.

The breakers appeared as intermittent flashes of pale gray in the darkness. Anthony watched them for a while. *"Cara'o."* He scrubbed his hand through his hair and squinted his eyes shut. He had sworn to himself not to become involved in this damned case, but he had to, if only to get Gail out of it. She was prepared to go down every last cul-de-sac in the maze. She would bash herself against stone walls for Kenny Ray Clark. And time would run out.

What to do.

"Anthony?"

He turned and saw her sitting up in bed.

"Here I am." He left the door open for the sound of the sea and came back inside. "I was looking at the stars."

"Are they still there?"

"Every one."

She lay back on her pillow. "I couldn't remember where I was."

"You are here with me. Always." He undid the belt to his robe.

Grasping the edge of the comforter, he slowly pulled it away, watching her soft curves appear. His senses were intoxicated, coming over him in waves. He buried his face in her. He could die drowning in her sweetness.

3/14/01

Dearest Gail,

I hope you can read this, I'm writing it by the light of the TV. I told the guard to turn the sound off and just put on the picture. You know on death watch they put it outside the cell, right? He asked me if I wanted a cigarette or a soda. It's funny that since this warrant is hanging over my head they treat me alot better. At our meeting the other day you asked me how I was feeling. Truthfully I'm a wreck. Before you came I was used to the idea of dying although I didn't kill anybody. Now I can't sleep and I can't eat because I keep thinking I might get out of here, and if so what would I do my first day of freedom? Stay out of Martin County for sure. Only the Man Upstairs knows how this will all turn out but I have my fingers crossed.

Kenny

CHAPTER 17

Tuesday, March 20

"Maybe he'll talk to me. They haven't been his lawyers for years, Larry. Don't go into detail, just ask him to call me."

Larry Black was a senior partner at Gail's former law firm, Hartwell Black, one of Miami's most established. Larry had contacts throughout the highest stratum of the legal profession, including, as it turned out, Hadley and Morgan of Palm Beach, erstwhile counsel for J. Whitney McGrath. Larry had gone to law school with one of the partners, William Shumway. Gail wanted to know from Shumway why his firm had fired Gary Dodson. Whatever he told her, if he told her anything at all, might not help, but the thread was there, and she couldn't let it dangle.

"All right, I'll see what I can do," Larry said. "And Gail? If you want to come back to the saner side of the practice, let me know. The door is always open."

"Thank you, Larry."

She hung up and made a check mark on her list. She tacked the sheet of paper back onto the bulletin board that now hung on her office wall. Boxes were shoved underneath the folding tables that ran along the other side of the room. On top of the tables were stacks of papers that would eventually be part of the many copies of various motions or petitions to be filed in any of four separate courts. Legal opinions, police reports, affidavits . . .

The snitch, Vernon Byrd, had signed his affidavit yesterday. He had driven all the way down from Stuart. Gail didn't see why Jackie had warned her away from him. Mr. Byrd had been cooperative, even apologetic. He had said he would be happy to testify for Kenny Ray Clark.

The gloom Gail had felt over the weekend had lifted. She walked slowly past the papers laid out on the table, taking a mental inventory. Byrd's affidavit. The affidavit from Tina Hopwood giving Kenny an alibi. More alibi affidavits from two men who had seen Kenny Ray at Lougie Jackson's house in Port St. Lucie the morning of the murder. Affidavit from Bess Grigsby, who knew of trouble between Amber and Gary. FBI studies showing rates of error in eyewitness identification.

Gail hoped to hear from Vivian Baker, former director of sales at River Pines, to see what she knew about McGrath and Amber. Hector had located her working at an interior design studio in Richmond, Virginia. Gail had left messages, but so far, nothing.

Go to Florida State Prison on Friday, get the client's signature on the motion under Rule 3.850. Spend the weekend putting it together. File the motion on Monday, argue it on Wednesday, March 28. Possible denial, go to Florida Supreme Court, oral arguments on Monday, April 2 —

The execution was set for April 11.

The thought sent a tremor through her, and she leaned on the table for support. Kenny had written her this week. He'd said she had raised his hopes — the very thing he hadn't wanted. What a cold wind it was that howled in the gap between hope and despair.

An hour or so later, working at her computer on the petition for *habeas corpus*, Gail heard a knock at her open office door. Anthony held up a box. "Time for lunch."

"You brought me lunch? That's so sweet. Come here, let me kiss you. Just one, though. That's all I have time for."

He pushed the door closed with one perfectly polished black shoe. He was dressed in charcoal gray Brooks Brothers. His stealth suit. He'd been negotiating a plea in federal court this morning. She stood up and they met over the desk. He put his hand around the back of her neck and held her there, making it last.

"Okay, okay, that's enough." She smiled and sat down, working on the brief for the Florida Supreme Court while he unpacked the box. Prime rib, baked potato, salad, bread. "I can't eat all that!"

"You're losing weight," he said. "I noticed at the hotel last weekend. You bruised me with your hipbones." He withdrew an envelope from his inside pocket. "Read this. I appear to have been wrong about Gary Dodson."

Gail stopped typing and turned around to look at Anthony. "You? Wrong?" She took a letter from the envelope. It had been signed by a Dr. Kevin Mannheim, the forensic pathologist.

Anthony summarized. "Mannheim won't pin down a time of death, but he went over Dr. Snyder's detailed notes on air temperature, body temperature, the victim's size, degree of blood clotting, and so forth, and based on that, and on the autopsy photos, Mannheim can't say that Snyder was wrong. Snyder's opinion was that Amber

Dodson died between 10:00 A.M. and 2:00 P.M., and Mannheim finds it entirely consistent with the evidence." Anthony dropped a pat of butter onto his potato. "Go ahead. Say 'I told you so.' "

With a dismissive wave, Gail read the letter herself. "Well, well. Gary is in the clear." She lifted the letter to look at the invoice attached. "Twelve hundred dollars?"

"He gave us a break because he knows me. You have the money, don't you?" He pointed with his plastic knife. "Eat, it's delicious."

Gail dragged the carry-out container close enough to eat while she worked. "I'll ask Miriam to mail him a check." In a couple of weeks, she added silently.

Anthony stood up and swiveled the computer monitor so she couldn't see it. "We're going to talk, and I want you to pay attention. This is important. A friend of mine, Al de la Torre, has experience in capital appeals. He would be glad to file a notice of appearance as co-counsel in the Clark case. His fee is negotiable. And no, I am not paying for this. I want you to talk to him. And please don't argue with me."

Gail shook her head. "We've had this discussion already. I'm not giving this case to another lawyer."

"Did I say that?" Anthony held up a hand. "I knew this would be your first reaction, but no death penalty attorney with any choice in the matter works alone. There is too much to do. One person cannot write the motions, prepare the exhibits, take phone calls, investigate the case, study the opposing briefs, argue in court, and at the same time deal with the clerks, the state attorney, the witnesses, and the client. You have less than a week to file this motion, and assuming the judge denies it, and we both expect him to, you will have only two weeks left to move the appeal through the courts. You have *no idea* what this will take out of you."

"Fine. You want to help me so much, you do it."

"I don't do capital appeals."

"You're one of the best lawyers around. You can't do this?"

His expression was stony. "I told you before, I don't have time."

"You can't squeeze it into your schedule? What happened to, 'Anything you need, sweetheart, anything I can do to help. Just tell me.' "

She could see his jaw tighten. He said calmly, "I am going with my grandfather to Cuba on the first of April. I can't put it off."

"Fine. Go ahead."

Anthony threw his napkin on the desk. "This is not a choice between you and Ernesto. I can't do both. I can't do everything. Neither can you, Gail. *Por amor de Dios,* when will you admit it?"

The intercom buzzed, and Anthony scowled at it. "I told her not to disturb us."

"She isn't your secretary." Gail picked it up.

Miriam said that William Shumway was on the line.

An hour and a half in a bubble of quiet, floating up the turnpike. Gail had promised Anthony that on the way to Palm Beach she would think about letting his buddy Al help on the case, if Al could reduce his fees.

She plugged in her cell phone and called the office. "Miriam, it's me. Let's get to work."

Miriam told her that Karen had called to remind her to pick up a video on the way home so they could watch it together. Gail made a note on her legal pad: *Call home re video.* She would ask her mother to take care of it.

Miriam said Ruby had called back.

"Would you mind?" Gail said. "Just see what she wants, okay? And let me know."

Vivian Baker had called.

"Great." Gail wrote the number. "Wait a minute. That area code is in South Florida. I thought she'd moved to Virginia."

She was visiting friends in Boca Raton.

"That's lucky. Now if she'll just talk to me." Gail's messages had only alluded to "an old real estate matter in Martin County," for fear that Vivian Baker would otherwise slam the phone down if she knew Gail wanted to talk about Whit McGrath. "I'll call her on my way home. What else?"

Miriam told her that the photo lab had finished with the crime scene photos, and the balance came to $285. "He says you can pick them up there, or he can send them over to the sheriff's office."

"God, no. Tell him somebody will go by the lab. I'll probably send Hector Mesa, if that wouldn't be beneath him. Call the lab back and ask if they take credit cards."

"One more thing," Miriam said. "What about Key West? Do you want me to call the hotel and get your deposit back?"

"Key West?" Gail remembered the trip she'd promised Karen for spring break. "I can't go. There's no way."

"I didn't think so. What are you going to say to Karen?"

It wouldn't be enough to say, "Mommy

has to work that week." Karen knew there was a client on death row, but Gail hadn't sat her down to explain what that really meant. She hadn't explained that every minute of the day had to be thrown into saving him, and that instead of ambling through the tourist shops on Duval Street she might be at the prison looking through glass at a man strapped to a gurney. "I don't know what to tell her."

For the next hour they worked on the *habeas* petition. Gail used her new headphone attachment so she could talk and drive at the same time.

After Miriam ended the call to work on the draft, Gail jotted notes on a legal pad. Questions for William Shumway. He'd been willing to talk to her over the phone, but she wanted to see him in person. Experience had taught her that more could be obtained from face-to-face conversations.

Her phone rang. She glanced at the caller-ID. *"Hola, chica."*

Miriam said, "The bank just called."

Something was wrong. Gail said, "What?"

"Ay, Gail. The check you wrote to the copy service? They don't want to honor it."

"What? They have to. We have at least eight thousand in the office account."

355

"Not until that settlement check clears. They say you already went past your overdraft limit."

"Oh, my God."

"What are we going to do? I put all those checks in the mail this morning. The office rent and the computer lease —"

"Oh, my God." The road ahead of her blurred for a moment, and Gail took a deep breath. "Okay. Call them back. Get an advance on my MasterCard, as much as they'll give me. Transfer it to the office account."

"Gail?" Miriam's voice sounded tight. "You don't have to pay me right now. Danny and I have enough saved —"

"Of course I'm going to pay you, Miriam. You've been working your butt off. Stop crying." Gail clenched the steering wheel. "Call the bank, let them handle it, and get back to work. I want to see that *habeas* when I get back. Okay? It's going to be all right."

Pressing the END CALL button, Gail began to laugh. She wondered what Anthony's buddy, the capital appellate specialist, was going to say when she told him he had to work for nothing. Thanks, but *adios.*

Hadley and Morgan looked out on Palm Beach's famed Worth Avenue with its pink stucco, tile sidewalks, and topiary in clay pots. The building itself was catercorner from Chanel. Past beveled glass at the entrance and the reception desk tucked behind marble arches, Gail was led up wide, curving stairs.

William Shumway warmly took her hand — "Larry has spoken so highly of you, Ms. Connor" — and asked his secretary, a young man in a pinstriped suit, to bring tea. Shumway's skin seemed suspiciously taut for his age. He wore a soft gray mustache that turned up at the corners, like a smile. He showed Gail to a sumptuous leather chair by a satin-swagged window. Shumway took the divan, where beside him, its head lifted toward Gail, sat an ugly little dog with a wrinkled black face, wheezing through its short nose. Its eyes were not unlike those of its master: brown, lustrous, and sparkling with eager curiosity.

"I must tell you, this is nothing like what comes into *my* office, day in, day out. I specialize in estate planning, so death is always close at hand, but *this*. A client facing the gallows, as it were. My clients are close to the end too, but they are very old, with live-in attendants and scores of relatives circling overhead on black wings."

Gail had laid out the situation for him,

and Shumway leaned toward her. "The rules of ethics will limit what I can say, but I see no bar to my telling you what I know of Gary Dodson's departure from this firm. Just forget where you heard it."

"Of course," Gail said, sipping her tea.

Shumway petted his little dog's floppy, triangular ears. "Gary Dodson was hired in 1984 to work in the branch office in Stuart. He specialized in real estate title examination. He lived in Stuart and had few friends in this office. Mr. Hadley, who's in charge of the big real estate projects, assigned Dodson to River Pines. Around 1985, Whitney McGrath and the other partners of JWM had begun acquiring property in western Martin County. There were dozens of parcels. Most of the land was vacant, although there were some small farms and a few homes. JWM developed part of the property, then in June or so of 1988 applied for a loan with the Bank of Palm Beach for two million dollars to begin building. As you know, to obtain a loan you need clear title. That was Gary Dodson's job, to examine title and assure the bank that JWM did in fact own all the land on which they intended to secure a loan. The bank had its own legal department, naturally, but we've dealt with them for years, and they rely on our word.

"The loan went through. However, one of the paralegals at the bank couldn't find the deed to one small tract, ten acres or so. The owners of record were a husband and wife called Mendoza. Dodson said it had to be an oversight, and he would find a copy of the deed. Several days passed. The bank's title company became impatient, so they checked and found that no deed from the Mendozas to JWM had ever been recorded. Dodson said he'd ask the Mendozas' attorney, who had probably neglected to send it to the recorder's office. Still nothing but excuses. Finally Mr. Hadley demanded to know what was going on. A few days later, the deed appeared in the county records, dated *before* Dodson's title opinion. There was no attorney for the Mendozas. The deed had been prepared by a notary. Mr. Hadley hit the roof."

The dog sneezed and shook its head. Its flat face resembled that of an old man. "This firm has a reputation for honesty. Mr. Hadley wanted to make sure that the Mendozas had actually signed the deed, that it wasn't . . ." Shumway seemed unable to say the word.

"A forgery?" Gail said.

"Mr. Hadley would have slit his own

wrists in shame. He asked Whit McGrath for proof of payment. McGrath produced a copy of a canceled check made out to the Mendozas. It seemed all right. We had to assume so. But this was *not* the way we do business. Mr. Hadley asked for Dodson's resignation."

"Did Mr. Hadley ever speak to the Mendozas?"

"They moved away. McGrath said they'd moved out of the country. I think they were from Guatemala."

The little dog panted softly, its wide mouth in a pink grin. The tip of its tongue curled up, not down.

Gail said, "When did your firm's relationship with Mr. McGrath end?"

"July of 1988, I believe."

"About the same time that Mr. Dodson left the firm. Was it Mr. McGrath's decision to find new attorneys?"

Shumway hesitated. "I really shouldn't comment."

"Did Mr. Hadley believe that McGrath had directed Gary Dodson to give a clear opinion of title before the Mendoza deed was signed? And then to backdate the deed?"

Shumway straightened his dog's curlicue tail. "I don't think I can comment on that, either."

"It must have been hard to give up such a wealthy client."

"We have many wealthy clients. Many, many."

"And you didn't need one who would jeopardize the firm's reputation."

"Can't comment." The points of Shumway's mustache twitched.

"The firm was forced to accept McGrath's version because there was no other choice. After Gary Dodson left, you severed your relationship with McGrath and closed the books on the matter."

The dog's eyes had closed, and its chin rested on its stubby front legs. "A question for you now," Shumway said. "How is this information, which I have not given you, in any way relevant to the murder of Amber Dodson?"

"I'm not sure it is, but I assume Amber knew that her husband and McGrath were engaged in . . . a possible forgery. Gary was fired because of McGrath. He opened his own practice, but he was failing at it. What if Amber demanded compensation from McGrath?"

Only the lips moved, as if someone might be listening. *Blackmail?*

Gail shrugged. "Gary Dodson has been working for McGrath ever since this firm fired him. Did you know that? He gets the crumbs, but it's enough to keep him alive. McGrath told me that he's been directing his employees' legal work in Gary's direction basically because he feels sorry for him. Based on what you know of Whitney McGrath, does this fit?"

One of Shumway's brows rose sharply. "No comment."

They finished their tea and chatted awhile longer about a few friends whom they unexpectedly had in common. Finally Gail thanked him for his time and promised to keep him posted. Shumway escorted her to the door of his office, and the dog leaped off the divan to trot at his heels.

"Mr. Shumway, could I ask you for one more favor?" Gail had just thought of it. "Does the firm have a copy of the Mendoza deed?" When he hesitated, she said, "The deed is in the public records. Nothing confidential there."

He agreed that she was correct and gave instructions to his secretary. The young man looked up something on his computer, then escorted Gail to the records department downstairs, where he asked the woman in charge to do a search.

Gail went over to the windows, looking out at a landscaped parking lot with at least three Rolls-Royces. She watched a woman loaded with shopping bags get into one of them, put the top down, and drive off.

"Ms. Connor?"

The woman from the records department held up an envelope. Gail took it, thanked her, and opened it as she walked down the hall toward the lobby. A copy of the deed was inside.

Ignacio Mendoza and Celestina Mendoza, his wife, grantors. JWM Corporation, grantee. Legal description. Date: June 23, 1988. But the deed hadn't hit the recorder's office until about two weeks later, July 7. Something was definitely wrong. In the normal course of business, a deed would be filed in the county records as quickly as possible, preferably the same day it was signed.

Gail glanced at the bottom of the document, seeing two indecipherable scrawls on the lines for witnesses.

Her steps slowed. The notary's signature was clear, strong, and feminine, with wide, looping capitals.

Louise Bryce.

CHAPTER 18

Tuesday evening, March 20

They sat in Jackie's Isuzu Trooper in the parking lot of the Flamingo Restaurant on South U.S. 1. Jackie had propped the deed against the steering wheel. She stared at it as though the clear evidence of her mother's involvement could be erased by force of will.

"Apparently no one at Hadley and Morgan connected the name with your father," Gail said, "but he wasn't the sheriff then. If this comes out now, people might notice. I have no idea what was going on, but I have to follow it up." She had made the short drive from Palm Beach to pick up the crime scene photographs. After some debate with herself, she had called her cousin. Jackie said she could meet her; with a rotating shift, she had gone back on days, seven to three.

"It might be that Aunt Lou was the Mendozas' real estate agent. The deed could have been signed and misplaced for two weeks, just as Gary Dodson said."

With a soft laugh, Jackie folded the copy

back into thirds. "Sure. That's what I'd like to think too."

Gail said, "Maybe I should ask Gary. 'Was your wife trying to blackmail Whit McGrath?'"

"If she'd done that," Jackie said, "Whit would have fired Gary as his lawyer."

"Why would Amber care? She was planning to leave him."

"Good point."

"Gary is off our suspect list, by the way. Anthony showed the medical examiner's records to a top forensic pathologist, who said the time of death was accurate, as far as he could tell."

"So you're looking at Whit."

"He's all I've got. I can't ask *him* about the Mendoza deed. He might send Rusty after me."

"Jesus. I can't believe Rusty did that to you and Anthony. I always thought he had a crazy streak, but that's over the top."

"What is it with him and Whit? They couldn't be less alike."

"Only on the surface. Underneath, they're not that different. There's this story, which is probably BS, that in high school they used to hate each other. You know, preppy rich kid versus redneck. One day they went target shooting to see who was better. A wild boar attacked Rusty, and Whit shot it right between the eyes."

"Really." Gail remembered what McGrath had said. "Whit was kicked out of a posh private school in Palm Beach, and his dad shipped him to Martin County High as punishment."

"That fits. Anyway, Rusty and Whit are pretty tight. As long as I can remember, Whit kept horses out at the ranch, and Rusty took care of them. Diddy was friends with Rusty's father, who was a drunk till he got religion. When Diddy decided to sell the ranch, Rusty bought it. He built a house in the woods, near the canal, and he's got this fourteen-foot gator hide over the fireplace."

"Did he shoot it himself? Or strangle it to death with his bullwhip?"

Jackie gave a short laugh. "No, he shot it, right there on the ranch. He's got plenty of room out there, and access by canal, so he can do pretty much what he wants, and nobody bothers him. Whit McGrath, same thing, in his way. Nobody bothers him because he's so damn rich. That's what I mean. They're not all that different."

"Flip sides of the same coin," said Gail.

Jackie played with the end of her braid, curling it around her finger. "Okay, what about that deed? Maybe we could track down the Mendozas and find out what was going on."

"McGrath told his law firm that they cashed the check and went back to Guatemala."

"Then . . . why would the deed be a forgery?"

"It wouldn't," Gail said, "and there goes my theory that Amber was shaking down Whit McGrath. Assuming that Whit is telling the truth."

Jackie looked at her. "And if he's lying . . . where are they?" The way she phrased the question said that the grim possibility of death had already occurred to her. "I don't guess Gary Dodson would tell us."

"I guess not," Gail said.

"You think Whit is giving Gary legal work to keep him quiet about the forgery."

"Well, it's not because Whit's a nice guy."

Jackie asked, "Could I get a copy of the deed?"

"Keep this one. When I picked up the photos, I used their copy machine."

Jackie put the deed in her shoulder bag. Light glinted for an instant on steel: her off-duty weapon. "If the Mendozas are still around, we should find them. I'll run Ignacio and Celestina Mendoza and see what comes up. Maybe someone in the area knows them. The Guatemalans are close-knit."

"Are there a lot of them in the area?"

"Not as many as Mexicans, but yes, some. They came to pick citrus, and some of them stayed illegally. The Mendozas weren't migrants, though, not with ten acres of property. Who's that guy working for you? Hector?"

"Hector Mesa."

"Tell him to call me. The Latinos around here hate badges."

The glass front of the restaurant reflected an orange sky. Gail looked at her watch. "I've got to go. It's late, and I still have another stop to make."

"Gail? Last weekend . . . did Aunt Irene tell you what she and I talked about?"

Irene had told her everything, and Gail knew that her cousin didn't like evasive answers. "She told me your mother had an affair, and that's why your parents broke up. I didn't know about it before."

"The guy was Whit McGrath."

"Oh, no."

"Aunt Irene doesn't know because my mother never told anyone. I sort of put two and two together and came up with Whit. My mother's name might be on this deed because she did it for him."

Gail reached for her hand.

"Mom didn't go around having affairs, according to Aunt Irene. Whit wanted her, he took her. She was a beautiful woman. She was smart enough to figure out what she meant to him, so she broke it off. Dad wouldn't forgive her, though. She never told him who it was. I mentioned it because you're going to see Vivian Baker tonight. If she knew about my mother and Whit McGrath, she might tell you, and I didn't want you to find out that way."

"I'm so sorry this is happening."

"Yeah. What I hope . . . I really hope that if it *is* a forgery, my mother just . . . you know, notarized it as a favor."

"I'm sure that's the reason. Aunt Lou couldn't have *known* it was a forgery. Never." Gail wasn't sure of that at all and could feel the same thoughts raging in Jackie's mind. "I think Whit manipulated her into it."

"Think so?"

"Yes, I do. Really, Jackie, that could be why she broke up with him, because she saw what he was."

"Bastard." She looked around at Gail. "May I go with you to see Ms. Baker? Unless you'd rather work alone. I can understand that, but I'd like to hear what she has to say." Jackie wanted answers, even at the risk of pain to herself.

Gail said, "Sure. You can come."

It took forty minutes to get to the Boca Raton address that Vivian Baker had given her, not one of the fancy condos on the intracoastal but a two-story building a mile inland. Gail and Jackie parked their cars on the street and walked to the gate at the entrance. They could see a courtyard inside with a tiny swimming pool and some concrete tables and benches.

Gail pressed the buzzer for apartment 204 and said who she was. A voice said to wait there. A minute later a thin woman in jeans and sandals and a loose white shirt came down the stairs on the opposite side. She held on to the railing to steady herself. Her dark hair was pinned at the nape of her neck, and tendrils of it had come loose. Gail tried to fit this woman with the description in the police report: an attractive brunette; business suit and diamond earrings.

"Hi. I'm Vivian." She opened the gate. "Sorry, I don't have much time. My friend has some people up there, and we're about to eat." The slur in her words said they'd already had happy hour.

"Is there somewhere we could talk?" Gail asked. They were standing in a dim entryway between the mailboxes and the manager's office.

"Umm . . . over there. Okay?" The patio was deserted, and she led them to one of the tables. The lights were on.

In a brief phone conversation earlier that day, Gail had explained that she was representing a man on death row. She was reinvestigating his case, and an old deed could hold clues. It involved property at River Pines that Ms. Baker might know about. Gail had feared saying anything more would bring an immediate *no*. Vivian Baker had said, "All right. I'll look at it if you think it would help."

As they sat down, Gail introduced Jackie as simply "Jackie, who's working with me on the case." She took the deed out of her shoulder bag. "My client is Kenny Ray Clark. He was wrongfully accused of the murder of Amber Dodson in 1990. You worked with her at River Pines."

"Amber?" Large hazel eyes focused on Gail. "Yes. Oh, my goodness." Her mouth opened. "Amber. He didn't kill her? Your client, I mean. I thought —"

"He didn't do it," Gail said. "His alibi witness was pressured not to testify at his

371

trial. Clark was nowhere near Amber's house when she was murdered, and his execution is set for April the eleventh."

Apparently Vivian Baker was still trying to comprehend this. She frowned, and deep creases ran between her brows. "Oh, my God. What can I do?"

This woman had lied for Whitney McGrath during the original investigation, but Gail couldn't think of a way to keep him out of it. "Next week I have to go into court and argue that my client is innocent. I have to give the judge some other reason why Amber Dodson was murdered. She was working at River Pines, and this deed . . . I can't say it was forged, but something very odd was going on. Amber's husband was a real estate lawyer working for Hadley and Morgan. They were Whitney McGrath's attorneys at the time. Gary Dodson issued an opinion of clear title *before* this deed was recorded and probably even before it was signed. The law firm fired him and severed its relationship with McGrath. You don't work for McGrath anymore. You may still feel some loyalty, but please. If you could give me any information, anything."

Vivian Baker's face, whose red splotches had likely been put there by drink, faded to an ivory pallor. "All right. Let me see it."

Head bowed over the deed, she murmured, "Mendoza. To JWM. Yes, I see. JWM was buying up property."

"Have you ever seen that deed before?"

"No. I wasn't part of that. I sold lots. I showed model homes and matched the people up to architects and interior designers."

Jackie reached over to touch the signature at the bottom. "Did you know the notary, Louise Bryce? She was a real estate agent. Some of her customers bought homes there."

"Louise Bryce. The name sounds familiar, but I can't put a face to it. I guess I'm striking out, huh?" Vivian glanced toward the second-floor balcony. "Is there anything else?"

Gail went on, "Amber Dodson wasn't working at River Pines at the time, but she came back six months after her baby was born. Remember?"

"Yes."

"A friend of Amber's told me that she had an affair with Whit McGrath before she left, and I believe she could have come back because she was still in love with him. Is this true? Were they involved again?"

"No, they weren't."

"Ms. Baker, please."

"It's the truth."

"They were never involved?"

"They *were*, but . . . not after she came back." Vivian Baker pushed a strand of hair behind her ear. Her fingers were trembling. "I'm only here for a week, visiting my friends. I thought I'd get through it without hearing his name. I saw an article in the paper on Sunday. I used it for the dog." She laughed self-consciously. "Amber wasn't sleeping with Whit. Two women in the same office would've been a little much."

Gail waited, then said, "You and Whit."

"Believe it or not. Have you ever met Whit McGrath?"

"Both of us have."

"Then you know. He's probably the most attractive man I have ever met, but dig under that, you find out how evil he is. I thought . . . well, he's just a tough businessman. A man has to be tough. It makes him sexy, all that power. My therapist told me that."

A door opened along the balcony, and music spilled out. A woman appeared. She held a drink in her hand. "Viv? How much longer? The boys are getting hungry."

Vivian called, "Go ahead, start without me. It's okay." After a moment, the woman went back inside, and the door closed. "There's an extra guy up there, but I'm not really interested." She crossed her legs. They were so thin she could wrap her foot around the other calf. She leaned on her knee.

"Whit would have told me to fire Amber, but he was afraid she would embarrass him. At least with *me* he didn't have to worry. I was married. Such a slut." She forced a smile. "I'll talk to you, but that's it. I can't go to court for you. I can't do that. And if you mention my name, I'll deny I ever saw you."

Gail and Jackie exchanged a glance. Gail said, "Fine. We only want to know what was going on. Your name doesn't have to come up."

Vivian looked at them both as if to make sure, then unfolded her arms and drew the deed back across the table. "Mendoza. I remember hearing that construction might be held up because the owners of one little tract wouldn't sell out. These are the people? Ignacio and Celestina. Only ten acres. Was it a farm? He probably ran them right off the property."

"What do you mean?" Gail asked.

Her voice was as wispy as her body. "They couldn't build River Pines and have little ten-acre farms all over it, could they? If you wouldn't sell, Whit would drive you

375

out. He would send gravel trucks up and down the road all day and night and fill your house with dust. He broke a couple of water lines, always accidentally of course. He told me about it. He thought it was funny." Vivian handed the deed back to Gail. "Does that help? I don't know what else to tell you."

Jackie said, "We're thinking the Mendoza deed was a forgery, and Amber knew about it. Her husband lost his job because of what he did for McGrath. We think McGrath hired him to keep him quiet, but Gary Dodson still wasn't making enough to suit Amber. She came back to work at River Pines so she could get money out of McGrath. Is that possible?"

"Amber wasn't like that. I mean, are you suggesting she would blackmail someone? It would never have occurred to her. No, she was very sweet. All she wanted was Whit. He didn't want her. He wanted . . . he wanted her to leave him alone." Vivian stared at the table, where broken pieces of ceramic tile had been laid in a random pattern. "Oh, my God, my God." Her lips continued to move, then she looked up. "He killed her. If your client didn't do it, Whit did. No, not Whit. He's too smart. He hired someone. Money. That's all you need."

Jackie said, "If she wasn't blackmailing him, why did he want her dead?"

"Listen to me. She wouldn't leave him *alone*. He told me. She called his *house*. His wife answered. That was crossing a line, don't you see?" Vivian looked from Jackie to Gail as if comprehension would surely dawn on them. "He knew she was home that day. Her husband called to say she wouldn't be in. I took the call, and Whit was standing there, so he *knew*."

"What time was the call?" Gail asked.

"About eight. I usually got there at eight, and Whit had a meeting with the construction supervisor that day."

Exchanging a glance with Jackie, Gail said, "So . . . you think he might have had her killed because she was bothering him?"

"You don't believe me." Laughing softly, Vivian Baker wound a strand of hair around her finger. "I bet you don't even believe he was sleeping with me. Do you? You're young and pretty, and you're saying to yourselves, what would Whit McGrath see in *her?* Well, I was forty years old but I looked damn good. I fell in love with him the minute I saw him. He was only thirty. I was married, but my husband was older. You know? I would have done anything for Whit. Anything. One day we were supposed to meet, and he never showed up. When I finally got in touch with him, he said it was over. Just like that. Don't bother coming in tomorrow, I'll send you a check. I didn't believe it. I went to his office, but they said he wasn't there. I left notes on his car. I called and called. I even called his house. Finally he said he'd meet me."

Vivian's soft monotone kept her words in the small circle where the women sat.

"There was a place we used to go, a fishing camp on Whit's property. He said to meet him there. It was about eight o'clock at night, and I could see his car. The door of the house was open, and a light was on. I went inside. Whit wasn't there. It was a friend of his, a disgusting redneck I'd seen at the sales office a few times, picking Whit up to go fishing or whatever. God knows."

"Did you know his name?" Jackie asked.

"I never knew his name, and I don't want to know. He knocked me down and tied my hands and feet, and put a gag in my mouth. Then he sat on the floor beside me, and he had a knife. He said he was going to cut me up, cut my breasts off, then my hands. He unbuttoned my shirt and sliced my bra apart. Then he . . . he held the point of the knife right on my breast. And he said . . . if I bothered Mr. McGrath one more time, then he'd come after me. If I called the police, he would kill me. He would hunt me down and cut me to pieces. Then he untied me and told me to get out. I drove to my best friend's house. I had to clean up. I'd messed myself. I wanted to die."

Pressing her lips tightly together, Vivian paused till her voice came back. She cleared her throat. "I never told my husband. Never. But we were never the same after that. Sam died four years ago of a heart attack. I think I killed him."

Gail felt cold inside, but sweat had dampened the back of her neck.

Jackie said, "The man who assaulted you. What did he look like?"

"It doesn't matter anymore."

"If we ever see him again, it might."

"Skinny. Long hair. Early thirties. I don't know."

"Any facial hair?"

"No. He had a ponytail. I remember that."

Jackie nodded. "Okay."

With a sudden release of air from her lungs, Vivian Baker shuddered and wrapped her arms around herself. "He was there with Whit that day. When Amber's husband called, I mean. I don't know why he was there, but he was. No, wait. Whit came out to give him a bridle or something, for his horse, I suppose. That man was there, so Whit must have told him to go kill Amber. Don't you think so?"

Neither Jackie nor Gail responded to this.

Vivian was still trembling. "I'm leaving tomorrow. I won't come back here again, ever. Stay away from Whit McGrath. Don't try to accuse him of murder, because he'll destroy you and get away with it. He gets away with everything."

They leaned against the side of Jackie's truck for several minutes without speaking. A television was on somewhere. The apartment building was quiet, no one going in or out the gate.

"That was some story," Jackie said.

"I believe her."

"Yeah. Good old Whit." Jackie turned around and kicked her tire. She was wearing her cowboy boots. "Son of a bitch. Son of a *bitch*." Her braid swung on her back.

"Jackie."

She put her hands on her hips. "I'm okay."

"You don't have to get involved."

"I already am." She walked slowly back and forth. "What about Whit killing Amber because she wouldn't leave him alone? Do you believe that?"

"No, but Vivian does. I can't see Whit going that far. A threat, maybe, but murder? He would have just paid her off. Jackie, when did Rusty start wearing a beard?"

"A beard? A couple of years ago, I guess. Why?"

"Mrs. Chastain — Amber's neighbor — saw a clean-shaven man in the yard."

Jackie hooked her thumbs in her back pockets. "But she might have seen Lacey Mayfield, too. You said she could've gotten all the details confused?"

"Maybe she didn't." Night had fallen. Gail stared at the lighted windows in the apartment building. "Rusty was there at the sales office when Gary Dodson called. That's interesting."

"Because Whit could send him right over to Amber's house?"

"Yes, that, but what if Whit didn't send him? What if Rusty had his own reason to want Amber dead? I wonder who he sold his property to? I mean the land he inherited from his father."

The thought registered on Jackie's face. "I bet he sold it to Whit's company. I don't know for sure, but it wouldn't surprise me."

"Me either. Is he — or was he in 1989 — part of that corporation, JWM? If so, he'd have something to lose if Amber opened her mouth about the forgery — assuming it is a forgery. I'll check state corporate records, but they might not name all the principals. See what you can find out, okay?"

"Sure. You still want me to track down the Mendozas?"

"Definitely. If they signed the deed, there go all our theories about who killed Amber Dodson."

"Tell Hector to call me."

"He'll do it tonight." Gail reached into her purse for her car keys. "I just had this wild thought that we're finally getting somewhere."

"Hey, Gail? If you want to leave the crime scene photos with me, I can take a look at them."

"Would you? I don't have much time, and you're better at it than I am."

"It's a good idea," Jackie said, "not to speculate too much until you're sure of the evidence."

Gail unlocked her trunk. The photographs were packed into a banker's box. She hadn't looked inside but assumed that some of them were hideously graphic. Jackie asked for copies of all the police reports too, and Gail promised to fax them.

The cousins embraced tightly before Gail

got into her car. Jackie told her to be careful. A few minutes later, heading south on the interstate, Gail found herself glancing into her rearview mirror, looking for the high, bright headlights of a black pickup truck.

CHAPTER 19

Tuesday night, March 20

Jackie carried the box of crime scene photographs toward her apartment over the garage. She had one foot on the stairs when she heard the sound of water hitting foliage in the side yard. The light from the house revealed a ghostly spray and a shapeless old bathrobe. She set the box on the bottom step and walked over. Her grandfather was standing under the oak tree with a garden hose.

"Hey, Diddy."

"Evening, officer." He slowly moved his arm back and forth. Drips ran down his forearm into his sleeve. "What's the news?"

"Not much. It's a little late to be out here watering, isn't it?"

"Ain't rained in two weeks. The grass is all dry."

She checked to see if he had his shoes on. He did: a pair of moccasins with sheepskin linings. "Is Dad in his study?"

"I believe he's on the porch."

"Diddy, back in 1988, was there a family that lived out west of the turnpike named

Mendoza?" Jackie had noticed that her grandfather's memory of the past was often as sharp as her own recollection of what had happened only weeks ago. "The land would be in River Pines now. Their first names were Ignacio and Celestina."

"I don't know nobody called Mendoza."

"Back in 1988 you don't?"

"Was they pickers?"

"I don't think so. They owned ten acres."

"Don't come to mind. Why do you want to know?"

"It's a case I'm working on. It's kind of important. If you think of anything, tell me, okay?"

"Ten-four. I hope we don't get another dry summer. Remember all them fires last year?"

Jackie took the hose from him and tightened the nozzle so it wouldn't drip. "Don't stay out too long." She kissed his cheek and went in search of her father. At night he liked to sit on the porch and smoke. Her mother had never allowed it in the house, and he had never broken the habit of going outside to light his pipe, turn on a lamp, and read.

The porch wrapped around to the back of the house, which faced the river. Her boot heels sounded on the wood floor, and when she turned the corner, Garlan was already looking up from his issue of *The Sheriff's Star*.

She sat in the next chair. "Can I talk to you for a minute?"

"Sure, honey."

"I was with Gail just now. She gave me the crime scene photos in the Dodson case to look at. I'm going to help her out. I believe her client is innocent."

Garlan tossed his magazine onto the ottoman next to his sock feet. "I thought you were staying out of this."

"It's hard to stand by and see a man get executed for something he didn't do. If you'd like, I can tell you the facts."

"I believe I have a pretty good grasp of the facts, since the case was directly under my supervision. That doesn't matter to you, that it's my case?"

"Yes, sir, it does. That's why I'm telling you straight-out."

He lifted his brows. "Thank you for being so up-front."

"Clark has an alibi, Dad."

"According to who? An ex-drug addict with a felony record? Did you talk to this woman yourself?"

"No. Gail did."

"Gail did. Good lord."

Jackie hadn't thought this would be easy, but her words weren't coming out anywhere near the way she'd expected them to. "I believe Ron Kemp thought he was right, but he leaned on the witness too hard. He scared her off, and it contributed to the conviction of an innocent man."

"You're real sure of yourself, aren't you?" Her father seemed halfway between amusement and disbelief. "You're not doing this on Stuart PD time, I hope."

"No, sir. My own time."

"You could get some flak from your fellow officers."

"I don't intend to run around talking about it."

"You think they won't find out?"

"Well, I guess they'll have to think what they want to. That's their problem."

"No. It's your problem. They're going to ask, Whose side is she on? Ours or the bad guy's? They'll say you're soft. As a woman, you've already got that battle to fight. But that doesn't bother you, does it?"

She said, "I'm sorry if it reflects on you."

"I don't give a damn about that. I care what happens to you, Jackie, even if you don't. Believe what you want about Kenny Ray Clark, but you can't be an effective officer if you're perceived as trying to undermine a solid conviction."

Jackie stood up. "I wanted to let you know, that's all. I didn't want to argue about it."

"Hold on. Did you tell Gail Connor what you and I discussed in my study last week?"

It so surprised Jackie that this would occur to him that she laughed. "No, Dad."

"Are you telling me the truth?"

"Yes, sir, I am." She felt the blood in her face. "I've never lied to you."

He continued to look at her.

She said, "If you don't trust me, maybe I should move out."

Her father picked up his magazine. "This is your home. Do as you please. You're making your own decisions now." Smoke drifted up from the ashtray. He took his pipe off its holder and stuck it between his teeth.

The branches of the oak trees shifted in a sudden puff of wind, and light seemed to dance through the leaves. The moon was out, glinting on the water. Jackie thought about her mother. Curling up in a chair with her drink. *Isn't the river beautiful with the moon dancing on it like that? Come over here, baby, and sit with me.*

"I guess I'll see you in the morning, Dad."

"Good night."

★ ★ ★

Coming across the side yard, Jackie had her head down, and she didn't notice someone sitting on the garage stairs. When the figure shifted, she jumped back, gasping.

"Diddy! You scared me. What are you doing here? I thought you went to bed."

"You was asking about Mendoza. It came to me." The fabric of his pajamas had become thin and soft. He rested his veiny hands on his knees.

"They was a migrant family, a husband and wife, her old daddy, and a teenage boy. They stayed in a little house out at Charlie Beck's grove, and picked his fruit. Charlie got cancer real bad and found Jesus on his way out, and he gave them the property. I went to see him in his last days. He told me about it."

"Rusty's dad? When was this?"

"Oh, let's see. Charlie died around Thanksgiving, 1987. I took him some turkey and dressing, but he couldn't eat it."

"Where are the Mendozas now?"

"Never heard nothing else about 'em."

Moving his plaid robe out of the way, Jackie scooted in beside him on the step. "The Mendozas lived on the property that Charlie Beck owned."

"Yep. He gave them some of it, where the house was. He was going to give the rest of it to the church, but he died before he could get around to it, so it went to Rusty."

"Who did Rusty sell it to? Whit McGrath's company?"

"Sure did, soon as the probate went through. He got four thousand dollars an acre. I remember when land out that way was going for two or three hunnerd." Diddy pulled on his ear. "I told Rusty he could get the groves back in shape, but he said he didn't want to be a farmer, might as well sell it."

"Do you know if he was ever part of the JWM Corporation?"

"What's that?"

Jackie reminded him. "They developed River Pines. Whit McGrath is the general partner."

"Is that up near Vero Beach?"

"It's out west of the interstate, Diddy."

"That's right." Diddy laughed. "I can't see Rusty in no corporation. He don't wear a suit and tie too good. I borrowed him one to wear to his pa's funeral. He didn't even want to go. He and Charlie hadn't talked to each other for years. Poor Charlie. He was a good old guy."

As Diddy talked on about Charlie Beck,

facts began to settle in Jackie's mind, creating connections. Rusty Beck and the Mendozas. The Mendozas and Whit McGrath. A forged deed. Amber Dodson's murder.

"Hey, Diddy, do you remember what kind of truck Rusty was driving in 1989?"

He stared blankly down the driveway for a minute, then nodded. "Sure. It was a 1988 Ford One-fifty. Brand-new, loaded. Before that, he always drove used trucks, but this one he bought right off the lot. He has that big black one now, bought it new too. A waste of money, if you ask me."

"What color was his other one?"

"Blue."

"What shade of blue? Light? Dark?"

"Kind of a midnight blue. A real nice paint job. Rusty bought it after he got the money off his daddy's land. He didn't have two dimes to rub together before that."

"Did Rusty get into any accidents in that truck?"

"Let me think." Diddy's wrinkled eyes squeezed shut. "He had to get the front bumper replaced. I believe he said somebody ran a red light, and they dented the bumper. Kind of picky of him to get a new one, but he loved that truck."

"Anything else? Maybe fender damage?"

"A lady in a van backed into him at the Wal-Mart and nicked him in the right rear fender. I was there with him. It wasn't too bad. After that, he sold the truck and bought himself another one, a red Dodge, straight off the lot."

Jackie asked, "When did he get rid of the blue truck?"

"Oh, I don't know exactly. You want me to ask him for you?"

"No. In fact, don't mention we talked about any of this, okay? Promise?"

"Ten-four."

"Thanks, Diddy." She helped him up by an elbow and kissed his cheek. "Go to bed."

He patted her shoulder. "You're a good girl, Jackie."

Her apartment was a single large room and a bath over a wood-frame, two car garage. A screen set off the sleeping area and a tiny kitchen took up one corner, but the rest of the space was open.

Jackie picked up the coffee table and set it upside down on the sofa, then pushed her lounge chair out of the way. Her boots sailed toward the bed — thud, thud. She pulled her shirt out of the waistband of her jeans, getting comfortable.

Her plan was to lay the photographs out

on the carpet in a way roughly corresponding to the Dodson house. It took her awhile to open all the envelopes and figure out which group of photos went where. The exterior shots had all been taken at night. Front yard. Street. Rear of house, view of woods. West side of house. Bedroom windows. Old air conditioners through the walls. Driveway and carport. Kitchen door.

Coming in closer. Interior of kitchen. White cabinets, white tile floor. Blood smears and spatter on floor. They'd used a six-inch ruler to show scale.

Interior of living room, dining room. Dark wood chairs, all perfectly aligned. Family room. Sliding door to back patio. Close-ups of white rock fragments on carpet. The expert at the trial had said they were commonly found at construction sites. That was a joke. They were found everywhere.

Jackie sat back on her heels. She'd been out to Rusty Beck's place. It was more like a hunting lodge than a proper house. There were pine trees. Hard ground, white rock coming through the pine needles. The samples taken from the Dodson house would still be in the evidence room. Would they match?

Had Rusty still owned his dark blue

pickup truck the day of Amber Dodson's murder? Could it have been the truck the fisherman saw at the park that morning?

Would Rusty have committed murder for Whit McGrath? Would he have done it to keep from losing a $600,000 deal? No doubt.

He carried a hunting knife on his belt. He had held the point of it against Vivian Baker's breast.

"Stop that," Jackie said aloud. She got up and went over to her refrigerator and opened a soda. "No preconceptions."

A speaker at a seminar had preached to the attendees about that. So many cases screwed up because the cops had an idea going in. Best keep an open mind. Just use your eyes. Pay attention to the evidence. It will speak to you.

She walked around the room looking down at the photographs, which already were taking up most of the floor. Making more room, she moved a stack of books to her desk, where she saw the snapshot taken on Uncle Eddie's boat, Fourth of July, 1988. Louise Bryce, laughing. Her arms around her children.

Tears burned Jackie's eyes, and her throat tightened. She hadn't cried for her mother in a long time. She quickly wiped her cheek on her shoulder, grabbed a pushpin, and stuck the photograph to her bulletin board where she could see it. She stood there looking at it awhile.

She'd hated her mother for leaving. Hated her, when she should have grieved.

Whit McGrath came into her mind. He had destroyed her mother, had seduced and used her. Jackie stopped herself from thinking about him. Anger wasn't good. It could affect your judgment.

Jackie put a frozen dinner in the microwave and went back to the photographs.

Bending from the waist, she laid down the series going from the kitchen toward the master bedroom. The hallway. Bathroom. Baby's room. The crib. Close-up of mattress. Jackie picked that one back up. There were two bottles in the crib. Her first thought was that Amber had wanted to sleep, but she reminded herself: no conclusions. Another close-up, pool of soured milk. The baby had caught itself between the mattress and crib rail, then choked on its own vomit.

Down the hallway. More blood. Some hair. Blood smears on doorjamb, on back of door. Views of bedroom. Light wood furniture, white curtains belling inward at windows, dresser with jewelry box knocked over. Nightstand on its side.

Bed pushed out of its casters. The victim, lying on white sheets, blue comforter. Blood seeping out from body. Red silk panties. Legs parted. No semen, Jackie remembered. Panties had been pulled down postmortem, according to the blood smears. Red silk top pushed up over breasts.

Blood on chest, dark red and clotted. Many slashes, bone exposed. One cut directly through right breast, laying it open.

Clock cord around victim's neck, pulled tightly. Blood on clock, white plastic case. 10:23.

Close-up on face. Mottled gray. Camera flash in her eyes. Blond hair matted with blood. Gleam of a gold chain, disappearing where it sank into her neck.

Violence. The kind of violence that enjoys itself, feeds on itself. A violence beyond cold calculation.

No conclusions, Jackie reminded herself. *Let the evidence speak.*

Irene was in her bathroom brushing her teeth. She looked in the mirror at Gail, waved with her other hand, then bent over and rinsed her mouth. A terry-cloth band kept her auburn curls off her face, which gleamed with cold cream. Her bright blue eyes seemed undefined without their usual coat of mascara.

"Hi, Mom." Gail leaned against the door.

"Have you eaten? There's some pot roast. You look like you could fall over."

"I went through a McDonald's drive-through on the way home."

"Please don't tell me that." Irene pulled some cotton balls out of a crystal dispenser on her vanity. "Did you speak to Karen?"

"She's asleep. Was she awfully mad at me for deserting her tonight?"

"I tried to explain, but it's difficult when there's a list of things I'm not supposed to mention." With quick, sure movements, Irene cleaned her face. "Jackie made the wisest suggestion to me last weekend. She says you should tell Karen what's going on. I agree with her. You don't have to be too explicit, but she should know. Darling, it's not just for Karen. It would take some of the worry off your shoulders. This isn't *your* death row appeal, it's affecting all of us." Leaning closer to the mirror, she patted under her chin. "I think it's time for a little tuck."

She swept the band off her head and turned out the light.

Gail sat on the end of the chaise longue while her mother got into bed and arranged her pillows. A biography of Maria Callas waited next to the lamp.

"I'm overdrawn on my office account," Gail said. "The bank is getting nervous."

"Oh, no. How much?"

"It's hovering around three thousand dollars. It would be higher, but I got a cash advance on a couple of my charge cards."

"Darling, don't *do* this. Ruby said she would take care of everything. She told me she had plenty of money. You have to give her a bill."

"She doesn't have anything left. Your and her conceptions of 'plenty of money' obviously differ. Mom, I hate to ask, but if you could help me with this, I'll pay you back when I get things straightened out."

"How much do you need?"

"Five thousand?"

Irene hesitated only a moment. "I'll go to my bank in the morning. Are you sure that's enough?"

"It had better be."

"Does Anthony know about this?"

"Oh, please. He would rub it in so deep."

"You don't give him much credit."

"Yes, I do. He's helping more than I could have expected. If I can just get past the next three weeks."

"You will." Irene patted her cheek. "I'm

so proud of my girl. This is war, and you're just as valiant as any soldier. Kiss me good night, I'm going to read for a while."

Gail had not raised the topic of Aunt Louise's signature, nor did she plan to until she knew for sure whether the Mendoza deed was genuine, or coerced, or a complete forgery. And perhaps not even then would she bring it up. Her mother had only good memories of her sister, and Gail thought they were worth preserving. Not everything had to be revealed.

And yet her mother's advice replayed in her mind as she passed the door to Karen's bedroom. She had tried to protect her daughter and had only built a wall between them. She turned around. The door was open a crack, and she pushed it open far enough to see inside.

The shape under the blanket was absolutely still, as if it were holding its breath.

She went in and sat on the edge of the bed. "Karen?" She waited. "Sweetie? I want to apologize. I'm sorry for not being here tonight or the night before, and working all the time when we went to Stuart last weekend. It's going to be like that for the next few weeks, and I want you to know why. I should have explained before this, but . . . I still think of you as a little girl, and I shouldn't.

"You know about my client, Kenny Ray Clark. You know he's on death row for killing a woman. He didn't do it, but people believe he's guilty. I have to change their minds, but it's so hard, and there isn't much time because the governor signed his death warrant. When you asked me what that was, I avoided telling you. A death warrant gives a prisoner about a month to live, then they put him to death for his crime. Kenny has about three weeks left, and unless I do my best, he's going to die for something he didn't do. Do you understand? I can't let that happen.

"I'm going to Stuart next week to explain to the judge, and if he says no, then I have to fly to Tallahassee to speak to more judges. I hope they'll say stop, let's not kill this man until we're sure he's guilty. Then I'll have more time to find proof that he didn't do it. But the next three weeks are going to be very, very hard, and I won't be home as much. Grandma is going to be here for you. I need your help, Karen. Please do what she asks you to and be good so I don't have to worry. I've got to think about Kenny Clark right now. It won't be for much longer.

"We can't go to Key West for your spring break. I know I promised, and I'm really sorry. When all this is over I want to take you somewhere special, just you and me. Not even Anthony along, okay? Just us. I love you more than anything. Think about what I've told you. Please try to understand."

Karen lay there until she was sure her mother had gone away. She rolled over. There was no one at the door. She heard the shower go on in the bathroom down the hall.

Today she had called her father. She'd asked him if he could fly to Miami and take her somewhere for spring break. He'd said he would think about it. Karen had decided not to tell her mother anything. She would pack a suitcase, and when her dad showed up, she would just leave.

That was what she had planned. Now she wasn't sure.

The shower went off. A minute later she saw her mother walking down the hall in her robe with a towel around her head, and she quickly closed her eyes.

Karen had already searched *death penalty* on the computer at Molly's house, so she knew very well what it meant. They'd found a picture of a gurney. It looked like something in a hospital except it had leather straps. Molly had wanted to do a pretend execution. She'd wanted to flip a coin to see who got to die first. Karen had said no.

She heard her mother's door close. A little while later, her voice. Karen couldn't tell what she was saying, but at this time of night, there would only be one person she'd be calling.

Karen swung her legs off the bed and at the hall looked both ways. No light came from her grandmother's room. Her mother's voice was soft, then louder, then soft again, like she was walking back and forth.

She tiptoed to the door and listened. Her mother was talking about Aunt Louise. An affair. A man so evil he had destroyed her without a second thought.

Karen put her ear to the crack.

". . . can't tell Mother. Seeing Jackie's face was bad enough . . . what he did to Vivian Baker. Oh, God, that poor woman. . . ."

Karen shifted to get closer.

". . . not irrelevant, the Mendozas are my only chance to find the person who killed Amber . . . she was murdered for a *reason*. . . . What do I have? Tina Hopwood's and Vernon Byrd's testimony, and basically that's all there is. . . ."

". . . have to get his signature on the

motion. Would you go with me to the prison? . . . I don't want Hector, I want you. . . . Dammit, don't tell me you don't have *time*. You want someone with no time, look at Kenny Clark, they're going to kill him in three weeks. . . . I *am* calm. I am *fine*. . . . No. No, I'm not fine. Oh, God. . . . Anthony, it's really bad. I need your help. I am so overdrawn I can't pay my bills, and Miriam is working for nothing. I didn't want to tell you, and I would rather die than ask you for money, but I have to. I'll pay you back, but I can't begin to say when. Mother's going to lend me five thousand dollars, but it won't be enough. The evidence isn't enough, nothing's going to be enough. I'm running out of time, and I keep having these nightmares that they'll kill him because I missed a deadline by one day or forgot to cite one case. . . . No, don't come over. Please, it's all right. . . . Really."

She started crying again, and Karen couldn't stand it anymore. She went back to her room and closed the door and sat in bed looking out the window at the street. She would see Molly in the morning at school and tell her about this. No. Molly wouldn't get it. Nobody in the world would understand. Nobody.

After a long time not hearing any noises at

403

all coming from her mother's room, Karen began to be afraid of what might have happened. She had seen a movie where a woman was so upset she fainted and fell down some stairs and broke her neck.

Karen hurried down the hall and opened the door.

Her mother was lying across the bed in her robe with papers all around her. A pencil had fallen out of her hand. Her hair was still damp from the shower. She was asleep.

Karen quietly gathered the papers and put them in a stack, which she set on the desk. She found a spare quilt in the closet.

"Who is it?" The words were all run together, and her eyes barely opened.

"Me." She pulled the quilt over her. "Night, Mommy."

Her lips moved. *Good night.*

Karen turned off the light, but instead of leaving, got into bed and curled next to her mother's side. She whispered, "I'm sorry for being a pain."

There was no answer, only her mother's soft breathing.

CHAPTER 20

Thursday, March 22

It was early when Anthony arrived at his grandparents' house. Digna was still asleep in her room. Ernesto's ancient sister, Fermina, who always rose before dawn, took Anthony to the back patio, where his grandfather sat in a lawn chair reading the newspaper. The nurse had pushed his wheelchair out of view so the old man wouldn't have to see it.

Fermina brought them *café con leche* and guava pastries. The light came through the trees in shafts of mist. The coral rock fountain bubbled and splashed on the ferns that had sprouted at its edge. The air was still cool.

Anthony said, "I am sorry to disappoint you, but I have no choice."

Ernesto gazed through his glasses toward the golf course, visible through the ironwork window in the heavy wooden gate. "People say that when they have *made* their choice. When I saw your face, I had an idea what you were going to tell me. I considered being angry about it. I tried to build up the energy to yell at you, but . . ." His hands went outward in a shrug. "My brain is so moth-eaten that everything leaks out. Even so, I can't say I'm not a little disappointed."

"We can go in May," Anthony said. "I made some calls. It could be arranged."

The old man sighed. "Maybe I should stay home. If I went back to Cuba, would it still be there? I don't know. The older I get, the less I know. When I was your age I had all the answers. Things seemed so clear to me then. Those values in which I believed — the rightness of our position, the evil of theirs, the honor in shedding blood — Where are they? I tell you, old age is a strange place to be in. Everything becomes gray. Everything."

He leaned over to pull a weed from between two of the paving stones. "If the man is innocent, I suppose you have a duty."

"It's Gail who needs me," Anthony said, "not her client. I am sorry for him, but there is little anyone can do. Gail can't accept that. I tried to persuade her to give this case to another lawyer, but she wouldn't. I can't force her, and I was wrong to think she would listen to me."

"They never do. Your grandmother pretends to, but she does what she wants. Years ago, she would lie to me. Now she doesn't bother." Ernesto laughed. "The old girl has her spurs in my ribs now." He reached over and patted Anthony's knee. "Go. If she needs you, go to her. It isn't weakness that draws you, I can see that."

Ernesto finished the last of his *café*. "May isn't such a bad month to be in Cuba. I will try to last that long."

At 10:30 A.M., in the clerk's office of the Martin County courthouse, Anthony filed a notice of appearance in *State v. Clark*. Gail had not asked him to do this; it had been Anthony's idea. Seeing the clerk time-stamp the document, he murmured to Gail, "It feels like getting married. I'm stuck with you now."

She squeezed his hand.

Next they went to Judge Willis's office to inquire about resetting the hearing date for the 3.850 motion. His judicial assistant said the judge would have to approve, and to come back at noon, when his honor came off the bench.

The postponement had also been Anthony's idea. With what they had now — a new alibi witness and a retraction of testimony by a jailhouse snitch — he put chances for success at less than fifty percent. They needed more, and Gail thought she had found it. She had drawn a dotted line from the victim, Amber Dodson, to a forged deed, then to a multimillion-dollar real estate project. Amber had known too much; she had been murdered to insure her silence. The theory relied on the assumption that the deed was in fact a forgery and that Amber had known about it. Aside from Whitney McGrath or Rusty Beck only one person had the answers: Gary Dodson. Gail wanted to talk to him again. Anthony doubted he would cooperate. The other source was the Mendozas. Jackie Bryce had found a traffic citation for Ignacio Mendoza on January 4, 1988, still unpaid. No later information appeared. Hector Mesa was talking to other Guatemalan families in the area to see if any had known the Mendozas. So far, nothing. Gail had said she feared finding them. If they were alive, and the deed was genuine, there was no crime, no motive for murder. No alternate theory of who had killed Amber Dodson. No way to save Kenny Ray Clark.

Gail had thrown herself into his defense with surprising ferocity. Anthony had seen her fight for a client before, but not to this degree. She worked with an astonishing single-mindedness of purpose. She breathed quickly, as though being pursued; ate little;

slept less. When she closed her eyes, the restless movement continued beneath her eyelids.

Through hard experience Anthony had learned not to become so lost in his cases; it was safer that way. He had told her, but she couldn't hear him. She was too far from shore, swimming in heavy seas. He would keep her from going under if he could.

In Judge Willis's chambers they sat at the long table perpendicular to his desk. Anthony let Gail talk. She revealed nothing about her theory of the murder, only that she needed more time to find witnesses.

Judge Willis was turning red to the roots of his white hair. He unzipped the front of his robe as if he needed to breathe. "Unbelievable. You folks sashay in here at the last minute —"

"This is a complicated case that I took on only two weeks ago, your honor. I've had to read several boxes of pleadings, reinvestigate the facts, prepare a 3.850, a brief for the Florida Supreme Court, a petition for *habeas* — I beg the court's understanding. My client's life is on the line."

"Ms. Connor, I've bent over backward for you, trying to be accommodating. This court does not exist for the convenience of the lawyers. You said you would file your papers on Monday, I expect you to do so. I'm hearing this case at two o'clock next Wednesday."

"I won't be there."

"You what?"

"I won't be there. I refuse to be pushed into doing a half-assed job just so everyone can say Kenny Ray Clark had a lawyer and now we can get on with his execution. There are witnesses with crucial evidence, and there is no way I can find them, speak to them, finish the motion, and argue it by next Wednesday. If this court won't allow me sufficient time to prepare, I will withdraw, and you can send an innocent man to his death unrepresented."

Anthony nearly gasped at the brazenness of it. He leaned close to Gail, his face momentarily hidden from the judge, and whispered, "What are you doing?"

Judge Willis stared at her. "This is outrageous."

"Yes, it probably is, your honor, but I have no alternative."

"Are you behind this, Mr. Quintana?" The judge was shouting. "Is this the way you people do it in Miami?"

Anthony felt Gail's eyes on him. "With all due respect, I absolutely agree with Ms.

410

Connor. We need a little more time. For your part, simply moving the hearing date to Friday would demonstrate fairness to the defendant and reduce the chances of reversal."

"I don't give a damn about being reversed." He slammed his hand on his desk. "Get the permission of the state attorney, and I might consider it."

Gail said, "Judge, it's my motion. The state shouldn't have to give their approval."

"Other people besides you are involved here."

"But of course they're going to say no."

"Don't push it, counselor."

Anthony stood up, taking hold of Gail's elbow. "Thank you, judge."

In the corridor Gail leaned against the wall and took deep breaths. Anthony put his arm around her. Gradually she stopped shaking and the color returned to her face.

He said quietly, "Do you want to explain where that came from?"

"Anthony, you know I wouldn't withdraw. I wouldn't. But it worked. Didn't it?"

"You got what you wanted, but you may pay a high price for it."

"What else was I supposed to do? I couldn't file the motion with what we had, and he was going to make me do it! He doesn't care, it's all rules to him —"

"Gail, stop."

"Rules and procedure and his goddamn schedule. Who cares if a man is going to *die?* If it doesn't fit into the schedule —"

"Gail!"

She pressed her fingers to her cheeks. "I have the worst headache." The polish on her nails was chipping off. The delicate skin under her eyes had darkened with fatigue.

Anthony wanted to yell at someone. He wanted Kenny Clark to hang himself in his cell. He had sworn to her not to lose his temper. Had sworn it. He kissed her, leaving his face pressed to hers for a moment, not caring about the glances from other people in the corridor. "Come on, we'll find you some aspirin."

She closed her eyes. "I'm so glad you're here."

Sonia Krause, state attorney for the Nineteenth Judicial Circuit, was a woman in her late forties, gray-haired and physically smaller than Anthony had expected, but in no way less formidable. She had heard of him. She asked if he was going to argue the motion.

"No, I'm here to assist Ms. Connor."

Ms. Krause rocked her chair forward to look at her desk calendar. "So essentially, you want the hearing postponed to . . . let's see . . . Friday, March 30. I have no problem with that. Is eight o'clock all right? We should have a ruling by early afternoon, giving Judge Willis time to fax the order to Tallahassee the same day."

Through a tight smile Gail said, "You obviously expect him to rule in your favor."

Ms. Krause's silver-framed glasses turned toward her. "Every death penalty case that comes out of this circuit comes back to us on a motion to overturn the conviction, but it rarely changes the result."

"Then let's do away with appeals altogether."

"Ms. Connor, we aren't on some kind of crusade to execute your client."

"I know that. It's not a crusade, it's a conveyor belt."

Patiently Ms. Krause said, "I don't like capital punishment, but it's necessary. Life without possibility of parole is a lie because legislators can change their minds and let these people out. There are no recidivists with the death penalty. If we save one innocent life, it's worth it."

Gail moved to the front edge of her chair, and color flamed in her face. "I really don't care about theories. All I'm concerned about is one man, my client, who happens to be innocent."

"You'll have your chance to prove it." Ms. Krause penciled in the new date.

"I'm curious," Gail said. "How can you be absolutely certain he's guilty? You were at the trial. You heard the testimony. An alleged statement to a jailhouse snitch. An eyewitness who was out of town for more than a week before looking at mug shots. Someone who saw Kenny in Fort Pierce at ten-thirty, no blood on him. If he hadn't had such a lousy lawyer, he would have been acquitted. You must know this."

"I've lost quite a few guilty defendants because they had good lawyers. That argument isn't persuasive."

"So you have no doubt of his guilt? None at all?"

"No, I don't." Sonia Krause looked at Anthony. "Is there anything else?"

Gail said, "Do you really believe that? *How?*"

"Thank you, Ms. Krause." Anthony pulled Gail up by an elbow. "We'll see you next week."

On the sidewalk, Anthony said sharply, "Get in control of yourself. I thought she

414

might throw us out and tell us to forget changing the hearing date. You argue with the judge, now the prosecutor?"

"I'm sorry. It was just so *insane*. She can't believe what she says."

"Yes, *corazón,* she does. She has spent years convincing herself that your client is guilty, and that the system works perfectly. You won't change her mind. They never admit they are wrong, not even if you show them a videotape of your client at Disney World when the crime was committed."

He turned Gail toward the parking lot where they had left his car. The day was bright, and he put on his sunglasses. Gail squinted unhappily. "We need to call the Florida Supreme Court," he said.

"I was just thinking about that," she replied. "The death clerk."

"Do you want me to do it?"

"No, I will."

"All right, but don't yell at her."

"I won't!" She opened the passenger door before he could get to it.

The car was hot, and he turned the air conditioner to high. He dropped his head to the headrest.

"I have a message," Gail said, showing him the blinking green message light on her phone. "Maybe they've changed their minds. They're switching the hearing back to Wednesday because I was such a pain in the ass." She pressed a button and looked at the screen. "It's Miriam." She hit her speed-dial. "Hi, it's me, what's going on? . . . Really?" Her eyes went to Anthony. "What did he say? . . . No, I don't. What is it?"

She wrote a number beginning with 561. A local area code. When she hung up, Anthony asked, "Who is that?"

"Whit McGrath. He called about an hour ago." She stared down at her notepad. "He said to call back. I don't know why. Should I call him?"

Anthony thought about it. "Later. Make your call to Tallahassee."

Gail looked at the numbers for McGrath and entered them into her phone. "He's going to inform us that there's a stick of dynamite under your car, and he wants to hear it go off." She put the phone to her ear, listened, then shrugged. Her mouth formed the words, *No answer.* "Mr. McGrath, this is Gail Connor returning your call. Sorry I missed you, but you can reach me on my cell phone." She left the number.

"That's very strange," she said. "I wonder what he wants."

"Call the clerk, Gail, get it over with."

She took her address book out of her purse and turned the pages. "Supreme Court. Supreme Court. I am so eager for more humiliation." She slowly punched in the number and put the phone to her ear. She closed her eyes, and her lips moved.

"What are you doing? Praying?"

"Marcia Turner, please. This is Gail Connor on the Kenneth Ray Clark case." She waited, taking deep breaths. Her hand reached across the seat and grabbed his. Her fingers were cold. "Ms. Turner, hi, this is Gail Connor. I've had to reset the 3.850 hearing to Friday, March 30. The brief for you is due the same day, but I don't think I can have it for you until Monday, and if we could move oral argument to Tuesday —" Her face was bloodless. "I thought it was a *tentative* date. . . . I apologize. . . . Yes, I know they have other cases, but I *can't be there* on Monday. I'm about to find the person who actually committed the crime. My client is *innocent,* Ms. Turner, please, I'm begging you —"

She nodded and cleared her throat. "Yes, that would be fine. . . . Of course I will. You're so kind. I am eternally grateful. And again, my apologies." She disconnected.

Anthony could feel his heart thudding. She was making him insane. He spoke

417

calmly. "When is it?"

"Two o'clock, Tuesday, April third. They had a cancellation, otherwise it would've been impossible. I have to file the brief on Saturday by noon. She said the justices don't like hearing cases so close to the execution date. It puts them under a lot of pressure." Gail laughed. "They have no *idea*."

For the convenience of having a place to work, Anthony had rented a third-floor hotel suite on Hutchinson Island, facing the Atlantic. He and Gail stopped for groceries, then unloaded the car. She had brought along office equipment and several boxes of files. They would drive to Florida State Prison in the morning so that her client — *their client* — could sign the motion. More accurately, the client would sign a page to be added next week, as soon as Gail finished writing the motion.

While she took a shower, Anthony hung up his coat and tie and fixed a drink, a scotch on the rocks. Gail's cousin would soon arrive with the crime scene photographs. She had called to say she had something to show them. Anthony intended to let the women talk while he put his feet up for a while.

The Atlantic was the color of lead. Clouds were moving in from the north, and the beach was deserted. Anthony had just settled into a chair on the patio when the doorbell rang.

"*Coño.*"

It was Jackie Bryce with the box of photographs. He offered a drink. She said she would take a beer. She sat at the counter that separated kitchen and dining area, running shoes on the rung of the high chair. Her sleeveless white top and blue shorts revealed her arms and legs, with their sleek, hard muscles.

Anthony could not decide, even upon this third meeting, what he thought of her. The girl had a tough, cool, almost masculine demeanor that Anthony couldn't easily respond to. She was a cop; he was predisposed not to like them.

Jackie seemed to regard him with the same uneasy appraisal.

He gave her a smile. "Gail should be out in a few minutes." The box sat on the end of the counter where she had dropped it. A few raindrops dotted the cardboard lid. From politeness he inquired, "Well. Did you find anything interesting?"

"There's a few I looked at twice." She pulled the box closer and took out an enve-

lope, withdrawing several color enlargements. She laid one on the counter. "This
shows the supposed entry point, the sliding
glass door. Those rock fragments on the
carpet were taken into evidence. But the
reason they zeroed in on the back door was
that it was off the track. That's what drew
their attention. They found scratch marks
outside, see? Here on the aluminum frame."
She showed him another photograph, a
blowup. "It's not that unusual to have
scratches. Anytime you lose your keys, you
can get in that way, if you don't have a safety
bolt, and they didn't."

"And what is this supposed to mean?"

"I don't know. I'm just saying, how are we
sure it was a break-in?"

Anthony drank his scotch. "Because the
door was off the track. I believe that some
assumptions can be made."

Jackie gave him another photograph.
"This is a close-up of the clock showing the
hands at 10:23 A.M."

The clock cord vanished off the right side
of the frame, presumably toward Amber
Dodson's neck, but the face of the clock was
clearly visible, with smudges of dried blood
across the plastic.

"Your point is that the police assumed
she died around 10:23," Anthony said.

"They were skeptical at first, but setting that aside for the moment, if you are suggesting, and I think you may be, that Gary Dodson set the hands ahead and opened the back door on his way to work to simulate a break-in, there is a problem. Amber died between ten and two. My forensic pathologist could find nothing wrong with the ME's estimate."

"I know," Jackie said. "Gail told me." She rummaged in the box again. "Here's a shot of the body. Notice the panties. They were pulled down postmortem, see how the smears go? She wasn't raped. What if, and I'm just playing with the facts here, what if the killer was trying to make the police think it was a sexually motivated attack that happened between ten and ten-thirty?"

"I can buy that," Anthony said. "Theoretically. What is this next one?"

Jackie held up a wide shot of the bedroom. "Tell me what you see."

"I've seen this one," he said. "The state introduced it into evidence. There's the bed, which is knocked aside. Night table turned over. Lamp on the floor. Book. Framed print on the wall. Curtains. Awning windows. Chair."

"Are the curtains open or closed?"

"Open."

"What about the windows?"

He leaned closer. The aluminum frames tilted outward. "Open."

Jackie put the photograph on the counter facing him. "Lacey Mayfield told Gail that she went around to the side of the house about nine-thirty and knocked on the window to see if Amber was awake. She couldn't see in because the curtains were closed. The windows had to be closed too. If they had been open, she wouldn't have knocked. So the windows were closed when Lacey got there."

Anthony grabbed for a logical answer. "The police opened them later."

"No, the police report says that Kemp asked Gary about the windows. He said they usually slept with the windows open at night, and they were open when he got home."

"All right, but what do you conclude from this?" Anthony did not like to be led along in a blindfold.

"Nothing. It's just interesting," she said.

"One could say, I imagine, that Amber got up, closed the windows to keep the room quiet, and went back to bed. Her sister came and knocked on the glass. When Gary called at ten o'clock and woke Amber up, she opened the windows."

Jackie nodded. "That makes sense." She put the beer bottle to her mouth and tipped it back.

Anthony poured himself a little more scotch. "Theories are useful if they lead somewhere. I don't see where this one is going."

"Maybe nowhere, but Gail got me to thinking, that day at the ranch when she was talking about Amber's sister. The ME said Amber died between ten and two. Lacey gave aerobics classes from ten until four, but she was gone about forty minutes for lunch. The studio was only a mile from Palm City. I checked."

"You suspect Lacey Mayfield?"

"Look at these pictures of the baby's crib. Two bottles, see? One's full, one's half empty. It's probably nothing. I asked a friend at work, and she said that she does that sometimes. Her baby was a big boy, and he'd get hungry, so if she wanted to sleep, she'd fix him two bottles."

Anthony circled his hand for her to go on. "And?"

"Lacey was the baby's aunt. If she killed Amber, she wouldn't want the baby to get hungry before Gary got home." Jackie kept her eyes on him as she took another swallow of beer. She said, "It's just a thought."

"One that we have no time to pursue," he said.

"What I was trying to do," Jackie said, "was to find other scenarios. Gail said she needed some alternative theories to argue in court."

"Do you know, Jackie, you're constructing a good case against Gary? He faked a break-in, adjusted the clock, and put two bottles in the crib because he wouldn't be home until late that afternoon." Anthony lifted his hands, palms spread. "I could have had Kenny Clark acquitted, proposing such a theory to the jury, if I could have made them ignore the medical examiner. But at the moment we need proof, not theories, and the proof lies with the Mendoza deed, Whit McGrath, and Rusty Beck. Or so I thought."

Jackie looked at him coolly. "It's a good idea to keep your mind open."

Twenty-five years old. How fortunate to be that age, to be a police officer, to know so much. Taking another deep swallow of scotch, Anthony became aware that a telephone had been ringing for some moments.

Jackie glanced at her bag. "Is that your phone? It's not mine."

It was Gail's. She had left it in her purse on the table in the dining area. Anthony took it out and checked the caller-ID.

He flipped the phone open. "Yes?"

A male voice said, "Hey, this is Whit McGrath. I met Ms. Connor last Saturday. I guess you must be Anthony Quintana. Do I have that right?"

He set his glass down on the table. "That's correct. Ms. Connor is unavailable at the moment. Why do you want to talk to her?"

"Listen, I owe you folks an apology. I mean it. I got a little stressed at the party, and then a friend of mine who lives out that way called and said he saw some people trespassing near Pines Road, and I said, well, ask them to leave. Then he called me back later and told me who they were — you and Ms. Connor. I should've let it go, and if he inconvenienced you in any way, I'm sorry."

Qué mentiroso. Anthony said, "Thank you for the apology. I should send you a bill for my jacket, which Rusty Beck ran over in his truck and ruined."

Silence. McGrath wondering how they knew the name.

Jackie, who had initially pretended not to be listening, had turned around on her chair. She slid off it and walked toward him.

McGrath's voice said, "Absolutely I'll pay

for it, absolutely. Hey, listen, how about you and Gail coming over to my place tonight? The wife is having some people in, but that's her thing, and I could use an excuse to duck out. We should talk."

Gail came out of the bedroom in jeans and a T-shirt, and Anthony held up a hand to keep her quiet.

"I confess to you, Mr. McGrath" — Anthony pointed to the phone — "that I am curious what it is you want to discuss." Gail's eyes widened.

"Call me Whit. What I would like very much, with all humility, is to ask a favor of you and Ms. Connor relative to that case you're working on. Come on over, say six, six-thirty, we'll have some drinks. It's not far, a little ways down on Jupiter Island. How about it?"

"I'll get back to you after I talk to Ms. Connor. But first I have a question."

"Okay."

"How do you know we are here and not in Miami?"

"How? Ms. Connor's secretary said she was in Stuart."

"Ah. Of course."

Ending the call, Anthony wondered if he had missed spotting the black pickup truck behind them today. He had left his pistol in

426

the glove compartment of his car and thought he would probably go down and get it.

The women were staring at him.

Gail said, "Anthony, what is going *on?*"

He repeated his conversation with Whit McGrath.

For a long moment the only sound was the faraway breaking of waves on the beach below them.

"There's no reason for both of us to go," Anthony finally said. "You have to work on the affidavit for Kenny Clark tonight. I'll go see what he wants —"

"You're not going without me," Gail said. "Whit McGrath isn't going to *do* anything. Not at his house, with his wife and all those people around." Gail looked at Jackie. "You know him. What do you think?"

Jackie stood with her hands in the back pockets of her shorts. "I don't think it's dangerous."

Gail looked back at Anthony, waiting for him to speak. She wasn't waiting for his approval. He picked up his scotch. "I want Hector to go with us. He went to Indiantown today, looking for friends of the Mendozas, but I can have him back here within an hour."

"If Hector is there too, McGrath might not talk to us."

"Hector's being there won't make any difference. We'll go, we'll listen. McGrath wants a favor, but I doubt it's anything we would be willing to give him. He called you, so you take the lead. I suggest we tell him nothing. We don't mention the Mendoza deed, and we don't reveal our suspicions that Rusty Beck killed Amber Dodson."

Frowning, Gail shook her head. "I don't know. It's just so useless to go there and say nothing. What do we gain from it?"

"If you know what he wants," Jackie said, "it would help with your strategy."

"Exactly," Anthony said.

"No," said Gail. "That's not enough." She was breathing quickly again, and color flooded across her pale cheeks. With short, jerky steps, she began to pace. She whirled toward them again. "I'm not going to go over there and do nothing while Whit McGrath toys with us. The man is evil. He thinks he's in control, but he needs to be shoved off balance. Kenny Ray Clark is going to *die* unless we start pushing somebody, *hard*. Why should we hide what we know? Why? There's nothing to lose. Why don't we threaten to turn Whit McGrath in for the murder of the Mendozas? He forged the deed, and now they've disappeared. Do any of us really believe that they're still

428

alive? Or that McGrath wasn't involved in their deaths? Even if the police do no more than investigate, the publicity could ruin him."

"Gail, we can't provoke him for the satisfaction of doing it." For support, Anthony looked at Jackie.

A shadow passed over Jackie's brown eyes, and her face seemed less young than it had five minutes ago. She said, "You should do it. Push him."

CHAPTER 21

Thursday night, March 22

It was past six o'clock when they left the apartment, crossing the bridges to the mainland. Heavy clouds dimmed what little light remained. The bridge to Jupiter Island was several miles farther south.

Gail could hear Hector's voice. He sat directly behind her in the backseat, able to look at Anthony. It was Anthony to whom he spoke. Gail knew she had no status with Hector Mesa.

He had spent the past two days around Indiantown, a one-stoplight town near the canal dredged from Lake Okeechobee, where Spanish was heard as often as English, and migrants lived in shacks without screens on the windows. Hector said he had dressed the part: mismatched old clothes and cheap, dusty sneakers. A harmless little gray-haired Chicano.

He had found a Guatemalan woman named Maria who had known Celestina Mendoza.

"Maria worked at a Mexican market in

Indiantown. Celestina used to go there to shop and to buy money orders to send home. Maria says the Mendozas came to Florida about 1985, after a few years in Texas. First they lived in a camp in Belle Glade, and then they came to Martin County to pick oranges during the season. There was the husband, Ignacio, and Celestina, and their son, Jose, and Celestina's father, Ramon. The boy, Jose, was a teenager but . . . *idiota*. What is that?"

Anthony said, "You mean mentally disabled?"

"Yes. They had another son, but he was murdered by the paramilitary in Guatemala, so they came to the U.S. They worked for the old American man you told me about, and he gave them the property, as you know. Celestina told Maria that a man came to the house and wanted to buy their property, but Ignacio said no. They had moved too many times already, and no more. The man came back and said if they didn't sell, there would be trouble."

"Who was the man?"

"She doesn't know. Maria didn't see Celestina for a long time. She didn't notice at first because they weren't close friends, but then she thought they must have sold the property and moved somewhere else.

She told me the name of Ignacio's brother and the town where Celestina sent the money orders, San Cristobal. I have a friend in Guatemala, and he went to see what he could find out. The brother, Felipe, is dead, but his wife says that after July 1988 the money orders stopped. Ignacio had no telephone, so Felipe wrote letters. Nothing. He was going to come look for them, but he died before he could get a visa and save the money for the trip."

"Rusty Beck," said Anthony.

"*Sí, es seguro.*"

"That's horrible," Gail said. "Beyond horrible. A family murdered for ten acres of land. Do you think they were buried near their house?" She turned her head to hear his answer.

"Maybe. It's too late now to find them. The shopping center at River Pines was built there."

A sharp laugh hissed through Anthony's teeth.

Hector murmured more softly, "*Van a pagar.*" They will pay.

Gail pretended not to have understood. Revenge produced only more violence, but in her current mood, to utter such an opinion would have been the height of hypocrisy.

★ ★ ★

At a small park on the ocean Anthony turned right, and the narrow road took them through a golf course, deserted so late in the day. Gail turned on the map light. Jupiter Island was a long and narrow strip of land that extended south to Palm Beach County. Dense foliage obscured any view of the water. There were no side roads, only driveways. Small signs of a common design contained a last name or sometimes only a three-digit number. A few indicated the service entrance. Some of the houses came into view, but most were hidden behind gates or the curve of a driveway. There was very little traffic.

McGrath had said he lived on the intracoastal side. Gail had expected another immense set of gates but saw only the name and an opening in a hedge of bougainvillea. The initial impression was misleading. The brick-paved driveway led between a double row of royal palms, then to a house that resembled an Italian villa, whose mahogany-framed windows gave glimpses of beamed ceilings, chandeliers, and a curving staircase. A dozen other cars had found places along the circular drive. As Anthony put on his jacket and straightened his cuffs, he stared at the house, and Gail thought he might be sharing her fantasy: a smoldering heap of rubble.

She checked her lipstick in her compact. "Okay, let's go."

Hector, in his dark business suit, trailed a few paces behind, up the wide steps and across a patio tiled in antique terra-cotta. Anthony pressed a buzzer. The door opened almost immediately, and a woman with a French accent took them through the entrance hall, across an indoor courtyard with a fountain and statuary, then up some stone stairs flanked by carved columns. Voices came from below them: a party. The woman tapped at a door, then opened it and stood aside to let them enter.

The room was obviously McGrath's private lair, overdone with dark paneling and red leather. The floor was parquet, the fireplace stone, and horned animal heads decorated the walls.

Whitney McGrath himself, in tux and black tie, his hair boyishly mussed, rose to his six-foot-plus height from the embrace of a brass-studded leather chair. "Hey, come on in. No trouble finding the place, I hope."

There were handshakes, introductions. Hector, introduced only as "an associate of ours," nodded and remained several paces away. McGrath didn't ask what this odd little man was doing here; perhaps he knew. Drinks were offered and declined.

"What an impressive house," Gail said.

"Taylor gets the credit — my wife. She's a terrific decorator. We've been here sixteen years, ever since we got married." McGrath explained about the dinner party down-stairs. Some friends visiting from New York. Others sailing back north. Couldn't spend too much time away from his guests. An hour, and then Tay would send out the search party.

The muscles along Gail's spine felt like twisted ropes.

McGrath's brow furrowed nicely. "First let me offer my most humble, most sincere apologies. Ms. Connor, I am sorry. Mr. Quintana. I talked to Rusty Beck, who gave you that little scare. He's very sorry. So am I. How much was your jacket? How much? Seriously."

Anthony insisted that it didn't matter. He had others; it wasn't that much. Gail knew how much: the suit had cost over a thou-sand dollars, useless without the jacket. She hadn't expected Anthony to accept com-pensation: McGrath's money was toxic.

"Rusty Beck is a friend?" Anthony made a polite smile.

"Yeah, I've known him, jeez, probably

twenty-five years. We were in high school together. He takes a sort of vicarious interest in my property, I guess you could say. That's no excuse for what happened, though."

Hector Mesa's black-framed glasses tilted toward the bristled head of a boar mounted on wood over an ornately carved cabinet. Long, yellowing tusks lifted its snout.

McGrath noticed Hector's interest and grinned. "Ugly beast, isn't it? I got it near Pahokee when I was a kid. In fact, Rusty and I were out target shooting, and this baby came charging out of the woods. It headed for Rusty, and I had to kill it."

Hector walked closer to inspect it. "What did you use? A shotgun?" He reached up to touch the bristles on the animal's left cheek.

"I know, bad choice of weapon, but it was all I had." McGrath opened the cabinet, which lit up when the double doors swung back. The red velour interior shone with the barrels and gleaming wood of a dozen or more large guns.

Gail glanced at Anthony, who shrugged slightly. McGrath showing off his toys. He rummaged through a drawer at the bottom. "Oh, here it is. A Remington auto. I got off one good shot, and that stopped him, then I let him have a couple more. That's why his face is messed up. Most people don't notice that."

"You were lucky to have a five-shot magazine." Hector raised the gun easily, planted it against his shoulder, and sighted down the barrel.

"This one you'd like better." McGrath pointed to another gun standing upright in the cabinet. "It's an Arrieta side-by-side. I picked it up in Spain. Or this. A Piotti, sixteen-gauge, Italian. I had it custom-made."

"Beautiful." Hector murmured something about automatic ejectors and slid his fingers along the satiny, burled wood stock.

Gail wandered to the open French doors, and Anthony followed. Beyond was a balcony, a view of the intracoastal and the mainland a couple of hundred yards away. Landscaping lights illuminated a pool, a dock, a fifty-foot sailboat. The sky had darkened.

His arm pressed against hers, and she felt the warmth of it. Her hands were icy. Softly he said, "Do you want me to talk to him?"

"I think I'm okay." She took a breath. "But if I start screaming, take over."

His lips formed a little kiss. Then he turned to say, "Mr. McGrath, we don't want to keep you from your guests."

Leaving Hector Mesa to continue gazing

at the guns, McGrath brought his drink across the room. They sat in three red leather chairs facing the balcony, Gail in the center. A slab of marble rested on the tops of three Doric columns, probably hauled in from Greece.

McGrath put his elbows on his knees, hands loosely clasped. Onyx studs marched down his pleated shirt. "I think you're like me, you don't like to waste time, so I'm going to get right to the point. You're in Martin County to appeal a conviction in a capital murder case. Kenneth Ray Clark. He murdered an employee of mine twelve years ago, and you say he didn't do it. I happen to disagree with you, but never mind that. I believe that your strategy is to create doubt, and that means creating a doubt about somebody else. I believe you've decided to throw suspicion on me. It isn't fair, and it isn't right. I had nothing to do with Amber Dodson's death. Nothing."

McGrath let out a breath and lowered his eyes. "I'm going to be honest with you. Amber and I had a fling at one time. I don't know how you found out, but you did. I swear to you, it was over, long over by the time she died."

He picked up a framed photograph. Did he usually keep it there on the table? Gail didn't think so. He held it for a while before turning it around. "This is my family. Tay, Melissa, Billy. I love them very much. In the past, I've done some things I regret, but these three people mean the world to me. My wife and kids. I think about what they'd go through, if people started gossiping and pointing fingers, and let me tell you, it scares hell out of me."

Gail glanced over at Anthony, whose dark eyes were steady, as calm as deep water. Certainty flooded through her as though transmitted by a touch.

"Mr. McGrath, I'm sure you care about your family," Gail said, "but let me guess that you're also worried about the vote in the county commission next month. It's going to be close. A couple of the commissioners are looking for any excuse to vote against Phase Two of River Pines."

He set the framed portrait back on the table and looked at Anthony. "I have a question. Who's in charge? Ms. Connor is the attorney of record. What's the deal here?"

"The deal is, it's her case," Anthony said quietly, "but I filed a notice of appearance this morning as co-counsel."

"Okay." McGrath leaned back in his chair. "You don't like bullshit. I don't either. I asked a lawyer about the odds of winning this case. Not good. You know that. At least you do, Quintana. Ms. Connor here is a civil practice lawyer, but *you*. Come on. You know this case is a loser, no matter what tricks you pull, and that includes trying to make me into a scapegoat. You could get disciplined by the bar, trying shit like that, and I would be forced to sue you for slander. But what do I gain? The publicity will already have killed me. You have me in a bad spot, you see? I'm willing to pay to get out of it."

Anthony's casual posture in the chair was the same, but his interlaced fingers tapped slowly on his chin. "What do we do in exchange?"

McGrath spread his arms. "Forget I exist. Don't mention my name. I didn't kill Amber Dodson. I had nothing to do with it, and if you imply I did, everyone will be hurt. I don't want to come after you. I don't. Let's work something out. I can be generous, as long as you keep it within reason."

Gail had learned Anthony's moods. His anger was often signaled by utter stillness, and he was barely breathing. He looked at her. "What do you think?"

"I think he should keep his money."

"Do you? Yes, so do I."

"Show him the deed," Gail said.

Anthony withdrew a copy of the Mendoza deed from his inside pocket and handed it across the low table to McGrath, who unfolded it.

"On June 28, 1988," Gail said, "Ignacio and Celestina Mendoza supposedly sold ten acres to your corporation, JWM. The deed was recorded on July 7. We believe it's a forgery."

McGrath's face had reddened. "What are you talking about? I don't know what this is."

"You needed the property because it sat right in the middle of River Pines, but the Mendozas wouldn't sell. And then they disappeared. There are no traces of them after July 1988, and their family in Guatemala haven't heard from them. Gary Dodson had this deed recorded for you. He was fired from Hadley and Morgan because of it, and the law firm ended its relationship with you, but you continued giving Dodson scraps of legal work. Was it to insure his silence? We believe that Gary told Amber everything. What she learned about the Mendozas made her dangerous to anyone with an interest in River Pines."

"Are you out of your fucking mind?"

Gail's mouth was dry. She wished she had

accepted the offer of a drink. "We believe we know who killed Amber Dodson, and so do you. The morning Amber died, the woman across the street saw a man with long hair and a denim jacket going behind Amber's house. A fisherman at a park nearby saw a dark-colored pickup truck with fender damage. Rusty Beck owned a dark blue truck at the time that had been in a minor accident about the same period. Amber was stabbed to death with a hunting knife, and he carried one on his belt. He still does."

The image of Vivian Baker on the floor of the cabin came into her mind, but she had sworn not to mention her name. "Rusty Beck is a violent man. We had wondered if you had sent him to threaten Amber, make her back off. You had bought Gary Dodson's silence by giving him legal work to do. Amber was planning to leave Gary, and she could have been a problem for you. But her word would have been nothing against yours, and besides, you're too smart to have someone murdered in the middle of the day, in her own neighborhood. Rusty Beck isn't that smart or that careful. If it came out that the deed was forged and the Mendozas were dead he had a lot to lose. So do you. The police would assume that you were somehow involved not only in Amber's murder, but the murder of the Mendozas. You have two choices: Give us Rusty Beck or go down with him."

McGrath stood up, looming over her. "You bitch. Get out of my house. All of you." He suddenly focused past Gail's shoulder, and she glanced around to see Hector Mesa standing a short distance away. His hands were loosely clasped at the front of his open jacket. The lamplight reflected off his glasses, obscuring his eyes.

"Let her finish," Anthony said.

The blood in Gail's head pounded against the bone. "We're willing to forget about the Mendozas. We're willing to forget that you benefited from their deaths. What we want from you is a phone call to Governor Ward. He's a friend of yours. He'll talk to you. Tell him that Kenny Clark is innocent. Tell him that you believe Rusty Beck killed her. Say whatever you like. Say that Rusty Beck confessed, or that you've just figured it out. Say you can't live with yourself if you let an innocent man be put to death. I don't care what you say, as long as the governor issues a stay of execution for as long as it takes to do a proper investigation."

McGrath was breathing as if he had just run up the stairs.

"If you refuse, we will make everything public. Everything. The Mendoza deed, the disappearance of four people, and your connection to Amber Dodson. People will say you ordered Rusty Beck to kill her. The vote in favor of Phase Two will probably be as dead as she is. Think about it, Mr. McGrath." She stood up, and Anthony rose with her. "You don't have to give us an answer now. You know my number. Call before the weekend is out."

A light rain was falling, silvering the windshield. Gail trembled, and her jaw was so tight her teeth chattered. She dropped her forehead into her hands.

As Anthony closed her door and went around, Hector's voice from the backseat said, "That was very good, *señora*."

She laughed weakly.

Anthony got in, started the engine, then leaned over and kissed her. "You were beautiful. Let's get out of here." At the road he waited for a car to pass, then pulled out, heading north. "I want a drink. And a steak, very rare."

Drained of energy, Gail couldn't speak.

Hector's voice came from the dark. "Did you see the guns he had? That Piotti you can't buy for less than twenty-five thousand dollars. Such beautiful wood. I've never seen a gun made so well. Like a piece of art. But you know, he ruins them. They all have his name engraved on them, every one, even the old Remington. *Qué bárbaro.*"

Gail took a long breath. "He won't go for it. Why should he? We can't prove the Mendozas are dead, and if we can't, he will sue us for every dime we have, and he'll win. He's got to know it's a bluff."

"We'll see," Anthony said. "We'll wait and see."

"I have to talk to Gary Dodson," Gail said. "He stays in that office like a prison, afraid to come out. Now I see why. I have to get through to him, Anthony. Even if he doesn't testify, if he would just tell me whether Amber knew. What if she didn't, and McGrath *knows* she didn't?"

"Gail, let it go." He picked up her hand and pressed it to his lips. "Please. You had him completely rattled, so let's wait and see what he does."

"God, my head is killing me."

The tires hissed on the wet road, and taillights appeared from a driveway some distance ahead, turning in the same direction.

A car behind them threw light on the rearview mirror, making an oblong patch of light across Anthony's face. His eyes shifted to her. "Gail, I have to ask you something. It's been bothering me for a couple of days now. Do you remember, when we were talking to Tina Hopwood, she told us that on Friday, the weekend of the Fourth of July, 1988, Kenny Clark and Tina's husband — What was his name?"

"Glen."

"Yes. She said that a man gave Glen a hundred dollars to chase some migrants out of an orange grove. Glen took Kenny with him, and they came back covered in dirt. They refused to talk to Tina about it. She said she was afraid of what had happened."

Gail sat silently for a few seconds, then said, "Yes. It occurred to me too, but I put it out of my mind. It's unbelievable to think that Kenny was involved in that. I don't think I could handle it if it were true."

"Yes. An unbelievable coincidence." Anthony reached up to adjust the mirror, but his eyes remained focused on it. He glanced in the sideview mirror. "Hector. *¿Qué hay atrás?*"

The headlights were on high beam.

"No puedo ver," Hector said.

A car coming the other way passed by, and the brief flash of light illuminated the vehicle behind them. Hector said, *"Una camioneta negra."*

A black pickup truck.

The cry that came to Gail's throat caught there. The Cadillac leaped forward, pressing her body into the leather seat. The speedometer moved toward seventy. The lights dropped back for only an instant, then closed in. "Oh, my God. Anthony, we can't go so fast on this road!"

The taillights ahead of them were rapidly growing nearer. The Cadillac swept around the slower car, and the high-pitched beep of a horn faded away. Low branches clattered on the roof of the car. The headlights grew brighter, then shifted. The truck was coming alongside. Two sets of lights pierced the blackness, and the narrow road rushed toward them. The speedometer was at eighty. The black truck seemed to fill the windows on the driver's side, and only a few feet of distance separated the vehicles. Rain streaked the glass.

Hector said something in Spanish to Anthony about releasing the window lock, then moved to the left side of the seat and pressed the button. The window slid down, and air and the noise of engines and tires rushed through it. Hector put his hand into his jacket.

Anthony reached under the front seat. His pistol was already out of its leather pouch.

Gail stared at it. "Oh, my God."

"Déjalo pasar," said Hector.

Anthony braked, and the Cadillac slowed, throwing Gail against her seat belt. Mist swirled from the truck's tires. Taillights glared, and the truck fell back into the left lane, engine popping. Anthony slowed to forty, thirty. He accelerated again, and the truck kept pace. Gail heard country music coming through the truck's open window.

Someone laughed. "Hey, slick! What're you trying to do, man?"

Anthony shouted to Hector, *"Tira la goma."* They were going to shoot out his front tire. Hector stood on his knee and aimed out the window. She saw a flash, heard a gunshot. The light shifted. Rusty Beck had fallen back, but the path of the truck didn't waver. He was still behind them, closing in again.

The ceiling lit up. Anthony pressed on the accelerator, and the wheels skidded around a curve. Rocks hit the wheel well.

There were taillights ahead.

Hector yelled out, *"¡Cuida'o!"*

A horn sounded, and Anthony hit the brakes. Rusty Beck's truck shot past them. The car swerved and slid sideways on wet grass. Bushes snapped. There was a solid thump, and Gail was thrown against the door. The car came to a stop, tipped at a sharp angle.

Anthony reached for her. "Gail, are you all right?"

"Yes, yes. I'm fine. Really."

The interior lights came on when Anthony got out. Gail struggled with her seat belt. The men shouted to each other in Spanish, and she gathered that Rusty Beck had kept going. She tried to open her door, but it swung open only partway, hitting the ground. She crawled toward the driver's side.

Anthony was taking umbrellas from the backseat. He tossed one to Hector, who stood at the front of the car, cell phone at his ear. It was raining harder now. Anthony turned the hazard lights on and the headlights off, then helped Gail out of the car.

He embraced her. "We came around a corner, and another car was ahead of us. I had to go off the road." Rain ticked on the umbrella. He looked toward the rear of the car. The fender had swung into the trunk of a palm tree. *"Que pendejada."*

"What do we tell the police when they get here?"

"Hector isn't calling the police," Anthony said. "Come on, stand out of the way, in case some other idiot runs into us." They walked a few yards down the slope and stopped at a wooden fence marking someone's property.

The surf pounded behind them in the darkness, and the rain steadily fell. Hector finished his phone call and stood by the car, vanishing then reappearing with each amber glare of the hazard lights.

"He wants to kill Rusty Beck, doesn't he?"

Anthony laughed. "So do I." The steady red flash of the taillights let her see his face. He looked at her, and his eyes widened. "Not yet. We need him alive for a little while longer, no?"

"For God's sake." Gail buried her face in his shoulder.

"I'm sorry." He kissed her and smoothed her hair. "So much excitement, it makes me a little crazy. No more jokes. Hector is calling some of his friends to get us back to the hotel safely. In the morning I'll rent a car, and we can be at the prison in plenty of time to see Kenny. And you know we'll have to ask him what happened in the orange grove that night."

CHAPTER 22

Friday, March 23

The trip to Florida State Prison, including a brief stop for lunch, would take about five hours. Anthony rented a car, asked Hector Mesa to have the Cadillac hauled to Miami, then headed north on the interstate. He drove; Gail plugged in her laptop computer and worked on the appeal. She had insisted on bringing five boxes of pleadings, documents, and legal research. From time to time she would carefully set the computer on the floor and lean over the seat to look for something. She was wearing shorts. Anthony committed the error of sliding his hand up the back of her leg; she told him to stop it, she was busy.

With a sigh he opened his cell phone and took care of some business at his office. He had arranged for most of his cases to be covered in his absence. This wasn't difficult; aside from the partners, Ferrer & Quintana had six associate attorneys and several paralegals. Gail A. Connor, P.A., was only Gail and Miriam, her secretary. Yesterday Anthony had asked how she was managing.

I don't want to think about it. He had called Miriam and told her to get some help and send him the bill.

Gail slid back down in her seat, picked up the computer, and set her fingers on the keyboard. In every motion, petition, or brief she wrote, she was leaving space for a section to be filled in later: naming the actual killer of Amber Dodson. She was waiting for Whit McGrath to come through and give up Rusty Beck. If he didn't, she would omit that part. It would be insane to make an accusation of murder on what little evidence they had now against Beck. He would promptly hire an attorney and sue them, successfully, for slander.

By the time they passed Orlando, Gail had finished drafting the appellant's brief for the Florida Supreme Court. Next she worked on an application for permission to file a *habeas* petition in the Eleventh Circuit Court of Appeals, in case she decided to go that way. That court wouldn't let her appeal unless it had first decided the case was appealable. Rules.

After lunch near Ocala at a Cracker Barrel restaurant whose calico decor and smell of cinnamon set Anthony's teeth on edge, Gail turned her computer back on and drafted the petition for *certiorari* to be filed in the

U.S. Supreme Court.

She was working from the checklist supplied by Kenny Clark's former attorney, Denise Robinson. How cleverly that woman had dumped this on her! She had sniffled into her hanky, and Gail Connor had come to the rescue. But Ms. Robinson, with her promises of legal research, editing, and advice, had vanished, sucked into the whirlwind of five or six other death row appeals.

Anthony and Gail had spent very little time, either last night or in the car this morning, discussing Kenny Ray Clark's possible involvement in the disappearance of the Mendozas. Gail had changed the subject. She was too busy to think about it. She had work to do. Anthony knew what this was: the need of a defense attorney to believe in his client. He himself had represented men with pasts so dark he didn't want to know about them. He kept his professional distance. But Gail couldn't do that. She had a soft place in her heart for her clients. She couldn't imagine that *this* client, whom she had come to like, had brutally murdered four people and buried their bodies.

Anthony could imagine it, but he would wait to hear what Kenny Clark had to say. The question had to be asked. If Gail wouldn't do it, he would.

As they sped by the exit to Gainesville, Anthony glanced over toward the passenger seat, then shifted to see what she was working on. The pleading was titled "Emergency Motion; Capital Case; Death Warrant Signed; Execution Scheduled for April 11, 2001 at 6:00 P.M."

In the interview room at the prison, Gail asked Kenny Clark if he was over his cold, and he said he was. She told him he seemed upbeat, and he replied that in general his spirits were good, although he'd been depressed after Lucius Brown had been executed on Monday.

"You make friends in here, and it's hard to lose them. Yeah, Lucius was a pretty funny guy, always cracking little jokes. I'm the only one on death watch now. Got the place all to myself. I can't say the room service has improved, though."

With a little laugh, Clark glanced at Anthony for his reaction. Anthony sent back a polite smile, and Clark once more settled his gaze on Gail. She was his shining hope, his lifeline, his angel; Anthony Quintana was the dark intruder.

Kenny Ray Clark's prison-pallor skin stretched over the sharp angles of his face.

His bright orange shirt was the only color in the room. Gail had changed into a plain gray pantsuit. Anthony noticed with dismay how loose it had become.

Clark said, "Hey, girl, you look a little worn down. Are you doing okay? I feel bad, making you work so hard."

"I'm doing fine, Kenny." She was looking through a folder for the pages he would sign. She gave him a pen and an affidavit. *I am innocent of the murder of Amber Lynn Dodson. On the morning of Monday, February 6, 1989, I was with Tina Hopwood. . . .*

Gail told him it would be filed with the 3.850 motion. His signature was slow, the letters small and careful. Next she put a copy of her draft on the desk and let him read it.

"This is great," Clark said. "What you have here about Tina and me, it's exactly what happened. And Vernon Byrd. I don't know how you got him to turn around, but you did. That's amazing. It looks good, real good." He ventured another glance at Anthony, who said nothing.

Gail showed Clark where to sign.

He bent over the page with the pen. "I was thinking last night what I'd do if I got out. First thing, I'd take a hot bath, then have some pizza and cold beer. Maybe a little R and R with a lady. Hey, Gail, you re-member that spotted dog over at Ruby's house? That was mine. His name was Barney. I'm going to get me another dog like that and buy a car and drive to Alaska. Make sure I get out in the summer, will you, 'cause I don't like cold weather. I'll send you a postcard."

She let him talk for a while, then said, "Kenny? I want you to hope for the best, but you need to know it isn't going to be easy."

"I do know that." His smile lingered. "It's fun to think about, that's all."

"Here's what we're facing. Even with two strong witnesses, there's still the neighbor, Dorothy Chastain, who believes she saw you. The judge can use that for a reason to deny us. I'm hoping the Florida Supreme Court will grant a stay. But in case they don't, we go to federal court, and probably straight to the U.S. Supreme Court. The problem is, they don't want to hear claims of innocence. They only want to know if the rules were followed. Were you denied due process of law? But if, during all this, we can find absolute proof that you are *actually* in-nocent, we'll be okay. But we have to prove it."

The smile was gone. He nodded.

"Okay, here's some good news. We're

pretty sure we know who killed Amber Dodson."

His back straightened, and his eyes opened wide. "You're serious? Who?"

"A man named Rusty Beck. He's a friend of Whitney McGrath, the developer of River Pines, where Amber worked."

"Jesus. How did you — Was he robbing her house?"

"No. We think he wanted Amber dead because she knew something that could have ruined him. Did you ever meet Rusty Beck?"

Clark looked to one side, frowning. "No. Why'd you ask that?"

Standing further back at an angle, Anthony could watch Clark's reactions. There was no doubt about it. The man was lying.

Gail said, "You worked at River Pines for a while. I thought you might have met him."

"Never heard the name. How did you find out he killed her?"

"We put some assumptions together. Here's what we think happened."

Anthony sat and listened to Gail tell Kenny that they had originally suspected Whit McGrath, but now believed that Rusty Beck had killed Amber on his own, and why. She went on to explain about the forged deed and the disappearance of the Mendozas.

Anthony crossed his arms and tapped his closed fist slowly on his mouth. He wanted to say, *Gail, stop!*, but it was too late. She had already given away everything, and if Clark had killed these people, and had an IQ above sixty, he would know where this was going. He was staring blankly across the desk, and the shutters had come down over his eyes.

Gail was still talking. "Last night we told Whit McGrath that we would reveal everything unless he helps us. We told him to call Governor Ward. They know each other. McGrath has to tell him that Beck killed Amber. We expect him to deny his own involvement, but that doesn't matter as long as he persuades the governor that you're innocent. It's risky, but it could work. Do you see?"

After a few seconds, Kenny nodded.

"We're your lawyers," Gail said. She put her hands over his. "We're on your side. Whatever you tell us won't go any further than this room. You know this."

"Sure. I know."

"The last time I was here, I asked you about some trespassers that you and Glen chased out of an orange grove. Someone paid Glen a hundred dollars, and he took you with him. When you got back to the trailer, your clothes were all covered with dirt. Kenny, what happened that night? Who were those people?"

Clark laughed. "Hey, wait. Are you thinking — Uh-uh. They weren't the people you're talking about. No way. Like I said before, we told some migrants to clear out. They were trespassing. Three men. I didn't see a woman or a kid. They got in their car and drove off."

"And that's all."

"Yes. I swear." Sincere. Bewildered. Brows tilting downward.

Gail looked across the desk into a dead end. She knew no more now than she had five minutes ago.

Anthony leaned a shoulder casually against the wall of the narrow room. He smiled down at Kenny Clark. "What were their names? The Guatemalan trespassers."

Clark let go a little puff of air and shook his head. "Glen never told me."

"He must have told you who hired him."

"No, he didn't."

"What kind of car did they drive?"

"Who?"

"These trespassers. What kind of car?"

"I don't remember. A beat-up old car."

"What did these people look like? What age? Did they speak any English?"

"Yeah, they spoke some English. I don't know how old they were. Maybe forty."

"Were they living in a house or a trailer?"

"I don't remember."

"You previously told Ms. Connor it was a house."

"I'm not answering any more of these stupid questions." Kenny Clark looked at Gail as if she might save him, but she had dropped her forehead into her hand. He glared at Anthony. "What are you doing here? I didn't hire you."

Anthony put both fists on the desk. He spoke in a low voice, never sure if these rooms were bugged. "Let me explain something to you, Kenny. You are under a death warrant. Ms. Connor and I are trying to save your skin. Maybe you were there when the Mendozas died, maybe not. I don't care. We need to lean on Whitney McGrath, do you understand that? If we can't prove these people are dead, we have nothing. What happened to them? Where are the bodies?"

Clark stared at him in sullen defiance. Anthony wanted to backhand him.

"Where are they?"

Still nothing.

Anthony said, "If you expect to rely only

on the testimony of Tina Hopwood and Vernon Byrd, you will die on April eleventh as scheduled. Is that clear enough for you?"

Clark leaned against the wall and straightened the knee of his blue cotton pants. His leg irons clanked on the floor. "I'll take my chances."

They had parked in the lot outside the administration building. Anthony turned on the engine but didn't back the car out. Gail was crying silently into a tissue. She looked through the side window at the men in prison uniforms planting fresh flowers along the walkway. A guard stood in the shade of a tree.

Anthony took her hand. "Gail —"

She pulled it away. She was angry. At what? Angry at him. At Kenny Clark. At how this had turned out.

He said, "I've been in your position. When I started in criminal law, I used to believe in my clients. Then I found out most of them lied to me. I hated them for it, for disappointing me, until I realized that it wasn't my job to like them, only to defend them."

"I didn't take this case because it's a *job*."

"You wanted an innocent client." Anthony leaned his head against the headrest. "Not only innocent of this crime, innocent

461

of any crime. You could feel good about saving him."

"Don't make my reasons sound so damned trivial."

He muttered, "I knew this would happen."

"You've been waiting to say that, haven't you?"

His own anger let go. "Why don't you stop feeling sorry for yourself?"

She looked around, reddened eyes in a pale face. Her lips seemed swollen. "Anthony, I'm just learning something about you. For all the passion you show in some areas, you're very unfeeling. It makes me wonder what you *do* care about."

He could feel his control begin to slip. "You asked for my help, and I gave it. I have given it generously, and this is what I get in return? Kenny was right. What am I doing here?"

"You don't have to be here. I'll drop you off in Jacksonville and you can fly home. It's faster."

"Whose case is this, Gail? I filed a notice of appearance yesterday. It's *our* case. I am stuck with it now."

"No, you aren't. File a withdrawal."

"*Jesucristo, me vuelvo loco.* What do you *want?*"

"A little understanding! Is that too much to ask? That you not be so goddamn superior? I'm doing the best I can!"

"You want me to *care?* Why should I? You resent it when I am the *only* one to maintain an emotional distance, without which, *querida,* a lawyer becomes unbalanced, and he cannot do his job!"

Through the window he saw the guard watching them, smiling. Two people screaming at each other.

Anthony put the car into gear. "Let's go."

"Wait." She put her hand on his arm. "Please?"

He threw it back into park.

"Maybe we're just . . . on edge. Or tired. Do you think?"

He laughed.

Her voice was meek. "I'm sorry for what I said."

He looked at her awhile. "Is this what our marriage would be like?"

She thought about it, and a smile curved her lips. "Maybe not. We're getting better at arguing. We know when to stop."

"I am not *detached,*" he said.

"Of course you aren't." She leaned over to put her head on his shoulder. "What should we do about Kenny? I have no ideas left."

"Neither do I, at the moment."

"Why wouldn't he talk to us?"

"Because he's afraid to. He doesn't trust lawyers. Don't take it personally, sweetheart. If you were on death row for eleven years largely because of an incompetent lawyer, you might feel the same."

"I can't see Kenny murdering four people in cold blood. A family."

"Maybe he didn't. We don't know what happened. Even if he was there and did no more than watch, he could be charged with felony murder. It's a weak case, but the possibility is there. From his perspective, it would be stupid to tell us anything."

Gail was silent for a while. "What about Whit McGrath? We can't do anything with him now, can we?"

"Realistically . . . no. If we mention Mendoza, he will point at Kenny."

"We need to find out what happened."

"When you think of a way to do that, tell me."

She sat up straighter and looked at him. "We'll talk to Glen Hopwood."

Monday, March 26

"Tina feels bad about Kenny, like it's her fault, what happened to him. I said no,

464

some guys just draw trouble. He draws it in spades. Christ almighty. At least I'm in for something I did. I got twenty-six years to go, and it's not anybody's fault but mine. Kenny, though. Man."

Glen Hopwood spoke through the thick glass that separated them. Hopwood was heavy, all neck and jowls, a corpulence encouraged by prison food. His voice came through a hole with a metal grill over it.

"The fact is, I didn't do him any favors either, you know? This thing you asked me about. He didn't have a part in it, not directly, you know what I'm saying? It's hard to . . . you know . . . to converse about certain things. If you're asking did he or didn't he, it's definitely no, he didn't."

Were there no other details he could give them?

"Things in the past . . . it's like a basement full of spiders you don't want to go into, you know what I mean? It's hard. . . . Well, maybe I should tell you a story I heard from a guy that used to be in here. He knew this guy named Rusty. They met in a bar and went out drinking a couple of times. The first guy — Joe — he ran into Rusty one day, and Rusty said he needed a couple of guys to go with him to put the fear of God into some Mexicans. He said they hadn't paid

465

their rent, and the owner wanted them out. So Joe got a friend of his. Johnny.

"They all went in Rusty's truck. They had some beers first and waited for it to get dark. Joe and Johnny had baseball bats, and Rusty had a shotgun. He said it was for show, to make sure there wasn't any trouble. There was a big dog, but Rusty said it was chained up on the front porch. They parked the truck on a side road and walked through an orange grove to get to the house. Rusty banged on the back door, and they got everybody outside. Four people. Rusty said he had their money for them, and they'd get it soon as they were in the car. Joe and Johnny thought that was kind of strange, but they didn't say anything. Rusty said, take what you can fit in the car and don't stop till you get to Mexico. The woman said they were from Guatemala, and Rusty said he didn't care if they were from China. They spoke a little English, except for the old man. The boy didn't talk much. He was retarded. He looked kind of funny in the eyes, and he walked slow. But he was big as the dad.

"Rusty made the boy stand out in the yard with him so the others wouldn't get any ideas. The car was by the side of the house, and these people started putting their stuff in it. Clothes and things. The woman was crying, and the dog was making a racket. Rusty kept saying hurry up, hurry up. The old man dropped a box, and Johnny helped him pick it up, and he said he was sorry about everything. Rusty said okay, slick, you help them load the car.

"Joe was standing by the back door. He saw the kid jump on Rusty and try to get the gun away. Rusty hit him in the head with it, hard, and the kid went down. The woman started screaming. The dad took a machete off the porch and ran across the yard. Rusty shot him. Then the old man. The woman got on her knees, and he reloaded and shot her. The boy was already dead, but he made sure. Fifteen seconds. Maybe less. Joe couldn't believe it. He could smell the gunpowder. It was hanging in the air. Johnny was over there on the ground crying and throwing up.

"Rusty said he had to do it, there wasn't a choice in the matter. He told Joe and Johnny if they talked they'd go down for murder, no question. He shot the dog and said that's you if you open your mouth. He made them clean everything up and put the bodies in the trunk. He made Johnny drive it. They pushed the car into a lake. . . . Where? Someplace south of Bryce Road, where they're building all those houses. . . .

Yeah, River Pines. I mean, that's what I heard, but the guy who told me . . . he's long gone. You tell Kenny I said good luck. I'll be thinking about him."

CHAPTER 23

Friday, March 30

Every seat in Judge Willis's courtroom was taken, and more people waited in the corridor to replace anyone who left. Few did. Before the doors had opened, the prosecutors had reserved seats for family and friends of the victim, police officers, and anyone else with half an interest in the outcome. Overflow had to go across the aisle and sit behind the defense lawyers. Jackie Bryce was sitting on that side by choice. Her cousin had saved her a seat in the front row.

Jackie had expected a crowd after so much media coverage all week. Channel 5 had gone back out to the scene: "Twelve years ago this quiet Palm City street was rocked by the brutal stabbing death of a young mother." They had replayed the footage of Kenny Ray Clark's arrest and explained why death row appeals took so long: "Even a convicted murderer has rights under the law." There had been a TV interview with the lead detective, Ron Kemp, and another with the Mayfields, who had sat together on their living room couch holding a framed photo of Amber. Amber's husband hadn't shown up on TV, but he'd been quoted in the newspaper: "praying that this will be over soon." The eyewitness, Dorothy Chastain, had been interviewed as well: "I have searched my mind many times, and I wish it weren't so, but he was the man I saw."

That morning's *Palm Beach Post* said that "a source" in the state attorney's office had revealed facts about Tina Hopwood, the star witness for Clark: "Prosecutors believe that Tina Hopwood's past drug use and felony arrest will affect her credibility." An editorial in *The Stuart News* had mentioned Clark's lawyers: "A high-powered, high-priced team of Miami criminal defense attorneys, Anthony Quintana and Gail Connor." Gail had said she liked that one.

The state attorney had put the sheriff of Martin County in the front row on the other side, on the aisle. He'd glanced up when Jackie passed by. They made eye contact but didn't speak.

Amber Dodson's parents sat just behind the prosecution table with Amber's sister, Lacey, who watched the proceedings as though lions were about to devour the Christians. At breaks in the proceedings she would whisper to Sonia Krause, and Ms.

Krause or her chief assistant would turn around and lean over the railing and see what Lacey wanted. Gary Dodson sat nearer the wall, half hidden behind two other men in dark suits, probably younger prosecutors. For days Gail and Anthony had been trying to get to him and ask about the Mendoza deed. How much had Amber known about it? But he'd been a ghost. His secretary had given excuses: out of the office, in conference, out of town.

Jackie had gone over to the hotel last night to borrow the crime scene photos again, and she had stuck around awhile. They weren't counting on a favorable ruling from Judge Willis. They were putting their hopes on finding more evidence to tie Rusty Beck to Amber Dodson's murder. They had some proof, but not enough. Their investigator was showing Rusty's driver's license photo around Amber's neighborhood, but so far nothing. The plan to force Whit McGrath to turn on Rusty hadn't worked out. The only word from McGrath had been a phone call from his attorney threatening a lawsuit.

It was unfortunate that Glen Hopwood hadn't been able to remember where they'd dumped the bodies. It was also unfortunate, Jackie thought, that the Mendoza boy hadn't grabbed the shotgun away from

Rusty Beck and let him have both barrels.

This courtroom was familiar to Jackie, who had testified on several felony cases. Like the rest of the building, it was typically modern. White walls, acoustical tile ceiling, rows of blue-upholstered chairs bolted to the floor. The judge sat behind a raised, oak-paneled dais with two flags behind him and a state seal over his head. He rocked slowly in his beige upholstered chair, and now and then he would pull back the sleeve of his robe and glance at his watch. "Let's move along, counselor."

Presently on the stand was the state's last witness, a sheriff's deputy who said that a few months ago he had arrested Tina Hopwood's son, Jerrod, and that Hopwood had been "extremely angry" about it. They were trying to show that Tina Hopwood had made up the story about Kenny's alibi because she wanted to get back at the police.

Tina had been the first witness on the stand. She had long, straight black hair and pale, angry eyes. Anthony Quintana had held open the swinging door in the railing for her, and her dress had swished like a cat's tail as she'd stepped up to the witness box. She'd been nervous at first but settled down as Gail took her through what had happened. Gail asked her about her past, getting it out of the way before the prosecutor could make her look bad. Sonia Krause had tried to, but Tina had given it back to her. Gail had coached Tina to keep her temper and to hide nothing.

Anthony Quintana took the next witness, Vernon Byrd. He was dressed in a suit, and except for his size, Jackie wouldn't have recognized him. He swore that nobody had promised him anything to testify. "I shouldn't have made up that story about Kenny Clark, but I wanted to get out of prison. The prosecutor said he'd be grateful if I told the truth, but I didn't. I lied, and I'm sorry."

Sonia Krause's assistant hammered on Byrd's credibility.

After that, the defense called the two men from Fort Pierce who'd seen Kenny Clark so soon after the murder that it was unlikely he could have done it. Gail's voice was getting husky. She started coughing, and had to go back to the desk to get some water. Anthony stood up, spoke to her quietly, and she nodded, then sat down. Her skin was flushed. From her seat in the front row Jackie mouthed the words, *Are you okay?* Gail gave her a little smile. Anthony finished questioning the witness.

After a break, the state's case began. Ron

Kemp testified that he didn't know where Ms. Hopwood had come up with this story, but it was absolutely not true. She had been drunk, had cursed him and Detective Federsen. They had let her sober up, then had come back, and she'd told them that Mr. Clark had left the trailer around nine-thirty that morning. Federson got on the stand to say the same thing.

Anthony Quintana cross-examined both of them, and it was blistering. He had looked into personnel files, found other incidents where witnesses complained that Kemp or Federson had pushed them around. Kemp nearly lost his temper. That scored some points, Jackie thought.

Then Sonia Krause put on the deputy who had arrested Tina Hopwood's son.

Jackie glanced over at Gary Dodson again. He was slouched in his seat, head in his hand, hiding his face. Jackie decided she would talk to him. The reporters would be all over Gail and Anthony, and they wouldn't be able to get out of here fast enough, but Jackie thought she could catch up to Gary.

Finally the deputy was excused.

"If there are no other witnesses," the judge said, bringing his chair around, "I'm going to allow you-all to make a short summary, but please make it quick. It's past six-thirty, and we need to move along."

Gail had wanted to give the summation. Jackie saw her reach over and squeeze Anthony's hand. He smiled at her, then rose to his feet, buttoning his suit jacket as he strode to the lectern on the defense side. His wavy hair was tamed straight back off his forehead, his suit was conservative gray, and his cuffs closed with buttons, not gold cufflinks. Every other time Jackie had seen him, he'd been wearing three rings. Now there were none. He put both hands on the lectern. His voice was strong and resonant, with a slight Spanish accent. Jackie had come to like it. She thought it made him sound more dramatic.

"Your honor, this is a case about actual innocence. Kenneth Ray Clark did not kill Amber Dodson. The evidence proves it. A witness, previously unknown to the defense, now says that Mr. Clark could not have committed the crime because at the time of death, he was with her. She didn't come forward twelve years ago because she was afraid. The lead detective, Ronald Kemp, and his partner, Tom Federson, came to her home, where her children were sleeping in the next room, and threatened to plant drugs, to revoke her probation, and send her to jail if she told the truth. This is outrageous police misconduct, by itself enough to justify a new trial.

"Two other newly discovered witnesses have testified that they saw Mr. Clark at ten-thirty on the morning of the murder, which fits perfectly with Tina Hopwood's statement that Mr. Clark left her trailer at ten o'clock. He could not have committed this crime because it was a physical impossibility for him to be in two places at once.

"The prosecution's original case was also built on the testimony of a jailhouse snitch, Vernon Byrd. You have heard him admit that he fabricated Mr. Clark's inculpatory statement. There was no such statement. Mr. Byrd lied to earn a reduced prison sentence. A year after the trial, Mr. Byrd was released.

"There are in the file affidavits from three jurors who say that had they known all of this, they would never have voted to convict. I myself filed an affidavit based on my conversation with the eyewitness, Mrs. Dorothy Chastain. She saw someone in the victim's yard at 10:05 A.M. the day of the murder. She believes that she saw Mr. Clark. She is mistaken. She confused Lacey Mayfield with someone else who may have come by at that time. Seven days later, after these details had become muddled in her mind, she was shown a photo display, a method so suggestive that it is no longer in use by the sheriff's office. She was shown six photographs. One of the men had long hair. That man was Kenny Clark. It is no surprise that she identified him in the lineup the next day.

"We have also submitted with our motion several studies, including one from the U.S. Justice Department, which all indicate an extremely high error rate among eyewitnesses."

The judge shifted in his chair and pulled back his cuff. "Mr. Quintana, the hour is growing late."

Anthony acknowledged this with a nod. "At the trial there was no physical evidence tying Kenny Clark to the crime. None. There were no fingerprints. The victim's blood was not found on his knife, nor was her missing jewelry found in his possession. The trace evidence found at the scene was not conclusive. All they could say was, 'It's not inconsistent,' which is the same as saying, 'We don't know.'

"Mr. Clark is an innocent man, the victim of police misconduct, the lies of a jailhouse snitch, and a mistaken identification. He was wrongfully arrested, tried, found guilty, and sentenced to death for a crime he did not commit. He has spent the last twelve years of his life either in jail waiting for trial or on death row, and his time has dwindled to twelve days. If this trial were to be held today, a verdict of acquittal would be the unquestioned result. I believe that the court must recognize this. Based on new evidence of Kenny Clark's innocence and in the interests of justice, the conviction must be set aside."

The spectators murmured among themselves. Gail turned her head far enough to see Jackie. They exchanged a smile. Jackie knew that the entire appeal could turn on what Judge Willis decided.

"State? Your summation, please."

Sonia Krause stood up, a short, gray-haired woman in a black suit and high-heeled pumps. She put her notes on the lectern, then glanced at the defense table as she began speaking.

"With all due respect to counsel for the defendant, this is not a case about innocence. It's a blatant attempt to overturn a verdict of guilty and have another shot at it because they didn't like the first result. The defense is asking the court to disregard the jury's decision and substitute its own. I'm sorry, but this isn't the way the system works.

"Putting that aside for a minute, let's take a look at their case. First, Vernon Byrd. He testified at trial, and he was cross-examined thoroughly by the defendant's lawyer. Mr. Byrd stuck by his story. And now he's changing his mind. Why? Isn't it a little strange that a man with such a long criminal record would open himself up to charges of perjury? Are we really expected to believe that Mr. Byrd would come forward out of the goodness of his heart? He has denied receiving any compensation, but frankly, we find that incredible.

"As for Tina Hopwood, look at what she alleges. Sheriff's office investigators threatened to plant drugs in her home if she told the truth. Incredible. And why would she suddenly, after all this time, come forward and point her finger? Her teenage son was arrested by the sheriff's office just a couple of months prior to her making these accusations. Was that a coincidence? I don't think so.

"The defense claims that if the case were tried today, the jury would have to vote for acquittal. That isn't true. Can we say that the jury could *not* have found Kenneth Ray Clark guilty? No. Take away Vernon Byrd's testimony entirely from the first trial. The jury still could have voted for guilt. Let's assume that these other so-called alibi witnesses had testified at trial. Could the jury have disbelieved them and voted for guilt? Yes. And if Tina Hopwood had come to court, and if she had testified as she testified today, could the jury have disbelieved her? Of course. They could have found her as unpersuasive as I do. They could have doubted her motives, as I do. They could have relied on the other evidence in the case. Mr. Clark was put at the scene by a responsible, reliable eyewitness who had time to observe him clearly. His face was imprinted onto her mind. She identified him not just from a photo display, but in a physical lineup —"

"I know all this, Ms. Krause," the judge said. "Sorry to rush you, but let's get to the legal points, shall we?"

"Yes, your honor." The state attorney turned a page in her notes. "Kenneth Ray Clark was, and is, a violent man. He had been arrested for a knife attack. He had been arrested for burglary in the same area as the Dodson house, just a few months prior. He and the victim worked for the same company. There is ample evidence then, which I will dispense with restating, and there is ample evidence now. When a jury votes for guilt, all the state's evidence must be taken as true. All of it, and on appeal the defense can't pick and choose what it wants to disregard. The jury's verdict establishes that not only did the eyewitness actually see Kenneth Ray Clark, and that not only did Mr. Clark make a confession to his cell mate, but *all the physical evidence* must likewise be taken as proven fact. They can't come in here and say that the trace evidence and the knife don't matter.

"They say that another jury, trying this case again, would vote for acquittal. This is *not* the standard for review. That is not what this court must consider. As a matter of law, the court must ask two questions. First, is the evidence *newly discovered?* No, it is not. There is nothing here that could not, in the exercise of due diligence, have been discovered before. Second, would this evidence, if presented to a jury, result in a different verdict? As you have seen, the answer to that is no.

"Defense counsel would disregard the rules. We must have rules, or the entire system falls into chaos. We would never have finality to any case. Each one could come back and come back, litigated forever. When does it stop? When does it stop for Amber's husband or for Amber's parents and sister, who have been waiting for twelve years? When does it stop for the victim herself, who still awaits justice?"

Several spectators applauded, and voices rose in the courtroom.

"Order!" the bailiff shouted.

Jackie saw Gail suddenly let go of Anthony's arm and stand up. She walked to the lectern. "One minute for rebuttal, your honor. My client is due to die in twelve days. I think he deserves to be heard for one minute."

"All right, Ms. Connor. One minute."

Walking toward the lectern she straightened her blue scarf, the only color on her slim, cream-colored suit. She pulled the microphone toward her from the level where Anthony had put it. Last night she had complained to Jackie that she wouldn't have time to do more than wash her hair. It shone beautifully, parted on the side, curling under at her collar. She cleared her throat, but the huskiness was still there.

"Your honor. The prosecution talks about rules, and I think it's because they don't have anything else to talk about. They can't talk about right and wrong, so they rely on procedure. I agree that we need to have rules, but not when they're used to obscure the truth. Can anyone with an open mind really be sure about Kenny Clark's guilt? Sure enough to send him to his *death?* Can *you* say that, your honor? Can you, not as a judge, but as a human being, sit there and say that you don't care that in twelve days a man will be strapped to a gurney and killed for something he didn't do? Step out from behind the robes, your honor. Don't put the responsibility on the prosecutor, or the jury, or the governor, or the executioner. It's *your* decision. You know that something is very wrong here. I ask you, I beg you, not to be a cog in the machine. You're going to retire soon. You said this was your first case as a criminal court judge, and your last. Do you want your last memory of this profession to be that you helped the state kill an innocent man?"

As Gail went back to her seat, Jackie stared at Judge Willis's face, which had turned red. His white hair seemed to glow.

"Ms. Connor," he said slowly, "if I did not believe that you are under an emotional strain, I would hold you in contempt. The court would like to hear your apology."

She stood up again. Her voice was raspy. "Would it affect the ruling?"

"No, it would not."

Jackie's heart rate increased. Anthony Quintana stood up, ready to intervene.

Gail said, "If knowing my client is innocent, and trying to prevent his execution, have caused me to give any offense to the court, I am sorry."

The judge stared back at her, then swung toward the state attorney. "Ms. Krause, you don't want another minute too, do you?"

"No, judge."

"All right, then. The state attorney is right, I can't substitute my judgment for that of a jury. On the other hand, I will admit to you that if this evidence were presented to me now, today, and the jury voted to acquit, I wouldn't say they were unreasonable in doing so. But the fact is, the law is the law, and I am obliged to follow it. I can't go willy-nilly second-guessing the elected legislature of the people of the state of Florida or disregarding the legal precedents of the appellate courts."

Sonia Krause stood up with a piece of paper and walked to the bench. "Judge, we have prepared an order, if that would help."

Anthony Quintana walked around the table. "This is improper. We object to this. It is the function of the court to render a decision, not to receive the state's argument in the form of an order, then sign it."

Ms. Krause said, "Defense counsel is free to submit their own proposed order."

"Both of you, sit down." The judge

scowled at them. "In view of the fact that it's nearly seven o'clock and the defendant's brief has to be filed tomorrow by noon in Tallahassee, I'm going to go ahead and issue a ruling from the bench. A written version will be faxed to your offices, along with portions of the transcript relevant thereto. Make sure the clerk has your fax numbers."

He looked down at his desk. Jackie didn't know if he was reading from his notes or was unwilling to look Gail and Anthony in the eye.

"This court finds that the two defense witnesses from Fort Pierce could have been and should have been discovered before trial, and therefore their testimony must be disregarded. This court finds the testimony of Vernon Byrd lacking in credibility. That leaves the testimony of Tina Hopwood, which this court finds does qualify as newly discovered evidence. However, under *Jones v. State,* the standard is that the evidence must be of such a nature that it would probably result in an acquittal on retrial. The defense has failed to carry its burden of proof. Therefore, the motion for postconviction relief is denied."

The courtroom broke into applause. Lacey Mayfield leaped up, hands over her head. "Thank you, God!"

The bailiff shouted, "Order! Quiet!"

"Court is adjourned." Judge Willis brought his gavel down on its block and went out through the side door to his chambers.

In the corridor, TV cameras closed in, and lights came on. Anthony Quintana spoke in clipped, angry tones, answering a reporter's question. "Of course we're going to appeal. This is an innocent man. We have no doubt of it. If Kenny Clark is killed by the state based on the testimony of one mistaken woman, then God help us all."

Briefcase in one hand, he took Gail's elbow in the other, and they made their way to the stairs. Gail motioned for Jackie to come with them. Having lost sight of Gary Dodson, Jackie gave up trying to find him and followed her cousin.

She had learned last night how eight copies of an appellate brief could get to Tallahassee so quickly. Gail had e-mailed most of it already. She had a friend with a major law firm up there. He would print it out, sign it as a courtesy, and take it over to the clerk's office before the noon deadline.

Their footsteps echoed on concrete until Anthony pushed open the door on the ground floor. They walked out into the space between the courthouse and the adjacent county office building. Night was falling. The lights in the courtyard had come on, and people were still milling about. A group of them had gathered on the long, landscaped walkway that led to the parking lot. TV lights were on.

"The self-congratulatory press conference," Anthony noted.

"Let's go the other way," Gail said. "Really, I'd rather. I can't stand looking at those people. I need to call Kenny, then I want to go talk to Ruby."

"No, *amorcito*, you have done enough for today." Anthony touched her forehead. "You don't have a fever, but I think you should go to bed."

"You were wonderful," Jackie said, giving her a hug. "You both were."

Anthony said, "In the courtroom, I thought I would have to bring her toothbrush to jail for her." With an arm around Gail, he said to Jackie, "We're going home in the morning. Hector will stay here, in case anything turns up on the investigation. You have his number. And ours."

They were both exhausted, Jackie thought. She said good-bye, then looked toward the crowd in the courtyard. "I'm going to see if Gary Dodson is still here."

*   *   *

He was. Lacey Mayfield had a grip on his arm, and though he leaned slightly away from her, his eyes on the ground, she wouldn't let go. The Mayfields were there, as well as another older couple beside Dodson, probably his parents. There were Ron Kemp, Tom Federsen, some other detectives, and a few uniforms. As she came closer, Jackie could see a Stetson hat. Her father usually stuck around for these things. Good PR, he'd told her. Palm trees on either side put the group in a frame.

The state attorney was speaking into the microphones held in her direction. Jackie didn't know what the question had been. Sonia Krause said, "The evidence just wasn't there. We're confident that the conviction will stand."

Someone asked what she thought of Gail Connor's last speech to the court. Ms. Krause smiled. "Well, Ms. Connor and I see things from a different perspective. I certainly don't like capital punishment, but it's necessary and appropriate in some cases. This is one of them. You will notice that the crime rate has dropped now that we're more serious about the death penalty in this country."

"Sheriff Bryce, do you see any chance

Clark will get a new trial?"

He stepped forward and at the same time noticed Jackie standing among the crowd. "Chances of a new trial are pretty slim, and it would be a shame to put the victim's husband and all the relatives through that a second time, but we're ready."

"Did you ever have any doubt that Clark did it?"

His eyes rested on Jackie. "That isn't for us to decide. We turn the evidence over to the prosecutor, and they take it from there. But personally? I have no doubts. And I want to commend the state attorney's office for the fine job they did this afternoon."

There was some handshaking all around. Jackie stared off beyond the parking lot, past the City of Stuart water tower. She thought about what the prosecutor had said. Seeing things from a different perspective. They weren't out to get anybody. Just doing their job. Everybody sure of the truth.

When Jackie looked around again, she saw her father making his exit. More handshakes. A clap on the back for the detectives. He didn't glance her way as he left.

The lights were on Lacey Mayfield. She said this was the happiest day of her life. "No, I take that back. The happiest day will be when my sister's killer dies for what he did, and we can get on with our lives. Those fancy lawyers are clogging up the system with their little tricks and technicalities. A person should get one appeal, and that's it."

"Will you be a witness at the execution, Ms. Mayfield?"

"I'll be in the front row, holding up a picture of Amber. I want her face to be the last thing he sees on this earth, just like his face was the last thing she saw." Lacey Mayfield's parents, gray and old, stood behind her, leaning on each other.

As Lacey spoke, Gary Dodson, released from her grip, had sidled away through the crowd. Jackie spotted his dark gray suit and thinning hair. He embraced his mother, shook hands with his father, and then walked quickly in the gathering darkness toward the parking lot.

Jackie followed at a run, holding her shoulder bag against her side to keep it from swinging.

He was in his car with the engine running, reaching for the door, when she got there and held it open with a hand on the upper corner. He drove a dark green Oldsmobile sedan several years old. Jackie could feel the AC blasting out of the vents. The inside of the car smelled moldy.

Gary Dodson jumped a little in the seat.

He squinted at her. "What do you want? I already said what I had to say."

"I'm not a reporter. My name's Jackie Bryce. I'm a City of Stuart police officer, in case you've seen me around, but I'm not on duty right now."

"Is your father the sheriff?" Dodson craned his neck to look at her. His scalp shone in the weak interior lights. "I heard the sheriff's daughter was a police officer."

"That's me. Listen, Mr. Dodson, could I ask you a question? It won't take too long." When he didn't immediately say no, Jackie went on, "My mother was Louise Bryce. She died in September of 1988 in a car wreck, so I can't ask her. There was a deed from Ignacio and Celestina Mendoza to the JWM Corporation. You lost your job because of the deed. My mother notarized it. Who asked her to do that? Was it you or Whit McGrath? I don't know who else to ask."

"Where did you get this information?"

"Gail Connor. She talked to somebody at your old law firm. I'd appreciate it if you'd tell me."

Dodson took hold of the steering wheel, and Jackie saw his nails. She'd gotten a description already from Gail. His hollow eyes closed for a moment. "Mr. McGrath delivered the deed to me. I sent it to the recorder's office. That's all."

"The deed was a forgery, wasn't it?" Jackie spoke as if she was sorry to have found this out. Dodson didn't reply. She squatted on one heel beside the open door. "What I wanted to ask you is, Did my mother know? Please, Mr. Dodson, I don't want to think the worst of her, but I'd like to have the truth."

"I believe . . . my impression is that she notarized the deed as a favor for Mr. McGrath. It's done, you know, sometimes. Notarizing documents like that, on someone's word. It's improper, but . . ."

"I'm aware of their relationship at the time," Jackie said. "Did you know my mother? Did you ever meet her?"

"Once. A lovely woman. Your mother asked me about the deed. She came to my office. That's when we met."

"When was that? Before she notarized it?"

"Oh, no, after. Several months after. It had been on her mind for some time. She was concerned that she'd acted improperly. I told her she hadn't."

"That wasn't exactly true."

"Yes, but she seemed so distressed. I tried to put her mind at ease. I hope I succeeded. I heard about her accident just a few days after that. My sympathies, Miss Bryce."

"Thank you." Cold air drifted through the door. The condensation from the air conditioner was leaking from under the car, running toward Jackie's foot, but she didn't want to move. "How did you find out it was a forgery?"

Dodson's teeth were bad, and the smile creased one side of his face and not the other. Softly he said, "You're working for Gail Connor. She's trying to free the man who murdered my wife."

"Yes, sir, I am, but the fact is, Kenny Clark didn't do it. Everything you heard in that courtroom today is the truth. I'm helping Gail because she's my cousin. Our mothers were sisters. I know Gail, and she wouldn't lie about anything. If we don't find out who really killed your wife, Mr. Clark is going to die for a crime somebody else committed. We believe it was Rusty Beck. Do you know who I mean?"

"My God." Dodson's hands slipped off the steering wheel into his lap.

Jackie said, "He knew your wife was home sick that day. When you called the office, Vivian Baker answered. She was Amber's boss, if you remember. McGrath was right there, and so was Rusty Beck, and they overheard the call. I could list the evidence

493

we have against Beck, but what I need to ask you is . . . and this is *real* important, Did Amber know about the Mendoza deed?"

Dodson laughed, a quick burst of sound, and his mouth remained open. "Did she know about the *deed?*"

Jackie stared up at him. "Yes, sir. Did you tell her about the forgery?"

"No."

"You didn't?"

"*No.* Tell her *that?* I wasn't exactly proud of falling so low, Miss Bryce. I loved Amber more than the world, and she worshipped me."

"Then how did you explain getting fired?"

"I . . . I . . ."

Jackie shifted a little, getting closer. "Let me explain. We're looking for proof that Beck killed her. Anything you tell us might help. We've got twelve days. Less than that, actually, before they put Kenny Clark to death."

Gary Dodson sobbed. "Yes, I told her. I said, Amber darling, it was only a favor for Whit McGrath. You see, he and I were going to be partners in a land deal. It was all set, but then he wouldn't do it, and it was too late. He ruined me. He's capable of any-thing, Miss Bryce."

Jackie played with the strap of her shoulder bag, which she had set on the ground. "Sir, you're aware that the Mendozas are dead, aren't you?"

He went completely still. And then the fabric of his dark gray suit, which had stretched over his shoulders, fell loosely as he sat up and looked at her. It was ages old, she thought, and several sizes too big.

"They're all dead," said Jackie. "Ignacio, Celestina, Ramon, Jose. The whole family. Rusty Beck killed them with a shotgun, and then he got rid of their bodies. That's why Whit McGrath had to forge the deed. Were you aware of this, Mr. Dodson? Did Amber know about it too?"

Dodson's eyes seemed to burn in his face, and his skin had turned gray. Even with the AC rushing out of the vents, he was sweating. "I have to go now."

Jackie said, "We need your help. If we can lean on Whit McGrath, he might give up Rusty Beck for your wife's death. Will you help? You want to bring her true killer to justice, don't you?"

"Excuse me," Dodson said, reaching for the door handle. "Please move out of the way. *Please.*"

When Jackie reluctantly moved, Dodson slammed the door. The interior lights went off. He backed out, and the car bounced as he hit the brakes. He stared back at her, and through the window she could see the dash lights making a greenish glow on his face. Muffler rattling, the car streaked out of the parking lot.

Jackie swung her purse over her shoulder, then quickly held it up to look at it. "Dammit." The leather bottom was soaking wet.

CHAPTER 24

Tuesday, April 3

After argument at the Florida Supreme Court, a lawyer coming out of the courtroom would walk onto the terrazzo floor of the rotunda, circled by eight green marble columns, and see the clerk's office down a wide corridor to the left. Gazing in that direction, Gail told Anthony that she wanted to make sure the clerk had all their contact numbers.

"We faxed them a list," he said.

"Let's make sure they got it."

She remembered having sent it, but last night, after finally falling asleep around three o'clock, she'd had a bad dream. The court had ruled, and they needed to give her the order, but they couldn't find her, and she couldn't get into the building. All of the high, metal doors were locked, and if she didn't get the order in her hands, it would be too late. The guards were standing outside Kenny's cell. *Kenny? It's time to go.*

Anthony gave one of his little sighs. "All right, we'll make sure."

Gail bit her tongue to keep from asking

497

him to stop it. He was being wonderful. He'd bought two first-class airline tickets because that's all there was available, and they'd stayed at the Doubletree in downtown Tallahassee. She had argued the case; he didn't even have to be here, but he wanted to be with her. He was carrying her briefcase. He had rubbed her back last night.

She took his hand. *"Te quiero mucho."*

Blinking as if surprised, Anthony said, "I love you too." He felt her hand. "You're perspiring. Are you all right?"

"I'm fine."

In the airy, modern clerk's office, they waited at the counter, and presently the death clerk came out to see them. Gail had expected a woman dressed in black, but Marcia Turner was a pretty blonde with a sweet nature. "I have all your phone numbers, so don't worry."

"How soon will they rule?" Gail asked. "Do you have any idea? This afternoon, do you think?"

"Oh, I don't think so. It could take a few days."

"A few *days?* But the execution is scheduled for April eleventh —"

Anthony was smiling at Ms. Turner. "Thank you for your help."

"— and my client is *innocent*, you see, and we need time to appeal. We're going straight to the U.S. Supreme Court —"

"Yes, ma'am."

Gail felt a sneeze and pulled out her tissue just in time.

"God bless you," Ms. Turner said.

"Gail, let's go," Anthony said.

They went out through the rotunda, heels tapping on the floor. She asked Anthony to wait, wait just a minute. She walked over to one of the doors leading into the courtroom. The justices were probably back on the bench already, hearing another case. Gail thought of the things she had wanted to say, but it had all gone so fast. Had they even read the brief? Two hundred pages, argument and exhibits and citations.

Eighteen minutes for the appellant, then twenty for the state. Then another two minutes for rebuttal. The red digital numbers on the lectern had relentlessly counted down. Then the court had thanked her and sent her on her way. The seven of them, two women and five men in black robes, had vanished through the curtained doorway behind Chief Justice Harding's chair in the center.

"They asked a lot of questions about the standard for review, didn't they?"

"You handled it very well, I thought."

"Did I?" She turned to him. "Did you notice how Shaw and Pariente kept asking about the claim of innocence? Shaw was talking about the totality of the circumstances. I think we have their votes. We only need two more."

Anthony took her arm. "Are you hungry? Let's find something to eat."

"The AGA was such an *idiot*," she said. " 'I'm fixing to answer y'all's question, Justice Quince.' Or this: 'If we go down that road, no tellin' where we'll end up.' He sounded personally insulted that we'd even filed an appeal."

"It's a routine for them, sweetheart." Anthony pushed open the door, and the wind at the top of the steps fluttered his tie and lifted her hem.

"I should have mentioned Rusty Beck. I should have *told* them."

"You couldn't. It wasn't in the record."

"Screw the record. They *wanted* more evidence of Kenny's innocence. I hinted that we had someone else, but I should have been specific. I should have told them. Too damned late now." Gail opened her purse and took out her cell phone. "I need to call Kenny."

Anthony sighed. "Gail, please. You know

how long the prison keeps you on hold. Wait till we get to the office. It's three blocks away."

They had dumped their overnight bags with a lawyer in town whom Anthony knew. Gail agreed it would be better to wait until they had a quiet room, and they went down the steps. It was a lovely, small-town day, and the dogwood trees were in bloom, like white butterflies caught among the fresh green leaves.

Gail made a note to herself: Call Ruby. She'd promised to let her know how the oral argument went. They had spoken yesterday. Ruby had told her not to worry. *Jesus will save Kenny Ray.* I hope so, Gail said to herself, because I'm not doing so well.

Call Kenny. Call Ruby. Check her offices for messages. Had she paid Karen's tuition this month? Call her mother.

At the sidewalk, Anthony turned left, but Gail grabbed his arm. Across the street was another set of steps that led up to the state capitol. "You know what? We should check at McLaren's office and see if he got our message."

Earlier this morning, over Anthony's protests, Gail had gone to the office of the governor's assistant general counsel in charge

501

of death cases to see if the governor would possibly be open to a stay of execution, if absolute proof were presented to him of Kenneth Ray Clark's innocence. A legal assistant to Mr. McLaren had come out to say that the governor was aware of the case. Obviously he was aware, she had replied. He had signed the warrant.

"Forget it. He isn't going to talk to you," Anthony said.

"What harm could there be in trying?"

He took her hand and pulled her along, and an edge came into his voice. "There comes a point when you have to accept that you have done everything that you can do."

"I have an idea," she said. "Let's get the media on our side. Governor Ward won't listen to us, but he reads the opinion polls. We should have done this before! Let's call the *Miami Herald*, *The New York Times*, CNN, *Forty-eight Hours*, *Nightline*, everybody we can think of. Let's say we know who did it."

"What?"

"Anthony, we have to name Rusty Beck as the killer or nobody would give a damn. We can't keep Whit McGrath out of it any longer. It would be a huge story. 'Palm Beach socialite implicated in death of young mother.' We won't *say* he's involved, we'll just let the reporters draw their own conclusions."

"Gail, we can't —"

"There would be such a clamor that Ward would be forced to issue a stay. And it doesn't matter if Rusty says Kenny was with him when the Mendozas died, don't you see? He would only implicate himself. We have him in a no-win position."

Anthony set down the briefcase and took her by the shoulders. "Listen to me. We have no *proof.* If you make unfounded accusations, they will sue the hell out of us."

"I don't *care!*" Gail felt the heat in her face, her neck. Her blouse was soaked. "All right, then, withdraw as attorney of record, and they can sue *me.* I haven't got anything they can take."

He shook her. "Stop this!"

"What else can I do? If we lose here, do we rely on the U.S. Supreme Court? Look what they did in *Herrera v. Collins.* They said innocence doesn't matter, all they care about is rules —"

She broke down, sobbing.

"Niña, no lloras." Then she was in his arms, pressed tightly against his chest. He stroked her hair.

"Anthony, I can't let him die. I can't."

"Por favor, corazón, deja de llorar. Todo va a salir bien."

Anthony sat by the window so he could lean against the bulkhead and Gail could lean on his shoulder. An airline blanket covered them both. He had put his jacket in the overhead compartment and loosened his tie. She slid her hand over his shirt, tracing the outline of his muscles.

She'd just finished her second glass of wine. Free in first class. The leather seats were roomy and soft.

"How do you always make it look so *easy?* You snap your fingers and people walk out of jail."

He laughed softly. "I like to brag about my victories, but I assure you, there have been defeats as well."

"Anthony, have you ever witnessed an execution?"

"Once."

"When?"

"The summer before my last year of law school. I was working for a pro bono capital attorney in Philadelphia."

"You never told me about that." She picked her head up. He was looking out the window. The sun had set, leaving only an afterglow. His eyes were intensely dark, nearly black. She waited, then settled her head back on his shoulder. "Can you talk about it?"

"The attorney had chest pains, but he'd promised the client that somebody would be there, so . . . I was the lucky one."

"Was it terrible?"

"The client was guilty, which was some consolation. Henry Lamar Williams. A twenty-six-year-old black man with an IQ of seventy. He raped and murdered a thirteen-year-old white girl. There was no doubt, because the police found her body in the shed behind his house, and he confessed. He said he didn't mean to kill her. We argued that it was cruel and unusual punishment to execute someone who was retarded, but the state said he wasn't officially retarded. He had one too many IQ points. So they put Henry in the electric chair. He saw me and smiled. Then they dropped the hood over his head. *Zzzzzzt*. The next thing I remember, they were loading me onto a stretcher. For months afterwards, I dreamed about it. But maybe it did me some good. I have defended more than a dozen murder cases since then, and none of my clients has been sentenced to death."

"You fainted?"

He put his lips to her ear. "Don't let this

get around, but . . . I am not superhuman."

"Yes, you are." Gail kissed him and smiled. "*Mi macho.* Listen, if . . . you know, *if.* You won't have to be there. They only allow one lawyer, and Kenny asked me if I would, and I said yes."

"I wouldn't put you through that," Anthony said.

"Whose case is it?"

"Ours, so I thought."

"Sorry, but I have seniority," she said. "Ha-ha."

Her hand went under the blanket, and he let some time go by before lifting it out. He rubbed his nose across hers. "I think you're a little drunk, *señora.*"

"I deserve to be." The stars in the window seemed to shift suddenly downward. The jet was making its turn toward Miami, coming in from the west, the black and endless Everglades below them.

A little while later, the lights in the cabin came on, but Gail couldn't begin to rouse herself or open her eyes.

"Sweetheart, sit up, we're about to land." Anthony gently shoved her off him.

She hid a yawn behind her hands. "I've been thinking. What about Gary Dodson? Maybe he knows where the bodies are. The way he acted with Jackie, he knows something, Anthony. It would explain why McGrath gives him legal work, to keep him quiet."

Anthony pressed a button, and his seat came up. "If that is true, Dodson isn't getting much for his silence."

"God, if we could just get through to him. What about Hector? He was amazing, getting a retraction out of Vernon Byrd."

Anthony glanced at her. "No, Hector isn't right for someone like Dodson. Is your belt fastened?" She clicked it shut. He leaned over and nuzzled her neck. "Come home with me tonight."

"Can't. Sorry. I need to be with Karen. I promised her I would, and then I have to get up early and work on the Supreme Court stuff."

He sighed.

"Anthony, I want you to do something for me."

He looked at her sideways. "What?"

"I want you to go see Kenny."

"Why? You just spoke to him."

"Make him come clean about the Mendozas. You could do it. You're a guy. Beat him up if he won't talk. Make him tell you where they dumped the car. He drove it, he has to remember. Tell him we have to *find* them."

Anthony focused somewhere over her head. "I don't want to get back on an airplane in the morning. What good will it do, hearing his lies?"

"Please?"

His eyes shifted to fix on hers. His full lips pursed into a kiss. "I'm keeping a list of all these things I do for you. Oh, yes. And someday, *señora,* I am going to collect."

Wednesday, April 4

The guards came to the death watch cell with the cuffs and leg irons and said his lawyer wanted to see him. Kenny put out his cigarette — no more Top tobacco; he was using up the last few dollars in his trust fund on Marlboros, living large. The moke out in the corridor made a note: *2:25 P.M. Inmate puts out cigarette.*

He rolled off his bunk, ready to go: *2:26 P.M. Inmate taken from cell for legal visit.* Between two guards he shuffled down the long corridor to the attorney visiting rooms, thinking he'd see Gail Connor.

He was wrong.

It was her Cuban boyfriend on the other side of the desk. They unhooked the cuffs from the waist chain, and Kenny sat down across from him.

They closed the door.

"Where's Gail?"

Quintana said he was sorry Gail couldn't come, but she had to finish some papers that had to be sent to Washington. *Bullshit,* Kenny said to himself.

"I want you to sit there and listen to me. Don't interrupt." Quintana looked over at the glass in the door, then leaned closer and spoke quietly.

After a while, Kenny sat up straight and stretched his shoulders. He looked around. Through the glass he saw guards bringing somebody else through. Blue shirt. Population inmate, a young black guy. The door closed in the next interview room.

Kenny put his arms back on the desk. "The prison chaplain came to see me this morning. He said he'd come every day if I want. Get right with God. You believe in that?"

"Not really."

"Me either." He bounced his knees and listened to the jingle of metal. "How's Glen doing?"

"Not bad for a man with twenty-six years left on his sentence."

"I never thought he'd rat on Rusty. Usually a guy who rats, you don't respect him." Kenny waited to see what Quintana would say about it.

He said, "I think Glen has his priorities straight."

"Yeah, maybe. What's the word from Tallahassee?"

"Nothing yet."

"Gail told me it was fifty-fifty, and to keep my hopes up. Is she wrong?"

Quintana looked straight at him. "Probably. There isn't much chance. I would guess five-to-two, maybe four-to-three against us. The problem is the eyewitness. The jury believed her, and the appellate courts don't second-guess a jury. We'll file the appeal in the U.S. Supreme Court, but they rarely grant it, even with a claim of innocence."

Kenny knew already, but it was like a cold river going through his guts when he let himself think about it. "How come Gail tells me fifty-fifty?"

"Because she believes it. She has to believe it, and I won't tell her otherwise, not now. It would be too much. She is exhausted. Her heart is skipping beats."

"Does she have a bad heart?"

"No, no, it's tension. I tell her to rest, but she won't. She won't eat, she won't sleep. She works. She ignores me."

"Not getting any, huh?"

"Not lately."

"When are you and her getting married?"

"I don't know. She won't give me an answer."

"Buy her a big ring. And get her pregnant. That way, she can't say no."

Quintana laughed. "Maybe I should try that."

Kenny heard muffled voices through the wall. "Are you sure Rusty killed Amber Dodson?"

"Not completely." Quintana shrugged.

"Are you sure I didn't?"

"Yes, I am sure of that." He asked again, "What about the Mendozas?"

"Do you think Whit McGrath is going to give up Rusty Beck?"

The dark eyes looked back at him. Didn't blink. "I doubt it."

"Then why should I tell you a damn thing?"

"Maybe I'm wrong. I'll give you another reason. Rusty Beck should pay for what he did."

"I like that reason."

"Here are four more. Ignacio, Celestina, Ramon, and Jose. They need to go home to Guatemala to their family. They should be buried properly, in a grave. Someone should say mass for them."

"That's true." Kenny closed his eyes, and he could hear the scrape of metal over rocks.

"Glen told you the truth. Rusty shot them. He told me to get in the car and drive. I followed him to the sinkhole back in the woods, and we pushed it in."

"A sinkhole? Glen said it was a lake."

"No, it was a sinkhole."

"Do you remember where it was?"

"Not right off. We ended up pretty close to where we started, but Rusty drove all over hell and back trying to find a good spot. He was pretty freaked out. I thought he was going to shoot me and Glen too."

"You followed his truck?"

"That's right." Kenny could see the next question coming, so he said, "I could have got away, but I didn't. I could have veered off and drove to the police station. But I said, damn, they'll arrest me for murder. Glen too. Who's going to believe us? I was scared. I was a scared kid, but I can't make excuses. I could've done something. Soon as I saw Rusty had a shotgun, I could've got out of there. But I didn't. I shouldn't have let him hold it on the boy, but I stood by and let it happen. I was a coward. That's what it was. If you look at a thing like that real hard, you see how you can't blame it on somebody else. I had no business being there at all."

Kenny expected Quintana to argue with

him, say he was forced, but Quintana nodded. "This is so. We are responsible, even those who stand by."

"Yeah." Somebody in here before him had scratched some letters on the desk. M-I-C. Kenny wondered what the guy's name was. What had he used? The edge of his cuff, maybe. Kenny put his wrist to the desktop and started scratching. Quintana noticed, but he didn't say to stop.

"You'd be surprised, a lot of the guys in here believe in the death penalty. I do too, for some cases. Like Danny Rolling. He killed five college students. Cut them up. When he goes, I'm not gonna cry about it."

M-I-C-I. Kenny turned his wrist to finish the *K*. "And this guy in the cell next to me, he told me he beat his girlfriend's son to death, three years old, to get back at her for cheating on him. Should he die for that? You ask most of the guys on the row, they'd say, hell yes. But what do you do with an ordinary guy? How do you decide if he snapped or if he's bad through and through? It's not easy to tell."

"That's true," Quintana said. "It isn't easy. When will I hear from you?"

M-I-C-K. Maybe the next guys in here would finish it. MICKEY MOUSE. Kenny sat back in his chair. "Call me when you get to Miami."

Quintana reached out his hand, a big hand with two rings on it, and some gold shining under his cuff. Kenny took it.

"*Vaya con Dios.*" He had a good grip.

"You too. Take care of Gail."

"She makes it difficult, but I'll do my best."

Kenny's throat felt tight, and he laughed. "Boy, she's a fighter. She's like Ruby. They both think I'm going to walk out of here. Maybe they're right."

Quintana nodded. "Maybe they are."

The guards took Kenny back to Q wing. The moke at the desk scribbled on his chart: *3:45 P.M. Inmate returns to cell.*

Kenny lay on his bunk and the thought came into his mind again. Seven days. Ice water ran inside his arms and legs and made his hands shake.

He got up and asked the guard for a pen. The guard came over and handed him a flex pen through the bars. Kenny sat down on his mattress and picked up the letter from the prison chaplain. *If you find yourself in need of spiritual guidance —*

Kenny turned it over to the blank side and tried to visualize the west part of the county.

The way to the Mendozas' place. How he and Glen had followed Rusty through the orange grove. The moon coming through the branches, the light and shadow on the ground. The shuffle of leaves under their feet. Glen finishing a beer, tossing the bottle. How the glass had clinked on a pebble.

He remembered the thick black hair of the woman, her white blouse. How she fell to her knees, praying in Spanish. Now Kenny knew what she was praying for. She'd seen her husband and boy and father die. She wanted to get it over with.

Kenny stared at the empty paper.

They were all there in his memory, somewhere, buried way down. He'd tried to forget, but they had come back in his dreams, and in the last few weeks they'd shown up every night, standing just outside the bars, waiting for him.

He had seen the car float, then go nose forward and disappear. Bubbles boiling up, then fewer of them, then none. The moon had jumped and swayed on the dark, rippling water, and he was down there with the dead, locked in the trunk.

CHAPTER 25

Monday, April 9

Jackie waited at the end of the road while the others walked down to the gate. It was locked with a heavy chain. A slight clanging noise filled the silence: a NO TRESPASSING sign, moving in the wind. She put on her sunglasses to cut the glare.

They looked out over the rocky field, broken up by a few puddles from the thunderstorms last night. Gail stood in the middle between the men. Anthony had his jacket off and his sleeves rolled up, but Hector Mesa wore a gray suit. He had a holster under it, and one on his ankle, but Jackie had pretended not to notice.

Her shift had ended at three o'clock, and she'd turned in her car and followed them out here in her own vehicle, not taking the time to change out of uniform. They had waited around till she could come too, so if Gail and Anthony decided to stand here all afternoon, that was all right with her. They had a lot to mourn.

Late Friday the Florida court had announced its decision: four-to-three, stay of execution denied. The bottom line was, four justices thought Kenny Clark was guilty. If they'd thought he was innocent, they could have found a way around the rules. Kenny would be dead in two days, unless something happened.

A solitary hawk drifted overhead, gliding on the wind, wings perfectly still. The field, dotted with pine trees, stretched to some woods about two hundred yards away. An old construction trailer was out there, and some piles of brush. About halfway between the road and the woods was a small body of water. A little lake. The future fountain at the entrance to the River Pines Hotel. Jackie couldn't see it for the trees, but Gail and Anthony said it was there.

They drove up from Miami this morning. Hector Mesa had been here a couple of days already, talking to local geologists and looking at aerial maps. Nobody could say for sure — yet — if it was *the* sinkhole, but there weren't that many in the county. There was only one way to find out.

From her higher vantage point on the shoulder of the road, Jackie saw the black truck before the others did. It appeared first as a plume of dust, then the shiny grille of a new Ford 150. It slowed coming by the rental car and Jackie's Isuzu Trooper, then swerved over to the left lane. Rusty's arm rested on the open window. The sun picked up the red in his mustache and goatee. A Browning twelve-gauge lay in the gun rack, and his bullwhip was coiled around one of the hooks.

Jackie walked over to see what he wanted.

He turned down the music. A smile lifted the corners of his mustache and cut lines into his skin. "Officer Jackie. What's going on?"

She looked at him through her sunglasses, her face level with his. "Just a little sight-seeing. You have a problem with that?" Up close, she could see the pockmarks on his cheeks. She thought of Vivian Baker with a knife at her breast. The people down there in the mud.

Rusty said, "This is private property."

"The road is a public thoroughfare," Jackie said, "and you're driving in the wrong lane."

"It's not your jurisdiction, sweet thing."

"I could make it my jurisdiction. Why don't you move along?"

Over by the gate, Anthony Quintana was keeping Gail behind him, an arm extended to the side.

Rusty cupped a hand at his mouth. "Hey, slick. You get that car fixed yet? Officer

Jackie, you ought to see the way this guy drives. He's loco. Big Miami lawyer, thinks he owns the fuckin' road."

During this, Hector Mesa had casually walked up the slope and now stood a few yards away.

Rusty reached over his shoulder with his left hand and lifted his bullwhip off the rack. He whirled the end of it. "Come on, Pedro. Let's see if I can snatch them ugly glasses off your face."

Hector smiled.

Jackie came closer. "Be glad I'm here, Rusty. Real glad. You better get going."

He shrugged, then saluted her off the brim of his cowboy hat. "See you later, darlin'." His tires screeched making the turn, and the truck went back the way it had come, engine popping and rumbling.

Jackie glanced around at Hector Mesa. He was looking after the truck like somebody had taken his toy away.

"Hector?"

"Yes, *señorita?*"

"Don't even think about it."

Jackie said she would drop Gail off at Ruby Smith's apartment. They were going to visit for a while and maybe have dinner together, depending on when Anthony got back from wherever he was going. He and Hector took the rental car, Hector behind the wheel, the car kicking up some gravel, then getting smaller down the long stretch of road. It had to be doing eighty.

"Where are they going?" Jackie asked.

"West Palm Beach. Hector has some friends in the tropical fish business. Scuba divers."

Jackie smiled. "They're going into the sinkhole."

"I hope they have better luck there than they did finding my engagement ring."

Gail had told Jackie about that. They'd had a laugh over it, Gail saying it was all she could do, laugh.

Right now she wasn't doing much of anything. She had her eyes closed and her head leaning on the head rest. Jackie thought she might be asleep until she said, "I wish Rusty Beck hadn't seen us. He could get on a bulldozer and push enough dirt in that hole to make it disappear."

"The way he acted, he's not worried about a thing," Jackie said. "You gotta know Rusty. In fact, it wouldn't surprise me if Whit McGrath doesn't know what's down there."

"He has to know. Rusty must have told him."

"Why? Would you? 'Hey, I just dumped a car with four bodies in that sinkhole on your property.' Gail, the hole wouldn't still *be* there if Whit McGrath knew. I mean, that's what I think."

Gail was pressing hard into her chest with the heel of her hand. She saw Jackie looking at her. "It's nothing. My heart flutters sometimes."

"You should rest."

"I will, as soon as this is over."

The plan was to get some underwater photos of the sinkhole and show them to Whit McGrath, force him to give up Rusty for the murder of Amber Dodson. The last time they'd gone after Whit, they'd been bluffing, and Whit had known it. With hard proof, he'd be backed against the wall. Whit McGrath would have to imagine a chain hooked to the axle, the car coming up out of the mud, and a news helicopter circling overhead, waiting to see what the police found in the trunk. And then he'd have to figure the chances of getting Phase Two past the commissioners after they saw *that* on the six o'clock news. Forget Phase Two. He'd have to explain what the bodies were doing there. If this didn't work — if the sinkhole was empty — they'd be out of options.

"Oh, God, Jackie. Two days. I don't want to see Ruby right now. Can you take me to the hotel? Maybe there's something I could work on."

Jackie said she would, then listened while Gail called Ruby Smith on her cell phone and apologized. Ruby must have told her not to worry about it. Gail said she'd be there for breakfast instead, then told her she loved her and disconnected. "The Lord is watching over me. I wish I could believe that." She put her phone away.

"Gail, why don't you come to my place? You could relax awhile. It's quiet there and a lot closer."

"I don't think I could take running into Garlan."

"He usually doesn't get home till seven or eight. I'll fix us a pitcher of margaritas."

"Well, in that case. Thanks." Gail squeezed her arm. Jackie noticed how cold her fingers were.

Jackie wondered why Whit McGrath hadn't done what they wanted. He could have lifted the phone and called the governor. He could have asked Ward for a stay of a few months, that's all Gail and Anthony wanted, a little time to build the case against Rusty. Maybe Whit was more involved than they thought. Or afraid of Rusty turning on him, pointing the finger. Afraid of Rusty? Why? Whit's money could hire lawyers and PR people to build a wall around him. Whit couldn't be touched.

Why had he thrown Gail and Anthony out of his house? Jackie wondered if Whit knew something they didn't. That Rusty wasn't the one.

"Gail, something's been bothering me. You remember those two baby bottles in the crib?"

Slowly Gail's eyes came open, but only halfway. "Yes."

"Why were they there? Rusty wouldn't care if the baby starved."

"Amber put them there so she could sleep."

"Yeah, but she was up at ten o'clock, remember? Gary called her. She'd have checked on the baby, wouldn't she? Why did the police find two bottles? One empty, one half full?"

Gail's eyes turned to her. "Anthony says you asked him the same thing. You said Lacey Mayfield spent her lunch hour killing her sister. She reset the clock and made it look like somebody broke in. Jackie, do we *need* another theory of who did it?"

Slowing at a traffic light, Jackie said, "If you look at the evidence against Rusty, it's more guesses than fact. A fisherman saw a truck with fender damage in the vicinity. You want to know how many pickup trucks in Martin County have fender damage?"

They were coming into Stuart, working their way across U.S. 1.

"What about this," Jackie said. "On a street like White Heron Way, people notice anyone who doesn't belong, like a man with a long red ponytail. Who *wouldn't* they notice, particularly? A woman."

"Stop it, Jackie. He did it. You know he did it."

"I *think* he did it. Ron Kemp thought that Kenny Clark did it."

"Well, he was *wrong*." Gail shifted restlessly in her seat. "Lacey Mayfield as a cold-blooded killer, hacking away with a knife. I can't see it. What motive could she have?"

"Jealousy. She was hot for Gary." When Gail rolled her eyes, Jackie laughed. "Hey, I don't know. Last week I had to pull two sisters off each other in a domestic because one borrowed a dress without asking."

"I do feel a little sorry for Lacey," Gail said. "If Kenny dies her life will be over. She'll have no one to hate anymore."

"Break my heart," said Jackie.

The shady street curved along the river,

and soon the house came into view, the wide porch and oak trees in the yard. A small red pickup truck was just pulling into the driveway. "Hey, it's Diddy."

Gail opened her eyes. Diddy stood by his truck, waiting for Jackie to park. He was wearing an old ball cap, and his jeans were covered in dirt. He lifted a hand in greeting. Gail said, "He is the sweetest thing. Do you think he'd mind if I gave him a hug?"

"He'd mind if you didn't."

She got out and went around. "Hi, Diddy, remember me? I'm Gail."

After a couple of seconds his tangled white eyebrows shot up. "Gail! Hot dog. You're a picture. Where you been?" When she hugged him, the top of his head came just to her shoulder. "Last time you was here, Karen was in didies. How's Irene?"

It amazed Jackie what he could remember on a good day. She picked a piece of straw off Diddy's plaid shirt. "What have you been into?"

"I had to go to the ranch. Whit McGrath is getting himself a new horse this week, a filly, all the way from Kentucky. I helped the boys clean out a stall. I told Whit I wouldn't charge him nothing to keep her, except for feed. It gives the place some class." He laughed.

Jackie smiled at him. "Such a deal."

"You girls come on in. We'll rustle up some supper."

The apology was forming on Gail's lips, but Jackie spoke first. "Well, Diddy, we can't right now. We've got some stuff to talk over, but we'll be down in a while. Go ahead and get cleaned up, okay?"

"Ten-four." He turned back around and winked at Gail. "See you later."

"Bye."

They watched him go. When the screen door had banged shut, Gail leaned heavily against the side of Jackie's truck.

"Margarita time," said Jackie.

But Gail's blue eyes were unfocused, staring at the trees. "What you said about Lacey Mayfield. It bothers me. Before Anthony risks going onto McGrath's property, I want to be sure we're right. I've got to talk to Gary Dodson about Lacey. Do you want to come with me?"

Jackie looked toward the house. "I better not." She reached into her uniform pants. "Here. Take my car."

She stood out of the way while Gail opened the door and got in.

"Gail? Do me a favor. When I talked to Gary Dodson at the courthouse, he said my mother went to him to find out about the

Mendozas, and she was distressed. He used that word. Distressed. He said she died a few days later. I was wondering how she was. Her state of mind, you know?"

"I understand," Gail said.

"What did she say? Did she mention anything of a personal nature? Did she mention me or Alex? Would you ask him about that?"

Gail could have used her cell phone to make sure Gary Dodson was in, but she decided not to. She didn't want to give him any advance warning. Jackie had said to look for a dark green Oldsmobile sedan about ten years old, and Gail saw the back end of it as she came around the corner. Dodson lived over his law office, converted from an old house. She recalled the shabby furniture, the worn carpet, and the curtains pulled across the windows, keeping out the light. Time had stopped for him twelve years ago. Both he and Lacey were imprisoned in the past, the sister trapped inside her anger, Gary in this tomb. Kenny's death, if it came, would not release either of them.

She parked across the street and looked around for a black pickup truck before taking the keys out of the ignition. What she noticed was Dodson's secretary turning into the driveway, struggling to get her bulk out from under the steering wheel, then walking up the steps. She carried a folder with papers inside; perhaps she had been on some errand.

Gail quickly got out of the Isuzu and ran up behind her, practically forcing her way through the door the moment the woman pushed it open.

"Hello again. I need to see Mr. Dodson. Would you please tell him Gail Connor is here?"

The woman frowned at her. "He's not in."

"Oh, but I'm sure I saw him." Gail moved toward the hallway. "I'll just announce myself. You wouldn't mind, would you?"

"Hey, wait a minute!"

Quick footsteps carried her to the door at the end. She knocked, then pushed it open. "Mr. Dodson?"

He was working on some papers at his desk, exactly as she had left him more than two weeks ago. This could have been the same somber suit, the same starched white shirt with fraying cuffs. He stood up and waved his secretary quiet.

"Never mind, Nelda. It's all right." He took off a pair of gold-rimmed glasses.

"What do you want, Ms. Connor?"

"I'd like to ask a question. I won't take more than a minute. Please."

"All right." With a sigh Dodson laid down his glasses, squaring up the frames with the edge of his file. "Nelda, wait. Did you get the agreements signed? Leave them on your desk, and I'll look at them later. Don't forget to lock up when you leave."

"Good night, Mr. Dodson." The woman went out, closing the door behind her.

A sliver of afternoon light came through the curtains, and a brass-shaded banker's lamp illuminated Dodson's desk. As before, the corners were taken up with stacks of old files with peeling labels, and Gail wondered if he kept them there to create the illusion that work was actually done here. She doubted he had any cases other than the pittance McGrath tossed his way.

"Have a seat, Ms. Connor."

She took one of the walnut jury-box chairs across from him and set her purse on the other. "Thank you." Amber and the baby smiled back at her from the framed portrait on the credenza, and the same lite-FM music was playing on his radio. "Forgive me for disturbing you, but I need your help. Kenny Ray Clark lost his appeal in the Florida Supreme Court, and the execution is scheduled for Wednesday. That's two days from now."

"I'm sorry the decision wasn't in your favor." The springs in Dodson's chair squeaked in a steady rhythm as he rocked in it. His head went in and out of the lamp-light. "I was at the hearing last week. Had I been the judge, I would have ruled the other way. You've come up with an interesting theory of who killed my wife, but regret-fully, I have no influence over Whit McGrath. As I explained to your cousin, Miss Bryce, I can't help you."

"Yes, she told me about your conversa-tion. What I wanted to ask you was, how well did your wife get along with her sister?"

"Strange question." He lifted his hands briefly from the chair. "Fine."

"Any arguments in the weeks leading up to her death? Any rivalry between them?"

"No. They weren't best friends, but they got along all right." A smile creased his cheek. "My goodness. Do you suspect Lacey too?"

"I wanted to rule her out." A cool breeze came from the vents, and Gail crossed her arms for warmth. "As long as I'm here, Mr. Dodson, I have a question about my aunt, Louise Bryce. Jackie said you'd met her." Gail hesitated, then dove into the subject.

"Louise died in a single-car crash in Palm Beach County in 1988. Jackie was only twelve at the time. She was told that the crash was an accident, and that her mother had been drinking. I think she has always feared it was something else. That her mother sped into that turn not wanting to come out of it alive."

The soft squeaking of springs continued. The lamplight carved shadows into Dodson's gaunt cheeks.

"You told Jackie that her mother was distressed when she came to see you, and that she died a few days later. You seemed to be saying that Louise was distressed about having notarized the Mendoza deed for Whit McGrath. What did you mean, exactly? Did she seem to be in a mental depression?"

"No, I wouldn't say so. By distressed, I meant . . . agitated. Excited."

"Excited?"

"Worried. Concerned. I thought I'd made it sufficiently clear to your cousin."

"What was Louise worried about?"

"The deed. She wanted assurances — and I gave them — that the deed had been properly signed. That the people who signed it had not been forced to do so."

"Why didn't she ask Whit McGrath?"

"Oh, she did, but they weren't communicating very well at the time. They had split up. I remember she was angry at McGrath, but not depressed, not to the extent of ending her own life. Please tell your cousin, and again convey my condolences."

Angry. Gail let the word float through her head for a moment. She shivered. Her short-sleeved linen dress did little to ward off the frigid air from the vents. "What did you tell Louise about the Mendozas?"

"I said they'd gone back to Guatemala. That they had signed the deed, accepted a check for the property, and there was no way to contact them."

"Had she been trying to?"

"Louise Bryce was concerned, as I said, because she had broken the law. It was a petty crime, to be sure, but a crime nonetheless. When Mr. McGrath shut her out, she came to me. What was *I* supposed to do? She started screaming at me. She demanded to have an address for the Mendozas. What a scene. But I was able to calm her down. After all, she wasn't blameless, was she?"

"You told her she could go to jail?"

"I had to tell her something. She was threatening to go to the police."

"Because she suspected the Mendozas were dead."

Dodson stopped his chair. The bones in his face seemed sharper, the skin more pallid. With a quick movement, he pushed back his frayed cuff to check his watch. "You know, Ms. Connor, I have some things to do this afternoon."

"Wait. I've just got one more question. Jackie told you why we suspect that Rusty Beck was responsible for your wife's death." When Dodson made no reply, Gail said, "We think Beck was afraid Amber would talk about the Mendozas. Beck murdered them, put them in the trunk of their car, and pushed the car into a sinkhole on Whit McGrath's property. The only leverage we have against McGrath is that he knew about it. He knew, didn't he?"

"Ms. Connor, I'd really rather not discuss —"

"A man is going to *die* if I don't get some answers. Just a yes or a no. Please."

Dodson blinked, then made a quick nod. "He knew."

"And Amber? Did she know?"

He pressed on his forehead with stiffened fingers. His cuticles were raw. "I never told her. She knew about the deed, but . . . nothing else. Please leave, Ms. Connor. I can't discuss this anymore."

Gail moved forward to the edge of his

desk. She spoke softly, sensing that if only she could put this the right way, he would let go. "How did you find out the Mendozas had been murdered? Did McGrath tell you?"

"He didn't have to. It was obvious."

"Why was it obvious?" Gail waited. "Mr. Dodson?"

Staring down at his desk, he leaned his forehead on an open palm, and after a few seconds, he began to speak. "When the deed wasn't delivered by a certain date, which had been promised, I became concerned. Mr. Hadley, my supervising partner, wanted an answer, and I had none. I couldn't get any information from Mr. McGrath, so . . . I drove out to speak to the Mendozas. Mr. Mendoza said he'd never sell. Never. And I'd already written the title opinion! I said to him, 'I'll make sure you get double your price.' He said, 'No, we won't leave. This is our home.'"

Dodson's lips trembled, then moved again. Gail leaned closer to hear him. He could have been reading from the pages of a book.

"Two days after I spoke to Mr. Mendoza, the deed was dropped off at my office with a note from Whit McGrath. 'Have this recorded.' It wasn't right. I had to find out what was going on, and I drove to their property. No one was there. I looked through the windows and saw furniture still in the house. Dishes in the sink. The dirt around the house had been raked. There were no footprints. No tire tracks. I couldn't move. I felt sick. Terrified. As if . . . they were there. Watching me."

From his pocket Dodson produced a folded handkerchief, and he pressed it to one eye, then the other.

Gail released a breath. "What did you do then?"

"Drove to Whit McGrath's office. I told him what I'd seen. I was outraged. Four people. I thought he *couldn't* know. But he did." Dodson cleared his throat. "He said they'd cashed the check and gone back to Guatemala. It was a lie, of course it was a lie, but he couldn't admit it, could he? I *knew*, and he *knew* that I knew."

"You never told anyone."

"No." Dodson unfolded his handkerchief and wept into it. "I did nothing. They were dead . . . murdered . . . and I did nothing. Mr. Hadley asked me . . . where they were. I lied. I said . . . Guatemala."

"Why?" The enormity of this lie, the staggering weight of it, forced the question to her lips. "Why did you lie for him? Four people dead, and you said nothing?"

He sobbed. "I had already recorded the deed! I couldn't embarrass the firm. I had a job, a family. Amber wanted so *much*. Always making *demands* on me. Buy me this, buy me that. What could I do? I couldn't bring them back. It was too late. Go ahead, say it. You're disgusting . . . weak. You pitiful example . . . of a man."

After a fast shower, Jackie changed into shorts and an old police academy T-shirt. She usually ran five miles after work, but today it would have to wait. Gail would be back soon. Jackie unbraided her hair and shook it out.

"It's *cold* in here." She saw that she had flipped the AC temp control down all the way. She turned it off and opened the windows. A strong breeze came through, and the photographs she had left on the kitchen counter started sliding to the floor. These were exterior color shots of the Dodson house. She'd been looking for something the crime scene techs might have missed. A patch of flattened grass, a button, a shoe print, anything.

Gathering them up, she noticed the photo of the west side of the house. The windows in the master bedroom were open. The four-paneled aluminum frames were tilted outward. But the other windows were closed. Three sets of windows, a hedge underneath. Living room, baby's room, master bedroom. Closed, closed, open. She hadn't really noticed that before. Jackie went through the photos to find the back of the house. The master bedroom windows there were open also. The third bedroom and the kitchen were closed. A big AC unit hung through the wall in the master bedroom. Jackie brought the photo closer. There was a vertical white line underneath.

She went to her desk for her magnifying glass, then to the window, where the light was brightest. She focused. It was nothing. A PVC pipe for condensation. The flash glistened on the concrete drip pad underneath. Water. The AC had been running. That was funny, she thought. The temperature had only reached the low seventies that day.

Jackie picked up the photographs again and shuffled through them. She found a close-up of the ground under the rear bedroom window, which also showed half of the concrete pad. She looked through her magnifying glass. The concrete was wet. Not just wet, flooded. The dampness extended to the outline of mildew and algae that always built up in the summer, when ACs were let run all day. This one had been running for a long time. Who had turned it off? And when? According to Dodson, the windows had been open when he had arrived home.

The crime scene reports were in a folder on her desk. Jackie flipped through pages until she found what she was looking for. Exterior photographs. Taken between 9:00 and 9:30 P.M. But still the puddle was there. It hadn't had time to evaporate.

Raising her head, Jackie looked at the open window of her apartment. She felt the warm air coming in.

Last Monday at the courthouse she had sat on one heel talking to Gary Dodson through the open door of his car. She remembered how cold it had been inside. The AC had been turned up high, and condensation had run out from underneath. The bottom of her purse had been soaked.

"Oh, my God."

Jackie threw down the photographs and ran to the counter for her keys. They were gone. She grabbed her cell phone and her pistol and pounded down the stairs yelling for her grandfather. "I need to borrow your truck! Diddy!"

As Dodson had continued to talk about

his own failures, the logic of the odd relationship between him and Whit McGrath had begun to make sense.

Gail said, "After you were fired from Hadley and Morgan, Mr. McGrath's company continued to give you some legal work. It's because he didn't want you to talk about the Mendozas. That was why, wasn't it?"

He wiped his eyes. "You're making it sound like blackmail. It wasn't. I'm a good lawyer. It wasn't my fault they fired me. I lay it all on his doorstep. McGrath owed me, don't you agree?"

"Maybe so, but he wouldn't care about that. He wouldn't be easily intimidated, either, unless . . . you had proof. Do you? Do you have proof of what happened to the Mendozas?"

His thin lips trembled into a smile. "No. What proof? I can't show you a photograph. I didn't see them die."

"But you could help us, couldn't you? Because you know the truth."

Again his eyes filled with tears.

Gail reached across the desk, touching his sleeve. "Please. Kenny has two days to live. You can't let him go to his death for someone else's crime. What can I say to convince you? Mr. Dodson, please."

Her cell phone rang in her purse. She let it

ring. The noise was muffled.

Dodson didn't appear to have heard. He retreated, leaning his forehead on his hands. The frayed white cuffs hid his face. "I can't. I told you, I can't help you."

"But why? You don't have to be afraid of him."

"I'm sorry. I don't want your client to die, but I can't."

Gail could hear her phone ringing again, but Dodson was paying no attention, either to her or to the tears that had begun to spill down his cheeks.

"Why can't you?" Gail wanted to shout at him, scream, pound on his desk, and the effort of remaining calm was making her dizzy. "Why are you so afraid of him?"

The voice was small and choked. "He — He would tell."

"Tell what? That you recorded the deed for him? It's going to come out eventually. Please don't wait until another innocent person is dead."

"No. No, no, no, I can't." Gary Dodson put his head down on the desk. "I don't deserve to live."

Intending to shut off her phone, Gail took it out of her purse. She noticed the number. Jackie was calling.

She murmured, "Excuse me." She spoke

softly into the mouthpiece. "Jackie. I can't talk now."

Gail could hear a car door slam and an engine start, then Jackie asking her if she was with Dodson.

"Yes, in his office."

Dodson raised his head, and his forehead creased into deep lines. He stared at the cell phone.

Jackie said to make some excuse, leave as quickly as possible, don't show a reaction, just say you have to go.

"Why? What's wrong?"

Telling her not to ask any questions, just *go*. The tension in her voice came through clearly.

"All right. I'll leave now. Be home in a couple of minutes."

Jackie said not to hang up. Let me hear you leave.

"Okay. Sure."

Dodson said, "That was your cousin? The police officer?"

"An emergency. I'm so sorry. I need to go." She reached for her purse and stood up. "Thank you for your time."

She heard a drawer slide open, and from it came a revolver. The lamp glinted on the long, shiny barrel. She could see the chambers. The bullets in them. The immense black hole of the gun.

"Sit down."

"What —"

"I said *sit down*."

She stumbled into the chair.

Jackie's voice came from far away. *Gail, are you all right? Answer me.* Dodson stood up, reached over the desk, and took the phone out of her hand. He closed it and pushed it aside.

"Move and I'll kill you."

Terrified into immobility, Gail could only stare up at him.

He laughed. "That sounds funny, doesn't it? Move and I'll kill you. I must have heard it on TV. But I do mean it. Please don't get up, Ms. Connor, oh, please don't, because I probably would shoot you. Just sit there and let me think."

Her mouth had gone dry. "I don't understand."

"Yes, you do. She told you, didn't she?" He burst into a laugh. "It's so funny. It really is. Rusty Beck. You want me to help you get him. You want him executed instead. So much death." Suddenly moaning, Dodson ran a hand over his head. The barrel of the gun jerked erratically. "I don't know what to *do*." His fist came down on a stack of files, and they slid to the floor.

Gail's heart fluttered in the fragile cage of her chest. "Please don't. Please."

"They're probably on their way. We have to leave." He began to open drawers. "What can I take? Nothing. *Nothing.*" He slammed the center drawer, then swung the gun toward her. "I said don't move!" He bared his teeth, and his eyes glittered.

"Oh, my God. It was you."

He picked up the portrait of his wife and child. "This is the only thing I want to take with me. It's all that matters. Amber. Sweet angel." He pressed his lips to the glass.

There were sirens in the distance, coming closer.

Gail moved slowly forward in her chair, ready to slide off and run.

Arm extended, Dodson swung the pistol, aiming it directly at her. "We're leaving now." His face was splotched red with emotion and shiny with tears. "You have to come with me. I can't do this alone."

The piercing wail of sirens surrounded them, and finally, he heard.

"They're coming. It's too late." He hugged the portrait to his chest. "God forgive me."

Jackie bailed out of the pickup truck in the middle of the street. She had reached the scene first, but a patrol car hit the brakes behind her, and another squealed around the corner at the end of the block, emergency lights flashing.

She took the steps in one leap.

"Bryce!" One of the officers shouted across the yard. "Hold on. Wait for backup!"

The door was locked. No one was inside the office. She slammed the butt of her Glock 19 through the glass and reached around for the dead bolt. "Dammit, dammit, come on."

Just as she turned the bolt, she heard a gunshot. She pushed the door open. Holding the pistol extended in both hands, she ran for the entry to the hallway and pressed herself against the living room wall. Three officers came in after her, guns drawn. More sirens were closing in.

She shouted, "Police! Drop your weapon and come out, hands on your head. Now!"

Gail's voice screamed back at her. "Jackie!"

She looked quickly into the hall. Gail stumbled through a door at the end and dropped to her knees. The front of her dress was flecked with blood.

"He's dead." She leaned against the wall, weeping.

CHAPTER 26

Monday evening, April 9

It was past nine o'clock when Anthony was finally able to free Gail from the detectives at the City of Stuart Police Department. They had questioned her like a potential suspect — customary in such cases. They had swabbed her hands for traces of gunpowder and listened with professional skepticism to her disjointed explanations of why Gary Dodson had put a bullet in his brain.

Returning to the hotel on Hutchinson Island, Anthony turned on the light and locked the door. He told Gail to go take a hot shower and change her clothes. No reply. She paced across the living room to the glass patio doors and back again, twisting her hands at her waist. Her dress was spattered with blood: rust-colored spots on pale blue linen.

"If only I had lied to them. I could have said he confessed. It might have made a difference." Her hair was wild and uncombed. She had rinsed out the blood in the law office bathroom before calling Anthony on her cell phone. She told him what Jackie had found: The air conditioner in the Dodson house had been running all day, chilling Amber's dead body. *Anthony, please hurry.*

Breaking speed limits to get there, Anthony created the murder scene in his mind. Dodson and his wife had argued that morning, another in a series of arguments between a frustrated, unhappy young woman and a man staggering under the weight of his financial, sexual, and moral failures. It started in the kitchen. He grabbed a knife and stabbed her. She ran for the bedroom. In the hall he nearly caught up, ripping out a handful of her hair. She tried to close the door, but he pushed it open, and the impact sent her staggering backward. He knocked her onto the bed, raised the knife, plunged it into her, again and again, blood flying from the point of the knife across the headboard, up the wall, to the ceiling. She was dead, this young woman in her red silk panties and top, and he kept stabbing until he was exhausted.

What then? Sanity returned.

He ripped the clock cord from the wall and wound it tightly around her throat. He reset the clock. Then a shower. A shave. Dressing for the office as if this were any other morning. A call to Amber's work — the call overheard by Whit McGrath and

Rusty Beck. A call to the baby's day care center. Two bottles in the crib. And before leaving, Gary closed the bedroom windows, pulled the curtains, and turned the air conditioner to its lowest setting. He made sure during the day to remain in sight. At 10:00 A.M. he faked a phone call to his wife. Returning home at the normal time, he turned off the AC, opened the windows, and went to check on his son. The anguish in the call to 911 had been real. Grief and shock disguised his guilt, and a mistaken eyewitness turned the police in another direction.

Only Jackie Bryce, twelve years later, had noticed the great quantity of water under the AC drip pipe. But what did a puddle of water prove, when Kenny Ray Clark had been tried and convicted of the crime?

"Gail, please. We're going to call Governor Ward in the morning. You should get some rest."

"But he won't listen," she cried. "He won't. I'm the lawyer for a guilty man. He'll think I'm lying. You saw how the police reacted. They almost laughed in Jackie's face. The governor isn't going to pay any attention." She fumbled for his hands with trembling fingers. "Anthony, we've got to do something. It isn't fair! We can't let this happen!"

He brought her hands to his chest and held them tightly. "We will talk to Whit McGrath. He knows Kenny is innocent. He's known it all along."

"You're right," Gail said. "Now. Let's go to his house now." Gail looked around for her purse, then noticed her dress. "All this blood. I don't care. Let him see it. That should give him a shock."

"Not tonight, tomorrow," Anthony said.

"We've got less than two days!" She took a shaky breath to quiet her voice. "All right, tomorrow. But you go. Please. You can do it. I'm afraid I'd screw it up. I shouldn't have taken this case. I had to be strong. I don't know why, but I don't care about that anymore. We have to save Kenny now."

"*Amorcito,* of course I'll go. Whit McGrath has to listen this time. He doesn't have a choice. Hector will have the photographs of the car by tomorrow morning. Don't worry. I'll talk to him."

"Do you think it will work?" Gail's eyes fixed on him, moving back and forth on his. She wanted hope, but not to be lied to.

Anthony was surprised to hear the words come so easily, even more surprised to find that he believed them. "Yes. I think we have a good chance." He kissed her forehead. "A very good chance. Let me take care of it."

Sometime in the night Gail slipped out of bed and closed the door softly behind her. Taking her cell phone, she went out onto the balcony. Her view was a heavy black sky and stars that seemed to pierce through it with a strange blue intensity. She slid the glass door shut and sat down to dial Jackie's number. She answered on the second ring.

"Jackie, it's me . . . No, I'm fine. Sorry to call so late . . . You too, huh? Well, Anthony is sleeping like a rock. Listen, I didn't get a chance to tell you this earlier, with everything going on. I love you. Really. You're so great. You were wonderful today, oh my God, coming in there with your gun drawn, but even more than that, how you stood by me. I mean, there I was, babbling away like a crazy woman, and you took such good care of me. . . . No, you *are* wonderful. And you're my cousin too, so I'm entitled to be gushy. . . . I want to tell you what's going on. Tomorrow Anthony is going to see Whit McGrath. . . . He says he can probably talk him into it, and I've got my fingers crossed, but this case has been so tough, right from the start. . . . Jackie, in case it doesn't work, we're going to be up against the wall. . . . The chances of the Supreme Court granting a stay are extremely remote. So I was wondering if you could talk to Garlan. . . . It's a long shot, but he might, if you explain it to him. . . . I don't know what else to do, Jackie. I've never been through anything like this in my life. I'm so damned tired. It's made me think about who I really am, and what I do, and whether I want to keep on being a lawyer, and I don't think I do. . . . Seriously. I used to think I was pretty good at this, but . . . No, things don't always look better in the morning, unfortunately. . . ."

Gail leaned her head on her updrawn knees and stared out at the ocean. "What would I do? I don't know, Jackie. I don't know."

Tuesday morning, April 10

Sunlight slanted through the open patio doors, and a slight breeze lifted the curtains. Anthony poured a cup of coffee from the room service carafe and kept an eye on the television. He kept the volume low. Gail was still asleep.

The NBC affiliate based in West Palm led with the Dodson story. A woman news anchor said, "Yesterday in Stuart the husband of a murder victim took his own life as the attorney for his wife's convicted killer looked on." There was footage of Dodson's law office, the body being taken out on a gurney, a small crowd watching from behind yellow crime scene tape. "Gary Dodson, forty-four, a Stuart real estate attorney, was said to be despondent over the 1989 murder of his wife, Amber, and their baby son. The man found guilty of the crime, Kenneth Ray Clark, is currently on death row, scheduled to die by lethal injection on Wednesday."

Kenny's face appeared, taken from the Department of Corrections Web site, a sullen man in a bright orange shirt. Anthony said, "So now you are accused of murdering the baby too."

The reporter's voice continued, "One of Clark's attorneys, Gail Connor, was in Dodson's office discussing the case when Dodson allegedly took out his gun and inflicted the fatal wound. In a surprising twist, Connor and her co-counsel, Anthony Quintana, both of Miami, say that Dodson was actually his wife's killer, and that their client is innocent."

Anthony looked at his own face under the glare of lights. The station had edited out most of what he had said. "Dodson got away with it for twelve years, but when he realized that Ms. Connor knew the truth, he shot himself. Kenny Clark was wrongfully convicted and sentenced to die for another man's crime."

The reporter reappeared on the screen. "Martin County Sheriff's Office Lieutenant Ronald Kemp was the lead investigator in the Dodson case."

The picture switched to Kemp, who said, "There's no evidence whatsoever linking Gary Dodson to the murder of his wife. Ms. Connor claims that Dodson acknowledged his guilt. Unfortunately he's dead, and we have only her word to go on."

The reporter came back. "Keep it here for further developments at noon. In other news, brush fires in western Palm Beach County continue to —"

Anthony turned off the television. He had seen enough. Police and news media were disregarding everything Gail had said.

He stood in front of the decorative mirror over the wet bar in the living room to put on his tie. His shirt was spotless white-on-white, custom-tailored. His cufflinks were monogrammed gold. He wore only one ring, an onyx and diamond, and his slim Cartier watch. He pulled back his cuff. The watch said 7:12. McGrath customarily arrived at his company's main office in West Palm Beach at 8:00.

There was time for another cup of coffee.

Anthony needed a jolt of *café cubano,* but this weak stuff would have to do. Room service had brought the morning newspapers along with breakfast, and he laid them out on the counter in the small kitchen.

The Stuart News. Front page photograph of the gurney being taken down the steps. Smaller photos of Dodson, Amber, Kenny Clark. LOCAL ATTORNEY COMMITS SUICIDE AFTER ACCUSATION THAT HE KILLED WIFE.

"I see," Anthony murmured. "It's Gail Connor's fault."

The story continued inside, but there was nothing about the crime scene photos, the extra bottle of milk, the hands of the clock that had been set ahead. Reporters had uncovered Jackie Bryce's connection to the story. The irony was too good to pass up. Sheriff's daughter involved in defense of man her father put away for murder. Gail Connor's cousin, twenty-five-year-old rookie on the Stuart Police Department, working for Clark's attorneys. "Police sources say that Officer Bryce had access to official crime scene photographs. Bryce alerted Connor about the condensation from the air conditioner, which led to Connor's belief that Dodson had cooled his wife's body to confuse the time of death."

A terse comment from Garlan Bryce: "My daughter has no access to our files. The photographs were obtained by Ms. Connor through a court order."

It was too bad about Jackie. She was already beginning to suffer the consequences of being on the wrong side.

Anthony closed *The Stuart News* and opened *The Palm Beach Post*. Same basic story. MURDER VICTIM'S HUSBAND COMMITS SUICIDE. DEFENSE LAWYERS FOR WIFE'S KILLER ACCUSE HUSBAND. FAMILY SAYS DODSON DESPONDENT OVER DEATH OF WIFE.

He found what he was looking for, the official reaction from the state attorney's office. Sonia Krause: "A jury found Kenneth Ray Clark guilty of the murder of Amber Dodson, and last week the Florida Supreme Court once again reviewed the evidence and once again upheld his conviction. It is unfortunate that Clark's lawyers are interpreting this tragic event as evidence of their client's innocence."

The Florida Association of Criminal Defense Lawyers had issued a statement to the press: "We support the call to stop this execution and order a full investigation."

Lines were being drawn. The police and prosecutor denied that anything had changed. The condemned man's lawyers had introduced a potentially dangerous challenge to the accepted version of the facts. Governor Ward would have to respond, if he wanted to maintain the legitimacy of Clark's execution.

But first, the governor would get a call from his friend, Whit McGrath.

The JWM Corporation occupied a Mediterranean-style building overlooking downtown West Palm, the sparkling blue intracoastal, and the island of Palm Beach on the other side. Whit McGrath's office took up a corner of the top floor, a massive expanse of marble and glass.

A large man in a suit stood just inside the wood-paneled door, his hands loosely clasped in front of him. He had patted Anthony down before letting him into the office. Anthony found this to be more an amusement than an annoyance. It proved that McGrath was a coward.

The size of the office prevented the man at the door from hearing Anthony tell McGrath why he had come, or from seeing the six black-and-white, eight-by-ten-inch photographs laid out in a row on the desk. Hector's friends had been busy last night, thirty feet down in murky water. The flash illuminated weeds, rocks, rotten vegetation, and a car resting upside down under a thick layer of silt.

Giving McGrath time to grasp his situation, Anthony went over to the windows to watch the boats going up and down the intracoastal. Tinted glass muted the glare of morning sun. He could see his own reflection and that of McGrath standing at the desk.

"Well. This is déjà vu. When you and Ms. Connor came to my house with your threats, I thought I'd seen the last of it."

"Then we didn't have the photographs. Now we do." Anthony turned around. "You have no choice, McGrath. Call the governor."

Making a noncommittal noise, McGrath glanced at another photograph, then spun it to his desk. "That car could be anywhere. There isn't a canal in South Florida without a car in it."

"It isn't a canal, it's a sinkhole, and it's on your property."

"You didn't open the trunk."

"We didn't want to be accused of tampering with the evidence. You know what is in the trunk. What you should be thinking about is what the police will make of it. They will see that you needed title to the

Mendozas' ten acres to finalize a two-million-dollar loan. The Mendozas wouldn't sell. You instructed Dodson to falsify his opinion of title. You forged the deed, then you told Rusty Beck to kill the Mendozas and dispose of their bodies. Four people. An entire family."

Slouching against his desk, arms crossed, McGrath shook his head. "That's a pretty wild story, Quintana."

Anthony calmly went on. "Gary Dodson might eventually have turned you in, but you had something to hold over his head — the knowledge that he murdered his wife." Anthony spread his hands apart. "And there it is. Make the phone call."

With a low chuckle, McGrath paced along the edge of his oriental carpet, then back. The man at the door watched. McGrath patted his coat pockets, then took out a crumpled pack of Marlboros and a scuffed Zippo. He tapped the cigarette on the side of it. "What am I supposed to say?"

"That's up to you. We've been through this already. Just make the call." Anthony picked up McGrath's desk phone and turned it toward him. "You probably have the governor's private number in your book."

The Zippo flared, sending a brief flash of

orange across his face. "Just call him, right?" McGrath pulled in smoke and squinted over the cigarette as he exhaled. "Trust Kenny Clark to forget about it."

"Meaning what?"

"He's going to be pissed off, isn't he, sitting in prison for twelve years? If he got out, he'd start looking for someone to blame."

Anthony laughed. "He doesn't care about getting even with you, McGrath. What he wants is to live past tomorrow, and if he's lucky, to walk out of prison."

Smoke drifted over McGrath's head then vanished in the soft breeze from the vents. "So you say. I think he'd try to shake me down, cause me some grief. A guy like that. A criminal, a degenerate. If he wasn't in prison for Amber Dodson, he'd be in for something else, just like his buddy, Glen Hopwood."

"Take the photographs and negatives," Anthony said. Impatience was beginning to heat his voice. "Fill in the sinkhole and build your fucking hotel on it. But call the governor. *Now.* Tell him what you know about Dodson, or within an hour I will be talking to Garlan Bryce."

A slow smile put dimples in McGrath's tanned cheeks. "Jesus, you Cubans are pushy people. You come in here, dictating to me. I don't like that. I don't like you." He lifted his cigarette to his lips. "It might be interesting to see what Bryce would say, if you run to him with this story. He might throw you out of his office."

Anthony came closer. "You want to try it? You want to explain four bodies to the police? Or to the media? What will you say when they pull the car out of the water and open the trunk?"

McGrath's smile deepened, and Anthony saw what it was: predatory delight. "Why, I'd be as surprised as anyone else. 'All I know, sheriff, is that they signed the deed, cashed the check, and went back to Guatemala. Maybe someone robbed them and pushed their car in the hole. I can't explain it, sheriff, and Rusty Beck can't either. I don't know what Quintana is talking about. Where's his proof?' "

"Are you crazy?" Blood began to pound in Anthony's head. "You are tied to the Mendozas, both you and Beck. You benefited from their murder."

McGrath's eyes were like low blue flames. " 'Rusty told me, sheriff, that he never went near the Mendozas. Ask him.' "

Anthony stared at McGrath. "You would let an innocent man be put to death because you are afraid of what he would say?"

"Kenny Clark is a murderer. He killed Amber Dodson. Her husband shot himself because he was depressed. You and Ms. Connor drove him to it. I won't be extorted. I won't help you set a killer free. I won't do that."

The world contracted to a narrow view of Whitney McGrath's face.

"Que malo. Un satanás verdadero."

The face spoke. "Take your pictures and get out."

The fibers the paper was made of began to let go. Anthony twisted the envelope still further and the glued seam tore open. His sweat had dampened the creases, and his fingers clamped tighter. The muscles in his forearms burned, but no less keenly than the knowledge that he had accomplished nothing. Less than nothing. And that Kenny Clark would soon be dead. Hatred for Whit McGrath had become a tangible thing, an animal clawing at his ribs, demanding release.

"Señor Anthony, you are bleeding." Stopped at a traffic light, Hector looked at him from the driver's seat.

Anthony turned his hand over. The thin metal clasp of the envelope had sliced into his palm. It had not been sweat he had felt, but blood. He tossed the red-smeared, twisted envelope, with the photographs inside it, to the floor of the car and took out his handkerchief. The wound began to sting, now that he was conscious of it.

The light changed, and Hector drove forward. "That man. Someone should remove him."

The blood seeped from the cut. Anthony pressed down firmly with his handkerchief. The pain wasn't bad.

"Tell me what to do," Hector said.

"Nothing. Not now."

"When?" The angled sun sent the shadow of his heavy glasses across his face.

"I do not know."

"You can forget what he has done?"

"No, Hector. I won't forget." Anthony carefully lifted the cloth. The bleeding had stopped. "It's better not to be ruled by emotion. You make bad decisions that way. A man with a bullet in his head causes problems."

"He has a horse. He could be thrown." Hector guided the car onto the northbound ramp of the interstate. He waited for Anthony to speak.

Anthony refolded his handkerchief. "I have a better idea."

Gail knew when he opened the door. It must have been written in his eyes. She slipped off the stool at the counter, barefoot, still in her robe.

"He said no, didn't he?"

Anthony took her into his arms. Her small breasts were warm and fragile against his chest. Her hair was damp at the crown when he pressed his lips to it. "Sweetheart, I'm sorry."

"Oh, God, Anthony, I thought he would do it. I thought —"

"So did I." He held her tightly. "We have to face the truth, *cielito*. Unless some miracle happens, Kenny is going to die. It's over. There's nothing more we can do." He closed his eyes. "I'm sorry. I promised you I would take care of it, and I couldn't."

"Please don't blame yourself." Gail tilted her head up. "Jackie said she would talk to Garlan."

"Well. It can't hurt."

"She wants copies of the photographs."

"I'll tell Hector." Anthony took a breath to steady himself. "You see, Gail? I told you, it's not good to care so much about a client. Something like this happens, and where are you then? We should call Kenny. He should know."

Gail tilted her face up and stroked Anthony's cheek. "In a little while. Come back to bed with me."

"Now?"

"Please. I need you, Anthony."

CHAPTER 27

Tuesday night, April 10

It was past eleven o'clock when the head-lights on Garlan's Jeep Cherokee finally swung into the driveway. Jackie stood up from the kitchen table. Her father's heavy footsteps came across the porch, and she opened the back door before he got to it. He squinted as if the light hurt his eyes. Exhaustion bowed his shoulders.

"You're up late," he said.

"I need to talk to you." Jackie closed and locked the door. "It's important. Sorry it can't wait till tomorrow. I know you're tired."

He let out a breath. "Yeah. Quite a day." He poured himself some water. "Has this got something to do with Kenny Ray Clark? If so, maybe we don't need to get into it again."

Last night he had given her the lecture about the young cop who got involved in something that was none of her business and deserved the hell she caught from her chief. Jackie had listened, biting her tongue.

"Mostly I wanted to talk to you about Whit McGrath."

He set the empty glass in the sink. "I had a call from the chief down in West Palm this afternoon. Seems that Quintana paid McGrath a visit and offered him cash to call the governor and ask for a stay. Nobody wanted to press charges, but he thought I'd be interested to hear about it. Is that what you've got on your mind?"

"He never offered money." Jackie picked up the envelope from the kitchen table and followed her father down the hall to his study.

He unbuckled his gun belt, a leather one he'd had longer than she could remember, an old-fashioned Sam Brown that hung low on his hips. He put it over a peg on the rack. His Stetson went on the top shelf. He ran his fingers through his short gray hair.

"Where is Quintana, by the way?"

Jackie said, "He and Gail left for the prison this afternoon. They picked up Kenny Clark's grandmother. They're coming back late tomorrow, maybe the next morning, depending. Are you going to be there?"

To witness the execution.

"No. Ron Kemp will represent the office." Her father tossed his jacket over the arm of the sofa. "I think Sonia Krause is going as well, maybe a few more people. I don't know." He glanced around at her. "I'm tired. What do you want to tell me?"

Jackie took the photographs out of the envelope.

He had his tie halfway out of his collar. He pulled it the rest of the way. "What are those?"

She handed them over. She had thought for a long time how to begin, but suddenly the words became jumbled in her head. "The reason Anthony went to see Whit McGrath was about those photos. They were taken at the bottom of a sinkhole on undeveloped property in River Pines. That car belonged to a Guatemalan family named Mendoza. They were murdered by Rusty Beck in 1988. He put their bodies in the trunk."

Her father stared at her, then shuffled quickly through the photographs. "Jackie, what the hell is going on?"

She told him. She spoke for nearly half an hour, stopping only when he asked a question or told her to slow down. He sat in his lounge chair, elbows on knees, and Jackie leaned on the edge of his desk.

"You suspected Gary Dodson at first, too, but his alibi threw you off." Garlan let out a breath and rubbed his fingers over his chin.

Jackie went on, "When Gail was at Dodson's office, I realized how he had manipulated the time of death. By the time I got there, he'd killed himself."

"God almighty."

"Whit McGrath knew that Dodson was guilty. Anthony talked to him this morning and told Whit to call the governor or else he'd turn him in for the Mendozas. But Whit wouldn't do it. He wants Kenny Clark dead so he can't talk."

Her father had to get up and pace around for a little while. Finally he said, "There's still Glen Hopwood. He could talk."

"Right, but it's better to have one guy talking than two. If there's only one, and he's in prison, who's going to buy it?"

Her father picked up the photos and went through them slowly. "What have you got to link McGrath to this?"

"Nothing direct. We have oral statements from Clark and Hopwood. We know that Whit needed the property to be able to start construction."

"Can you prove he forged the deed?"

"No."

"That's not enough."

"With the photographs, can you get a search warrant for the sinkhole?"

"Maybe, but it won't be easy. I'd like to

see what's in that trunk, but you know, Jackie, we could get shot down on a motion to suppress."

"Whit McGrath thinks he's above the law," she said.

"No one is above the law."

"Will you investigate based on what I've told you?"

"Absolutely."

The relief hit Jackie with such force that it left her momentarily breathless. She reached into the back pocket of her jeans, where she had put a folded sheet of paper. She had debated with herself whether to tell him, but decided there was no way around it.

"Dad? There's something else you should know. This is the Mendoza deed. Look at the notary."

He held the paper under the desk lamp, then leaned closer. She saw his jaw sag. "My God."

"Mama knew Whit McGrath from her real estate office, and I remember seeing him at the ranch. They were friends. She notarized it as a favor."

Her father handed the paper back. "Louise wouldn't have notarized a deed unless she'd seen the people sign it. Are you sure it's a forgery?"

With dismay, Jackie saw that she could hold nothing back. "Yes, sir, I am sure. Gary Dodson told me himself. He said Mama did it as a favor for Whit, but she didn't know the signatures were phony. Whit and Mama — She was in love with him. That's why she did it."

Her father stared at her. Jackie said, "Nobody told me. I sort of put two and two together. I'm sorry. If this comes out, I wanted you to know in advance."

His eyes closed and he turned away.

"People will talk, I guess. She's gone, so it won't hurt her, and the rest of us, well, there's nothing we can do about it. Dad, you can't blame her. I mean . . . not for everything. Whit McGrath seduced her. She called it off, but you wouldn't take her back —"

"You know nothing about this, Jackie."

"I do. Not a lot, but something. I know that she was torn up by what she did. She wanted to come back, but you wouldn't let her. She moved away, and we didn't see her because you got custody. I thought it was because she didn't care, but that's not true."

"Are you blaming *me?*"

"No, sir. I just . . . I wish you'd told us. Alex blames you. I guess because he doesn't know. Maybe you and he could talk about it someday." Jackie held onto the edge of the desk and forced herself to look at her father. "Everybody shares blame. I was mad at her. One time I told her I didn't love her. She cried, and I didn't care because I wanted to hurt her for leaving us. Aunt Irene said it was an accident, how she died. She said Mama wouldn't have killed herself. All I can do is try to believe it. But I know she was drunk that night, and I keep thinking she just didn't want to live."

"You're wrong about that, Jackie. She wasn't drunk. Not then, anyway. I made sure the sheriff in Palm Beach investigated thoroughly. You mother had been to a bar, and she'd had a couple of drinks. She drove out to the country to see about a real estate listing. She was there for two hours. The people said that when she left she was in a good mood, and they hadn't offered her anything to drink."

"But what about the bottle?"

"She had the bottle in her car, but her blood alcohol level was less than point-oh-two. There was some thought it could have been an accident, somebody hitting her from behind, because they found a dent in her rear bumper. But the only skid marks were her own tires. She was going seventy miles an hour into that curve, Jackie. The sad truth is, your mother was a victim of her own irresponsibility."

"Why didn't you tell me all this? I thought for all these years that she'd killed herself."

"You thought that? I didn't discuss it with you because you were young. And it never came up."

The room was silent for a while, and then Garlan said, "You shouldn't have thought your mother didn't love you. She did. It wasn't much of a marriage, though. We had some problems."

"Yes. I know that."

He let out a breath and picked up the deed again. "All right. This may well become public, but there's nothing we can do about it. I'll start looking into this tomorrow. Rusty Beck. Good God almighty. You write me a report, put down everything you know about it. I want to get a statement from Quintana and Connor as well. I'll probably interview Glen Hopwood myself."

"And Kenny Clark," Jackie said.

"Well, that's . . . not going to be easy, is it?"

"You can't let them execute him now."

He looked at her, smiling slightly as if she were making a joke. "I can't prevent it, Jackie."

"Why not? Call Governor Ward and tell him what you found out. He'd listen to you."

"Whoa. The fact that the Mendozas may have been — *may have been* — murdered doesn't prove that Clark is innocent. I couldn't give Bill Ward anything but hearsay."

"Ask Whit McGrath yourself. Go ask him," Jackie said. "Ask him why he didn't turn Gary Dodson in. Ask him."

"If I could read minds, I wouldn't need a detective bureau."

"But you *know* Kenny is innocent."

"I do *not* know that. Jesus. I spent two hours in a meeting at the state attorney's office this afternoon because the governor wanted to know what's going on. There were six of us. Me, Ron Kemp, a guy from crime scene, and three prosecutors. We went over the same photographs you looked at. We read Gail Connor's statement. All it proves is that the air conditioner had been on at some point. It may have been early that morning or the previous night. It's a question mark, but that's all it is. We reviewed the evidence for the umpteenth time. We considered Tina Hopwood's testimony, and we came to the conclusion that it just wasn't credible. Even if Kenny Clark did leave her trailer at ten o'clock, as she says, he could have gone straight to the Dodson house, and Mrs. Chastain could have been a little off about the time she saw him. There isn't an investigation in the world where everything fits perfectly."

"Mrs. Chastain was *wrong*."

"Was she? I sent Ron Kemp to her house. He asked her, 'Is there *any* possibility that you could have been mistaken?' She said no. She got a clear look at Kenny Clark in broad daylight. Who are we to say she was wrong and we're right?"

"Dad, please. If you're not sure he's guilty, how can you let this happen? Do it for me. A favor. Not for Gail or Anthony, for me."

"Jackie, do I make exceptions for myself? Do I have to live by the same rules that I expect everyone else to follow? If I make an exception for you, it's like doing it for myself."

"But I'm not asking you to do something wrong!"

"I know that, Jackie. You're not listening. A person in my position, and yours, has less freedom than other people. We can't pick and choose what parts of the law we like and what we don't, or the whole thing comes tumbling down."

"So you're going to stand there and do *nothing.*"

He looked at her a moment, then said, "Let's just call it a night. What do you say?"

She got to the door before he did and leaned on it. "Explain it to me, Dad. Tell me why a man's life doesn't matter."

"I didn't say that!" His broad face reddened. "Aside from the fact that it would be like trying to stop a freight train, I will not subvert a system that I have spent my life trying to uphold. Kenny Clark was tried and convicted by a jury, and the appellate courts have consistently refused to say they were wrong. I refuse to put myself above them."

"What you're saying is, 'It's not my responsibility.' "

"Let me lay it out for you. You want me to go to the governor and say I *believe* this man is innocent. Is that it? Tell him that the men and women who did their best on this and a thousand other cases can't be trusted to get it right. That's how the press would see it. The defense lawyers would love me. I would create mistrust and disrespect for my office and everyone in it. What's at stake here is the rule of law, and how the public regards that law, with respect and confidence."

"I don't want any more of your damned lectures!" Jackie pressed herself against the door. "How can you justify letting a man be executed so the system can avoid embarrassment? Because that's what —"

"Listen to me!" He spoke over her. "*Even if* Kenny Clark is innocent of Amber Dodson's murder, he was there when Rusty Beck shot the Mendozas, and that makes him guilty of four counts of felony murder. I'd have to arrest him for that, if he ever got out. Did that cross your mind?"

"He had to do it! Rusty held the shotgun on him."

"Nobody made Kenny Clark pick up a baseball bat and go out in the middle of the night to force these people off their land. If we started weeping and moaning over the rights of every last criminal, we might as well let them all out. But like you said, you don't get it. So far, you've done nothing but exhibit a total disregard for your job, your reputation, and what you supposedly stand for. I question whether you're fit to be in law enforcement." He pushed her out of the way and opened the door. "We're done. I'm going to bed."

She followed him through the hall. "A man is going to die, and you talk about some abstract principle of law, like you were trying to be God, but you *aren't*."

He went up the stairs.

"Tell it to Kenny Clark. See if he understands, because I don't." Jackie hung onto the bannister. "That's what drove Mama away! It's why Alex left! It's driving us all away."

Footsteps echoed in the upstairs hall. A door slammed.

Jackie slid to the bottom step, breathing heavily. She had never yelled at her father. Her hands felt weak, and she let them fall into her lap. "Oh, my God." She would have to move out. It was no use staying here anymore, avoiding him, knowing what he thought of her. She hated him equally. Pompous, cold, unbending.

She would pack her things tomorrow and find an apartment. Pack them tonight.

Jackie leaned against the dark oak finial post and wondered what to tell Gail. She had promised to call her first thing in the morning. *I'm sorry. I tried.* She wondered why she should give a damn what happened to Kenny Ray Clark. He was only a punk, a nobody, always in trouble with the law. But she did care. She cared about the damn shame of it all. She thought her father might be right. She wasn't cut out to be a cop. She wasn't sure where she belonged and she only wished she could ask her mother. *Oh, Mama, I miss you so much.*

From above her came the light shuffle of bedroom slippers. She looked around and saw Diddy at the top of the stairs. Hanging on to the balustrade, he came down.

"Hey there, Jackie," he whispered.

"Hey, Diddy."

He steadied himself on her shoulder and sat beside her. "What's going on?"

"Nothing. Sorry if we woke you. Go back to bed."

"Sounded like a bomb went off." He rested his hands on his bony, pajama-clad knees. "Everything okay?"

"Fine. Don't worry about it."

"Alex and your pa used to fight before he moved out. He went to Tampa. And Louise is gone. You're not going away too, are you?"

She took his hand. "I don't know."

"I hope you don't. I'd lose track of things." He grinned at her. He hadn't shaved this morning, and his whiskers were white. "Of all the things I've lost, I miss my mind the most. I heard that at the diner today."

She smiled at him. "That's a good joke, Diddy."

"Yeah, it's pretty funny."

"Go back to bed, okay? It's late." She stood up and tugged him off the step. "I'll see you in the morning."

"Nighty-night." He pursed his lips, and she gave him her cheek.

She locked the kitchen door on her way to her apartment over the garage. Not her apartment. Not her house, either.

She climbed the steps thinking about what she'd do if she could turn the calendar back a month to the moment she'd seen Quintana's Cadillac run the red light. She could let him keep going. Then they wouldn't have come out to the ranch or told her about Kenny Clark, and none of it would have happened like this.

Maybe not like this, but it would have happened. Some things were just bound to happen, and you couldn't hold them back. If Gail came to her again and asked for help, Jackie knew she'd say yes. It might come out just as bad the second time, but she would still do it.

CHAPTER 28

Wednesday, April 11

Gail and Anthony sat at one of the tables in the dreary waiting room adjacent to the maximum security visiting area. The table was a scuffed white octagon with four blue-upholstered stools bolted to the center post. An industrial fan stirred the air. At another table, a woman with a little girl on her lap gave her son some quarters. Gail watched the boy feed them into a snack machine.

Ruby was saying good-bye to Kenny. She couldn't hug him; a thick glass window would keep them apart. The guards had apologized. They had been courteous. The prison seemed quiet, expectant. Going through the main gate Gail had heard none of the muffled shouts that had accompanied her previous visits.

They'd been late getting away from Martin County because of calls to or from the governor's office, the death clerk at the U.S. Supreme Court, people with anti–capital punishment groups. Reporters had started banging on their door at dawn. The execution was leading the news. Copies of the crime scene photos had been published in the *New York Post*. KILLER CLAIMS AC PROVES INNOCENCE. A reporter from *The Wall Street Journal* wanted to know about Kenny's prior criminal history, and how much his family was paying to get the services of a top defense lawyer like Anthony Quintana.

Dorothy Chastain appeared with her lawyer on CNN: "I am absolutely certain that Kenny Clark is the man I saw outside the Dodson house."

On *Good Morning America* Governor Ward said, "I have reviewed the evidence. I have talked to experts about this air conditioner question. The defense lawyers are raising a bogus issue. Their real goal is to manipulate public opinion, but I will not back down. The people of the state of Florida believe in capital punishment. So do I. I believe it deters crime. It also affirms the value of life and sets a standard for a civilized society."

Anthony had pressed the remote; the screen went black. Through his teeth he'd muttered, *"Comemierda."* Gail thought she knew his moods; this one was icy, dark, and foreign, unlike anything she had ever seen.

They would hold a press conference this afternoon at their hotel in Gainesville, forty miles away. After that, they would return to the prison. Witnesses were to assemble at the administration building by 5:30 P.M. Rules would not allow the inmate's relatives to view his execution, so Ruby would wait outside with Anthony. As Kenny's lawyer, Gail would be taken with other official witnesses to Q wing. Thinking of what would happen there, she became sick with both shame and anger. Not only had she failed Kenny, her presence at his execution legitimized his death. The defense lawyer was a necessary part of the machine. I wasn't good enough to save him, Gail thought, but because I am here, the system is blameless. There is a lawyer to defend him, a judge to deny the appeal, four guards to buckle the straps, someone to insert the IV's, a physician to pronounce him dead. It's our job. We don't like it, but it has to be done.

The world had revealed itself as indifferent and random. People had not evolved; they were brutish Neanderthals with cell phones and computers who still clung to primitive rituals of death. Men like McGrath and Beck could walk away with blood on their hands and nothing could be done about it.

Gail clenched her fists, digging her nails into her palms. She refused to cry.

Ruby Smith came through the door a few minutes later leaning on her walker. An embroidered bag tied to the front swung to and fro. She kept what she called her necessaries in it. She wore a pretty, flowered dress and a small hat on her pouf of gray curls. Gail rushed over to her. "Ruby, are you okay?"

Exhausted from walking, Ruby took Anthony's arm and let him guide her onto a stool. "It wasn't easy," she said, "saying good-bye. I can't tell you that Kenny Ray's at peace, but he's resigned. We prayed together, and he accepted Christ. At least he said he did, and I have to believe him."

She pulled her walker around to find her Bible and magnifying glass in her bag. The old leather-bound book was crammed with notes and bookmarks. "Go on and say good-bye. He's waiting. Take your time. I'll be right here."

"Have you been watching the news?" Gail asked. "We were on TV this morning."

"You were?" Kenny looked at her. His skin seemed too tight for his bones, and his eyes were red and tired. "I'm sorry I missed that. I've had the TV off the last couple of days. It was getting pretty depressing."

"I know what you mean," Anthony said.

Gail said, "The Supreme Court could still grant a stay."

"Well, excuse me, Gail, but I hope they don't, because it wouldn't last, and man, I don't want to go through this again."

They all smiled, then were silent.

Kenny knew about Gary Dodson; they had spent an hour talking about it on the phone last night. It had been rotten luck that Dodson had shot himself before confessing. Kenny had made a joke about bad luck being the only luck he'd ever had.

Gail touched the mesh that covered the small round hole in the window. "How are you doing, Kenny?"

His shoulders lifted. "Ruby says there's a purpose to this shit, but I wish I knew what it was. How am I? Aside from not sleeping for about three days straight, and throwing up because of my nerves, I'm fine. Well, to be honest with you, I'm ready to check out. I want to get it over with. Listen. I got a couple of things to say, and I have to make it kind of quick because they're going to take me back to my hotel room in a minute. First, take care of Ruby. Okay? I guess she's all right living at that new place, but if you could look in on her every now and then, I'd appreciate it."

They murmured that of course they would.

"And I want to say thank you for everything you did, standing up for me and all. It meant a lot, and I'm not just saying that. Hell, I had it all figured out, this nice little speech, and it's gone. Oh, well." He smiled. "No offense, but both of you look like shit. After this is over, take a vacation."

Gail pressed her lips together. The muscles in her throat ached.

Slowly Anthony moved forward until his mouth was only inches from the window. Dark fire glittered in his eyes. He whispered, "Kenny. We know who is responsible for your being here. I swear to you, he will pay for this. There will be justice."

Kenny glanced at Gail, whose shock must have shown clearly on her face. He said, "Listen, Anthony, I appreciate it, but don't get yourself jammed up on my account, man. I mean, getting even with McGrath or whoever, I don't want that. It's not worth it. Don't let me go in there worrying about you."

The two men looked at each other through the glass. Anthony made a slight shrug and a smile. "As you wish."

"Yeah. I got some other stuff to finish saying right now." Kenny took a heavy breath and knitted his fingers together on the table. "If you could tell Tina Hopwood thanks for testifying at the hearing. Tell her I hope Jerrod and Michael stay out of trouble and study hard. Also get in touch with Glen. Tell him to hang in there."

Kenny leaned on his arms as though they were the only things holding him upright. "Also, last but not least, I forgot to tell Ruby this, but she couldn't do it anyway, so this is your job. There's this cypress tree down on the south end of Lake O, near the boat ramp at Port Myacca. The branches stick way out over the water. You can't miss it. It's about my favorite place in the world. It's shady, and the grass is nice and soft, and if you stand there and don't move the fish will come right up to you. Maybe it's gone, I don't know, but would you take my ashes down there and put them in the water?"

"I promise, it will be done," Anthony said.

Gail could only nod.

"Yeah. I liked that place. It's got some good fishing, if you like to fish." Kenny was silent for a moment. "Hey, listen, could I talk to Gail? I'll wave when we're done."

Anthony glanced at her, then said, "Of course."

Kenny watched him go, then turned his eyes on Gail, and it seemed as though he were trying to memorize her face. He leaned closer to the window. "I don't want you to think you didn't come through for me. Ruby said you feel real bad about it."

"I'm sorry. Oh, Kenny. I wanted . . . to get you out of here, and . . . I thought I could, but . . . I couldn't. . . . I'm so sorry." Her eyes stung.

"I wish you wouldn't cry."

"I'm not." She blinked.

"Yeah, sure."

She took a deep breath. "There. See?"

He smiled and shook his head.

"But I hate this so much," she said.

"Yeah. It sucks." He lifted his hand to the window. "Is it okay if I say I love you? I mean, in a spiritual way."

"Of course it's okay, Kenny. I love you too." Gail put her hand next to his.

"Well, it's mostly spiritual. Good thing we got this glass between us, Anthony might come over and beat me up. But he's okay. For a lawyer."

"You're right. He's not so bad."

"Let me talk to him for a minute. All right?"

Gail waited in the corridor, able to see Ruby at the table, reading her Bible through a magnifying glass, one finger following the text.

"Gail."

She turned, and Anthony was there. He held onto her arm, speaking softly. "Kenny wants me to be the witness. The rules allow only one legal representative. We can't both be with him. He wants to know if you would mind if I do it."

Gail glanced past Anthony's shoulder. "Really? Why?"

"I think he's trying to be chivalrous."

"He doesn't have to do that."

"Let him," Anthony said. "Kenny needs to make this decision and you have to let him do it. Allow him some dignity."

"What about you?"

"Don't worry about me. I'll be fine."

She looked at him closely. He needed his dignity as much as Kenny did. "All right. Ruby and I will wait for you outside."

They went back and sat down. Gail told Kenny that she hated to admit it, but she was relieved, really she was. She didn't want her last view of him to be shared by a room full of strangers. They talked for a while longer, then a guard came up behind them and said they had to leave. Gail leaned close and lightly pressed her lips to the mesh screen.

"Good-bye, Kenny."

Anthony put his hand flat on the glass. Kenny put his hand in its outline. "You-all take good care of each other."

"We will," Anthony said.

At the door, Gail looked over her shoulder. Kenny's eyes were closed. He's glad we're going, she thought. He wants to get back to his cell. Gail could see he was starting to let go.

"Gail, wait." Anthony pulled her closer to the wall. "There's something I have to tell you." He spoke as if a surprising and long-hidden truth had just dawned on him. "You're such a good lawyer. Better than I am."

"Don't say that."

"It's true. Your passion, your devotion. You are fearless. I have never seen such commitment. Not only to your client, but to everything you touch. Gail, this has been missing for a long time in my life. I was wrong to think I had all the answers, or that you should listen to me. This was your decision, and I should have respected that. No matter what happens between us, I will always love and admire you. You are the best woman I have ever known."

The tears finally slid down her cheeks. "Thank you."

There were several dozen anti–death penalty protestors carrying signs at the hotel when they returned. Anthony parked around back and asked to use the freight elevator. Gail helped Ruby to her room, took a couple of Excedrin, then went downstairs with Anthony to do the press conference.

They spent the afternoon resting and waiting for a call from the Supreme Court. At four-thirty they took the freight elevator back downstairs and left for the prison. The clerk at the court had both their cell phone numbers, in case. Ruby's hands were folded on her Bible, which she held in her lap.

Once again, they reached the small town of Starke, then turned northwest. The land opened up to flat green fields, and the sun was in Gail's eyes. Nearing the prison she saw the cars and vans already lining the road. There were three satellite trucks parked on the grass. They had to speak to a guard to get through the main entrance, a metal arch resting on stone pillars. FLORIDA STATE PRISON. Beyond were the high chain-link fences and coils of razor wire.

Anthony parked in the lot near the one-story brick-fronted administration building. Two Department of Corrections vans waited nearby to transport the witnesses over to Q wing. Gail saw Detective Kemp hold the door for Sonia Krause. There were some men and women carrying notebooks, and she assumed they were reporters. No one seemed to be talking. Most of them wore dark clothing. How appropriate, she thought bitterly.

Anthony sat for a moment looking through the windshield, then said he ought to go in. Ruby, who was in the passenger seat, reached over and hugged him tightly and told him not to worry. He kissed her and got out.

Gail walked with him as far as the front door of the building. "Anthony, are you okay?"

"Yes, fine." He took a breath and let it out. He embraced her.

With nothing else to say, she told him that she and Ruby would be across the highway and he could walk over there afterward in the crowd. She would be looking for him. She added, "I love you." He nodded. His mind was already somewhere else.

Leaving him at the door, Gail came back down the walk and nearly ran into the Mayfields. Amber's parents blindly continued walking, but Gail and Lacey Mayfield circled each other like dogs, hackles rising. Triumph shone from Lacey's eyes. Her mouth was small and pinched. Gail wanted to pull her hair out by the roots and stomp her bleeding body into the ground.

She should die an early and painful death, Gail thought, then immediately was ashamed of herself, imagining that Ruby had overheard.

She got back in the car. The windows were down, and the breeze came through. Ruby smiled at her through her heavy glasses. Gail curled her hands over the top of the steering wheel and rested her forehead on them. Ruby gently patted her back and Gail fell into Ruby's arms. Twenty-five years ago she would have crawled into her lap and rested her head on her bosom.

"Now, now. It's going to be all right," Ruby said.

"I don't know how," Gail said.

"You did everything you could, don't you know that? Kenny is saved. Maybe not in the way we thought he would be, but soon he'll be walking in a better place."

"Oh, Ruby. Do you really believe that?"

"My goodness, yes." Her eyes shone with certainty.

Gail felt that the world had gone insane, and she along with it. "Well, I guess you're right," she said to Ruby.

She started the car and drove off the prison grounds. Someone was directing traffic, and she found a place to park. She helped Ruby out of the car and unfolded her walker for her. Some of Ruby's women friends from the church had driven up to be with her, and soon they put her in a lawn chair and gathered around.

The grassy area opposite the prison was roped off into three sections. One for media. One for anti–death penalty protestors. One for advocates. The publicity had generated a crowd in the hundreds. Gail remembered she had promised some of the TV reporters she would speak to them, but turned her head away, and put on her sunglasses.

Ruby was busy talking with her friends, so Gail hid for a while behind a group of women with crosses on their breasts. They all held candles, which had not been lit and would in any event be useless in the bright sunshine.

People jostled each other and raised signs in the air. Gail craned her neck to read them. HOW CAN KILLING STOP KILLING? EXECUTION IS NOT THE SOLUTION. THOU SHALT NOT KILL. She read the ones on the other side of the rope. REMEMBER THE VICTIMS, which had a photo of Amber and the baby. HE EARNED HIS WAY TO DEATH ROW. A photo of Kenny with a red circle around it, and a line drawn through. WHOSOEVER SHEDS THE BLOOD OF MAN,

BY MAN SHALL HIS BLOOD BE SHED. GENESIS 9:6.

Someone bumped her, and she nearly stumbled across the yellow rope. She was drunk on lack of sleep, and her reflexes were slow.

A pickup truck drove by, and a man in a camouflage cap cupped his hands at his mouth. "What day is this? Fry-day."

"You dimwit," Gail said aloud. "They don't use the chair anymore."

The anti crowd booed the man in the truck, and some in the pro crowd cheered. Others told them to be quiet, that wasn't what this was about. Back in the media area, reporters stood in front of cameras. Their mouths moved, but Gail couldn't hear them. Another crowd had gathered around the trucks, watching the monitors inside.

A man's voice a few feet away said, "Shut up. Listen. The Supreme Court just denied his appeal." Someone turned up the volume on a portable radio, and the voice of the governor came through.

". . . have finally reached an end. Mr. Clark has received the due process that our Constitution affords him, but enough is enough. Twelve years is more than enough. We need only point to the tragic suicide two days ago of the victim's husband, who could no longer bear the heavy weight of his grief. To his family, and to hers, my deepest condolences. To Mr. Clark I say, I harbor no ill will toward you, sir, but you deserve the justice being meted out today. May God have mercy on your soul."

A cheer went up.

Groans.

The nuns began to sing "Amazing Grace."

Gail walked away, pushing past a man handing out buttons for Citizens United Against the Death Penalty. She stepped over the rope and stood with her back to the crowd. The ground sloped downward a bit, and another correctional facility was just to her left, but an area of grass stretched out ahead of her.

She reached for her shoulder bag and remembered she'd locked it in the trunk. She had wanted her cell phone so she could call Karen, who had been too little in her mind these last days. She'd wanted to tell her hello and say she would be home soon.

Gail walked a little farther, thinking of her promise. She and Karen would go somewhere, just the two of them. Not even Anthony. They wouldn't even wait until Anthony left to take his grandfather to Cuba. That would be later next month. The old man had been patiently waiting for Anthony to come home, something Gail had never thought he would do, wait patiently for anything.

A flock of birds flew by, and Gail turned to follow their progress. They were heading north. She supposed the snow had melted already. The days were getting longer. The breeze was warm.

She sat down on the grass. How fine it was, such long, tender shoots. Not like that in Miami at all. It had rained recently and the ground was moist. She gathered a handful of grass and held it to her nose. It smelled of earth, sweet and fresh.

Her shoe had come untied. She reached over to retie the laces.

CHAPTER 29

Thursday, April 12

The sun was going down. The hotel's shadow stretched across the sand, and the clouds over the Atlantic had turned pink. Standing on the terrace, cell phone at her ear, Gail listened to Anthony's voice telling her to leave a message.

"Damn." She snapped the phone shut and went inside. Anthony had left three hours ago, and she'd hoped to be home before dark. Karen was expecting her, and Gail longed to see the last of Martin County for a while.

"Still no answer?" Jackie was setting the last box on the stack of them by the front door. She had come to say good-bye, but when Anthony hadn't shown up, stayed to help Gail finish packing the suitcases, computer equipment and files in the Clark case.

"I don't know where he could be. He said something about going with Hector to pay the divers for those underwater photos of the sinkhole. I suppose they all got into a conversation about the good old days of the CIA, God knows what, and he forgot the time. Maybe he forgot to turn his cell phone on too."

"Did you try Hector?"

"His isn't on either."

Jackie's calm brown eyes followed as Gail put her cell phone by her purse and tapped her nails on the kitchen counter. "You're worried."

"Not really. He's with Hector. I'm just annoyed that he hasn't called me back." This wouldn't have bothered Gail so much if he hadn't been in such a weird mood the last couple of days. His face seemed carved out of stone, and he barely spoke. She had awakened in the middle of the night, and his side of the bed was empty. From the terrace she had seen the figure of a man walking along the deserted shore line, too far away to hear her call his name. Anthony, so careful to maintain his professional distance from cases and clients, had been swept into the dark vortex of Kenny Clark's execution.

Jackie said, "Well, I'll just stick around till he gets back, if that's okay."

"I'd like you to." Grateful to have her cousin's companionship, Gail said, "Something's going on with him. He's so angry at everything, and particularly at Whit McGrath. The last thing Kenny said to him was to let it go, it's not worth it, but he can't seem to get past it. I think time will take care of people like McGrath and Rusty Beck. That's what Ruby told me. I have to believe it, or I'd go crazy. Maybe getting the search warrant will help. Tell Garlan we appreciate what he's doing. Truly."

Jackie followed a few moments of silence with a little shrug. "He's just doing his job."

"It's more than that, Jackie. He's sticking his neck out."

Gail could tell that Jackie regretted having failed, on the eve of Kenny's execution, to persuade her father of his innocence. Even so, she had convinced Garlan of the possibility of four bodies entombed in the trunk of a car. He was using his clout to get a search warrant, hoping to find something that would link the bodies to Rusty Beck, the man who fired the shotgun. And if charged with murder, who knew what kind of deal Beck would ask for. He might turn on Whit McGrath.

In the morning Garlan Bryce would take the warrant to Judge Willis for his signature. Garlan would give him a copy of the Mendoza deed, the underwater photographs, and state records that showed who owned the car. It wasn't much. Gail could imagine Whit McGrath's lawyers and PR people lining up to fight the inference that

McGrath was connected in any way to what might be found at the bottom of that sinkhole. They would probably succeed. There was no physical evidence against McGrath. But the scandal of hauling up four skeletons would put a pall over River Pines and possibly cause McGrath to lose the vote on Phase Two. It would cost him dearly.

It wasn't enough, but it was something.

Gail put her hand on Jackie's arm. "Anthony and I were talking about a complete investigation, top to bottom, to prove who really killed Amber Dodson. There wasn't time before, but now there's no rush. Would you like to help?"

A smile appeared. "Sure. I'll help you."

"No matter what we find, we won't convince everyone, but Kenny deserves to have the effort made. It's what Ruby wants, and I think it's going to make Anthony feel better. Me too. If you could write down everything you know about the case, including that conversation you had with Gary Dodson —" Gail swung around on her stool. "Jackie, you wanted me to ask him about Aunt Lou, and I did ask, but I forgot to tell you about it with everything else on my mind. He told me that she came to his office a few days before she died. You wanted to know if she seemed depressed. Remember?"

Jackie nodded. "What did he say?"

"He said no, he didn't think so. She wasn't depressed, she was angry. She was angry at Whit McGrath for talking her into committing a crime."

"A crime?"

"Notarizing the deed when she hadn't seen the Mendozas sign it. She wanted to make sure it was all right, but McGrath wouldn't tell her where they were, so she went to see Gary Dodson. He gave her the standard lie, that they'd left the country."

As Gail watched, the color slowly left her cousin's cheeks. Her freckles stood out clearly against the ivory pallor. "Jackie, your mother didn't kill herself. It was an accident. That's what you really wanted to know, wasn't it?"

"She wanted to find the Mendozas?"

"Dodson told her they'd gone home," Gail repeated.

Jackie inhaled a long and not quite steady breath. "The night I talked to my father, I asked him if Mama was drunk when she went off the road. I'd always thought she was, but he said no, she was speeding. Gail, I don't remember my mother *ever* driving that fast, but he said she'd have to be going about seventy around that curve to fly off the road the way she did. He said her rear bumper was dented. They thought at first she'd been hit from behind, but the only skid marks were hers, where she put on her brakes. So they decided the bumper damage wasn't related, and she'd been careless."

Suddenly too cold, Gail crossed her arms. "Jackie, what are you trying to tell me?"

Her voice had the cool, uninflected tone of a police officer on the witness stand giving testimony. "When we were looking at Rusty Beck for Amber Dodson's murder, we wanted to know about fender damage, because a pickup truck with fender damage had been seen near the Dodson house. Diddy told me about Rusty's fender bender. He told me something else too. Rusty bought a new truck in 1988, and he replaced his front bumper after an accident. My mother died in September 1988."

"When did Rusty replace the bumper?" Gail asked.

"I don't think Diddy said." Looking to one side, Jackie tried to reconstruct the conversation, then shook her head.

Gail said, "It could be a coincidence."

Jackie raised her eyes to Gail's. "The night you and Anthony went over to McGrath's house, Rusty Beck nearly ran you off the road."

"He wasn't trying to kill us."

"Are you defending Rusty Beck?"

"God, no. I just think there ought to be some evidence before we assume he's guilty and make ourselves crazy with it. I mean, how could we ever prove such a thing?"

"He had a motive. My mother knew the Mendozas had disappeared, and she suspected they were dead. Isn't that what Dodson told you?"

"Not exactly." The memory of her conversation with Gary Dodson flitted just out of reach, but Gail could recall clearly one thing he had said. "He told me your mother wanted to go to the police, and he talked her out of it. He told her she wasn't blameless, so she shouldn't make trouble. My impression was, she dropped it."

"She wouldn't have dropped it," Jackie said fiercely. "My mother wouldn't have just let it go, not something like that. She was a good woman. She was honest and true."

"I know she was." Gail could see her cousin's emotions revealed in the gleam of unshed tears, the tightness of her lips, the rigid set of her shoulders.

"You're right, Gail. We can't prove it, not after thirteen years. But it so fits, doesn't it? In my bones I have this feeling, I *know*, that Whit McGrath said, 'Hey, Rusty, take care of this bitch. Scare her or something, like you did with Vivian Baker.' And Rusty went after her, but he didn't stop at scaring her. She knew too much. He slammed into her car, and she went off the road and died, and McGrath didn't say shit about it. Or maybe he wanted her dead too, and he told Rusty to kill her. That's possible, isn't it? I don't know what happened, and I'll never know for sure, but Jesus, I want to do something about it. It's funny. I'm the one who's always telling folks they can't take the law into their own hands. Trust the system. What does that mean? Nothing. It's words. I'm thinking, what if I had a chance to even things up and get away with it? Would I do it? I don't know. I might."

"No, you couldn't."

"Yeah." Jackie closed her eyes. "It might be that Mama was coming through that curve too fast, trying to get home, and that's all it was, but I hate McGrath and Beck for everything else they've done, so I want to nail them for this too."

For a long while neither of the women spoke. Gail's insides churned, and she could feel herself shaking, as if the temperature had plummeted.

Her cell phone lay on the counter where she had left it. She flipped it open. No messages. Dread descended on her, a dark premonition of disaster.

"I'm worried about Anthony."

"Why? You said he's okay with Hector."

"Hector used to be an assassin. Did you know that? It's true. I don't know how many people he's killed, but he's never been caught. He's with Anthony, and Anthony hates McGrath. He despises him. He promised Kenny he would let it go, but he hasn't. He can't. It's eating him up. Dammit, Jackie, *where is he?*"

"Give me the phone," she said. "I'll see if I can locate McGrath."

The surface of the water moved as if alive, but the smell was of stagnation and rot. Anthony stood on the shore thinking of what words might be appropriate for the dead that lay beneath. He didn't expect ever to see this place again, nor wanted to. Strands of algae clung like hair to the rocks and swirled slowly in the lift and ebb of ripples. The sky reflected gray, and the evening star had come out.

He heard the murmur of voices behind him and turned. The two men had stowed their gear and laced their boots. Lean men, quick and hard, even with gray hair and deep lines in their faces. Hector had given up only their first names to Anthony. They shouldered their packs, telling Hector they'd be in Miami on the weekend, they'd settle up then.

Anthony stepped away from the water's edge. There were handshakes. Then the men became shadows quickly moving west, keeping more to the trees than to open ground, until the foliage became more dense and took them out of sight.

Hector busied himself checking for evidence that anyone had been there. He scuffed his soft-soled shoe over a patch of dirt, erasing a print. Hector had said that earlier today McGrath's company had brought in the bulldozer and backhoe that now waited by the construction shed. There was little chance, however, that the sinkhole would be filled in tomorrow. Hector had removed a few parts that would incapacitate the machines without immediately revealing the cause. This would give the sheriff more time to get the search warrant, if the warrant could be obtained at all. Anthony hoped, but he had his doubts.

"Hector, *vamos*." Anthony was ready to get out of here. It was late, and they had left Hector's car some distance away. It would be necessary to walk through pine woods and scrub palmetto that grew in great, spiky clumps. Hector gave another look around, then moved east, taking the lead. Anthony didn't mind this. He was sure of his own ability to become lost in these woods.

Under his jacket, the butt of his pistol pressed into his ribs.

Jackie accelerated out of the parking lot before Gail had finished buckling her seat belt. Jackie had located McGrath — more or less. Using the name of a woman detective with the Palm Beach sheriff's office, she had learned from McGrath's wife, Tay, that he had gotten a phone call and left for River Pines almost an hour ago. He was going to meet someone. *Who?* Whit hadn't said, but he had seemed agitated.

Gail held onto the door grip as Jackie sped west over the bridges to the mainland. She wasn't afraid of a crash, only of being slowed by some grayhair or a deputy who didn't recognize the Isuzu Trooper. But luck and traffic were with them, and they sailed through town, over the south fork of the river, and past Palm City, picking up more speed on Martin Highway.

Jackie had already found out that McGrath wasn't in any of the business offices at River Pines. She was waiting for a call from the sheriff's office dispatch to tell her if anyone had seen McGrath's Land Rover. She was shamelessly pulling strings. They assumed that McGrath had gone to meet Anthony. They didn't know where, but with no other ideas at hand, they headed further west.

The reddening sun touched the horizon. They didn't have much time. Gail tried not to think about it, but the scene played out in her mind. Anthony confronting McGrath, beating him bloody. Hector ending it with a bullet. Weighting McGrath's body and sending it to the bottom of the sinkhole to join the four others. Or even worse: McGrath lying in wait with a shotgun. Anthony lifted off his feet by the blast.

She gnawed her thumbnail. They were out of the residential area, heading into grove land and ranches, the scenery blurring past. "Jackie, are we overreacting?"

"I hope so." Jackie kept her eyes on the road. She had told Gail not to get into a panic. If they found Anthony, and *if* he was in a situation with McGrath, Jackie would stop them. No need to assume that Anthony was in danger. On the other hand, Hector could be a problem.

Jackie's phone rang. She picked it up and listened, then thanked whoever had called. She braked so hard her wheels screamed and took a left at the next intersection, heading south. "They saw McGrath about fifteen minutes ago on Grant Road. It runs along River Pines Phase Two property. It's near the sinkhole, Gail. I think that's where they are."

Hector felt the strange tickle in his chest that signaled danger. He turned with a finger at his lips, and at the same instant a man in jeans and a denim vest stepped onto the path just behind Anthony. The man was bearded, and long, graying hair was tied behind his neck. He held a double-barreled shotgun. Rusty Beck.

"Hey, slick."

Anthony spun around. Hector froze. He kept his hands away from his jacket, not to signal that he was armed. But Anthony touched the front of his windbreaker.

"Try it, slick, I'll blow you apart."

A voice from the other direction said, "Hands up, both of you. Way up." Whit McGrath stood on the path ahead of them, blocking their way with a chrome-plated .44.

McGrath said, "Keep them up. Rusty, see what they've got."

This man liked to think he was in charge, Hector noticed, but he was wearing clean, pressed pants and leather-soled shoes. On these damp pine needles his feet might slip, if he were pushed. *"Para ahora, hagas lo que dicen,"* Hector said quietly.

"English," McGrath said.

"Yes, I am sorry. I was telling him to do as you said." *For now. Only for now.*

The redneck took Anthony's 9-millimeter, then searched Hector and found the .38 in the shoulder holster and the Beretta on his ankle. Hector didn't care about the revolver, but he hated to lose the little Beretta. It had memories.

"Let's go." McGrath turned them back in the direction they had come. "We're going to take a walk." At the point of his pistol, they moved west again.

"What do you want?" Anthony said, glancing over his shoulder. "If we disappear, don't you think someone will look for us?"

"Just walk."

"How did you find us?" Hector asked, curious to know what mistake they had made. *Had they also seen the divers?*

"We got lucky, Pedro," said Rusty Beck. "I saw your car." He guarded them from the side, easily sliding past the sharp points of the palmettos.

Presently they came out of the woods and stepped under the barbed wire fence. The field was vast and empty, scraped clean of everything but the biggest pine trees. It was not so dark here. As they walked, Hector thought about the men who held them. Rusty Beck was explosive. He would act without thinking. McGrath was intelligent, but slower. Hector longed for his knife, which he could visualize folded at the small of his back, waiting in his belt. The blade could slice through shoe leather.

Someone would die soon. Possibly himself. Anthony would go to the old man, and say, "*Abuelo,* Hector saved my life. He died as a man." But then Hector thought he would prefer to live, if that were possible. He might not be able to kill both, but surely one. He began to think which one.

A minute later they stood near the sinkhole, a gaping black mouth with ugly, weedy water. Rusty Beck backed them up to the edge and held the shotgun while McGrath went to look at his machines, the backhoe and bulldozer. He was careful and took his time, as if he thought they might have taped explosives to the engines. He found nothing.

Rusty Beck was smiling, impatient for them to make a move so he could kill them right away. He had ugly skin, marked with little round scars. Hector saw the bullwhip hanging on his left shoulder, circling under his arm. There was a knife on his right hip. Anthony's pistol in his waist. The smaller guns in his pockets.

Anthony's eyes had gone to the same place — the pistol. Very softly Hector made a long sound through his teeth. *S-s-sssss.* Not yet. Wait. Wait.

McGrath came back and pointed his gun at Anthony. "I know you were here. What were you doing?"

"Looking at home sites. But I have to tell you, the landscaping could be improved."

"Don't fuck around with me, Quintana. I asked you a question."

Anthony shrugged. "We were paying our respects to the dead."

"Bullshit," said Rusty Beck.

"And now we are going to leave before someone makes a mistake."

"You're not going nowhere." Beck raised the shotgun and pumped a shell into the chamber.

"That kind of mistake," Anthony said to McGrath.

Hector understood: Rusty Beck wanted them dead. McGrath had not decided what to do, but if Beck killed them, he would say nothing. He would protect Rusty Beck, as he had done before. Their bodies would disappear. Not here, but somewhere in these vast acres. He would say, *Maybe they went back to Cuba.*

McGrath's eyes shifted from Anthony to Hector and back again. "You and your bodyguard come onto my property, armed. Why?"

"I told you."

"And you're lying."

Rusty Beck uncoiled his whip and shifted his shotgun to his left hand. He moved his arm and leather whistled, then cracked. "Answer when you're asked a question. What were you doing here?"

Anthony glanced at him with contempt, then looked again at McGrath. "He has already caused you enough problems, no? How will you explain two more deaths on the four he has already cost you?"

The metal end of the whip slashed across the front of his jacket, sparking on the zipper, cutting open the fabric. Anthony flinched but didn't move. Hector saw how he shifted his weight, getting himself ready to grab the whip. Foolish. The metal could take off his fingers. Whit McGrath waited to see what would happen. He held his .44 carelessly, his elbow at his waist.

"You better get your mouth moving, buddy." The whip sliced across Anthony's upper arm, and he gritted his teeth and put his hand over the sleeve. Blood oozed through his fingers.

"Put down the whip. You don't have the guts to take me on without it."

"You're a stubborn son of a bitch." Rusty Beck laughed and whirled the whip over his head.

Hector decided Beck would die. First or second, it didn't matter.

McGrath watched, enjoying it too much to end it quickly. He liked to see blood, Hector thought. Good. He would see his own. Hector said quietly, *"¿Estas listo?"* Are you ready?

Anthony made a slight nod.

Whimpering, Hector fell to his knees and held his hands out to McGrath. "Please, *señor,* tell him to stop."

The whip lifted the edge of his suit coat. Hector felt the air move past his ear. The crack echoed back from the trees.

Hector yelped, then said, *"Señor* McGrath, I will tell you everything. Don't let him hurt me. Please." Cowering sideways, making himself small, he walked on his knees like a beggar toward McGrath.

"Look at the little spic." Rusty laughed and pointed.

The barrel of McGrath's gun, aiming at

Hector, dropped slightly as he approached. Hector shifted to plant one foot firmly on the ground. He turned his head up to McGrath, looking over his hands, which he flattened and pressed together. A prayer. The hole at the end of the barrel was six inches from his nose.

"Talk," McGrath said.

A big man. Big men were slow. They had soft bellies. Hector thought he might not die after all.

At the end of Pines Road, Jackie slowed and tires slid on gravel. She stopped just short of the gate, which was locked. There were no other cars anywhere.

"They aren't here," Gail cried.

"I'll have a look." Jackie automatically took her Glock from her purse as she got out of her car. The holster had a Velcro strap, which she quickly fastened around her belt as she walked to the gate. She put a foot on the cross bar and vaulted over. Gail in her skirt and sandals was slower, but she caught up.

They walked around the tangled bushes at the gravel tracks, then past some trees. The field stretched out ahead of them. There was still enough light for Jackie to make out four figures some two hundred yards away. Four men. One of them seemed to be holding a gun on a man kneeling in front of him. She couldn't tell anything more.

Jackie kept her voice calm. "Gail, go back to the truck and call 911. Tell them 'officer in distress, send paramedics.' "

Gail's eyes widened. "What —"

"Do it *now*." Not waiting to see if Gail did what she was told, Jackie ran. Arms pumping, she headed for the sinkhole. Dodging the bigger rocks, her legs ate up the distance. The features of the men became clearer. Whit McGrath holding the gun on Hector Mesa. Rusty Beck guarding Anthony.

She saw it happening in front of her.

Hector Mesa lunging forward, driving his fingers into McGrath's stomach. The gun went off, a flash of light. McGrath going down, Hector standing, bringing back his foot. A kick in the head. Another.

Rusty Beck moving toward Hector, then remembering Anthony, but too late. Anthony on top of him, dragging him down. Beck reaching for his knife, not fast enough. The two of them rolled toward the weeds that marked the edge of the sinkhole.

Jackie's sneakers pounded over the hard earth. She took her gun out of its holster.

Rusty looped something over Anthony's

head and pulled tight. A rope? As Jackie came closer she could see it: his bullwhip. He was choking him.

Anthony lay facedown at the edge of the sinkhole, Rusty with a knee between his shoulder blades. Anthony twisted, clawing to get his fingers under the leather. Rusty's muscles stood out as he pulled tighter. His teeth were bared.

Hector moved toward them. He reached behind his waist, under his jacket, and from fifty yards away Jackie saw the flash of steel. She screamed out, "Hector! Drop the knife! Stop!"

She wanted Rusty Beck alive.

In one motion Hector pulled back on Rusty's ponytail, reached around, and slid the knife across his throat.

Rusty fell to one side. His cowboy boots kicked out twice before he went limp. Anthony rolled over, coughing, dragging in air.

Jackie dropped beside the body. Rusty's eyes stared blankly at the sky. The blood looked dark purple in the gathering dusk. It flowed toward the water. "Dammit, Hector! I told you to stop!"

He wiped off his blade and clicked it shut. "I didn't hear you, *señorita*."

"Yes, you did."

"Why are you here?"

Ignoring Hector, Jackie reholstered her gun. She went over to McGrath, who lay moaning on the ground, holding his head. His eyes rolled, then focused on her. "Jackie. Christ, I'm glad to see you. Where's Quintana? They were going to kill us —"

She picked him up by the front of his knit golf shirt and shook him. "Did you send Rusty Beck to murder my mother?"

He stared at her. "What?"

"I said, did you send Rusty Beck to kill my mother? Did you? You used her, you bastard. You seduced her. You made her sign that deed, and you wanted her dead when she asked too many questions."

"No. Jackie, honey, she had an accident —"

"Liar!" She slugged him so hard she felt it all the way up her arm. "Was it you or was it Rusty?"

He touched his mouth and spat blood. "Shit. Jackie, have you gone crazy?" He struggled to sit up. "I loved Louise. I wouldn't have —"

The crack of a gunshot tore into his words.

Startled, Jackie stumbled back. Standing behind her, Anthony had fired over their heads. He lowered his pistol, aiming at McGrath.

McGrath scooted backward and collided

with the trunk of a pine tree. He held out his palms, warding off the next bullet. "It was Rusty! He told me she was dead. I didn't know! I swear to God I didn't know."

Jackie stared at Anthony. His face had twisted into something she could barely recognize as his. He wasn't listening to McGrath. He hadn't come over to hear about Louise Bryce. His left arm hung limp, and blood dripped from the fingers.

"Hijo de puta." His voice rasped from his throat, as though the whip had cut into his vocal cords. "You murdered Kenny Clark. The Mendozas."

"I didn't —"

The gun shifted slightly upward. A bullet tore a chunk out of the tree and ricocheted. "Say it."

"Jesus, what are you —"

"Say it." The gun fired again, closer.

McGrath covered his face. "Yes, yes, yes, I did it, whatever the fuck you want, I did it!"

Anthony would kill him. McGrath knew it. Jackie knew it, and she didn't care. She wanted him dead.

No. She didn't. This was insane.

"Anthony, stop it. Put it down."

A movement in the field caught her attention. It was Gail, running, her skirt whirling around her legs. She shouted, and Jackie made out some words. *Coming. They're coming.* Then she screamed Anthony's name, but it didn't register.

The gun moved to point directly at McGrath's chest.

"I said put it down! Don't kill him. You'll be arrested for murder. I can't lie for you! Stop!" Jackie fumbled her pistol out of the holster and held it with both hands. They were shaking, and the barrel jumped wildly. She stood at right angles to Anthony, less than six feet away. She screamed, "Drop your weapon! Now! I'll shoot. Don't make me do it!"

His finger tightened on the trigger.

Finally Gail was there, gasping, horrified, her eyes fixed on Anthony. "Oh, my God."

Jackie's voice cracked. "Tell him to stop."

McGrath was on the ground crying.

Gail walked closer and looked into Anthony's face. He made no sign that he knew she was there. She softly touched his shoulder. "It's me. It's Gail. Please, Anthony, you can't do this. He isn't worth it. They'd take you away from me, and I need you so much. Anthony, I love you. Please don't leave me."

As though it hurt to move, he finally dragged his eyes off McGrath and looked at

Gail. He let his arm fall, and the gun dangled from his hand. Jackie took it away from him.

Gail collapsed onto his chest and held him tightly. Anthony let out a breath and closed his eyes.

Along the road, in the gathering darkness, patrol cars sent flashes of light across the field. Jackie holstered her gun. It would take a long time to explain all of this, and maybe it would never be fully explained. She watched Hector take his guns from Rusty Beck's pockets. It was her duty to secure every firearm at the scene. "Screw it," she said.

Anthony walked past her and went over to Rusty's body and looked down at him. Rusty lay sprawled on the rocks at the edge of the sinkhole. Anthony put a foot on his chest and glanced around at Jackie. She knew what he wanted to do. She didn't stop him. He shoved, and Rusty Beck slid off the rocks and into the water. He floated for a second, then went down.

CHAPTER 30

Friday morning, April 13

Finally, the sun cleared the trees, sending some light down on the sinkhole. The divers hadn't wanted to start on the car till visibility improved. Garlan Bryce was weary in every bone of his body. He'd been at this all night. But they hadn't needed a warrant, not with a fresh body to retrieve.

A perimeter kept onlookers back by the road, but a chopper from Channel 12 had been up there since daybreak, its rotors ceaselessly beating the air. How these things got out to the media, he could never understand. Maybe it was the crane that had been trucked in on a flatbed at 5:00 A.M. That must have aroused some curiosity.

The divers had pulled Rusty Beck out of there about midnight. They'd also seen a car, a mid-1970s Plymouth. Garlan had turned around to Whit McGrath and said they had to pull it up. McGrath had done a pretty fair job of acting surprised. A car?

At the moment McGrath was standing over by one of the patrol cars, drinking a cup of coffee. Waiting, like everybody else. His face was bruised where Hector Mesa had kicked him. He'd been talking about suing Mesa. Quintana too.

The crane operator cranked up the engine, and smoke belched out of the exhaust. The big cable played out, making ripples on the water. The police divers were ready. They would hook the cable around the axle.

Garlan had told the paramedics to send two vans out, although he expected nothing but bones, after thirteen years.

The news copter was hovering closer. *Whap-whap-whap.*

Whit McGrath came over with his coffee. "Sheriff, I want you to know that I'll cooperate in any way. I've known Rusty Beck a long time, but most of what Quintana was saying last night came as a complete shock." McGrath shook his head. "You think you know someone."

Garlan kept his eyes on the sinkhole. "Your lawyers don't mind you talking to me?"

McGrath laughed, and he talked too fast for a man with nothing to hide. "I want to help, sheriff, trust me. I'm on your side. You've got to know about Anthony Quintana. He's out to get me. Jesus, that guy. Maybe he snapped, defending that convict. It's all very strange. What he said about Rusty and those people, the Mendozas, maybe I can buy it. But to turn around and accuse me as well? What's the matter with him? The way he threatened me at my office. I was willing to let it go, but Jesus. I should make a report, don't you think so?"

"It's up to you."

Garlan let him talk. He hated to admit it, but Whit McGrath would probably walk. He would waltz himself right out of this. He could put on an act, all right. Innocence, confusion. Garlan could predict how it would go. The state attorney would explain why charges wouldn't be filed: no way to win this one. Even so, it was satisfying to stand here on McGrath's property and think about what was going to come up out of that sinkhole.

McGrath was saying he didn't know what Rusty Beck had done, but if he did anything, it should be brought to light. Too bad Rusty wasn't still around so they could ask him. Maybe Quintana and Mesa had killed him to keep him quiet. Then McGrath started apologizing again about getting involved with Louise. "Just one of those things. Shouldn't have done it, such a great woman." And he was dismayed — another of McGrath's favorite words, dismayed — that Jackie would think he'd ever wanted anything to happen to Louise. "Jackie's a great girl, a credit to you, Garlan, but a little overwrought about Kenny Clark, but I can understand it, all the stories that Quintana was feeding her —"

"Mr. McGrath? I'm going to ask you to step back over there out of the way. I don't want to hear anything you have to say right now. Is that clear?"

One of the divers came up out of the water and signaled an *okay* with thumb and forefinger before paddling to solid ground. The diesel engine on the crane belched smoke, and the drum holding the steel cable began to turn. Nobody said anything. All eyes were on the cable coming up out of the sinkhole.

The car came out tail-first, pouring brown water through a cracked windshield and open windows. The crane operator waited till most of it stopped, then swung the boom toward dry land. It took some time to get the car positioned so it would drop onto its tires, which immediately flattened. A little more time to get the trunk open because Garlan insisted on raising a tarp first. The helicopter was hovering overhead with its zoom lens, and he wanted to give these people a little dignity — if they were in there.

They were. All that remained were bones and some scraps of hair and clothing. Shoes. A rusted watch around an arm bone. For the most part, the bones had turned black, covered with the crud that sticks to things so long underwater.

Ron Kemp was in charge of the scene, and Garlan stepped away so he could get the photos done. After making sure his face wouldn't give his emotions away, Garlan looked around at McGrath, who exuded shock and concern. One of the crime scene techs, standing by the front passenger window, called out, "Sheriff? Come take a look at this."

Garlan went to see. What he thought might have been a tree limb became, on second glance, an old shotgun. He said to Kemp, "Bring it out after they take some pictures." Kemp told somebody to bring some plastic sheeting. The door was impossible to open, so they fished out the shotgun by the trigger guard. A tech with his hands in latex laid it on the plastic.

It was a rusty, silt-filled, double-barreled Browning. The wood stock was black with rot. Garlan sat on one heel. A twelve-gauge. He took off his sunglasses and using only two fingers raised up the shotgun. He squinted and wiped the mud off the side plate. Some letters were engraved there. The metal was pitted, but he could make out a name.

Knees popping, Garlan stood up. "Ask McGrath to come over here." Garlan waited for him and, when he got there, asked him if he recognized the shotgun.

"No, I don't. Why?"

"It's yours."

"Mine? What do you mean, mine?"

"It's got your name on it. Look. J. W. McGrath."

"That's impossible."

"Let's get this to the lab." He pointed at McGrath. "Step back."

"That's not my shotgun."

Garlan signaled to Ron Kemp. "Ron, call Sonia Krause. Tell her what we found and that we could be looking at murder one. I want her opinion."

Ron took out his cell phone.

McGrath yelled, and his face contorted. "What is going on? That's not my fucking gun. They planted it! Quintana planted it. He's trying to frame me."

"We'll be talking to you about it," Garlan said. "Just step over there out of the way, but don't leave the scene."

Garlan happened to look across the field. He could see an Isuzu Trooper parked on the road, and his daughter standing beside it. She'd gone home about two in the morning after making a statement. She'd been distant with him. Professional. They'd both been distant since their big fight. But she'd come back. She wore jeans and a white shirt, and her hair was in a braid. She gave no indication that she saw him looking at her, but he knew that somewhere in that hundred-yard distance their eyes were meeting.

He still didn't believe Kenneth Ray Clark was innocent, but he had thought long and hard, and he had to admit one thing. Jackie had done some good work with those crime scene photos. None of his detectives had noticed the air conditioning drip. Relevant or not, they hadn't seen it.

Garlan had also thought about going back over to the Dodson house and finding out if the same AC unit was still there, and if it worked. He'd thought about closing the doors and windows and checking the temperature, and seeing how fast the air would warm up when you opened the windows.

He didn't know if he really wanted to do that or not. He wasn't sure he wanted to know the answer, even if the answer could be obtained twelve years later. The AC might not work the same, different time of year. What would it prove? And anyway, it was too late. Way too late.

What bothered Garlan was his own hesitation. He put a lot of value on the truth, so he shouldn't be afraid of it. But he was.

His daughter was still looking this way.

Garlan told one of the men he would be right back, and he started walking across the field. He didn't know what he would say when he got there. Or what she would say. But she wasn't getting into her truck and driving off. She was waiting for him.

CHAPTER 31

Saturday, May 19

Anthony chartered a Lear Jet to take him and his grandfather to Grand Cayman. From Grand Cayman they would get on a fishing boat bound for Punta de Cartas on the southwestern shore of Cuba.

The jet was waiting at a small airport in Marathon in the Florida Keys, and Gail played chauffeur. Ernesto sat up front with her, and Anthony shared the backseat with Karen, telling her the things he and his grandfather planned to do on their trip. Ernesto Pedrosa was going incognito, hiding behind a false set of papers and a neatly trimmed beard and mustache. His cheeks had turned pink with excitement. He rested his hands on the curve of his cane and gazed through the windshield as though Havana lay just beyond the next bridge.

With Ernesto and Karen in the car, Gail had been unable to ask Anthony a question that had been on her mind ever since she had read *The Miami Herald* that morning. It was another story about Whit McGrath. He had been arrested a month ago, but his lawyers had just issued a statement about the shotgun. They claimed he had never owned such a shotgun.

Reaching Marathon, Gail could see the airport from the highway. It was hardly more than a landing strip with a small concrete block building for a terminal and a few private planes parked next to a tin-roofed hangar.

Ernesto found a place to sit in the office, and the pilot let Karen come with him to do his preflight checklist. Gail helped Anthony put the bags and Ernesto's wheelchair next to the open door in the fuselage, leaving them for the pilot to load. Anthony's arm had been cut deeply by the metal tip of the bullwhip. It was almost healed, but a sudden exertion could still make him wince.

Gail said she had something to discuss with him.

They walked back toward the office. She asked if he had read the article in the newspaper this morning. Anthony said that he had.

She stopped in the shade of the roof overhang. Ernesto was visible beyond the glass. Turning to Anthony, she smiled at him. "Sweetie? How did that shotgun get into the Mendozas' car?"

Anthony's brows rose. He was wearing a

white T-shirt and a Miami Dolphins base-ball cap, and his hair curled from under it. "What do you mean, how?"

"Did you and Hector put it there?"

"*Alaba'o.* Of course not. Gail, the shotgun has been underwater for thirteen years. The police say the metal is rusted and the wood is rotten."

"I know what they say."

Anthony gave her one of his shrugs — palms up, shoulders lifted.

Gail said, "Hector noticed McGrath's guns the night we were at his house. They were all engraved with McGrath's name, just like the one found in the sinkhole. You swear that Hector didn't do it?"

"Well. I can't vouch for what Hector does."

"I'm afraid Whit McGrath will accuse *you* of putting it there."

Anthony drew an *X* on his chest. "I promise you, I didn't put it there."

The next question was on Gail's lips — *Do you know who did?* — but she didn't want to force him to lie to her.

"Sweetheart, McGrath is too smart to accuse me. He would have to explain my motivation, and that means explaining why he let Kenny Clark die. And this leads us back to the Mendozas, and his connection

to them. Whit McGrath would wind up im-
plicating himself, you see?"

Gail made no reply.

"*¿Qué pasa, chinita?*" Anthony kissed her
forehead.

"McGrath didn't kill them, you know."

"But he is responsible, as he is responsible
for Kenny Clark, and for your aunt —"

"We'll never really know for sure about
Aunt Lou, whether Rusty did it on his own
or because Whit McGrath asked him to.
Jackie wanted to be certain, but I doubt she
ever will be, unless McGrath comes clean,
and that isn't going to happen."

"Life isn't always certain, is it?"

"No, it isn't, but we shouldn't forget
what's really going on here. My point about
the shotgun, which you don't want to see, is
that after everything we've been through
with Kenny, to make false accusations
about one thing because we can't get him on
another —"

"I understand your point," Anthony said.
"I just don't agree that it matters." He
shrugged, waiting for her to argue with him.

She said, "Fine. Believe me, I'm not
crying about Whit McGrath. He deserves
everything he gets, but even so —"

"You have such a good heart." Anthony
put his arm around her shoulders. "Here is a

prediction. Whit McGrath has already hired a team of excellent criminal defense lawyers, who will cost him millions of dollars. These lawyers will allege he was framed by the police or that unknown enemies set him up, whatever. His expert witnesses, who will also collect enormous fees, will say that the engraving was done recently. Other witnesses will swear that they never saw that shotgun in Whit McGrath's possession. The jury will be left with a reasonable doubt, and they will come back with a verdict of not guilty. But in the meantime, McGrath will have spent six months or a year in jail waiting for the trial. His business will be ruined, his wife will divorce him, and when he gets out, he will be a pariah in Martin County."

"Really?"

"Absolutely."

Gail thought about it. "All right. I can live with that."

Anthony was looking past her at the Lear Jet. "The pilot is loading our bags. We have to leave in a few minutes."

The loneliness was already flooding through her, and Gail held him tightly. "I'm going to miss you so much. Please be careful. Take care of Ernesto."

"I will." He held her face in his hands.

"*Siempre te llevo en mi alma, querida.*" He kissed her, and she wished they were not in public view. Their good-bye last night hadn't been enough. Nothing would be enough until he came back.

"Oh, I almost forgot something." He reached into his pants pocket then quickly put both hands behind his back and brought them out again, closed. "Pick one."

"Are you serious?" She laughed.

"Go ahead."

Gail tapped his right hand. His brows drew together, and he looked at her sideways. "Are you sure?"

She tapped the other one. "This better be good."

His hand slowly opened. Lying on his palm was a diamond ring. The gold setting gleamed, and the stone sparkled.

"Oh, my God. Is that *mine?* Hector found it?"

"Just yesterday." Anthony held it up. "Hmm. It has a little scratch here on the band. Did you do that, wearing it? And there's a tiny bit of dirt under the diamond. We should take it to a jeweler and have it cleaned properly. We'll do it when I get back."

"Let me see. I can't believe this." Gail held it between thumb and forefinger, turning it this way and that. Amazing. It looked almost new. But why not? Other metals would tarnish or rust, but not gold. The diamond was perfect, brilliant, flashing with light. But a thought began to creep into Gail's mind that this wasn't her ring. That the tiny specks of dirt between the diamond and the setting had been put there. That this ring might not have been lying at the bottom of a golf course water hazard for nine months. Had Hector made a duplicate? No, it would have cost too much. Anthony had paid for it.

She raised her eyes. He was smiling, waiting for her to say something. Little lines bracketed his mouth. His expression was open and guileless.

Maybe it was her ring. If she asked, would he tell her the truth? Gail didn't know. But it didn't matter.

She smiled at him. "I thought it was lost forever."

"I told you I would find it. Well? Are you going to put it on or not?"

She gave him her hand.

ACKNOWLEDGMENTS

The list is long, my gratitude boundless. A special place at the top goes to my sister, Laura, my sounding board, my bulwark.

Without the inspiration and generosity of others, this book wouldn't have happened. Such as: Milton Hirsch, who sparked the idea; Leslie Curtis, who provided an early philosophical framework; and Michael Mello, author, professor, and scourge of Florida's capital punishment system, who threw his body across the tracks for an innocent man — read his book.

For complicated reasons, I set the story one hundred miles north of Miami, in Martin County. I am grateful to those who told me about the history and development of that area: Judi Snyder, Lisa Graff, Scott McNabb, and Carolyn P. Ziemba. Thank you, George Seaman, for the photos.

Detective Steven A. Graff (Officer of the Year, Stuart P.D.) helped me solve the crime. Thanks also to Deputy Jennifer Heard of the Martin County Sheriff's Office, and to crime scene detectives Salvatore Rastrelli and Jon Wright. Major

Karin Montejo and Detective Rupa Fitzpatrick (Miami-Dade Police Department) gave me a glimpse of the life of a female police officer. And as always, thanks to ace homicide investigator David W. Rivers, now retired. Medical examiners Reinhard W. Motte (Miami) and Frederick P. Hobin (Martin County) provided clues.

These lawyers taught me about the capital appellate system: Cherry Grant (Public Defender's Office, West Palm Beach); William M. Hennis, Rachel Day, and Todd Scher (Capital Collateral Counsel in South Florida); Jane Siegel Greene (The Innocence Project); and Jim Marcus (Texas Defender System). For stories of life in the trenches, Joseph H. Forbes (Gainesville). A view from the prosecutorial side: Penny Brill and David Waksman (Miami). Practicing law in Martin County: Jay Kirschner and Diamond Litty. Thanks also to Tanya Carroll, clerk at the Florida Supreme Court, and to attorney Jan Franklin, who answered stray civil practice questions.

Thanks to Claudia Laurence, error-catcher and cheerleader, who propped up my spirits. To Joe Fraga, for the Spanish. And to my editor, Audrey LaFehr, whose suggestions made it a better book.

My knowledge of death row was a gift.

Thank you, Judge Marvin Mounts, Warden David Lehr, and Florida State Prison liaison Randall E. Scoggins. Thanks also to Pam Scott, who answered the call to minister to men and women in prison; and Michelle Agans, founder of Florida Death Row Advocacy Group (FDRAG.com), which speaks out on issues affecting inmates, their families, and friends. Through the FDRAG site I met two men with inside knowledge. They asked to be remembered as John Huggins, who lives on Florida's Death Row, and Raymond Wike, a resident of "Hotel UCI" (Union Correctional Institution). Thank you for letting me in. Peace.

Little more than a year ago, I had never given much thought to capital punishment. Writing this book forced me to gather the facts, to weigh various opinions, and to acknowledge the deeply held beliefs on both sides. I have learned that no argument can erase the pain of the survivors of crime, and that police, prosecutors, and courts do the best they can with limited resources. Like any product of human invention, the system is fallible. Rules of procedure do not always correct its mistakes. Ultimately, however, this is a moral and religious issue, not a factual one. I now find myself among those who believe that capital punishment is primitive, arbitrary, and unnecessary.

Information about the death penalty is widely available in book form and on the Internet. For a copy of my reading list, check my Web site, barbaraparker.com.